The Last Dwarf

I0590243

B.D. Murphy

WorstAuthor LLC

B.D. Murphy

Website: https://www.authorbdmurphy.com
Facebook: https://facebook.com/bdmurph73
Cover design by Bryan Murphy

Contents

Author's Note

We have heard about mythical dragons, dwarves, and many other races and creatures. Stories usually show dragons and dwarves living in mountains, close to each other. There may be another aspect of the story that has never been revealed.

This novel started as an exploration of several questions.
1) A dragon buys nothing, yet it hoards gold. Why does the dragon consider gold plates, cups, and ornaments a treasure?
2) How does a dwarven city inside the mountains feed everyone with no farms?
3) Why is the city located inside that specific mountain?
4) Dragons and dwarves live in the mountains. Hmm. Is there more?

MAP

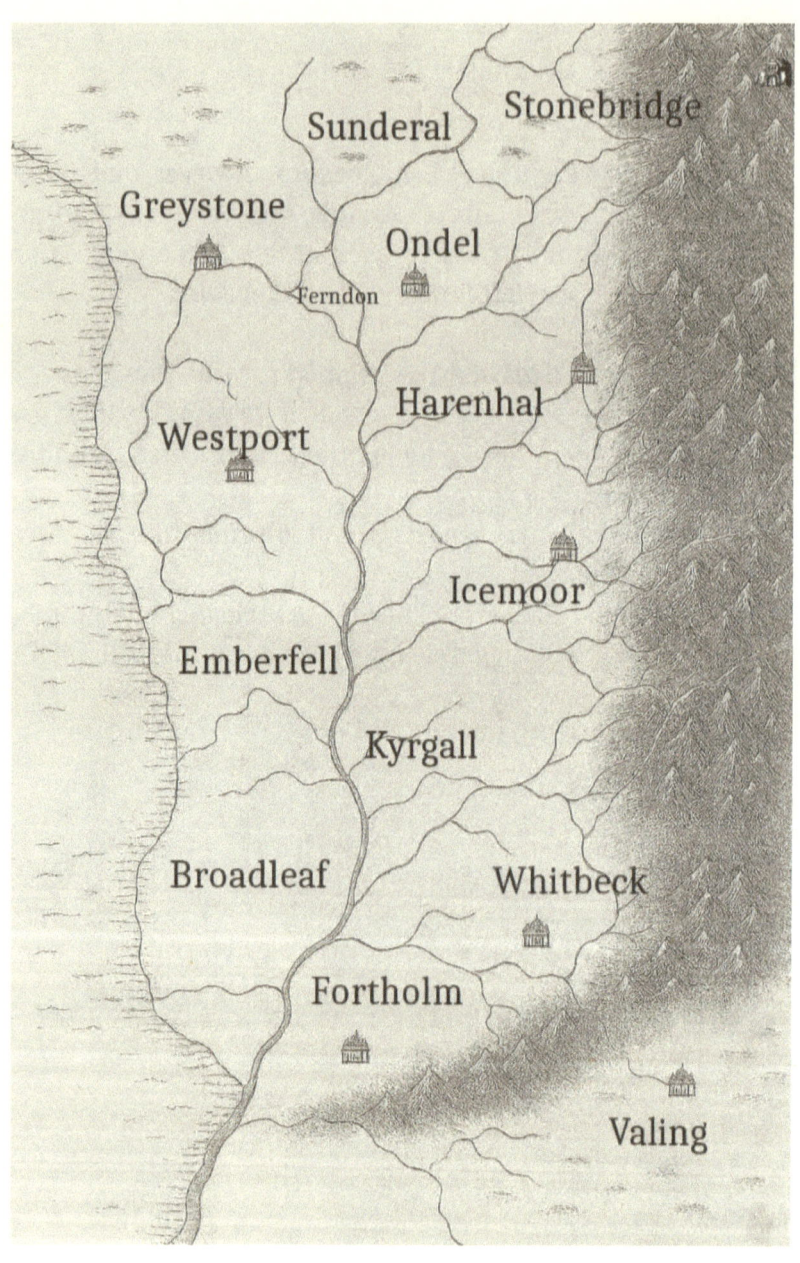

Tattered Dwarf

Humans can be trouble for him, so he sleeps out of sight and away from the road. Hallr is unrolling his blanket fifteen meters from the road, through the trees and brush, so that he won't be discovered. The old blanket has many holes, the largest measuring 4 centimeters across, as the weaving is unraveling. Sitting on his butt, he digs into his small and well-used pack and pulls out his last jerky. He looks at the dried meat, thinking, *"Last meal. Tomorrow, I should arrive at the battle area. I'll have food, or it won't matter anymore."*

He avoids starting a fire that might be seen from the road. He doesn't need a fire to keep warm this time of year. Before he can sleep, he needs to take care of himself. Taking care of his feet is essential, so he removes his boots. Looking at the holes in the boot uppers, his left little toe is poking out. He rubs his feet, thinking about how he will get the leather to repair them. His boots have worn soles, but they still work. His leather jerkin and pants are patched and will need more sewing soon.

He put his pack down as a pillow, shifts his great axe, his most prized possession, next to him. The double-bladed axe has been in his family for generations.

The tattered blanket goes over his body. He drifts off to sleep.

Hallr rolls over, suddenly awakened, after being kicked in the side. He exclaims, "What the hell?"

On his hands and knees, he looks up, thinking, *"They must have heard me snoring."*

The apparent leader bends down, looking at Hallr in the dark. He says, "What is this, boys? I don't believe it. A real dwarf. I thought they were all dead."

"Hallr, with his better low-light vision, is looking at four young humans standing over him. They all have short swords out. His large, two-bladed great axe is next to him on the ground. He won't be able to pick it up before they stab him. What do ya want?"

The leader on the right for Hallr says, "We want to be the ones to claim we killed the last dwarf."

"Ah. Ya want to slaughter me and claim a big fight victory? Typical human shit. If you want to claim you won a fight, there should be a fight."

The leader says, "He's right, surround him, boys."

The one on the left says, "The dwarf's great axe. We can sell that for some gold."

The big one says, "That is worth something."

Hallr says, "No one will give ya actual gold for that thing."

"How old are you, dwarf?"

"One hundred and sixty, give or take."

"Wow, that's old."

"What are you doing around here?"

"Heading to the fight. I can get food and get paid to fight."

"You still got fight in you, old dwarf?"

"Enough to scrape by. I'll kick your asses in a real fight."

Sarcastically, "Sure you would, old fella."

"You're gonna hold me and just stab me. Not a mark on any of ya while fighting a dwarf. You will all be called liars and thieves."

"No one will care."

"I think he's right. Fighting a dwarf and no marks on us. People will talk."

"No, stupid. After we kill him, we make small cuts on ourselves. Minor stuff, but we can say he wasn't good enough."

"Ya could make it look better if you killed me with the axe."

The biggest one, a healthy farm boy, says, "Hell yes."

He is second from the right of Hallr and next to the leader on the right. He reaches down for the axe. Grabbing the handle in one hand, he tries to lift it. "Sheeza, this is heavy."

Hallr shifts to kneeling. As he does, he shifts to face the large one.

The big guy hands his sword to the leader, "Hold this." He reaches with both hands and lifts the axe. "This thing must be 50 kilos."

Hallr jumps to his feet and takes two steps to the right. At 142 centimeters, he can't hit a standing human at 175 centimeters in the face hard. His left fist shoots out at the leader's side. His arms are strong from swinging the big axe, and when his fist hits, he hears and feels ribs crack. The leader crumples and falls backward.

The big one is trying to get the axe up while the other two are looking between Hallr and the leader. Hallr takes two steps to his left, his right hand back, and punches the big one in the side of his head. The big one stumbles and goes to one knee, but he isn't out. Hallr takes another step and punches him again. This time, the big one goes out, collapsing on his side.

Hallr looks at the other two as he reaches for the axe. The leader is moving and yells, "Don't let him get the axe."

Recognition appears in the eyes of the final two, who raise their short swords, looking at Hallr. Hallr has his hand on the handle close to the double blades and stands up straight. The axe comes off the ground with no visible effort.

Hallr shoves the axe forward hard, letting the handle slide in his hand to get more reach with the blade. The small, sharp four-centimeter-tall cone tip on the top of the handle, between the large blades, hits the young man on the left in the chest. He crumples backward. His sword flies out of his hand. After landing hard, he curls up into the fetal position.

Hallr has pulled the axe back and is holding the blades up. With the two large blades on either side of the handle, it covers Hallr's chest, going from shoulder to shoulder. Looking at it people see a shield.

Hallr takes a step forward as he turns the blade to face front, then shoves it forward. The young man put up his left arm to block the sharp Mithril blade. The blade cuts off his arm and then cuts into his chest.

He looks down at blood spurting from his arm and passes out.

Hallr turns to see the leader backing up and the large one shaking his head. The large one gets on all fours. Hallr steps over and shoves him with his bare foot. The big one hits the ground and yells, "Hey."

Hallr says, "The one surefire way to piss off a dwarf is to take his axe. Ya shouldn't try to take my axe." As he says this, he swings the axe in a circle and brings it down, taking off the big one's head.

The leader looks frightened and confused. "You'll regret this, dwarf. The witches will get you." He turns and runs off.

Hallr yells, "Tell me somethin' new. Witches are always trying to kill me."

Turning around, Hallr sees the one who had been in a ball has gotten up and is helping the one missing a hand as they try to move away. He is wrapping the cut-off arm stump with the end of the jersey.

Hallr checks the big ones' boots. They look newer and would do him well. Checking the size, they are too long and not wide enough. He can't wear them, but he can cut off the uppers as patch material. Sitting down, he puts on his boots, then, pulling his blanket over, rolls it up.

With his pack ready, he dons his footwear and consumes the rest of his water. He goes to the big dead one and searches him. He gets two coppers from his pouch. Leaving everything else, he heads toward the main road.

He is walking toward the border between Emberfell and Greystone. The word has spread that Greystone has defeated Ferndon and is now attempting to conquer Emberfell, seizing its resources.

He now has no food and two coppers to his name. A dwarf with a great axe can fight and get food. He will get paid for fighting for Emberfell. After the fight ends, he can scavenge a better blanket and pack from the dead before moving on.

4

The Last Dwarf

He has also heard that the king in Emberfell has a bounty on witches. Anyone caught doing magic gets the death penalty, which is good for Hallr. He could get lucky and collect a bounty for killing a witch.

He should reach the battle lines today. Many people are traveling the roads, with some leaving and others heading to fight. He likes to use minor roads and walk across open country to avoid humans. Because of dense trees and a river, he now has to use this road and deal with whatever comes.

He is walking on the road in the dark. He doesn't see anyone in the dark, which suits him.

When the sun is fully up, he hears humans talking behind him. He keeps walking at his usual pace. They are talking about how they will spend the gold they will have after the war.

When they get close, after realizing he is a dwarf carrying a large battle axe, they talk about him.

There are six young men of varying ages. They are still behind Hallr. Listening, Hallr can make out what they say.

The oldest says, "I'm sure that is a dwarf."

"I thought they died off," says the tallest.

The young one blurts, "Obviously not."

"Do we kill it?" asks the one with the biggest sword.

The oldest chuckles, "This entire group couldn't kill one."

"You know this, how?"

"A story from my grandpa. When he was a small boy, in his first battle, he was carrying water. At the end of the key battle, the king decided the dwarf needed to bow to him and become his warrior slave. The dwarf said No."

"So, they killed him."

"The dwarf killed hundreds of the army before they took him down. Dwarves are great fighters and hard to kill. Dwarves are not the enemy. They are trying to live just like us. Just keep walking."

"He's wearing rags. The only thing that looks good about him is the axe."

"These must be hard times for him."

"Another good thing about dwarves is that they hate witches."

"I heard a story that they go into a rage when a witch attacks them."

While still behind him, Hallr turns to check on the group. They watched him shift his axe, gripping it tighter. The tallest one shifts on the road to walk past Hallr, taking more distance. The others shift one by one as well. They continue to walk and, with their longer legs, eventually catch up to Hallr.

While they are directly next to him, one of them talks to him. "Dwarf, you're heading to the battle. The stupid Greystones think they can ruin their kingdom and then take this one. They have threatened Emberfell for years. That all ends tomorrow."

Hallr nods in greeting. "I don't have many details about what is causing this. Just need some coins for food. I heard there is food and some money for the fighters."

"Look for us, Dwarf. My mates and I will collect the bounty for the general and the king's heads."

Hallr perks up, looking at the speaker, and says, "There's a bounty?"

Another one of the six men says, "100 gold for each head."

Hallr nods. "I'll have to look for you. Maybe get one of those rewards for me."

"Dwarf, we will go fast and kill everything in our way. Your little legs will not keep up. That idiot king is going down."

Hallr smiles, "Good luck to ya. I hope to see ya after."

The humans slowly walked ahead and eventually disappeared around a turn.

When he arrives at the battle area, he moves from one tent to another, shifting to the next clerk and then to the next military level. No one wants to deal with him.

At an elaborate tent, where the smell of food fills the air, the guard looks at him and shakes his head. Hallr smiles and says loudly, "I've been told to report to the general in this tent. You think you're going to stop me?"

Inside, there is a voice: "Is that the dwarf? Let him in."

Entering the tent, Hallr sees a man sitting and eating with two others serving and attending him. He doesn't offer a chair or food. "Dwarf, good to have you with us. I was told you want a different deal. The standard plunder and take what you can carry doesn't work for you?"

"I can't carry away a bunch of shit. Your paid soldiers are getting ten coppers. I'll kill four times your best. Give me twenty coppers, and I'll walk away after. We both know you don't want me around afterwards.

The general puts down his spoon. "You have balls. All right, twenty coppers. You can get it from me when we win."

Hallr smiles, shaking his head. "Ten coppers now. You could be dead after the battle, and then I get nothing. Your next statement is going to be I need to keep you alive is shit. I will not be your nursemaid."

The general looks at Hallr with a smirk and a slight shake of his head, "No."

Saying nothing, Hallr turns and reaches for the tent flap. The general says, "That's it. No negotiating?"

Stopping, Hallr says, "You want to play games? Is that how you lead an army, by negotiating? That means your troops wonder about the right angle to play the situation and not fight like hell. Fifteen coppers now."

The general shoves his plate away and stands up, red-faced. He stops, takes a breath, and says, "15 coppers up front, and that's it. If you aren't killing dozens, I will have the army hunt you down after the battle."

Hallr nods. "Who pays me?"

The general nods, sits, and turns to one of the two others in the tent, saying, "Take him to the paymaster."

After receiving his money, he asks about food, and someone directs him toward the cooking area.

After paying four coppers, commenting about being robbed, and eating, Hallr takes the plate to the cleanup area. In this sizable area with many hungry humans, there is little waste. The pile of chicken bones on his plate is twice the size of everyone else's.

One girl helping asks, "They told me you get to have as much as you want. Do all dwarves eat like that?"

"Only when we have food. Usually, there is less to go around."

"Do you want more?"

Smiling, Hallr says, "No, lass. As it is, I'll be blowing up the latrine later."

"Mr. Dwarf, how old are you? Your face doesn't appear very old, even though you have a grey beard."

Hallr replies, "I don't know for sure. I tell people who ask, I'm about 160."

"Oh. How long do dwarves live?"

"When we don't get killed, we can live to over two hundred."

Hallr gives the girl the plate, saying thanks, and walks to the bench to get his axe and his kit. He was told to find any spot he wants to bed down, but he knows better. He heads to the area with the latrines and horses. The place with the worst smell is also where he will have the fewest problems with humans.

Finding a spot, he dropped his kit and started working on his axe. This was from his father. The axe is more than twice the size of the heaviest human axe. Double blades, heavy and simple. Crafted at the ancient dwarven forges from Mithril, commonly known as dwarf steel. It is stronger and lighter than human steel, and no one can make it. His axe is the deadliest blade on this battlefield.

He needs some rendered animal fat to rub into the leather on the axe handle. He also needs it for his leather armor. Digging through his kit, he finds the leather pouch, but it is empty.

He can't leave his stuff to get stolen, so he gathers everything and starts heading to the Smith area. As he walks, he hears humans calling to each other. The mood is good in the camp: no one calls or waves at him. A few people look at him, then comment to those close by.

At the smithy area, he sees a man working the bellows while

the smith shoves steel strips into the coals. They are both wearing leather pants and no shirts because of the heat. On the bellows, the man's black hair is in a tail going down his back.

The blacksmith grabs another handle with a glove and pulls out a bent sword blade. He puts the bright red blade on the anvil and grabs his hammer.

After a few minutes of watching and waiting, Hallr looks and motions to the man on the bellows. The bellows stop, and after a few more blows of the hammer, the smith stops. The smith looks at Hallr and then puts the much straighter blade back into the coals.

Hallr says, "I need some tallow for my gear. Do you have some, or do you know where I can get some?"

The smith goes to a bucket, grabs a cup hanging on it, dips it into the bucket of water, and drinks. Then he gets another cup, bends, and pours it over his head. The water shifted his brown hair toward his face. He stands, flinging his hair back.

He says, "I could use a break. Sit for a minute. I want to talk about your axe."

Hallr sighs, knowing the smith will ask about buying his ax. "The ax is not for sale."

"No, no. I would like to know more about dwarven steel. Where is it from? Where can I get it?"

Hallr gives a little scowl, smiles, and walks over. There is a worktable, and the smith pulls over a chair while the bellows worker pulls over another.

Hallr leans his axe next to the table with the blade up. "That is an interesting question. In all my years, I've had no one ask about just getting the metal. Most want my axe or others like it.

Gesturing to the forge, the smith says, "I make blades, and a blade is only as good as the steel that goes into it. "My name is Milfred, and that's Agnarr."

Hallr says, "I'm Hallr. Why aren't you two part of the fighters?"

Agnarr says, "The army needs working weapons. That means a smith who can make or fix weapons. I'm an apprentice. We have been busy the last two days fixing all kinds of weapons."

Milfred says, "Where can I get some of that metal?"

Hallr looks back at Milfred and says, "I do not know. This axe has been in my family for generations. I was told it came from the forges in Molgan."

Manfred says, "Molgan, the lost dwarven city. Haven't you been there?"

Agnarr stands and says, "I'll be back."

Hallr shakes his head, saying, "I've never been there. It disappeared long before I arrived.

Agnarr returns from rummaging in the supply wagon and places a small barrel on the worktable. He turns and walks away. Returning with three small mugs. Turning the small barrel on its side so the spigot is off the edge, he puts a mug under it and opens it.

After three mugs are mostly full, Agnarr says, "Something better than water."

Milfred lifts his mug in a toast. They clink mugs, and Hallr says, "Thank you." Taking a drink, Hallr tasted stale beer. He hasn't had beer in many weeks.

Agnarr says, "Stale, but wet."

Milfred stands and walks to his wagon. Shoving his arm into a box, he grabs something and returns to the table. He put a small pouch on the table in front of Hallr, saying, "Tallow."

Hallr nods, saying, "Thank you again. What payment?"

Milfred says, "Everything you know about the city, Molgan."

"I only have stories from family. No one in my family was ever there. Dwarves live three times longer than humans, but the city had been lost for years, even before my grandpa was born.

Agnarr asks, "Didn't you grow up close to the old city?"

Hallr says, "I grew up in Southern Stonebridge in the mountain area. We worked in mines getting iron and coal. No one knew about or talked about Molgan other than in old family stories."

Milfred says, "I'll take anything you can tell me. Finding any metal from those furnaces, I could make a few great blades."

Agnarr asks, "Aren't you interested in seeing the city?"

"Yes. I've no family, and one reason to wander is to find the city. The stories say it is in the mountains, but I can only search in the mountains during the warm months. But I can't search without supplies, that means I need coins."

Milfred asks, "How did it get lost? Maybe it was just locked and hidden. How does a forge make metal like what's in your axe?"

No one knows why they abandoned it. My family talked about a battle, and the battle destroyed a part of the city.

After a few more minutes of discussion, Hallr stands and pulls off his chest piece and jersey. Sitting, he opens the bag of tallow. Putting a small amount on his fingers, he rubs the leather on his chest armor. He says, "I don't have a problem talking with you, but I need to work on my gear."

Agnarr and Milfred look surprised to see Hallr's bare chest. The muscles of his chest and arms are massive. He can swing that enormous axe with power. There are scars on every visible part of his upper body.

Milfred nods toward Agnarr, then turns back to Hallr and says, "We're curious. It's not like we see dwarves every day to have these discussions."

Agnarr asks, "I always heard that dwarves speak with a heavy accent and are hard to understand. You are speaking normally, like everyone."

Hallr smiles, "My family grew up with humans, speaking with humans, not just with dwarves. The words and accent were at home with family."

Milfred asks a variety of questions about Molgan. Hallr slowly recounts everything he remembers being told throughout his life. After a time, Hallr puts down his chest piece and picks up his axe. He puts the blades between his legs, the handles up, and begins rubbing tallow on the leather.

Agnarr watches intently. After a minute, he asks, "Is that the original leather?"

"No. Each generation, when they pass the axe, the new owner

prepares and replaces all the leather. It is now the new owners. The workmanship and reliability are the new owner's responsibility."

Milfred asks, "Who will you pass the ax to?"

Hallr stops rubbing, looks at Milfred, and says, "No one. I have no kin left. I haven't seen another dwarf in years."

This puts everyone in a somber mood. After a time, Milfred says, "Bed down next to the wagon. I can hold your kit tomorrow during the battle."

Hallr says, "Have you seen any witches in the area?"

Agnarr says, "There are always rumors, but we have seen none. Why?"

I need to understand if someone might attack me during sleep or if I should go hunting.

Milfred says, "I heard dwarves kill witches. Why is that?"

"That is people talking about the results. Witches attack me. They always attack me. Then I kill them."

Agnarr says, "The story I heard was witches wanted dwarves to fight with them, and the dwarves said no."

"Maybe centuries ago. No witch has ever asked me or even tried to talk about fighting together. They want to kill me or hire some mercenaries to kill me."

Milfred says, "We need to get back to work. We have several hours before we finish. Like I said, bed down by the wagon."

Ready to Fight Like a Dwarf

Hallr was up early to pee. He just stayed up and got his stuff ready. Before a battle, this includes pulling his hair out and redoing the braid into a tight weave. He has never wanted the legendary dwarf ponytail with a barb in the tip that can be a ranged weapon. His beard gets a new weave. He has no beads or jewelry to add to the weaves, but these people don't care.

As a young dwarf, he was told that traditionally, members of a clan put an arrangement of beads and jewelry, a pattern to show their clan affiliation. On the battlefield, when everyone was wearing a helmet, you could tell clans and people apart.

In the food area, he was one of the first. He grabs only a chunk of bread; there isn't much else offered. He won't fill up on food before a battle. While eating, he stands away from everyone, watching. He wants to know who will be on the field with him.

He looks up, seeing light fog on the low hills kilometers away. Light winds are moving the mist across the flat fields. The battle will be in the fields. With light winds, archers will be effective. Good for archers, but bad for targets. The wind won't move the arrows in flight.

If the fog goes into this area, there will probably be more deaths.

From his location, 142 cm tall, he can't see the enemy camp. The tents of the Emberfell army blocked his view of the flat fields.

When he finishes his bread, he moves to leave, but stops. He turns to get two more chunks of bread and walks back to the wagon.

Agnarr looks surprised to see him return and even more surprised when Hallr hands him the bread. "We thought you were already heading to the front line."

"No. It will be several hours before the fighting starts. I don't need to stand around for several hours. I only need to be there to

encourage our line and scare the enemy.

A couple of hours later, tension was building as the battle approached. Those who have experienced battle are more relaxed, but not completely. Many are going to die today. The professional soldiers are moving people forward to the line. There is chanting, an attempt to remain upbeat. The speeches to encourage the scared and give them courage will start soon.

Hallr is walking slowly toward the front line. The officers will try to inspire the troops to crush the enemy. The enemy across the field is doing the same. He doesn't need speeches to encourage him to fight humans.

A young man moves past Hallr, adjusting an old, dented helmet that is too big. He stops, turns, and asks, "Mr. Dwarf. Do we have a chance of winning? Greys have defeated two other kingdoms."

"They defeated the weakest kingdoms. Now, their resources are strained. You also have me. Yes, we will win."

"Can …. Can I stay close to you? To help with whatever you need?"

Hallr has been expecting this. It happens frequently. A young kid wants to stay close, so he has a better chance of staying alive. He says, "Are you ready to kill? Around me, there will be lots of killing, more than in some other places."

The young man swallows, his face turning white. He pulls out the short sword that was given to him. Hallr says, "They gave you a sword because you know how to use it, or they ran out of pikes? Fighters with swords are targets. They will think you are an easy kill."

The young man's eyes went wide. He lets go of the sword. Looking down at it and then back at Hallr, he hyperventilates and shakes.

Hallr says, "HEY!" Watching the man jerk from being startled. "Pick up the sword and listen as we walk."

With his hand shaking, the young man reached down and picked up the sword. He has to dash to catch up to Hallr, who hasn't waited.

"All right, young buck. Currently, we are out of range of the enemy archers. Do you know why?"

The kid shakes his head.

"We won't get arrows constantly shooting and hitting us. As we move forward, the archers will start firing to hit as many targets as possible. When we engage, the pikes go first. The pikeman needs to hurry to get close. The archers will stop shooting when the engagement starts, so they don't hit their own. We want everyone to run to close the distance."

The kid nods, "Where do I go?"

"We yell for the pikemen to run and heel. Don't be in front of the pikes. Your job is important. At some point, the enemy will get through the pikes. When they do, they will start killing the pikemen from behind. That is when we could lose it all."

The young man is walking next to Hallr, listening. With Hallr's words, he nods and grips the sword.

"Your job is to kill anything that gets through the pikes. Don't let them attack the pikemen. They will focus on the pikemen as soon as they get through. You let them focus on the pikes, then stab them in the side."

Hallr puts his pointed fingers on his side to show the kid. "Here and shove hard. You want that blade halfway in. If you only give them a scratch with the tip or only a finger's depth, they will get mad and kill you."

"I understand," *the kid says.*

"If you kill someone and find a better sword, take it and use it."

"Will someone get mad at me for having a better sword?"

"Spoils of war. If they yell loudly, you put the pointy end into their belly as deep as you want. You keep it by fighting to keep it."

The kid is walking better. Nodding more naturally from Hallr, making it all a matter of fact.

"What else?"

"If they are on horseback, don't attack on your own. You need a group and preferably a pike or two."

"That makes sense."

"The last part is you have to make noise to keep the front line focused and fighting. Yell, hold the line, move, kill them a lot."

They reach the front lines, and Hallr asks, "Are you going to your unit?"

"I don't know where they are. I was told they would be around here."

Hearing them talk, a man carrying water to the line says, "Two groups marched off to the right about half an hour ago."

The kid nods and looks at Hallr, "Where do you need to go? Do you need a helper?"

Smiling, Hallr says, "I will go where the enemy is making the most noise. After encouraging our troops, I'll go to the weakest point to break their line. If you want to tag along, it will probably be the most dangerous place to be."

The kid licks his lips, with a breath, says, "I'll stick with the veteran."

A few minutes later, Hallr's growl causes the kid to jump. "What's wrong?"

"I hate waiting like this. It is more to whip up the scared conscripts. The speeches will start any minute."

The kid says, "My name is Aksenzo. People call me Enzo."

"Hello, Enzo. They call me shithead, scum, and sometimes dwarf. My name is Hallr."

Enzo says, "Hallor."

"No, Hallr. The last is growling r. Hallr."

Enzo nods, and before he can say anything else, someone yells down the line to the right. At first, they can't understand what they are yelling to everyone. Then they can understand the repeated lines. Hallr snorts, "He isn't building up to it. He is jumping to destroy the enemy. We will be in the shit soon."

People are moving around quickly. People are yelling. When a soldier with a sword and helmet walks by, he yells at Enzo. "Get your ass over close to those pikes."

Hallr says, "Naw. He is going to be my finisher."

The soldier stops and looks at Hallr, sizing him up. He says, "What the hell does that mean?"

"It is simple. I will fight through as soon as there is a break in their pikes. Everyone I hit that doesn't die right away will be his job. He will follow and kill the stragglers so that I can concentrate on the enemy in front."

The soldier looks at Enzo and laughs, saying, "That little shit is going to kill your leftovers."

Hallr says, "He'll do. You got someone standing around who would be better?"

The soldier looks at Hallr, then turns to Enzo, saying, "I can order him somewhere else. I could order you somewhere else, dwarf."

"Ya could try. I'm not paid to run around just cause you say so. I'm here to kill."

Hallr shifts his axe, looks up at the man, and continues, "In the heat of battle, swinging my big axe, ya could be hurt if you're too close."

The soldier looks at Enzo and says, "Kill all the Greys." He turns and walks away, yelling at the people he sees.

Almost an hour later, Enzo, following Hallr's lead, is shouting encouragement to the front-line pikemen and swordsmen. They alternate mostly with killing the Greys, and the Greys are cowards.

Stopping to drink water, Hallr says to Enzo, "Now we add something else. They need to hear a dwarf is commin', killin' two or three at a time. We want the front line to yell it, A dwarf is commin.'"

Enzo looks at Hallr, "I don't understand."

"This is to scare the Greystone troops and encourage our side. You make up shit like, veteran of dozens of wars, he chops people in half. The great axe of dwarven steel will kill."

Enzo and Hallr have been talking, yelling, and moving around for over an hour. Enzo is carrying his helmet instead of wearing it so he can yell and move better.

An officer on horseback rides up and listens, while looking across to the enemy side. "Dwarf, you're making the enemy move troops around. There are now twice as many troops facing us."

Hallr smiles and walks to the horse. "That is great."

"What the hell do you mean that is great?"

"They are taking those troops from somewhere else. Where is their line getting weaker?"

The officer gives Hallr a look, then, realizing why Hallr is smiling, he scans the enemy line to the sides. Nodding, he looks down at Hallr, "To our left. They have shifted troops from that side."

Hallr says, "That's where I'm going through. Time to get this party started."

"We aren't ready."

"Neither are they. Start yelling encouragement here. We have them scared."

Hallr turns and starts walking to the left. "Enzo, time to get to work."

The officer watches Hallr and Enzo walk off, "Dam dwarf." He then yells, "Everyone, we have them scared; they're shifting troops around. It's time to show the Greys why you don't attack Emberfell."

As they walk, he hears the officer telling the line that they are about to move. Even if they don't, the word will spread, and the Greys will react. Hallr says, "I'm not just going to stand around yelling all day."

Enzo is at his side and says, "What do we do now?"

"I need to get the line over this way to surge toward the enemy. Get ready to yell, mad dwarf."

"Mad dwarf? Okay."

Hallr jogs to move farther down the line. After about fifty meters, he spots one of the professional soldiers managing the pikemen. He turns toward him and starts yelling, "Attack, charge, go kill those cowardly Greys."

Hallr swings his axe up above his head and spins it just as

everyone turns to look at who is yelling. Hallr says, "Enzo."

Enzo is jogging behind Hallr and yells, "Mad dwarf! Move forward. Mad dwarf!"

The people in front of Hallr shift, some to the side, but many move forward. They are now pushing the line forward. The people at the front can't see Hallr; they hear a mad dwarf.

Hallr keeps jogging, and now, with his axe over his head, yells a battle cry. The line hears the battle cry, followed by Enzo yelling, "Mad dwarf."

Everyone surges forward to get away from the mad dwarf. This causes the Greystone line to shift, forming the pike wall that makes the Emberfell line form its pike wall. However, the mad dwarf is making the section of the Emberfell line surge forward.

Hallr is still jogging forward, yelling. He gets to the actual front as people continue forward or shift to the sides. The Greystone line sees the pikeman line part, and the dwarf coming charging through the line straight at them, swinging an enormous axe.

Several people on the grey line panic, turn, and try to run. Quickly, panic ensues.

The officers at the back of the grey line are yelling and then stab pikemen who are dropping their pikes and running.

The Emberfell line, seeing this, surges forward. In less than a minute, the grey line breaks as Hallr goes charging through, swinging his axe. Chopping the pikes and then the pikeman.

The discipline of pike-and-sword fighting, with charging mounted fighters, is in tatters. Chaos is now the norm.

Hallr and Enzo are behind the grey front line. Hallr is swinging his axe and wounding or killing someone with every swing. After several minutes, he has no one within axe range, and he stops, breathing heaving and sweating.

Looking back, he sees Enzo, with no helmet, pulling his bloody sword out of a downed soldier to finish him. Enzo is also breathing hard and sweating.

Turning back, Hallr walks toward a mounted officer he sees. When the troops shift, he sees a large man with a long sword. Hallr yells, "Hey, Shorty."

The man shifts toward Hallr and smiles. Hallr returns the smile. The big ones with long swords think they can best a dwarf with an axe.

In the last few meters, the man raises his sword above his head for a hard downward swing. As the downward swing begins, Hallr hops to the side, swinging his axe up and to the side to gain momentum. As the sword comes down, the axe swings in an arc, around and up. The man can't shift the big sword path fast enough; it slices down next to Hallr, putting the man's arm in a position to meet the upward-swinging axe.

His left arm falls to the ground, letting go of the sword. The man shifts and takes a step back as blood spurts from his severed arm. He dropped the sword to clamp his now free hand over the stump to slow the bleeding.

Hallr shifts to the three men with short swords who followed the big one. After dispatching the three, he pauses and looks back for Enzo.

He sees Enzo pulling his short sword out of the belly of the standing big man. As Hallr watches, Enzo looks down, then reaches for the man's sword.

Hallr cringes at the rookie mistake. He yells, "He isn't dead. The sword won't move. Kill him first, then get the sword."

As Hallr is speaking, Enzo stands with the heavy sword. He watches the big man pull a dagger and lunge at Enzo, stabbing him in the side of his abdomen. The man then draws the knife across Enzo's abdomen, slicing him open.

The man is wobbly as Enzo is looking at his guts spilling out.

Enzo drops the sword and tries to put his guts back in as the large man goes to his knees, then falls. Enzo collapses onto the man.

Hallr turns away and begins looking for another soldier or his next victim. He is breathing hard, gripping the axe tightly, and wants to kill something.

It is stupid. The army conscripted a dumb farm kid, who had

no real training, and sent him to war. He has seen the waste many times, and it always makes him angry. He channels the anger into the fight. Marching further behind the greys battle lines.

Fewer soldiers will fight and slow him down this far behind the lines. He can now be more selective with his targets to inflict the most effective damage and end this quickly.

Hearing something behind him, Hallr turns, expecting the enemy, and sees a dozen Emberfell troops with an older officer. They are fighting, and Hallr realizes they are following his path of destruction.

That is when the pain starts. Hallr immediately grabs his head with his free hand and bends at the waist slightly.

The group is close, and the officer comes over asking, "Are you injured?"

Hallr growls, "I have a pain in my head. This only happens when a witch is attacking."

One man behind the officer yells, "They are shifting toward us. They want the dwarf."

The officer yells, "There is a witch. She must be forcing them. I will give a gold coin reward to whoever finds and kills this witch."

The men all scowl when they hear witch, then their eyes get big when they hear one gold to kill a witch. That is enough for them to share.

Hallr says, "There are men who are controller witches as well, not just women."

With that, Hallr grips his axe and says, "Head toward their King's tent."

The fighting around Hallr intensifies, and the Emberfell men are yelling 'Witch,' so others know. The battle shifts toward the Greystone Kings' tent. When the word of the witch gets to the main line for Emberfell, the lines shift and focus on moving harder to the Greystone King.

Minutes later, the pain in his head is gone. Hallr pauses, turns to the officer who has stayed close to him. "The witch has stopped attacking me."

Looking over the battlefield, the officer says, "Our troops are almost at their king. The battle is done. The witch will hide now."

Hallr says, "I'll keep looking."

The officer nods and turns to his troops, "We are going to push to join the rest of our troops."

Hallr shifts his axe and continues walking.

After the Battle

The battle is done. There is still some fighting in places. Enemy fighters who won't quit. They refuse to stop fighting because they know their enemies will kill or enslave them. A few are overzealous victors. They believe they can take anything they want and attack others from their side to gain the loot they desire.

Hallr has been sitting on the ground, dripping sweat, for about fifteen minutes when he sees Agnarr and Milfred making their way through the bodies. He looks up at the sky. The fog never came to the battle. The wind is stronger, cooling him off after the fighting.

Agnarr and Milfred stop to check on some bodies. Hallr realizes they are searching for specific items on the bodies. They are taking better-quality weapons and pouches from some of the dead.

Hallr knows the pouches could contain valuable items, not just coins. Once, his spoils included a random pouch with a gold ring.

He stands as they get close to him. Agnarr says, "You are pretty deadly with that axe. The stories about dwarves making a difference are true."

Milfred says, "You should have asked for 100 gold."

Hallr laughs, "That would make me a target. I keep my purse light with what I need. I took a rest. Now I'll collect gear for my payment. People grab the best stuff right after the fighting. The scavengers will come, and fighting for the loot will start soon."

Agnarr scowls, "There is an order against fighting over loot. If they do, both sides will lose the loot into the common pool."

Hallr shrugs, "That's not reality. I'm heading toward the enemy medical area. Guys with good stuff and money get taken to the medical area first."

Milfred looks at Agnarr. He nods, saying, "That is experience talking."

When they reach the medical area, they can hear moaning and

yelling from a few beds. Sections divide the beds. The raised beds are sticks with woven nets. This is for the rich. The rest are simply straw beds on the ground.

You can recognize the people helping by their blood-soaked clothing, which are primarily women. They are walking, usually carrying something.

Hallr watches a woman carrying off a leg as they reach the edge of the bed. On the bed is a man passed out, missing a leg. Another man is wrapping rags around the stump. They all smell burned flesh where they burned the stump to stop the bleeding.

Agnarr asks, "Will he survive?"

The man looks up for a moment before turning back. He says, "Probably not. He is strong, but he lost a lot of blood before he got here."

Milfred asks Hallr, "Was that you?"

"No, I would have just chopped the leg off, not have him drag it back here to lose it."

Hallr then asks the man, "Where is his gear?"

The man turns, looking at Hallr, "He isn't dead yet."

"I could kill him. He is a living enemy. I could kill you as well."

The man stands straight. Looks at Hallr. "I'm the King's cousin. You can't touch me."

Hallr swings his axe up, showing the blade, and takes a step toward the man. The man backs up and says, "No."

"I asked, where is his gear?"

"The man points.

Hallr says, "Thanks."

Hallr turns and starts looking through the gear. Agnarr and Milfred look at the man. Agnarr says, "Why are you protecting him?"

"He's my brother. He will be angry that he lost his leg, but he will be alive."

Hallr is moving around the gear. He straightens and says, "This is his armor, but his weapons are gone."

The man says, "I wasn't watching. I don't know."

Milfred asks, "Can you describe his weapon?"

The man gives a vague description of a sword, except for the family crest on the handle.

Hallr says, "You will get more casualties until someone finds that sword. It has value so that people will fight over it." Pointing at the man on the bed, he continues, "If he has any surfs, boys, they need to be looking."

The man nods, "Wasn't that what you wanted? The sword?"

Lifting his axe, Hallr says, "Don't use a gigantic sword. I wanted to know if it was here. I want to know about his chainmail. His barrel chest could be big enough that it would fit me."

The man nods, "Sorry, he had none. He is too big for the standard armor, and chainmail is too expensive to be made special."

Hallr nods. As he turns away, he says, "Make him drink water. It helps when you lose a lot of blood." He walks away.

Agnarr and Milfred quickly catch up, and Agnarr asks, "What else are you looking for?"

Hallr stops and turns. "Blanket, a good pack, a pot, and other camp necessities. You two should collect the best weapons. You can sell or trade them. If anyone gives you a problem, yell. I'll set 'em straight."

Milfred asks, "Where do I put them?"

Hallr rolls his eyes. "Amateurs. Holy dragons, man! We just won the battle. Take a wagon. Get people to load it. While you search, I need an upgrade kit. Keep your eyes open for better blankets and a nice, small pot. A smaller pack that fits me would be great. Big human packs work but are awkward. I'm going toward the King's tent looking for chainmail."

The field is full of people wandering around. Some people have injuries, while others are searching for people or items. Hallr is looking at any fallen to see if they have chainmail or good weapons. He is heading toward the King's tent, toward the witch, and remembering there is a bounty on the King's head.

Still a dozen meters from the King's area, looking at what is happening. He sees a group away from the tent to the north. There are two sets of riders close together. One group is wearing simple brown leather, and the other is a much darker color. As he looks at the group, the two in brown leather turn north and ride away, while the others turn south toward the tents.

The pain in his head returns. It is distinctive for him. The witch is back. His focus is now on the tents, looking for where the witch could be hiding.

Shaking his head, he walks with purpose, spinning the axe as he walks. He passes close to others instead of avoiding them, and they notice. People comment, "What is the dwarf after?"

Between the tent area and Hallr, fighters gather, facing Hallr. There are Grey and Emberfell troops together, and this causes the Emberfell officers to take notice.

Hallr concentrates on reaching the royal area and locating the witch. He doesn't notice the cage wagon or the several riders in dark clothing as they leave the area. The unaffected Emberfell troops form into a group under the command of the same older officer. When the Grey forces move toward Hallr, ignoring the Emberfell soldiers, the old officer looks at Hallr with an intense gaze and walks toward the tents. He yells at Hallr, "What are you looking to kill?"

Without pause, Hallr says, "Witch."

The officer yells, "The witch is alive and after the dwarf, attack the Greys and get the witch."

The Greystone troops can also hear the officer yelling, but they ignore him. They are concentrating on Hallr. The Emberfell forces attack from the side, as the Grey's attacked Hallr. He kills two and then has to shift to defense. They ignore practical fighting techniques and try to overwhelm him.

After several grey forces fall from the soldiers' attack, Hallr can go on the offensive, and the battle concludes quickly after this point. The officer gets to Hallr, grabs his shoulder, and asks, "The witch?"

With the pain gone, Hallr looks at the officer and says, "Not sure. The pain in my head is gone. She stopped."

The officer turns to his men, "Find the witch. There is still the one gold bounty."

Two hours later, Hallr returned to the medical area. Agnarr notices him with a blanket rolled up under his arm. He asks, "Did you find any weapons?"

Hallr says, "A new knife, and a couple of pouches." He pulls a knife from his belt at the small of his back. Showing it, he put it back.

Hallr asks, "How is your collection going?"

Milfred wipes sweat from his forehead. "We've switched back and forth between gathering and helping with the injured. We are taking weapons from the wounded when they arrive."

Hallr nods and asks, "Gather anything good?"

Milfred nods, "Several good swords and a large bag of beans in the wagon we took."

"Now that is a find. Someone hid that bag. More injured I can search. I'm going to take a walk-through."

Agnarr joins him, and they walk among the injured, who lie on the ground. The critically injured are dead, passed out, or recovering.

The less injured are getting treated now as the helpers have time. Most are treating each other.

Looking around, Hallr sees an argument. He can't hear what is being said. He tells Agnarr, "That woman is helping and getting shit. This is the crap that pisses me off. Don't give someone helping you shit."

With that, Hallr walks toward the woman. As he approaches, he hears the argument. The man is saying, "Help him. If you don't save him, you're dead."

The woman replies, "I can't help him with you breathing down my neck. Back up."

Hallr walks up behind the man, reaches up with his right hand, and grabs the man by the collar. He lifts and pulls him backward. Now, on his tiptoes, the man yells, and swings his left arm to hit

Hallr. His arm completely misses, going over Hallr's head.

Hallr shoves, making the man stumble. When the man turns around, he sees Hallr spinning his axe in his left hand.

"Dwarf, you got a problem?"

"Yep. Leave."

Hallr takes a step toward the man, shifting his axe. The man's eyes suddenly get large. He turns and runs several meters away. Hallr says, "Stay there until she is done."

Turning back to the woman, Hallr asks, "Are you okay?"

The woman is standing in her simple dress, covered in blood, looking at Hallr. She walks over, using her wrist to shift her light brown hair away from her face. She looks down at him with brown eyes and says, "I've never seen a dwarf in person. Thank you; I'm fine. I need you to keep him back, but don't let him leave."

Hallr nods and says, "You help those who don't deserve it. They would just as soon rape you."

"It's what I can do to help."

The woman turns back to the man. Kneeling, she checks the dressing on his stomach. Agnarr kneels and talks softly to the woman while Hallr walks down the beds.

Hallr tells the man, "Walk with me. She's working on your friend." As they walk, Hallr kneels and goes through gear at certain beds.

The man asks, "What are you looking for?"

"Chainmail."

After checking the beds, Hallr says, "You stay away from her while she's working." He walks back toward Agnarr.

While walking back, he watches the woman open a pouch, take something out, and put it into the man's mouth. He has seen healers use medicinal herbs many times. Each has a secret recipe. She then places her hands on the man's wound and mumbles something, concentrating. That is what a witch would do.

When Hallr gets to them, Agnarr stands and looks at Hallr.

Hallr's knuckles are white from his grip on the axe. Through clenched teeth, he says, "I'll be leaving now. You need to get away from this area."

The woman stands and says, "You will just leave them? Stay and protect the wounded."

Hallr looks back at her and says, "The scavengers like to kill while people sleep. They will enjoy you. A woman, a healer, and from what I saw, a witch."

Agnarr doesn't look surprised by Hallr saying the woman is a witch. Hallr says, "You didn't react to her magic, which confirms you're more than a blacksmith apprentice."

The woman says, "Please don't talk about that."

Hallr's gut tells him she isn't the witch that was attacking him, but he twirls his axe, "Are you the witch that was attacking me earlier?"

The woman's face goes white, she takes a step back, "No. No. I don't do that."

Agnarr steps in front of her. "She isn't one of those. They aren't all bad. She has been helping."

Hallr looks from Agnarr to the woman, "Aye, right. I've spent my life avoiding and fighting your kind. I expect you will get the army to attack me if I stay. Magic is illegal in this kingdom. If I'm attacked while leaving, I will yell and get the scavengers and the soldiers on your ass."

She says, "Wait. Please. I will not attack you. I promise. Will you help me find some kids?"

Hallr turns to look at the woman, ready to swing his axe. After a second, Agnarr steps over to be next to Hallr and says softly, "The man and his friend know where three kids are being held. They will become slaves if people do not find and rescue them.

Hallr looks at Agnarr, then back to the woman, "That is why you were working on that one. Trying to save him to give you the info on the kids?"

The standing man says, "What the hell. How do you know about the kids?"

Hallr steps aggressively over to the man, grabs the front of his tunic, pulls him forward, and trips him. His axe is in his left hand. He puts one blade on the man's chest and pushes. The man tries to grab the axe handle and push it away. He says, "Stop! What are you doing?"

"You know where three kids are being held."

The man's demeanor changes. "Why do you care about some brat kids the king was buying as servants?"

"I don't like people making kids slaves. Tell me."

The woman says, "They are children. They aren't cattle."

Hallr pushes on the axe. The man is trying to push back, but he doesn't have leverage. As Hallr presses, he is having trouble breathing, and the blade is cutting into him. "Where?"

"A cage wagon close to the King's tent."

Hallr releases the pressure on the axe. The man breathes hard. Hallr looks at the woman. "I was in that area. The king's tent was being taken down, and there was no cage wagon."

"They must have moved them. We have to find them."

"No, we are several hours after a major battle. The scavengers are going to go through everything. They will take whatever they want."

"You can't just do nothing."

"I can and I will. Dying by being foolish doesn't work for me."

"Help me find them."

"Witch, I'm leaving. This area is going to be more dangerous than the battle soon. Scavengers don't just kill soldiers; they kill everyone. Let the killing happen and look for them afterward. I won't help a witch who will attack me when I'm not watching."

Hallr walks back toward Milfred with Agnarr and the woman following. Hallr is looking in the wagon, pulls out a small pot and some food, and starts putting them into a pack that Milfred hands him. Milfred says, "I need to return to my smithy wagon. Your gear pack is there. Will you walk with us to get the wagon?"

Hallr looks at the rest of the stuff in the wagon they took over.

It is full of weapons, gear, a barrel of water, and food. They have two yoked oxen ready to go. "I don't need that old gear. You need to be kilometers away before the scavengers kill you. The scavengers will start with the Grey camp, but they will go to the Emberfell area as well."

Looking at the woman, he pauses. He shakes his head and starts walking back toward the Emberfell tents.

Milfred asks, "What is your name, girl?"

"I'm Sheyla."

"Get in the wagon."

Agnarr whispers something to her. She nods and heads to the wagon.

Hallr is exiting the fancy general's tent. Even though Emberfell won the battle, the scavengers are going through everything. The scavengers probably killed the general. Looters have already looted the tent. He found a few pieces of jerky and half a loaf of bread, which he is putting into the pack. He hears Milfred yelling.

Hallr is walking toward the road south, not toward Milfred, yelling, but in that direction.

Now he hears, "My tools. They only left the really heavy stuff."

In the distance, he sees men searching the Emberfell tents, taking items to a wagon. As he walks and watches the scavengers, he sees a man who was hiding being dragged out of a tent. The man is holding a small pack to his chest.

Hallr takes notice of the pack's size. The pack is small, kid-sized, and a good fit for him.

The man is on his knees, clutching the pack, pleading with the two men. Hallr can't hear what is being said.

One man laughs, and the other stabs the kneeling man in the back.

Hallr shifts to walk toward them. The size of that pack, which is a much better size for him, has him interested. He wants to see if he can get that pack.

He can still hear Milfred yelling. Now the talk is about hitching two wagons together.

Walking faster than usual, Hallr watches the men toss the small pack into the back of the wagon. They then return to the tent.

Getting to the wagon, Hallr could hear the men in the tent talking about what to take. Hallr is too short to reach the pack. He places his axe on the back of the wagon, puts his hands on the board, and pushes himself up.

As he stands in the wagon, he feels intense pain in his head. The witch. It is always worse when he isn't holding his axe. As a dwarf, he has always been told he is resistant to magic, but he doesn't understand why there is intense pain in his head, especially without his axe.

As he reached down, he feels an impact on his left side, knocking him over on top of his axe—a new shooting pain in his side.

He grabs his axe and tries to jump off the wagon. Landing hard, his head is clearer while holding the axe. The pain in his side is less. Looking at this side, he sees blood, no knife or arrow.

He raises his axe as a shield when the tent opens, and two men with items appear.

They look at Hallr, drop the items, and pull out their short swords.

Hallr turns toward them, lifting his axe when he feels a hard impact and a sharp pain in his right leg. Looking down, there is a dagger sticking out of his leg. As he looks, the dagger flies out of his leg. Looking up, he sees it fly into the hand of an older woman who is wearing a long black leather coat and has grey hair.

Focusing on the two men who are closer, he shifts. The axe moves to be a shield as he steps to the side. He feels the pain in his head getting stronger. His leg has shooting pain as he steps.

The axe deflects the first man's blade as Hallr continues to shift. He wants to put this man between himself, the second man, and the witch.

He uses the cone point on the handle to stab the man in the chest, knocking him down. As he takes a painful step toward the second man, he raises the axe to shield himself from the man's sword when the witch's dagger hits and deflects.

Hallr swings the axe blades to the side to create a swing and chop this man. He gets the axe moving, looking at the man's sword and body movements. His much heavier axe has the advantage in a parry move.

The man's attempt to block the axe completely fails, and the axe knocks the blade out of his hand.

Hallr continues the motion, using the momentum of the axe with a new direction to start a big swing that will cut the man in half.

The axe hits the man in the side as he is trying to put his arm up to block it. As the axe slices into the man, Hallr feels another impact on his left side. With his injured leg and the heavy axe, he stumbles.

Hallr takes his left hand off the axe handle and reaches for the handle of the dagger sticking out of his side. His fingers grasp the handle as it slides out of him, throwing him off balance.

Stumbling, he falls at the feet of the second man, who is collapsing from the axe impact. He is dead; he just hasn't realized it yet.

As the man falls, Hallr tries to get to his hands and knees, but the man lands on him, and they both go to the ground. Trying to lessen the fall, Hallr lets go of the axe, and the pain in his head intensifies.

Hallr knows he is in trouble. He needs to get up and get his axe. Using his dwarven strength, he moves his hands under him to push the man up and off. The easy way to get him off is to put the body fully on top of the axe.

Hallr shifts to one knee, reaching for the axe handle when the dagger hits him again. This time it hits his right shoulder. This is the arm grabbing the axe, and the impact moves his hand away *from the axe handle.*

"The witch is trying to keep me from touching the axe."
Hallr is focused on the handle. He needs to get to his axe. One-on-one, he can kill the witch. He has done it many times before.

Reaching, another dagger struck his shoulder. The witch is walking toward him, smiling. The daggers fly back, one into each hand.

Hallr sees the witch toss one dagger in the air. It is turning, and as it comes down, she gestures, and the blade flies toward Haller. This one hits his right chest.

Hallr gets his hand on the axe handle, the blade is stuck under the dead man, and when the dagger hits his chest. Another pain, but this one, along with the shoulder wounds, makes it hard to move the axe.

Breathing hard, trying to pull the axe out, Hallr feels like a cough starting. The blade has hit his lung, and he will start coughing blood now. He has to end this quickly.

Jerking the axe handle, he moves it out from under the body, causing Hallr to fall backward. The next dagger flies over him as he falls.

He rolls to the side, gripping the axe tightly, and stands. The dagger hits his right side and knocks him over. The axe is on top of him as he lies on his back.

Hallr is on his back, angry, frustrated. He has killed dozens of witches who have attacked him like this. None of them has been this strong at making his head hurt, or flying daggers at him so strong and so fast.

On his back, looking up as the witch walks up. She says, "Well, now. After ruining my plan today, I thought I would have to hunt you down. Now I have the box and a dead dwarf. I just need to find the kids."

As the witch speaks, Hallr sees the first man stand. He reaches for his short sword when the witch, hearing a sound, turns to look at the man.

Her head snaps around, looking the other way, over Hallr at

someone else. She says, "A controller witch. What are you doing? I've defeated the dwarf."

The man takes a step toward the witch, raising his sword. The witch turns and pushes him with her magic. He stumbles back. The man recovers and begins walking toward the witch again. There is blood running down his chest from the axe cone that hit him. He focuses intensely, ignoring any pain. His focus is totally on the witch.

The witch is looking across Hallr and someone. She says, "You can't stop me, girl."

Hallr coughs. He can feel the liquid he is coughing up and knows it's blood. As the next wave starts, he shifts toward his left side and shoves the axe toward the witch.

Letting go of the axe, the pain in his head intensified, but the blunt part of the axe hits the witch in the ankle, making her stumble.

The man behind her raises his sword as he takes the last couple of steps toward the stumbling witch. The witch is recovering from the axe hit when the sword enters her lower back.

Screaming in pain, back arching as the man pulls the sword back, twisting it. She turns and angrily stabs the man in the gut several times.

The man looks at the witch as his face changes, as if he is suddenly looking at someone else when he falls.

Hallr has continued to roll over, and as she is stabbing the man, he has crawled to the axe.

Hallr stands with blood streaming out of multiple wounds, his chest covered in his own blood from coughing. He has the axe and shoves the cone into the witch's chest as she turns back toward him. She stumbles back and falls.

Hallr takes a step, swinging the axe up and letting it fall into the center of her chest. As he is raising the axe, he hears behind him, "No. I need her alive."

The witch dies, the great axe buried in her chest, with Hallr smiling down at her. As her eyes close, he staggers to the side, *begins coughing, and falls to his hands and knees.*

He hears footsteps, then hears Agnarr's voice. "We got you. Sheyla is a healer. We will ...."

Hallr yells, "No witches," and starts coughing again.

Struggling to take a breath, Hallr hears Milfred, "I can drag his axe to the wagons."

Sheyla's voice says, "He wanted that little pack, so did the witch. Agnarr, you take him to the wagon so I can heal him."

Hallr feels Agnarr grabbing his shoulder as he coughs again, and then blackness.

Teppo and his group are approaching the area from the west. They left the main road yesterday when the Emberfell patrols became more frequent. The king's patrols are searching, including looking for witches who might impact the battle.

The witch Anfisa left the group three days ago to make the final preparations and conduct negotiations. They dispatched her to the area to influence the flow of the battle. The Greystone king, friendly to witches, needs to win. The Emberfell king will see his army fail, not even realizing a witch was the reason.

What the Greystone king doesn't know is that he is also being manipulated. The king is told he can buy orphaned children with magical abilities to help his army fight. Teppo's group wants these special kids to train them in control magic and control the Greystone king from the shadows.

The kids need chaperones and trainers, which Teppo's group will provide.

The news that the battle is already over has Teppo in a foul mood. This group knows that means things didn't go as planned. The Greystone army lost the battle. When they heard a dwarf was in the battle, most of the group tried to avoid being close to Teppo.

Ranjeet, his second in command, rides up and says, "We can't find Anfisa. She isn't at the meeting point, and we can't sense her now."

Teppo is glaring at Ranjeet, "There was a dwarf, and the Greys lost. Any sign of the kids or the box?"

"None. The only reason Anfisa is not at the meeting point is that she is retrieving the box."

"We need to search the area. Have men spread out."

"They will fight scavengers."

"Kill whomever you need to. Find Anfisa, the box, and the kids."

Peace With the Enemy

Hallr hears one of the oxen, a jingle of the harness. Smelling smoke from a fire and cooking something. He opens his eyes and looks to the side. The mostly empty blacksmith's wagon is his bed. Hallr tries to sit up and feels shooting pain in his side, chest, and leg. He groans in pain.

Agnarr quickly climbs into the wagon and says, "Don't move."

"I need to get up."

"No, you don't. You almost died. You lost a lot of blood from the seven knife wounds."

"I killed the witch, but there is another one."

"Calm down. You don't have to worry. Sheyla is bringing you soup. She spent over an hour keeping you from dying, then we stopped to make the soup."

Hallr is breathing; his chest is better. The urge to cough is there, but it is on the edge. He can take slow breaths to make it easier. There is distant yelling, as if someone is being tortured.

Looking at Agnarr, he says, "Are we still close to the battlefield?"

"We are on the road. After traveling south a distance, we stopped."

Hallr says, "We need to get away from the battlefield. Scavengers will search and kill anyone they think has something of value."

"We will be okay. We will take care of everything. You don't need to worry right now."

"You mean you have a witch?"

"I don't do that," Sheyla says from outside the wagon.

"But you did with the guy behind the witch."

"I had no other way to stop her. I did that, or you would have died. You're welcome."

"Didn't ask for a witch to help."

Agnarr is looking at Hallr, takes his hand off his chest, and says, "Maybe we made a mistake saving you. You go wander with the scavengers around. Let them see a wounded dwarf with a Mithril axe and see how long you last."

Hallr lifts his head while staring at Agnarr. He hears from Sheyla, "Rip open the wounds, and I'm not spending all my energy fixing you again. That was hard enough with you being a dwarf."

Hallr puts his head back down. Agnarr nods, "Seven knife wounds. That is a lot for anyone."

"Why aren't I completely healed?"

"That isn't how it works. A healing witch gets your body heal itself faster. The witch can quickly heal a single minor wound. Your body does the work. That means your body must have the materials to repair itself. Seven major wounds take time."

Sheyla's voice says, "That is why we stopped to make soup. You need food. Your body needs materials to heal. Agnarr, give him this."

Agnarr reaches over and takes a bowl. Setting it aside, he says to Hallr, "You need to sit up so you can eat the soup."

Agnarr helps Hallr get adjusted. He is sitting up with his back to the side of the wagon. Agnarr hands him the bowl. The wagon sides are high enough that no one can see Hallr unless they are at the wagon looking inside.

Hallr says, "Put out the fire, get the pot onto the forge, and start moving. We need to get out of the area. Scavengers are dangerous."

He hears Milfred's voice, "Yep. I've got the wagons better tied together. The oxen will be slow, but they are strong enough to pull both wagons."

They had been moving for a few minutes when four men on horseback surrounded them. One of them is clearly on a horse for the first time. He is correcting every little movement of the horse.

Milfred says, "What can we do for you, fine men?"

"Are you a blacksmith?"

"Yes, that is my wagon that was looted. Can't fix shit without my *gear."*

Another asks, "With all the blood on you, girl, can you do healing?"

"I can only do simple stuff; otherwise, there wouldn't be this much blood on me."

"We need a healer; you need to come with us."

"Why?"

"We have injured people. You need to help them."

Agnarr asks, "What's in it for us. We go with you only to be robbed and killed. We can take our chances here, right now."

Hallr is quietly sitting in the wagon. He is low enough that the riders can't see him over the sides of the wagon.

The rider says, "You will come with us or die."

Sheyla replies, "You say something, and we just jump. If you kill us, your friends will die. If you force us, I wave my hand, but do nothing, and your friends die. The only path that works for you is if you agree to our safe passage and return the blacksmith's tools."

Agnarr says, "Think about it while your friends bleed to death."

"Agreed, now come with us."

Agnarr looks down at Hallr, who is sitting quietly with a bowl of soup in his lap. Agnarr says, "We leave the wagons. Sheyla and I will follow you with the healing items we have. You bring blacksmith tools this way."

Sheyla healed the dwarf but is staying away from him. He is angry at magi especially control witches. It was her only choice to stop the witch who was attacking him. She made a personal vow not to control, then she did it to save a dwarf that would just kill her if she blinked wrong.

But she saw him. How smart and aggressive he was during the fight. Wearing tattered rags, not just another ruthless scavenger. In return for his help with the brutes and for information about the kids, she was repaying him.

She requests Agnarr get items out of the wagon when they travel with the scavengers. She hopes the dwarf will rest and heal.

Agnarr wants to talk strategy as they walk, but he has to be careful what he says, "We need to heal and help as much as we can. Give the leaders priority. We talk to them and try to get them on our side."

Sheyla says, "Keep your eyes open. If they have the kids, they will be locked up or hiding in a tent."

"These guys will look for how they can exploit the kids. They will want money at a minimum."

Agnarr turns to a rider and asks, "How far do we walk?"

"Another kilometer."

Sheyla says, "I need one of you to ride ahead. I need you to get things to help. I need clean water and clean linen bandages. If I do all this work and they still get an infection, it would be a waste. If you have any alcohol, strong drink, the good stuff, I can use some of that as well."

A rider asks, "Anything else?"

Agnarr says, "If you have any healer supplies from tents, like herbs, bring them out."

One rider goes at a gallop toward the camp.

As they approach, they need to take a route through tents on the edge. This gives them a different angle across the camp. Agnarr is looking and whispers, "A cage wagon."

Sheyla looks over and then reaches out mentally. She initially detects nothing. Then she detects someone. They are elusive. She understands this. She has had to hide before; remaining hidden from other mages takes discipline. They are afraid.

"Agnarr, they are here. I don't know if they are in the wagon."

They arrive at a tent and hear a single person moaning. Agnarr is looking around. "I expected to see an open area with wounded people."

Sheyla walks up to the tent and asks, "Just the ones in here, or are there more?"

"These are the ones still alive."

Entering the tent, Sheyla sees four men lying on the ground. One is awake and moaning, holding his leg. No limbs are missing. Everyone has blood on them.

Turning to Agnarr, she asks, "Can you check the two on the left? I need to know how bad the wounds are. I need to focus on the worst injury first."

Agnarr nods and moves to the left. When one rider walks in, Agnarr asks, "What happened? I mean, what was used to injure them?"

"There were other riders, and they said they were looking for a woman. They found the only woman in the area dead near one of our wagons and two dead men.

"Riders searched for a woman, couldn't find her, and now your men are injured. What is the rest of the story?" asked Agnarr.

"Our men wanted their horses and gear. There was a fight."

Sheyla asks, "Who is the leader?"

The rider points to one of the unconscious men on the right. She kneels next to him and pulls up his leather shirt. "This looks like two arrows. You pulled them out, which way?"

The rider looks confused. "We pulled them out this way." He is just trying to show they pulled them out the way they went in."

Agnarr says, "That isn't good."

"What?"

"That does more damage. The arrowhead causes more damage if it is just pulled out. It is better to push the arrow through or angle it to the side and push it through. The little barbs on the side of an arrowhead rip you up when you pull it out."

Agnarr asks, "Where are those other men now?"

They got injured and rode off.

Agnarr nods, "They will probably be back with more men.

You should get ready."

Sheyla asks, *"Where are the supplies I asked for?"*

"Let me check."

When the rider leaves, Sheyla says, *"Riders looking for the witch."*

"Probably the kids as well."

Sheyla nods, *"I need to stop their bleeding, then we bandage them and get out."*

"They will not let us walk away. We need to give Milfred some time to create something."

Sheyla looks at Agnarr with a questioning expression. Agnarr says, *"I don't know, but he will do something."*

After they leave with the riders, Hallr picks up the bowl and finishes the soup. Putting the bowl aside, he moves slowly and crawls to the back of the wagon.

His axe, pack, and the little pack he was interested in are at the back of the wagon. He knows he has to get away from the wagons. Agnarr mentioned a wounded dwarf walking around; however, an injured dwarf sitting in a wagon is even worse.

Sliding off the back, he grabs the axe. His pack is heavy. Looking at the items, he can't take them all. Grabbing the little pack, because its size is better for him and his axe, he turns. He still doesn't know what is in the pack. He will dump the pack's contents later. The blacksmith is doing something in the first wagon and doesn't hear Hallr moving.

Limping off the road, into the trees, away from the direction of the camp, so he can't be seen. Now, the only evidence that he was in the wagon is blood. He doesn't sit. Getting up will be a problem.

Sitting the axe next to a tree where he can see the wagons, he shifts the pack and opens it. Inside, he sees a rectangle made of Mithril. The pack is too light for it to be solid. He reaches to pull it out when he hears horses.

They ride up to the wagons on the other side. He watches the blacksmith shift so that the wagons are between them. He is wearing a sword. From the look of the handle, it's one of the better ones they picked up.

One rider says, "Are you the blacksmith?"

"Yes."

The riders approach the blacksmith's wagon, look inside, then turn to the first wagon. He drops the item he is holding and moves away. The next rider brings his horse close to the wagon and does the same. Then the third rider. A hammer, tongs, and his thick leather gloves. "That was the bargain: blacksmith tools for healing."

Milfred says, "What about the rest? The bellows, the fine hammer, the iron stock?"

"These are the tools; that is the bargain."

With that, they turn and ride away at a gallop.

Milfred goes to the wagon to get the tools. He turns and looks at the woods. "Smart. You can come back."

Hallr doesn't move. He closes the top of the pack and latches it, then puts it down next to the tree. The riders were inspecting the contents of the wagons, deciding what they could take.

After stopping the bleeding, Sheyla is evaluating the condition of the four men. They are in awful shape from damage and loss of blood. She needs to concentrate on the worst wounds to use her magic. She says, "I don't think this one will survive; the wound is too big."

Agnarr is applying bandages to cover the open wounds. He says, "There is a non-magical healing thing I learned. It takes catgut and a needle."

"What? I've never heard of this."

"When you don't have healers, witch healers, you need to try other things. You basically sew the skin back together to help

keep the wound closed, and it heals better."

"That is interesting. Where do we get this catgut?"

"Large cities with apothecaries. The good ones know."

"Hidden magic. I'm starting on the belly of this one first. This could be a while."

After working about an hour on three of the men, they are people outside. The tent flap opens, and three children walk in.

The man holding the tent flap is heavily armed and armored. He says, "Here they are, Merial. I will wait outside."

Sheyla now focuses on the new arrivals and says, "Hello."

She is looking at the guard as he closes the tent flap. With the flap closed, she shifts to the kids. She feels the touch of another magi, and she squints at the older girl.

The youngest girl appears to be five, the boy ten, and the older girl twelve or thirteen. These ages are usually too young to express magical power fully. This is their training age.

The older girl says, "Hi. We..."

The boy interjects, "We want to go with you and learn magic."

Nodding, the oldest says, "You're a healer. Can you teach us?" while the youngest is nodding.

Sheyla glances at Agnarr and says, "Hi, I'm Sheyla. How did you get them to bring you to us?"

The youngest says, "I'm Merial. I asked him nicely with my powers."

Sheyla shifts, "Did someone teach you how to do that?"

"I've just always done it."

Agnarr says, "Hi, Merial. I'm Agnarr. How many can you ask at the same time?"

"Mostly I do one, but I did three to have them open the cage door."

Sheyla is sitting calmly, blinking. She is looking at a junior version of herself. This version has much darker hair and inquisitive brown eyes. This is how it started for her. She could ask, and people did things. Then, an old witch took her from her family to train her as a controller. She learned only later how bad that was.

Taking a breath, she says, "I will teach you healing. What are your names?"

"I'm Tanisha," says the oldest

The boy says, "Feliu."

"Merial."

Sheyla says, "Let's start with this man."

Looking at Agnarr, then back to the kids, she shifts so they can get closer and begins explaining.

Sheyla knows these children are exceptional. They do not know how powerful they are with magic. With little to no training, they can control people. Control covens will spend years searching for children like this; they can train them and corrupt them.

Agnarr concentrates on an injured person and bandages them. After a minute, the boy turns to Agnarr, "You don't heal with magic?"

"No, I can't do healing magic very well. I'm better at push magic. Women usually heal better. Men are usually the ones to do push magic. Where are you from, Feliu?"

"West of here, on the ocean."

"Is your dad a fisherman?"

Tears start rolling down his cheeks. The older girl turns and puts her arm around him. "Leave him alone."

"I was just trying to learn about you three."

"His family is dead, just like mine and hers. They killed everyone when they took us. No one to look for us. No one to go back to. We only have each other. We are family now."

Agnarr says, "I'm sorry. Were you going to learn to get training from someone?"

Feliu says, "They said they would evaluate us to become controllers."

The oldest girl says, "We will be controllers or support for controllers."

Sheyla asks, "Would you like to travel with us? Would you like to go somewhere to get training?"

Feliu nods, Tanisha nods after a pause, and Merial asks, "Learn to heal?"

"Yes, and more. But you won't learn to use control magic. Good magi do not do that."

Merial replies, "I'm a good magi. I need to learn good magic."

Agnarr says, "I know a village that can give them the training they need. The village will not take just any kids. They will want to evaluate how strong they are."

Tanisha says, "They don't want us because they see us as controllers." The guards at the wagon said someone would pay to get us because we are strong with magic. We can be their slaves to control others."

Agnarr smirks, then nods, "That is why you three were in the cage at the battle. You were being traded, sold."

Sheyla clenches her teeth. This isn't good for these kids. Turning to Agnarr, she says, "We need to finish with these four. Your friend Milfred needs to do whatever he is going to do, and we need to create a plan to get the kids out of here."

Merial says, "We can leave. The guard will help."

Agnarr says, "It would be nice to get the blacksmith tools."

Sheyla says, "First, the kids and I are going to heal these guys as much as we can."

Sheyla is talking to the kids, telling them what to think about to stimulate the body's healing. They don't need to understand all the details to start.

Sheyla is just getting the kids to ask good questions and to learn when they hear a hammer. A blacksmith's hammer hitting an anvil in the distance.

Agnarr says, "Whatever is going to happen, it is time."

Hallr has been watching the blacksmith. The blacksmith puts the pot of soup in the first wagon and then moves other things around *in the wagons.*

Watching the blacksmith, Hallr is tired. He knows if he sits down, he won't get back up fast or easily, but he needs to rest. Holding the tree, he slowly lowers himself. He put the small pack behind him as a prop to continue watching the blacksmith.

The hammer startles him awake on the anvil. He had fallen asleep. He looks for his axe and sees it still propped against the tree. His travel pack is now sitting next to the axe with a waterskin, within easy reach.

Hallr looks over to see the blacksmith hitting the anvil with his hammer, which the riders had dropped in the wagon earlier. He is not hitting any material; he is just hitting the anvil.

Hallr reaches over and pulls the waterskin over to take a drink. He must have snored when he fell asleep, and the blacksmith brought the pack and water.

Soon, riders arrive at the wagons. They are looking around and churning, circling the wagons, looking at everything. When the riders circle the wagon, he stops hammering.

The scavengers walking now appear. When a group has assembled, the blacksmith says, "The bargain was smithy tools for helping to heal your men. Giving me a hammer, tongs, and gloves isn't the bargain."

"What are you going to do about it?"

"Now that all of you are here, who's watching the camp? Who's protecting the loot? You didn't keep the bargain, so you need to deal with us, looting everything."

Sheyla looks at Agnarr. "What do we do?"

Agnarr shrugs, "Don't know yet."

They hear the people of the camp moving toward the sound. The camp seems to be drawn to the sound.

Merial asks, "Tommy, are you still there?"

From outside the tent, they hear, "Yes, Merial. I won't leave.

No one will get in. Go under the side if someone wants to get in."

Sheyla is looking at each of the kids, then at the wounded. "Should we go out?"

Agnarr is looking at Sheyla and nods, "I think we need to get out of the camp. If Milfred is drawing them to the wagons, there will be a fight, unless he can make them leave."

Sheyla nods, then stops. Eyes moving, thinking. "He drew them away so we could get out. Maybe we draw them back, so they leave the wagons, then we go back to the wagons and leave."

Agnarr nods, "That could work, or they could chase us."

Sheyla says, "We don't have many options. Kids, will you go with us?"

Feliu says, "Yes, we all will go."

The girls nod.

As Agnarr steps to the tent flap, they hear horses. A voice says, "Where is everyone?"

Tommy outside says, "They went to check some sound."

"What's in the tent?"

"Wounded."

"You need to guard the wounded."

"I'm guarding my friends inside the tent."

"I see. So, you're okay with us looking inside?"

"Why are you looking in here when there are all these other tents to look inside?"

"No one is guarding the loot in the other tents. Only this one."

They hear horses approaching. Outside, they hear, "Riders are coming." Then they hear hooves from the direction of the wagons, followed by yelling.

Agnarr shifts to the other side of the tent, stepping over the head of one of the wounded men, and kneels and pulls up the side of the tent. He waves to the kids and Sheyla.

Outside the tent, they move away, keeping the tent between them and the yelling riders.

<<<>>>

Hallr is smiling. The blacksmith has the scavengers confused and now mad at each other. Someone yells, "Why didn't you stay?"

Another says, "Now the camp is unprotected."

The blacksmith says, "You're arguing like grade-school kids. We are just getting more loot.

"What about this guy?"

"He is just one guy. We can catch him anytime."

The riders turn their horses towards the camp and ride off, quickly followed by the men on foot, some running, some walking. In a minute, the blacksmith is alone again.

Hallr takes another drink and considers how to get up. He looks at the human-sized large pack, the small pack, and the axe. Shifting, he attaches the small pack to the larger pack. Putting on the pack, he then grabs the tree to help himself stand. Slow, painful, using his hands to climb while standing.

There is pain in his side and in his leg. When he gets fully upright, he can feel blood running down his side and his leg. He picks up the axe, turns, and walks deeper into the forest, and then turns south.

In minutes, Hallr hears the wagons moving. Hallr is moving slowly and trying to keep his breathing controlled. His leg is oozing and painful to walk on. He needs to keep walking. Hallr is focusing on making slow progress to get out of the scavengers' area.

Hallr stops, listening, then looking toward the road, thinking, "He can't outrun the horseback riders in the slow wagons. The scavengers are going to catch up."

The wagons go by him on the road while he watches. He walks again, watching. The wagons continue to crawl. Walking slowly, he is less stiff and making progress. He can still see the wagons ahead through the trees and brush on the road.

Hearing the wagons stop, he pauses. Then a noise, then the witch, the apprentice, and three kids become visible.

He is on the other side of the road, but, shaking his head, he shifts a little deeper off the road.

Sheyla smiles when she sees the wagons. They hurry over, and she gestures for the kids to climb in. Agnarr helps them get into the first wagon. She goes to the smithy wagon at the back to check on the dwarf.

Getting to the back, she looks in and sees the dwarf is gone. She hurries up to the front, "Milfred, where is the dwarf?"

"He took off after you left with the scavengers. It was a good thing. When their riders showed up with the hammer, tongs, and gloves, they would have found him and probably killed him. Get in the wagon."

Agnarr says, "Sheyla, I introduced the kids to Milfred. Milfred, there were other riders at the camp. They were yelling when we snuck away. They will be after us soon."

Milfred says, "Our only chance is to disappear from this road, or get another group to fight them."

Sheyla says, "How do we do that?"

Hallr is walking better. Walking has helped with stiffness, but it has also made him tired. With the wagons stopped, he is now closer. He walks into an area of less dense growth. As he walks into this area, he realizes it looks like an old, abandoned road off the main road. He is just ahead of the wagons as he completes crossing the old road. Knowing he needs to stop, he is tired. He has been drinking water, and his skin is almost empty.

Feeling something in his head, not pain, not an attack, he immediately thinks, "Witch."

Turning back to the wagon, he sees the little girl swing her head around and look directly at him. It isn't in his direction; she is looking directly at him. She waves.

The wave throws Hallr off. No one waves to him. Witches actively ignore, shun, and attack him. This little witch did...did what? While he watches, she says something and waves.

Everyone turns to look at him. He looks at the position of the wagons, the old road, and then back at the kids. Sweating and tired, he takes several stumbling steps back onto the abandoned road.

Looking at the wagon, he can see the apprentice. His name is.....Agnarr. He is pointing and saying something. Hallr drops his axe. Looking down, he can see his empty hand. He doesn't let go of his axe.

Hallr collapses, unconscious.

Agnarr says, "He is standing in an open area. That is an old road. Turn the wagons. Let's take that side road and get away from the main road."

They watch Hallr collapse, and Merial says, "We need to help him."

Sheyla says, "Merial, he hates witches. Every witch he has met in his life has attacked him."

"Accept you?"

"Not me. I didn't attack; I worked to help him heal. He is harder to heal. Healing magic works best when we help the person feel better and make them believe they are getting better. Dwarves are resistant to magic, making them harder to heal."

Tanisha asks, "How did he get injured?"

"A fight with a powerful witch. She had grey hair and a long black coat."

The kids exchanged looks. Feliu says, "We saw her. She wanted to take us to get training."

Tanisha says, "She was talking to us when the war started. She turned, said dwarf, and walked away."

Merial is looking toward the dwarf. "Why did she attack him?"

Agnarr says, "There are stories everywhere that witches attack dwarves."

Sheyla says, "They attack because they are resistant to magic. Control witches can't control them, so they try to kill them."

Merial says, "He could be nice, and they still attack him?"

"Yes."

"I don't want to attack him. I'm a witch, and I want to help him."

Agnarr smiles, "Merial, we can try, but he has never met a nice witch before. Now there will be three, plus two nice wizards. He won't believe we are nice."

Milfred has turned the wagons, and they are going over the smaller brush and trees toward the road.

Merial looks from Agnarr to Sheyla, "I will be nice."

Hallr hears a voice whispering. He is thirsty. He shifts his right arm, and pain shoots through his shoulder.

A small hand touches his shoulder, and he hears, "Hi. I'm Merial. Are you hungry?"

Hallr opens his eyes and turns his head to see the little girl smiling at him. She has dark brown curly hair, brown eyes, and her skin is even darker than Hallr's when he has been in the sun. "You're a real dwarf. They said your name is Hallr. Are you hungry, or maybe thirsty?"

Hallr nods and says, "Thirsty."

Merial reaches over and brings a waterskin to Hallr. She pulls the cork and puts the spout to Hallr's mouth and drizzles.

After he finishes, Hallr looks at Merial and asks, "Why are you helping me." You're a witch."

Merial says, "I want to help. I'm a good person."

Hallr puts his head down and closes his eyes. "I can't stop you."

"Stop me from what? Maybe I can hug you? I like hugs?"

With his eyes closed, Hallr listens to the girl talk, half asleep. She doesn't stop. She talks about everything. The wagon, the trees, the *road, the birds, she keeps talking. Hallr has experienced nothing like this in his life.*

Agnarr climbs into the wagon, sits next to Hallr, and asks, "Things going okay?"

Hallr says, "This is the first witch that has tried to talk me to death."

"You are so single-minded. Not everyone is trying to kill you. You don't realize she's sitting next to you all this time, trying to heal you. The food is almost ready. I came to get Merial to take care of herself. She has focused on you for over a couple of hours.

"What about the scavengers? They came to the wagons. They won't give up that easily."

"Yes, we turned off the main road onto the side road you pointed out. It is old, overgrown, and not obvious. We traveled several kilometers before we stopped. We will only have the fire during the day to cook."

Milfred walked up to the wagon and put the food pot on the back. "Chow time. We got Milfred mush or jerky."

Hallr says, "I am hungry. Is the mush spiced?"

Milfred smiles, "Just for you, the spice is heavy to make the veg taste better. You ready to try it?"

Hallr nods. Agnarr asks, "Meriel, are you ready for some food?"

Merial smiles and nods, "Can I eat with Hallr?"

Hallr turns to her, "Why do you want to eat with me?"

"I've never eaten with a dwarf."

Agnarr smiles as he hands them both bowls. "Merial, I bet Hallr has never shared a meal with a witch before. He's probably shaking inside with excitement."

Hallr glares at Agnarr.

An hour later, Hallr is short with Merial. "I need to pee, and I'm sure you do as well. I'm getting out of this wagon and moving."

"You need to be careful; don't hurt yourself. I'll help you?"

"Where are the other two? Why are you always here and not

with them?"

"You need my help. Sheyla showed me the basics of healing. I needed to practice, and you're the best patient. I get to try different things, and you don't complain."

When Hallr moves, his leg surprises him. The pain is so much less; he isn't limping. It still hurts, but more like a soreness than a sharp, shooting pain. His right side is sore and not burning. He can breathe better, and his shoulder isn't shouting in pain.

Sliding off the back of the wagon. He stretches, looking toward the other wagon and sees Agnarr with the boy and Sheyla with the older girl.

The boy is at an age when he is portly, just before a growth spurt, with straight, light brown hair. The older girl is looking at him, so Hallr can see her eyes are blue and she has light hair. Her features are like those of the witch, Sheyla. They may have been born in the same area.

Sheyla says, "Hi, how are you feeling?"

"Better."

Tanisha says, "Merial, you look tired. Have you been trying to heal him all this time?"

Merial nods.

Hallr turns, saying nothing else, and walks toward the woods.

Agnarr watches Hallr walk away and Merial's face.

Sheyla says to Merial, "Let's walk together."

"Why is he so mad at me?"

"He has been alone, with no family, and every witch he has known has attacked him."

Merial replies, "We are the same. I have no family; witches killed them. If I don't obey witches, they will punish me."

"Maybe you could tell him that."

"You are the same. None of us has a family. Can we be a family together?"

"I'm not sure Hallr is ready to think about us differently."

"Yes, I'm sure. We searched the camp. We questioned people. I used control magic to compel them. The box is not in the camp," states Ranjeet angrily.

Teppo says, "And the kids?"

"Ran off, escaped. They are far enough away that I can't sense them. I don't sense any magi. The assigned guard said he was outside the tent, and they escaped while he was dealing with us."

"Where did they go? Where could they go?"

"Teppo, it is almost night. We will fumble around and get nothing. In the morning, we will get the scavengers to search."

"Have the scavengers search and bring everything here. Our men can range out. There was also a dwarf in the area. If they can find and eliminate him, we remove that threat."

"Agreed. It would be interesting to get the box and test what we learn on the dwarf."

"That would be a great trail, but given the choice, I would eliminate the dwarf threat if we get the chance."

<<<>>>

"Morning."

Hallr opens his eyes to see Merial kneeling next to him, smiling. She is holding a cup.

"I have water for you."

"Why are you being this way with me? You won't convince me witches are now wonderful."

"That isn't true. Some witches are evil, and some are good. I'm one of the good ones. Sheyla is going to train me to be a healer."

"You've met evil witches?"

Merial nods, "They killed my family. Now I don't have a family, just like you."

"Why are you a good witch?"

"I want to be good. I like being nice to people. Why are you so angry all the time?"

"Humans are mean to me. Why should I be nice when they are going to attack me, cheat me, and steal from me? Humans think dwarfs are lower, inferior."

"We both have no family. We both don't like evil witches. You were nice. I like you. Can we be a family together?

"I'm a dwarf. Humans and dwarves aren't family."

"Why not?"

"You don't want to be my family. Other humans and witches will be mean to you if you're my family. It won't be fair to you. I need to leave."

"You need to heal more. Then I will go with you."

"I don't understand why you would consider traveling with me. How will you learn to heal?"

"Family is more important. The witches were mean and killed my family. Now I'm older and understand. I won't let them hurt my family."

Hallr sits up, takes the cup of water, and drinks it. "Thank you. I'm sorry about your family. You should stay with humans and learn to be a healer."

Hallr hears Agnarr, "Are you ready to start the fire, Feliu?"

"Yes."

"To make it easier, you want to stack the small wood items with the smallest on the bottom, larger on top. The small ones will light the larger ones."

After a minute, Agnarr says, "That is a good start. Now concentrate on the bottom. Make the smallest one's move; make them hot."

After a few moments, "I see smoke. Good job, Feliu, now keep going. Make it hotter."

Milfred says, "Let's get a kettle going for some tea."

Sheyla says, "Now that everyone is up, we need to change the wagons. Move stuff to the back wagon so there is room for the kids and Hallr in the covered wagon."

Hallr says, "Don't do anything special for me."

Sheyla walks to the back of the smithy wagon and says, "You healed enough to walk around all day?"

"I need to leave."

Sheyla says, "So do we. If we're going the same direction, we can travel together."

Merial says, "I want Hallr to travel with us. It is safer."

Hallr says, "Safer for whom?"

"For all of us. If there are fighters, you can defeat them. If there are witches, Sheyla, Tanisha, and I can defeat them."

Hallr shifts around and slides off the back of the wagon. He lands and feels a sharp pain in his leg, his right chest, and his shoulder. He puts his right hand on his abdomen.

Sheyla says, "Yep, still some healing to do there. It still takes days for your body to heal fully, even with a witch's help."

Milfred walks over, "There will be tea in a few minutes. Not much time to prepare food. After tea, we will put the fire out. We won't have a fire at night that could spot us. We have jerky. Let's shift the stuff in the wagons."

Hallr says, "I don't need help."

Feliu says, "Why is he getting mad?"

Sheyla says, "He can't get comfortable with anyone helping him. The entire world is against him."

"Yes, it is."

Agnarr says, "Except for this little group. We have declared a truce. We will let the dwarf hang around for a few days. This would all go better if you relaxed and worked with us."

Hallr looks at the distinct faces. He says, "Truce for a couple of days."

Merial smiles.

Hallr says, "I'll work to unload gear from this wagon to make room for the moved items."

The first thing he pulls out is his axe and sets it down, leaning against the wagon wheel. Next, he grabs his large pack and puts it next to the axe. Now he grabs the small pack and pulls it out, holding it.

Milfred says, "That is a great size for you. What's inside? I never looked after we grabbed it. We focused on getting you into the wagons and out of the area."

Hallr says, "I don't know. Something made of Mithril."

The rest all walk over to see. Feliu asks, "Is it a treasure? Mithril could be a treasure."

Tanisha replies, "After the battle, the scavengers could have taken it from one of the rich people. Let's see what it is."

Hallr opens the pack, looking at the part he can see. He turns the pack over to dump the contents. A box falls out. It is all the dull sheen of Mithril. The way it lands appears to be bottom up, with the cover facing down. The cover is slightly bigger.

Feliu says, "It looks like a box. So, there is a treasure inside." He steps over and turns the box over. As he lets go, he says, "It feels dead, nothing. I can't sense anything."

Sheyla says, "Mithril disrupts magic. It appears to have writing on top. Hallr, can you read any of it?"

Hallr shifts the box, scanning. "There are simple words scattered; I can read some of them. At the bottom is Dwarven. It says, danger. do not open."

Sheyla asks, "May I look at it?"

Hallr shrugs and hands her the box.

Sheyla shifts the box around and begins scanning. "There are words scattered around, as if they are mixing languages." She is reading and then drops the box. Her face goes white; shaking her head, she steps away from it. "No. That is evil."

Tanisha asks, "What does it say?" as she reaches for the box.

Sheyla says, "Don't pick it up. It says, teach, control, dwarves. It's how to train a control witch to control dwarves."

Merial is scowling at the box, "Training in evil magic."

Milfred says, "If you're sure it is evil, we should destroy the contents."

Tanisha is looking at the box inscriptions, then turns the box, then shakes it. "I don't see any way to open it. Is it real?"

Agnarr is looking at Hallr, "It's Mithril. We can't use magic to open it. That must have been intentional. Made of Mithril so that a dwarf can open it."

Hallr is looking back at Agnarr, "I do not know how to open it. Wouldn't open it if I could."

Agnarr nods, as if satisfied with one detail.

Sheyla is breathing hard, sweating, "This is a nightmare. We need to destroy it."

Merial asks, "Why are you upset?"

Sheyla takes a breath, "If that teaches a witch how to control a dwarf, it will be something every control witch will want to possess. They will want it, so they learn and get more power."

"They will kill everyone necessary to get the box," says Agnarr.

Hallr is looking at the upset witch, the confused young ones. He doesn't know how, but he won't open the box anyway. No one will get the contents. "I will not try to open it."

Agnarr says, "It doesn't really matter. This was what the witch who attacked you was after. She didn't care if it needed a dwarf to open it. She was trying to kill you to get it."

Milfred says, "That is Mithril. We can't destroy it. I can't melt it with the hottest fire I can create. I would need the bellows and tools even to try."

Sheyla is looking at Milfred, then back at the box. "There has to be a way. Someone created it, so there must be a way to destroy it."

The only forges for Mithril are in the lost city of Molgan.

Sheyla says, "Then we'll take it there."

Hallr smiles.

"This isn't funny. That thing is evil, dangerous," says Sheyla, pointing at the box.

Agnarr says, "He's smiling because your casual statement to take it to Molgan can be humorous. We don't know where the city is. It is an ancient, lost dwarven city."

"If it's that dangerous, I'll keep it," says Hallr.

Sheyla is looking intently at Hallr, "And do what with it?

What if you're attacked again? I want to destroy that thing. It looks like I want to destroy it more than you do. Teaching magi how to control dwarves is bad; it's wrong."

"I'll find a place to hide it. If I'm the only one who knows, no one else can get it."

Agnarr says, "Sheyla is right. What if you're attacked again while you're traveling to hide it?"

Merial is watching the elders. She turns to Tanisha, has her bend down, and whispers. When Tanisha nods, Merial says, "We'll all go together."

Tanisha adds, "Merial is right. It is safer if we are all together. We can help each other."

Milfred says, "Molgan would be a good place to go. We can hide it there, protect it, or even destroy it. I've wanted to find Molgan. We can make Mithril tools; we can do so much more than destroy a box."

Agnarr asks, "Hallr, when we met, you said you were looking for Molgan. Milfred wants to find it. Now Sheyla and I want to find it. We can travel and search together."

Hallr looks at them, "And the kids. Searching for a lost city is not a way for them to live."

Sheyla says, "You're right. We need to find some place with teachers so they can learn how to use good magic."

Feliu says, "We want to go with you. You can teach us. Agnarr taught me how to start a fire. Sheyla has taught Merial how to heal."

Hallr says, "I've always traveled alone. I haven't even agreed to this. You all expect me to accept witches as traveling companions, just because."

Sheyla nods, "Yes."

Agnarr is looking at Hallr intently. "You still think we are going to attack you. After all, we've done, you can't just accept what you have seen and experienced to travel with us?"

Milfred says, "Hang on. Let's do this one step at a time. We are traveling to the east. Hallr, you need to head to the mountains, *which is traveling east. We can travel in the same direction for a few days."*

Hallr nods, "We can travel in the same direction."

Milfred says, "Good. I think you should put that thing in the supply wagon, at the front, under as much stuff as possible."

Later that day, they are in the wagons, traveling slowly with the two oxen. Hallr is sleeping. Merial asks Sheyla, "He is sleeping again. Is that okay?"

"Yes, when a body is healing, that much sleep helps."

Well past noon, they heard horses, then men shouting. They come up to the front and turn, stopping the wagons.

Feliu touches Hallr. When he doesn't wake up, he pokes him.

Hallr opens his eyes, sits up, and winces.

"There you are, blacksmith. You left the camp without getting your tools."

"I left because you would not give them back, anyway."

"Well, we found you. Now we can get back to our discussion. You have to pay to use the road. That wasn't part of the bargain."

Hallr shifts slowly to the back of the wagon. He is looking, searching for what is in the wagon he might use. Not knowing how many riders there are or what weapons they have limits him. He whispers to Feliu, "Do you know how many?"

Feliu nods and holds up four fingers. Hallr nods.

Tanisha leans over, asking, "What do we do?"

Hallr is thinking, looks at her, and says, "I need something to distract them while I get out of the wagon. I have to get up there with my axe."

Feliu says, "I can make their horses lie down."

Hallr looks surprised, then a tiny smile appears. He nods, reaching for his axe.

Traveling Alliance

Hallr nods when he is ready at the back of the wagon. Feliu closes his eyes, and they all immediately hear the horses shifting and complaining. The men yell.

Hallr is being careful; he gets out of the wagon by sliding off rather than jumping. Getting his axe, he walks toward the front and finds a pleasant surprise. Hallr sees four horses spread out in front of the wagon, and they are all lying down.

The humans shout and kick the horses.

This is an opportunity for Hallr. He walks forward toward the closest scavenger. When the man sees him, he yells and draws his sword.

Moving quickly, Hallr gets close and swings his axe, then immediately turns to the next scavenger, who has pulled his bow off his shoulder and is grabbing an arrow. The third man is already drawing his bow with a nocked arrow, aiming at the wagon.

Hallr shifts the axe to be across his chest as a shield as he moves toward the man. He is almost close enough to swing when the man draws his bow back to shoot Hallr.

Ready to shift the axe and deflect the arrow, he sees the man fly backward, landing hard, while the arrow goes up in the air.

Hallr looks back at the wagon to see Agnarr gesturing. Turning, Hallr sees the third scavenger flying backward. He shouts, "Bring them to the axe, not away."

In another minute, Hallr looks at Agnarr and says, "That was not a blacksmith's apprentice, and not a simple mage."

"You're welcome."

Feliu comes running from the back of the wagon, saying, "I'll get the horses. We can have a team for each wagon now."

Milfred says, "Not really. We need collars. The oxen use a yoke across their necks, but we need collars to hitch horses. Right now, *we just take them with us."*

Agnarr is at the archer, pulling off his gear. "Feliu, come over here and help."

Hallr says, "We need to get moving. The other scavengers will look for them if they don't return."

<<<>>>

Hours later, Ranjeet is giving Teppo an update. "One group of scavenger scouts has not returned. They were on the road south."

"What is south?"

"We don't know."

"Could they have just taken off?"

Ranjeet shakes his head, "I doubt it. We told them they would get ten gold coins to find the dwarf or the kids."

"Right now, that is the best we have. Tomorrow, we head that way if we get nothing better. A dwarf and three kids can't just disappear."

"And the box?"

"It must be with them. Unless you didn't really search everywhere else."

"We searched. We had the scavengers search."

Teppo says, "I need to check on Willow. She has been working hard today."

"She has. The scavengers were very compliant because of her control skills. Thank her for me."

"I will. Don't expect this level again tomorrow. You need to use the men and muscle to keep the scavengers inline."

"Teppo, tomorrow we'll take the best items we can find and leave. If the scavengers are a problem, we will eliminate the problem."

The next day, after finding the small trees that were broken, the group turned onto the side road. Scouts quickly came back to report.

"Ranjeet, we found a campsite with a fire. Further on this old road, we found the bodies of the four scavenger scouts."

Ranjeet says, "So they are over a day ahead on this road. Any idea how many?"

"We saw footprints of several adults, children, and what could be a dwarf. We don't have an accurate number."

When Ranjeet reports to Teppo, he asks, "Should we send men ahead to stop them?"

Teppo looks at the men. He has six men, ten women, Ranjeet, and himself in this coven. He can't afford to lose any men. Turning to Ranjeet, he says, "No. They killed Anfisa and four scavengers, so they are good at fighting. I don't want to risk any men. We need to be together when we encounter this dwarf."

They reach a streambed and figure out why people don't use the road. The deepest part of the stream bed features a small, broken, unusable bridge. Wagons can negotiate theMilfred began cursing when he walked up to look at the details. Sheyla says, "Language."

They all collected in front of the wagons, looking at the situation. Milfred says, "The oxen won't be able to pull two wagons on the other side."

Agnarr says, "We will need to do the wagons one at a time."

Hallr chuckles, "A good thing we don't have all the blacksmith gear. The wagon would be too heavy."

Milfred replies, "Not funny."

Sheyla asks, "Can the oxen pull the wagons over those rocks?"

Hallr says, "We need to move and break some rocks. If I had a mining hammer, it would be no problem."

Agnarr looks at Sheyla, who is looking intently at Hallr, then turns to Agnarr, away from Hallr, and makes an 'O' with her mouth.

Tanisha is looking at the adults and asks, "Was that important? What did he say?"

Agnarr says, "He will help humans with a problem that a dwarf *would be the best one to solve."*

Sheyla says, "I would get you a dwarven mining hammer if I could."

Milfred says, "I like the new camaraderie, but we need to have a clear plan. Sheyla is going to have to drive while the rest of us push. I don't think Hallr can give 100% yet."

Feliu says, "I can try using push magic to help. Tanisha can help with push magic as well."

Agnarr puts an arm around Feliu, "Good. We may push some rocks before we try the wagons."

Hallr says, "I've something I can help with."

Milfred says, "Really, what is that?"

"I will guide the oxen, get them to pull."

Feliu asks, "Will you use magic?"

Hallr shakes his head, "Of course not. Oxen will pull hard when they have a leader pulling hard."

Milfred says, "Okay—one more part. When the wagon is across the streambed, the road starts again, but it is narrow, winding, and leaves the flood area. We need to get the first wagon up, over the hill, then the second. The oxen will be tired, and pulling both up the hill won't work."

Hallr nods, "Aye. We need to be away from the streambed. When the wagons are going up the hill, I will stay at the stream in case we get company."

Agnarr gives a surprised look. "Okay. I'll stay with you."

"You help push the wagons up the hill. I don't want you close if a control witch comes."

Sheyla says, "You're not fully healed."

"I can fight now, but I can't fight a witch and any of you being controlled and attacking me at the same time. You go with the wagons while I wait."

Sheyla begins to say, "They..."

Hallr waves his arm, cutting her off. "I will stay alone, or with everyone."

<<<>>>

It is dark when they get the second wagon over the hill. They are tired, and Hallr says, "We're all tired, but the next bit of road is down-sloping. We should use that to make some progress before we stop."

"Why," asks Tanisha.

"The scavengers won't give up that easily. Worse, that witch wasn't working alone, looking for that box. They will be searching."

Agnarr's face goes from a smile to flat, then lipped. "He's right. My first thought was the dwarf who is paranoid of humans, then I realized he is right."

"Bein' paranoid doesn't mean I'm wrong."

Sheyla has been silent. Merial takes her hand, which startles Sheyla. She turns and walks with Merial down the slope, saying, "I grew up thinking about people differently. I don't understand his perspective on humans, all humans."

Merial says, "There are good humans and bad humans."

Sheyla smiles and replies, "It's more complicated. Part of it depends on your personal view. When I was your age, I thought witches were great. They were going to teach me to understand my abilities and to make things better. Then I learned some witches only care about making things better for themselves. They are good to some other witches and bad to most."

"Hallr hasn't known good witches."

"Yes, and most humans haven't been good either, but a few have. Otherwise, he won't be helping. He has a good heart."

"I can tell. I like him."

Sheyla turns Merial, so she is at her back and starts running her fingers through Merial's hair. "We need to get a brush for you. Has your hair always been wild like this?"

"Mama said I had hair like hers. It has a mind of its own."

"Let's braid it so it won't get so dirty."

Down the slope, they made camp. Hallr is lying under the wagon. He is exhausted and upset with himself, so his mind is churning, and he can't sleep. He has done more with these humans than any others in a long time. The box makes it worse.

His past tells him he needs to get away from them. Take the box and leave. They are susceptible to witch control and corruption. *"If the witches searching for that box get to them, I will be fighting every one of these humans."*

"The one bright spot is the kids. They got away. Feliu got the horses to lie down, which was great. Merial knows what control is, can do it, but is unfazed by the idea of someone doing it to her. Perhaps she can't be controlled in that manner. She has been asking, making him think about humans and dwarves."

Shifting to pleasant thoughts about having food to eat and not getting attacked, he drifts off.

Agnarr is sitting up to watch. Hallr said it was important, and he agreed. After a long time, he hears Hallr's breathing change. He is finally asleep.

He is thinking, *"That little paranoid dwarf has been through a lot. The only thing that seems to calm him is Merial. She is a powerful little witch. She doesn't really know; no one has yet discovered her true power."*

Sheyla is becoming a concern. She is doting on the kids, but he can see her looking at the wagon whenever someone goes in. Checking to make sure they don't touch the box.

He has been looking toward the stream, away from the small fire, so that the remains of the fire don't affect his eyes. He hears footsteps, then Sheyla says, "Can we talk?"

Agnarr nods.

Sheyla sits down next to him. "The kids are asleep."

"You should be, too. You're supposed to be the next watch."

"I have a problem. I can't sleep."

"Just one."

"Funny. One big one. That box."

"We have it. We need to keep it away from other witches until we can hide it or destroy it."

"I know. I really know how dangerous that thing is. My concern is that I've already broken my personal vow not to use control magic when I helped the dwarf. If there is another fight for the box, I will have to do it again. I also don't think Hallr understands the danger of the box."

Agnarr turns to look at Sheyla, "That is two things. First Hallr understands. I watched him before when he said he wouldn't open the box. He will never open that box, even if he knows how. He isn't interested in looking at it to figure it out."

"Are you sure?"

"We have never heard that dwarf lie. He wasn't lying when he said that. I'm sure. The second subject is you and your abilities. Tell me what you're afraid of."

Sheyla takes a breath, "Merial is a young me. I was taken from my parents, like her, to be trained, but I was in a coven. The coven taught me to control others from an early age. That she is here in my face makes me more concerned for both of us. Agnarr, I'm good at it. I can create a world in someone's mind that we both believe in. That is the good and the problem."

"I don't understand?"

"Control witches make people believe things with visuals, thoughts, sounds, and smells. It has to be something the witch believes. Over time, when all you do is control, you lose yourself in that world."

"You can't differentiate the real from the fake."

"Or good from bad, or friends or family. Old primary controller witches go crazy. They eventually don't know how to take care of

themselves. I don't want that to be my end."

"It won't be."

"I don't want my legacy to be controlling others. I want to help make things better."

"Like an old dwarf, wearing rags, who is helping where he can."

Sheyla blushes, "Yes. Speaking of him again. He hates control witches, hates them. If I do any controlling again, he won't want to stay. Then he will take the box. I can't let him take the box."

"Wow. Hang on now."

Surprised by Agnarr's reaction, Sheyla shifts.

"Stop, Sheyla, and listen to yourself. You and Hallr are so alike it is bad for all of us."

"What. No, I'm not."

"Single-minded about some things. Won't give the other a chance."

"I'm giving him a chance."

"He doesn't want any witch to have the box. Trust me on that part. You know it's true. That includes you. He will do what he thinks is the best thing to keep the box out of any control witch's hands. What he thinks is best."

"But...."

Agnarr holds up his hands for her to stop. "That dwarf sees us, all of us, as potential threats."

"I won't."

"But a controller could make you. That is what he knows. That has been his life. I've experienced it. A controlled human will attack him."

"Agnarr, listen to me carefully, because this is true, and you may not believe it. No witch can control me. That witch we fought, I could have done so much more."

"That is what you're afraid of. The power will take over, consuming your ability to judge."

Sheyla nods. "The only witch I've met that might challenge me one day is Merial. With training and experience, she will be a powerful witch. I don't want that to be a control witch."

"Hallr doesn't know our abilities. He doesn't trust us. We have to give him time, space, and trust him. I will also say that whatever it is in your past that makes you afraid, you won't talk about. That thing we all know and sense in you. He can tell."

"Like your past. I saw the way you pushed that wagon. You have power you don't show or use. Why do you think showing your power of push can be so bad?"

"Maybe one day I'll feel trusting enough to tell you. Not today."

"Not today. I won't talk about my past. Thanks for listening."

As she stands, Agnarr says, "We have to work to get the dwarf to trust us. What Tanisha said when we met is important. No one, none of us has a family. We need to become a family."

"What do I do?"

"We need to get the kids somewhere safe and stay focused on helping each other. It won't be easy to keep Hallr from wanting to leave. We have the best chance of surviving and finding Molgan together. Our best chance to destroy that box is together, to become a little family."

"If we become separated, they can target us;

"Exactly. Before you go, we haven't finished part of the discussion. You don't want to control anyone. Fair, and I respect that. Don't look at using control to defend your family as giving up, as giving into the bad."

"I'll think about that."

"See you in a couple of hours for your watch shift."

"I can see the tracks; they've got two wagons across this stream. We can do it as well."

"I agree, Teppo. It is going to take a lot of time."

"It slowed them. If we focus and get through it, we can make up time. Getting our two wagons, with horses to catch them, should be simple on the other side."

"All together we can get the box, the kids, and kill the dwarf. Tomorrow could be a great day."

An hour later, Ranjeet is cursing. The wagon the witches ride in broke a wheel getting across the streambed. The wagon can't move.

"Teppo, we need to leave it and catch the group."

Teppo is quiet. He has been talking with the witches since the wagon broke. They have been on foot, getting Willow across the streambed.

"The other wagon is full of supplies. If we leave the supplies to take the witches, they will only last a couple of days out here. We can't go back."

Ranjeet is looking at the group of women, knowing they are the key to defeating the group and getting the box. "We have to prioritize the witches."

"Can we fix the wheel?"

"It will take days. The best option is to go back to the scavengers and get a new wheel or another wagon. That should be a couple of days."

Teppo growls, fists clenched. He turns from looking at the wagon, "Send the men. Get a wheel or a wagon; I don't care which. We will camp here."

Kids to the Village

The group crossed the border between Westport and Icemoor, heading southeast toward Harenhal.

Milfred is talkative with people, trying to get the latest information, some call it gossip, about where they are heading.

His chatting has allowed them to trade the horses they had for a bellows and supplies. He can now do blacksmithing.

They learned Ferndon was one country Greystone had conquered. Many refugees in Icemoor are celebrating their independence and traveling back home. People in Westport are also traveling to return home.

At the border with Harenhal, a country with mountains on its eastern border, it is primarily flat farmland and forest. They get information about the local conditions.

Because of generations of civil war, fueled by surrounding kingdoms wanting to keep Harenhal weak, the only economy left is farming. The country is lawless, with the only government far to the east. No one finds it valuable enough to concur—sections function as fiefdoms, with marauders preying on travelers and the weak.

At the Harenhal border, soldiers are checking travelers. They stop the group. The soldiers ask Agnarr if the group wants to hire protection while traveling, "This countryside is dangerous. The country's government is in shambles. Army patrols stay close to the capital. There are no patrols or guards in this part of the country. We can recommend trustworthy men to ride with you and provide protection while you travel."

Hallr says loudly, "Good. Let the bandits come. We need two teams of horses for the wagons."

Agnarr says, "Thanks for the offer, but we will be fine."

"With a dwarf, you will get attention, and lots of dumb shits will try to best the dwarf in a fight. Good luck to ya."

The next night at camp, they are having a rare treat. Agnarr killed two squirrels with his bow. They stopped well before sunset at a flat area for camping and cooking the fresh meat. With Hallr's help, they have gathered local ingredients and created a stew. While they are eating, Sheyla says, "We should be at the village in a couple of days. We will get you three situated."

At the border, they traded with another group to get a comb. After Merial had taken out Tanisha's braid, combed her hair, and redone her braid, they shifted. Tanisha is now working on Merial's hair.

Agnarr says, "This country doesn't have a powerful government. It is really a bunch of fiefdoms. We are going to a village that will keep you safe and provide you with training. If there is a problem getting you settled there, we will find another."

The kids look at each other, and then Feliu says, "What if we want to stay with you?"

Tanisha says, "Merial, your hair is a mess. This will take a while."

Sheyla shifts, "Let me help."

Agnarr says, "It isn't safe with us."

Tanisha shoots back, "We got him," pointing at Hallr.

Hallr snorts. Milfred says, "She isn't wrong."

"You know what will happen when the gangs around here know there are little morsels like you three. Easy to do whatever they want."

Sheyla says loudly, "Don't go there. Don't just scare them."

"What? Keep the little darlings in the dark about the real world. I haven't heard who took them to the battlefield area. Their families were killed. Why would a gang not take advantage? They are safer in the village."

Sheyla stands, slowly shaking her head. Looking at Hallr, she says, "You don't know about the real world. About growing up on the street with no one. I do. This is an easy life. This is what kids should experience growing up."

Gesturing at the kids, she says, "They have abilities. They are exceptionally talented, going beyond the average magi. Their abilities can help many when properly trained. They are not property to be traded, and they can be more powerful on a battlefield than a single dwarf, and not by fighting."

Agnarr is looking at Sheyla, knowing some of what she says is about her own past, and says, "While young and not able to use their powers, they are vulnerable."

Hallr replies, "I know about magic. I've dealt with it. What I've learned is that humans do stupid shit. A solid blow from an axe can fell every gifted person. They are also easy to manipulate, so they do nasty shit to others. I've been thinking, and I should leave you when we get to the village."

Milfred says, "No. We are going to the village to find a place for them."

"Good. Then I've helped get them to a new home and can leave."

Sheyla says, "We are staying together while we hunt for Molgan."

Agnarr says, "We need to stay focused on the common goal. We agreed to find Molgan together. Hallr, you don't want to find it anymore, or you're going to find it alone?"

Nodding toward Sheyla, Hallr says, "She and I don't get along. I can search on my own. I wander anyway, searching to find the impossible works for me."

Sheyla is sitting, looking at the fire now. She doesn't look or respond, but Agnarr can see she is angry.

Meriel has been quiet, watching. At every opportunity during the day, she stays close to Sheyla, asking about healing. She speaks, "I want to stay with..."

She stops speaking and turns to look at the forest down the road. "They are going to attack."

Agnarr moves quickly to the wagon and grabs the bow and arrow quiver.

Hallr walks over and picks up his axe. "Are you sure?"

Meriel nods.

Sheyla says, "All of you get in the wagon and stay down."

Hallr is looking at the little one. "How do you know?"

"I can read them, sense them."

Sheyla says, "Hallr, she is young, and her sensing abilities are at their peak. When I was growing up in the coven, I had to be early in the morning watch because of my sensory ability."

As the kids get in the wagon, Milfred pulls out his belt with the sword and dagger. As Milfred shifted the belt, the dagger slipped out and fell. Milfred tries to grab the handle as it falls, bending over. The arrow hit the wagon where his body had been seconds before.

Hallr says to Agnarr, "Use magic."

Tanisha says, "They're trying to use magic."

Hallr turns to Tanisha, "How do you know?"

"I can't explain. It is a feeling, a thing I see, but in my mind. I know the archer is a mage."

Hallr comments, while shaking his head, "I'm not sure about all this. Witches talking and knowing what is happening."

Agnarr says, "They aren't attacking you. We are working together. Working together, we can be much safer."

Milfred says, "What will the other guy do with magic?"

Agnarr says, "He will use magic to make the arrows faster or try to hit more accurately. I have a surprise for them."

Hallr holds his enormous axe up as a shield. The next arrow hits the blade, and Hallr deflects it.

Agnarr nocks an arrow, pulls back the string, and moves the tip around, aiming. Releasing the arrow, it burst into flames as it flies. They watch it hit the archer in the chest.

Hallr watches the arrow and sees the panic on the faces of the other four marauders. He says, "Keep picking them off."

Feliu says, "They have horses; don't hit the horses."

Hallr walks down the road, saying, "I'm getting the horses."

Milfred looks at Hallr, simply walking toward four armed

men. Feliu turns to Agnarr and says, "He wants you to keep shooting flaming arrows. Can you show me how to do that?"

"Yes, I will show you tomorrow."

When Hallr returns, he is leading six horses. One has a pack of supplies.

They now have four horses for the heavy wagon and two for the lighter one. They tie oxen to the back, and the oxen follow.

The next night, Sheyla is adjusting the fire when putting the kettle back on the edge. "With the horses, we will be at the village tomorrow."

The kids are lying under the wagon with blankets, watching. The temperature is chilly at night. Everyone wants to be close to the fire and covered in blankets.

Agnarr nods, "We need to be up early and push. We don't want to get there after sunset."

Hallr asks, "What will happen when we arrive?"

Agnarr says, "Everything will be fine for us. They will not trust you two," as he nods toward Milfred and Hallr.

Milfred asks, "What should we do?"

"Stay close to the wagon and don't talk."

"How about I stay out of town? You don't need me. I will take my kit and keep walking. You can catch up to me."

Sheyla shakes her head, and Tanisha says, "This close to the village, stay together."

Hallr looks at her and asks, "Why is that?"

"It will be safer for everyone else. There are outcast magi who might try to attack you if you're alone. If you are all together, they won't attack."

Hallr replies, "I don't have a problem with that."

Agnarr says, "If you get attacked by a group of magi while alone, they can injure or kill you. It will be much harder than a single witch."

Hallr chuckles, and Milfred says, "You're protecting the outcasts. They don't get killed if they stay away."

Hallr nods, "They always think they are tough enough to take a dwarf. We are hard to kill."

Tanisha is looking at Sheyla and says, "I'm not joking. There are outcast magi in the area."

Sheyla blushes, turns to Hallr, and says, "Please stay with us until the village. Outcast magi can get desperate. Have you already forgotten about the witch that almost killed you?"

Hallr is looking at Sheyla. Her reaction to the girl saying 'outcast' is interesting. "I remember killing the witch."

Sheyla shakes her head and walks to the back of the wagon.

Agnarr says, "Are you two still mad about the argument yesterday?"

Sheyla looks at Agnarr without speaking. Her look gives him her answer.

Later that night, after the kids are asleep, Agnarr is fidgeting. He pokes the fire, adds more wood, and moves around the wagon.

Milfred says, "What is wrong with you?"

"We need to finish talking about the future." Looking at Hallr, he continues, "Before we split up, even though we agreed not to."

Hallr says, "What?"

"We talked about this, then the attack started. You don't want to talk about it when the kids could hear. Why won't you talk about this in front of the kids?"

"You want to talk about how wonderful it will be. The kids don't need dreams like that. Searching for Molgan is a quest when you have nothing else to live for. It will be dangerous, and we probably will never find it. If I leave, you can stay in the village with the kids."

Feeling agitated, Milfred takes a stick and pokes the fire, stating, "I'm not staying at the village. I'm going to search for Molgan. Will you travel with me? That would be the perfect place to hide the box."

Hallr asks, "Tell me why finding the city is so important to you?"

"They made Mithril weapons and armor in the city. Mithril of any kind is now very hard to find. We could make new weapons. There is also the old rumor about treasure."

Hallr is standing next to the wagon. He looks over at Milfred, poking the fire. Thinking about the time with these humans.

"There has been food and companionship. They have traveled well together. These humans are not the typical mercenaries or grifters he meets. Without the kids, the dynamic with the witch could be different.

She has not attacked him. She keeps insisting that she isn't like that. Hallr's only experience with witches is that they eventually attack him. Sheyla is the first witch he has spent more than a couple of days with, and she stays away from him. She dotes on the kids and helps with the camp. She is nothing like what he expected from a witch. Agnarr is something different. He can do magic, but he acts like a blacksmith's apprentice."

Hallr looks at Sheyla and asks, "If you're not the type of witch that attacks me, what kind are you?"

"I'm a healer. All magic people can do the same things, but you have to be disposed and practice to do some things well. I've trained and practiced being an excellent healer. You're considering leaving. I will not attack you. I share your goal. Hide or destroy that box. We are better together than separately."

He bends down, grabs the stick from Milfred, and tosses it onto the fire. He takes a breath, looks up, and says, "I'm old now. There are still some years left, but I'm slowing down. Finding Molgan will give me a last place to rest. A place to hide and store that box. If you will not stay in the village, we can find the city together."

The next day, they enter the region around the village, and there are fewer travelers. They have seen no one who might try to attack in two days.

When they see two men on horses at a distance, Tanisha won't take her eyes off them. When he asks, she says, "They are outcast magi. They are desperate for supplies, and they want power."

In the late afternoon, several men on horses showed up even before they arrived at the village. The leader says, "Keep on the road."

The two riders moved further away when the men from the village arrived. After they leave, the outcast riders move back closer to the wagons. Hallr asks, "Why are they outcasts?"

Agnarr says, "You won't believe it, but magi have outlawed the use of control magic. It is bad for everyone."

Sheyla says, "Some of them have done terrible things and have lost their ability to tell right from wrong. They are going crazy."

Agnarr is nodding. "They get sucked into their control illusions and can't get out. Obsessed with power and controlling others. They usually also lose their memory of friends and family."

Sheyla says, "Some old controllers can only control one target group. They only know the lives they create. Others have to feed, wash, and clothe them. They are like babies, managed so they can control someone."

Hallr looks between Sheyla and Agnarr and says, "Crazy sounds right. I'm having a hard time because my experience is that witches consider controlling humans or attacking a dwarf as normal, not bad."

Agnarr speaks, and Sheyla says loudly, talking over Agnarr, "I can see that view. When the rumors say witches are bad."

Feliu interjects, "Neither of you is what the rumors say. Why are you letting random people's words control you?"

Milfred says, "Nice wording. Letting random others control you."

Agnarr says, "Something to think about."

When there is a lull in questions from the kids about magic, Hallr says, "When we get to the village, you kids can't talk about the box."

Agnarr nods, "Good point. That box is very dangerous. The fewer people who know about it and its location, the better."

Sheyla asks, "Are the three of you okay with not talking about the box?"

Merial nods, then Feliu. Tanisha asks, "What if people thought the box was in the village, protected from other witches?"

Agnarr says, "That would put the villagers in danger. Anyone wanting to fight for the box will attack the village."

Hallr says, "It is better to stay with me and take it to the city. As we agreed, it is bad enough that there is a box people will fight over. We don't want to put an entire village, or you three, in danger by talking about it."

When they can see the village, Hallr furrows his brow. Then he puts his fingers on his temple. His head doesn't hurt, not like when witches are attacking him, but he feels something, like they are pressing on the inside of his head.

Merial says, "They want to read to you."

Hallr looks at the Merial. She turns to look at the village, concentrating. Hallr sees her lips moving but hears nothing.

Sheyla furrows her brow and looks from Merial, whom she was watching, to the village. "They will send out riders."

A minute later, men on horses charge out of the village, horses at a full gallop. When they get to the wagon, they surround it.

Merial says, "They are reading all of us.

This time, when they ride up, Agnarr doesn't just nod. He asks, "Is there a problem?"

One man on horseback says, "No one said anything about gifted young ones, or a dwarf."

Sheyla looks back sternly, "We will not shout about gifted children on the open road. We're not idiots."

Two of the riders are watching Hallr.

The lead rider is looking at Hallr and says, "Don't speak when we enter the village unless asked a direct question."

Hallr grunts and doesn't speak.

The village gates are wooden, natural, and only four meters high. They won't keep out an army, and they don't need to. An army would die from magic before they reached the gates.

As the wagon passes through the gates, Hallr looks back down the road. A dozen men on horses are watching. He rubs his temple, sitting on the back of the wagon with his legs hanging off the back.

Merial crawls next to him, hanging her little legs off the back. She says, "They know you're a dwarf and hard to read. They are arguing about us."

Hallr looks at the men on the road and asks, "What about them?"

"They call them outcasts. They don't follow the rules. No one explains to me how come, what they did, but I think they are broken. They aren't powerful, but they want power to control others. They are afraid of you."

Milfred says, "They could be trouble when we leave."

When the wagon stops, Hallr doesn't move. He hears a woman's voice speaking behind him. "Bring the children and the dwarf."

Men surround the wagon, and two walk up to Hallr, holding their sword handles with the swords still in their scabbards. Hallr says, "That's the way it is, you just attack."

The woman's voice says, "I didn't say attack. Dwarf, please join the children to speak with me."

The men let go of the sword hilts and step back.

Nodding, Hallr hops off the wagon and helps the kids get down. They all walk around the wagon toward the woman. Merial reaches her hand over and takes Hallr's hand, holding it. She is only about thirty centimeters shorter than Hallr.

The woman looks to be middle-aged, maybe fifty, because her hair is more than half grey, and the surrounding wrinkles grey eyes as she looks at them. She is wearing a long dress with a shawl over her shoulders. She is holding a staff that appears ancient, worn from the many hands that have held it over the years. Carvings of what appear to be three sides adorn the top of the staff. On the side toward him, he sees an eye.

When they stop before the woman, Hallr gives a deep nod but

doesn't bow or kneel. The kids are next to him, and the others are behind him. Watching Hallr, the kids all nod to the woman.

The woman says, "My name is Neriah. You're the first dwarf anyone has seen around here in many years."

"I haven't seen another dwarf in years. I may be the last. There are few because the dwarf deaths I heard about were from your kind."

Neriah looks seriously at Hallr, "That is concerning. The old stories talk about dwarves being friends. Why would you fight us?"

"Every witch I encounter says I'm the enemy." Nodding toward Sheyla, he says, "She hasn't attacked me yet."

"Do you think every magi will attack you?"

"That is my experience. According to the stories I heard, magic weakened the dwarves before someone killed them.

"Are you going to attack us?"

Hallr gives a raspberry sound, saying, "I would already be gone. You're keeping me here."

Neriah looks surprised. "You're right, and I apologize. I do not intend to hold you if you're not an enemy. We want to offer food and rest to thank you for protecting the young ones and bringing them to us safely."

Hallr nods.

Neriah asks, "What are the children's names?"

Tanisha says, "I'm Tanisha. He is Feliu, and she is Merial. We were all taken from different places and met each other a few days before the battle.

Hallr nods and looks down at Merial, who is holding his hand. He says, "You're going to stay here and learn how to use magic like her."

Merial shakes her head as tears well up. "I want to stay with you. You're going to find the great city."

Neriah says, "The great city. What are you saying?"

Tanisha says, "He is going to Molgan."

Several of the people around the group smiled. The woman says, "The lost Dwarven city. What will you do there?"

Milfred shifts behind Hallr, and Hallr says, "The forges can make tools and weapons."

Looking at Hallr, she says, "You and the blacksmith will do this?"

Agnarr says, "I will go with them."

Sheyla shifts and says, "I will join them as well."

Neriah shifts to Sheyla, saying, "The witch who betrayed our most sacred laws. Traveling with them is wise; you know you can't stay with us."

Sheyla stands up straight and says, "I broke the magi law so we could all escape, and I would choose to do it again. You can't accept that, and I will leave. I'm still alive because I destroyed the attackers and prevented the slaughter of witches."

"The way you did it is an example of why humans put bounties on killing magi."

Hallr's forehead crinkles as he hears Sheyla is an outcast controller witch. He turns to look at her. She is precisely the witch that would attack him, but she hasn't. She said she was a healer.

Several people look at each other in response to Sheyla's words. Neriah takes a slow breath, considering Sheyla's words. Tanisha steps away from Hallr and takes Sheyla's hand. Tanisha looks intently at Neriah, who looks back without speaking for several seconds.

Shifting her gaze to Milfred, Neriah says, "Thank you all for bringing us these extraordinary children. We need to get them evaluated to understand what the best training for them is."

Sheyla looks at Tanisha and nods. The girl goes to Feliu, takes his hand, and then reaches for Merial's hand.

Merial hugs Hallr and says, "I want to go with you and see the city."

Hallr says, "Stay, learn, and you can join me when you're older."

Tanisha takes Merial's hand and starts toward Neriah.

Neriah says nothing as she steps aside. After the kids walk past, she shakes her head in wonder and looks back at the others.

"Eat and rest. We will talk tomorrow."

Hallr nods and says, "Tomorrow? If we can get food and fill our water barrel, we will be on our way. You don't want us in your village."

Neriah nods and says, "Thank you for understanding. You should stay for the night under our protection from the outcasts. You will have whatever you need and can leave in the morning."

Teppo says, "Search the bodies and collect anything valuable. Bring their horses."

Ranjeet is wrapping a strip of cloth over his upper arm where the arrow was just removed. "I was able to get a weak one to talk. The dwarf and the kids are further ahead. They have horses for their wagons now."

Teppo nods, "How many men did we lose?"

"One is dead, two are wounded and may not make it."

"We are a coven; we can heal them."

"We are a control coven, not trained healers. An arrow through the chest is difficult to heal," says Ranjeet.

Teppo is clenching his jaw. "We need to get moving. The children are probably out of reach. Losing that girl is unfortunate. The reports of both girls' skill assessment meant they could one day be primary controllers."

Ranjeet nods, "Losing that little girl is a big disappointment. Our primary, Willow, is over seventy now. None of the others is close to her in control power. We need to find a new one to train."

Teppo says, "The outcasts were fools to attack us."

Ranjeet replies, "The dead man is the rider we sent ahead to ask about helping catch the dwarf. They must have thought we were easier than fighting a dwarf."

"They were fools."

"Those were fools; however, the magi in this area could be

recruits. We could use several more men."

"Ranjeet, would you trust any of them?"

"Not at the beginning, but they could prove themselves."

"I want to evaluate all the candidates."

The next day, after leaving the village, the group followed the road, trying to turn east toward the mountains. While at the village, Hallr asked for leather, and they gave him a whole deer skin.

Now Hallr is sitting in the back of the wagon as they travel, working on the leather.

Sheyla is sitting on the wagon seat but turns to watch and talk to Hallr.

"Hallr, while you're working on making new pants, I want to talk about the village and magic."

"You want to convince me you're good. You're going to tell me why you're an outcast?"

"No."

During the quiet, Agnarr says, "We are being followed."

Sheyla takes a breath. Hallr looks up to see tears running down her cheeks. "I'm not proud of what I did, but it was how we survived."

"I understand that. That is probably the only thing we understand about each other."

"I don't like that kind of magic. Once I learned what it really meant, what it really does, I decided not to do that kind of magic. I have been forced. But I wanted to be; I am a healer. I want to use magic to help, not hurt."

"But you know how."

"I know how to do it very well. The witch that attacked you was the first time I've done that level of magic in several years."

"Why is this important to talk to me about?"

"I'm not your enemy. I'm trying to be a friend. It is glaring to me that you never start a conversation with me. You barely talk *to me, ever."*

Hallr stops sewing on the pants leg and looks up at Sheyla. "My life, my existence, is dealing with witches. When will the next one attack me? When will some group of humans' faces change, and suddenly they attack me, the whole group, without warning? I don't like witches. Witches attack me and do evil things to other humans. I'm even here because you have been useful and haven't attacked me. I don't trust you, and I don't know if I ever can."

As he finishes and looks down at the pants, he gets a pain in his head. He glares up at Sheyla as he puts his finger to his head.

Sheyla looks and immediately says, "What is it?"

Hallr says, "Witches."

Agnarr says, "Outcasts are approaching from behind. We are going to fight. Milfred, get your sword. Sheyla, take the reins."

Sheyla is glaring at Hallr. She doesn't turn.

Agnarr says, "Sheyla?"

She turns to Agnarr and says, "Stop the wagons and get ready. This will be a magical fight. They will try to control Milfred." Turning to Hallr, she says assertively, "I'm mad. You're partially at fault. Don't get out of the wagon."

Sheyla shifts to look behind the wagons to see four men on horses approaching at a trot. She feels a twinge in her head. She knows what that means—barely noticed by most. Someone is trying to influence her, to make her see and believe what they want.

Agnarr shifts and looks at her as he puts his hand to his temple.

At that point, Sheyla realizes she has a problem. They are trying to control Agnarr, Milfred, and her. Milfred is already out of the front wagon and climbing into the wagon toward Hallr while reaching for a sword.

She immediately says, "Hallr, hold Milfred down. I need a second." She focuses on the four behind them as Agnarr grips the wagon seat hard and says, "They don't have complete control of me."

Hallr stands as Milfred climbs the wheel, throws his leg over the side, and pulls his sword. Hallr takes a step, wraps his arms around Milfred, and gives him a bear hug. Milfred can't swing the sword or attack. He grunts and tries to get free.

Hallr turns to look at the riders quickly approaching. Thet man in the back pulls his sword, charges forward, and stabs the man in front of him in the back. The man falls off the horse, which turns to the side.

Agnarr says, "No, Sheyla."

Sheyla replies, "Shut up."

The rider turns to the next man and stabs him. This man yells at being stabbed, which causes the rider in front to turn.

Sheyla says, "I'm making him think the other riders are Hallr. They need to stab him, attack."

Hallr has wrapped his arms around Milfred and turns to Sheyla. Her focus is on the group of men.

They all hear one man yell, "Bitch."

Sheyla feels the push from the leader as he extends his arm toward her. She adjusts her position, gripping the seat back more tightly.

Sheyla is focused, but she sees Hallr look at Agnarr. She hears Agnarr growl and shift next to her.

The second man has fallen off his horse, the attacker has dropped his sword, and the leader is looking intently in their direction.

Sheyla is holding on to the back of the wagon seat, focused on the leader. Her breathing is more labored as she concentrates. In her peripheral vision, she could see Hallr throw Milfred out of the wagon, grab his axe, and raise it above his head.

She says, "Hallr wait!"

Her arm shoots out toward the leader. The push causes him to jerk on the reins, and the horse stops.

"Now!" Sheyla is squeezing her hand into a fist. The horse is frantic, jerking, fighting the rider. She is trying to have the horse stay so Hallr has a still target.

Hallr has the axe as far back as he can get it and throws it into the air.

The axe arcs high in the air toward the leader. Sheyla sees him jerk back hard on the reins, making the horse step back, then rear up.

The axe hits the horse in the chest between its front legs and slices into its chest. It drops to all four hooves, which drives the sharp axe deeper into its chest. The horse doesn't even scream before it dies and collapses on top of the axe.

As the horse collapses, axe blades go through its chest. The spike on the end of the handle deflects off the spine, passes through the saddle, and up into the leader's groin.

It looks like it is kneeling with its head down. The axe handle is in the ground, with the rider is now cursing and holding his hand over the side of his groin. Blood is spurting out between his fingers.

Hallr says, "Damm. If the horse hadn't shifted, I would have cleanly taken out the rider."

Sheyla focused on the rider. She barely perceives the words after Hallr's axe throw. Now she wants to question the leader. Spent from the intense burst of effort, she shifts to climb down from the wagon. Slipping, she falls, landing on her back, face up, wind knocked out of her.

Hallr jumps out of the wagon, landing next to her.

Looking up, she sees his hand extended to help her stand.

As she stands, she says, "Sorry, that is taxing. I get mentally and physically drained, especially when I haven't done that in years."

Hallr is holding her hand after helping her, staring at her. "Thank you. From the village discussion, I know that was not what you wanted to do, but I'm glad I made you mad."

Sheyla blinks, shakes her head, and says, "That is an interesting thank you. I need to ask him some questions before he dies. I won't be healing him."

Sheyla walks towards the leader while the warlock she previously controlled stands up after his fall. Sheyla is shaking her hair to get dirt out. Before she gets to the leader, she wraps her hair into a loose knot to keep it out of the way.

Hallr looks at Agnarr, who nods. "I'm okay."

Milfred is now dirty, looking at Hallr and Agnarr, "What was that?"

Agnarr says, "Your latest experience with control magic."

Hallr turns to follow Sheyla, saying, "We need knives to carve my axe out of this dead horse."

The horse is kneeling, with the axe acting as a leg, holding it up. The leader, still in the saddle, totally focused on his bleeding artery. Sheyla says, "He is trying to use healing magic to stop the bleeding."

Hallr continues past the leader to the last rider. He has recovered from Sheyla's control and is now focused on Hallr. He looks around and strides to his fallen sword. Hallr follows with his dagger out.

The man turns toward Hallr after picking up a sword. He has become focused on Hallr and steps toward him. Agnarr's arrow hits him in the side, causing him to stumble. He looks to his side, then toward Agnarr when the second arrow enters his chest. This arrow is on fire when it hits him.

The man screams, drops the sword, and frantically moves around trying to put out the flames.

Hallr turns back to see Sheyla with the leader on the ground. The leader ignores Sheyla and focuses on his groin. Sheyla has the leader's sword, stabbing him in the neck. Hallr steps over, "Did he give you any information?"

"I wanted to know how many like him were in the area. Why are they in this area, as opposed to around some village they can dominate or control? He completely focused on you. They were told you needed to be dead. He said that without you, the village can't protect the artifact."

"What did I do differently suddenly, and what artifact?"

Sheyla says, "They were told to kill you. They must be thinking you will return to protect the artifact. Artifact can only mean the box. They think it is in the village."

Milfred is wiping dust off himself as he limps toward them. "I'll tell you what he did. He turned the battle, so Greystone lost. He let the kids escape. The friends of that witch you fought and killed now want you dead."

Hallr nods toward Milfred's leg and says, "Sorry about the leg, but I needed to get you away from me."

Milfred replies, "I get it. The pain from the injury helped break his control."

Sheyla says, "We will encounter more like him. We have to stay alert." Turning to Hallr, she says, "I understand what you meant before about always getting attacked. I'm sorry."

"Normal day for me. I need to get my axe."

It takes thirty minutes to cut up the horse enough to pull the axe out without having to break bones. Hallr also carves out the liver and a sizeable chunk of meat. "Mixed stew for dinner."

Sheyla's face scrunches, "I don't want to eat horse. They are beautiful and helpful."

Hallr replies, "I will not waste all this meat. We may not get more for days. I'm only taking what we can use for the next meal."

They get back into the wagons with three horses tied to the back. They will sell or trade these remaining horses. Hallr settles into work on the new pants.

Sheyla says, "We have to finish the conversation."

Hallr looks up at her and says, "After that encounter, I'm more trusting of you, but it will take me time. I have a question. I understand I pissed them off by helping Emberfell, but why before that? Why kill me?"

Agnarr says, "Probably because of your resistance to control magic."

Sheyla is concentrating, thinking, and says, "When I was young, I was trained to be a control witch. There was something they said about dwarves. Get the control target to attack dwarves first. Don't try full control with a dwarf in the area."

Milfred is finishing wrapping his ankle with a long strip of bandage and says, "The only things you can use to fight control witches are dwarves and Mithril armor."

Sheyla asks, "Is that something you heard?"

"Yeah. The old blacksmith who taught me talked about it. He wasn't specific about his experience, but he would say something about it every time witches came up."

Hallr looks at Milfred and asks, "Is this the real reason you want to find Molgan? You want to make both armor and weapons. There is another problem with that plan."

"Yes, I want to make armor. I also know that only dwarven craftsmen knew how to make armor with Mithril. We will figure it out."

Sheyla is thinking, and after a minute says, "The box is Mithril, so no witch can use magic to open it. That was the intention. Know how to get it open."

Agnarr says, "The only ones who could create that box are dwarves."

After wrapping his leg, Milfred climbed back into the first wagon to drive. He turns back and says, "If magic can't open it, there must be a key, or a puzzle to open it. Maybe there is a key in Molgan."

Hallr nods, "Haven't looked at it closely enough to see if there is a keyhole. Don't really care. It makes sense that a key would be in Molgan. If it is a puzzle, I can never solve it. I'm terrible at puzzles."

The Next War

The village was a week ago. They have been traveling south and east toward the mountains.

Sheyla says, "After we cross the river, we will be in the border area of Icemoor and Harenhal. There are mountains in the far eastern region. Because we are far from Icemoor City, the gangs will probably be more frequent."

Hallr says, "Good exercise. We also get loot. Selling their horses means we keep the wagon stocked."

Milfred says, "The real discussion is that we have been traveling south because none of us has been in the mountains to the south. We know the Molgan is in the mountains. We need to get to the mountains."

Hallr looks at Agnarr, "If everyone agrees, we need to follow one river that comes from the mountains."

Milfred, always talking to people and getting rumors, says, "There is fighting to the south with Kyrgall. The last group passed us was leaving the area. They didn't want to fight. They said people are getting conscripted to fight in the war."

Hallr frowns. "The stupid will fight. The smart and the wealthy will leave, and the marauders will grow bolder. I say we don't turn east at the next opportunity. We turn around and go back one day to the road east. It will get us to the closest river crossing."

"I agree with that," says Sheyla.

They have the wagons turned entirely when they see a traveling group of men. A dozen riders immediately go to a gallop to overtake the wagons.

"Where are you going?" asks the leader. He is in his early twenties, dressed in a nice linen shirt, leather pants, and boots. Someone who obviously knew how to cut his hair. He appears to be a member of a rich or noble family.

Agnarr says, "We passed a road to head east and the big river crossing."

"Where east?"

Milfred says, "I'm a blacksmith. I go to the villages and work wherever they need me. We heard there are more villages to the east and no war."

Hallr has been standing quietly. One man is staring at him. He says, "Hey, Tobias. I think this guy is a dwarf."

"Naw, no dwarfs anymore."

The man moves his horse forward, shoving Hallr. "Move away from the wagon, short man."

Hallr glares at the man, then slowly steps away from the wagon.

Tobias moves his horse around and looks at Hallr away from the wagon. "You look like a dwarf, but there are no dwarfs. What's wrong with you?"

"I've got a gland condition. On top of that, I was rude to a witch, and she hexed me to look like a dwarf."

Milfred smiles and looks at Sheyla, whose eyes are big, and then she smiles. She says, "That bitch said it was permanent."

Tobias nods and looks around at the others. He turns back to Hallr, smiling, "It's your lucky day. We are going to war, and having the Fortholm army think they are fighting a dwarf will be awesome."

"If I say no?"

"Then anyone who doesn't die right now will get to fight on the front line."

As he says this, the men pull out swords; four men notch arrows, and three load bolts into crossbows.

Milfred looks around and says, "If we stay together. We can provide support with fixing gear, healing."

Hallr is thinking, *"We can't go into a war with the box. We can't risk it being discovered and taken. If I go alone, the others can get the box away."*

Hallr says, "No, I'll go with them alone. This is what I do; this is how it works for me. I can put on the show to make them think a badass dwarf is going to chop them up."

Sheyla is playing along and says, "You have to be careful; looking like a dwarf is not the same as being one."

"I'll catch up to you on the east road when it is over." As he speaks, he goes to the wagon and pulls out his sword and scabbard. Leaving his axe covered in the wagon.

Agnarr shakes his head, looking at Milfred, "I don't like this."

Milfred and Sheyla, after seeing Hallr get the sword and not his axe, are squinting. He has something else planned.

Realization dawns for Sheyla; she says, "We will meet you when you've won their war."

Tobias laughs, "You don't make the terms. They all will fight."

Hallr speaks loudly. "If I'm fighting, I will get paid. You will pay them for my work now."

Tobias looks confused. "Didn't you hear what I said?"

"Pay them before you die. It takes dozens to kill a dwarf. You will be first."

The horses can sense the human's unease. They shift and snort.

Hallr stamps his foot while saying, "Pay them, and they leave."

This startles the horses close to him, and they shift away, ignoring their rider's direction.

Tobias' face is flushed. He is trying to control his horse, but not trying to get it closer to the dwarf.

Sheyla is watching and mumbles something. One horse prances suddenly to the side, swinging its head and tail as if a bug were harassing it.

Agnarr watches all this happen. He put his hand on Milfred and pushed him toward the front of the wagon, out of his way. He shifts toward Tobias, puts his hand out while focused on the horse, and says, "Pay me."

Tobias' horse is rearing up on its hind legs. He is holding on, yelling at the horse, which rears back and then lunges again. Tobias falls off the horse.

The band of men is struggling with their horses and cursing.

Now they laugh at Tobias.

"Forget how to ride."

Hallr walks over to Tobias. He has the sword in his hand but shows no aggression. Turning the sword blade to the side, he held out his other hand to help Tobias stand. He says, "You are right. I know how to make people think I'm a real dwarf. You don't need them for the show. They leave, and I will go with you."

The others calmed down, lowering their bows and crossbows.

A few minutes later, Hallr has a blanket, a pot, and his sword. He looks intently at Milfred, "Move out of the area. It would be better if they didn't have you to threaten. If they can, they will threaten you, trying to keep me in line. I'll catch up in a few days." He walks with the mounted group.

Sheyla says, "Don't worry about us. Stay well."

An hour later, Tobias says, "Walk faster."

"My short legs can't go faster."

"Tobias, we need to get him a horse."

Hallr says, "They don't like me. My feet can't reach the stirrups. I never ride a horse. I walk. Or you carry my pack, and I'll run. You ride ahead and make camp. I'll catch up."

Tobias becomes agitated after another thirty minutes. He says, "Give him your pack. You run and catch up, dwarf. We will hunt you if you try to leave."

After handing off his pack to a rider, Tobias put his horse into a gallop, and they all rode south.

Hallr begins a slow jog, carrying nothing. It is faster than walking, and Hallr can keep up a pace for several hours.

Running with no pack, three days later, the group reached the edge of the army. When they arrive, Tobias heads to one officer to show off his prize. Hallr stays with the rest of the group.

Soon after Tobias leaves, Hallr says, "Take me to the armorer. I need to see if he has better weapons."

No one in the group wants to cross Tobias, who said to stay.

"I'll find it myself. You boys don't need to leave. When Tobias gets back, you tell him I'm getting better weapons."

Hallr walks in the general direction where he has occasionally heard banging and screaming.

To the south, mountains mark the Fortholm territory. The Kyrgall camp is on the plain to the south and west. The Fortholm appears to have the positional advantage, but the Kyrgall army is over twice its size.

As Hallr walks through the camp, he sees the problem is that many of the Fortholm army are conscripts, like him. They lack the motivation to fight.

Getting to the Smith area, he finds out that many of the conscripts are being shackled because they have tried to leave. They are called deserters and are now shackled by their legs in groups of four.

Hallr gets directions to the lead weapon, Smith. The shackled people all looked at him and speak to each other softly. They are spreading the word that a dwarf is in the camp. The smith knows he is coming and is waiting with a small, single-bladed axe. "Word was you're looking for a big axe."

"I am. Something with some substance. Not that little toy."

"This is the biggest axe I have."

"Can you make something bigger? With two blades."

"That is crazy. It would be too heavy to swing all day. It would also take days to shape something like that."

Hallr looks around and walks to the stack of crappy swords in a pile. He rummages through them and picks out two shorter versions. He tosses them at the feet of the Smith and asks, "Where are your axes?"

The smith points, and Hallr walks over and pulls out two similarly sized axes. Walking back to the Smith, he says, "Make me an axe from these parts. Weld the two axe heads together with the blades facing opposite directions, one on top of the other. Take a sword and weld it to the blade of each of the axe blades. Better would be better to curve the sword blades before you weld them.

Harden the whole thing and get a handle that works."

"I can do that. The blades on the end of the axe heads will be weak and probably break."

"I guess I'll be careful. I'll pick it up tomorrow."

"Not going to happen."

As he says those words, Tobias rides up with an officer. Tobias says, "What are you doing?"

The officer looks at Hallr and says, "You look like a dwarf. Can you do anything like a dwarf?"

Hallr replies, "You want me to intimidate them, so they get scared a dwarf is going to chop them up. I need an enormous weapon. This will be the most enormous axe they have ever seen. The Fortholm soldiers will get scared.

The officer hears all this and says to the blacksmith. Make the axe.

The blacksmith inclines his head and says, "Okay. How long do I have?"

"Tomorrow. As soon as the dwarf can show the Fortholm army his axe, we will start the battle line assembly."

The blacksmith says, "I'll get you an axe."

The officer says, "And anything else he needs."

After the officer leaves, Hallr says, "Food?"

The blacksmith points and says, "You won't get much and won't like it, but go ahead."

Walking to the food area, Hallr passes through the deserter area. The men are all sitting around in groups of four. He is looking at the pathetic humans, knowing most will die in the battle. They are bodies to throw at the enemy. In the group, he sees an odd human. He is sitting on the ground, leaning back on his arm, and Hallr sees a very long arm.

Hallr stops and says, "Hey."

The man looks up, and Hallr sees a boy. Dark hair, dark eyes, a sharp nose, and a square chin. He isn't mature, probably a teenager. He is also skinny as a rail. As he stands up straight, he gets taller than the surrounding men, who are fully upright.

Another man in the group of four stands. He is tall and broad. The young man towers over him.

Hallr says, "Are you a giant?"

The young man replies, "They say so. My ma and pa are normal size."

"You look like a strong wind could blow you over."

"I'm strong. I can do all the chores around the farm."

"Hmph. Think about whether you want to fight with me. The dwarf and the giant."

Saying that Hallr continues walking toward the food area. After he has eaten, Hallr walks to the food, grabs a chicken leg and a hunk of bread, and walks out as the server yells at him.

Back with the deserters, they are all staring at him. The word that he is carrying food goes through the groups like wildfire. When one large man stands to block his path, Hallr shifts the bread as he walks straight up to the man and punches him in the stomach, hard.

The man flies back and doubles over in pain from the punch. After that, no one tried to stop him. He walks up to the giant and holds out the chicken leg. The kid grabs it and starts eating. In seconds, the meat is gone. He looks at Hallr, who hands him the hunk of bread.

Dropping the chicken bone, the man next to him grabs it and starts chewing. The bread is gone in two bites. Hallr says, "I'll be back in a few minutes for your answer."

Hallr turns and walks to the Smith. "I need tools to get someone out of shackles."

The blacksmith shakes his head, "I'm not supposed to do that."

"I'm going to do it. Show me where to get the tools."

The smith nods toward a bench, and Hallr grabs a chisel, hammer, and some leather. Back with the group, they all know something will happen, and you can sense the tension. Hallr walks up to the kid and asks, "Do you want to fight with me or stay here?"

"I'll fight with you."

Hallr says, "Put your foot there, with the shackle pin facing me."

The kid shifts his leg, so his foot is flat on the ground. Hallr shoves the leather between the shackle and his skin. He places the chisel's sharp edge against the rivet inside the shackle's straps. He says, "This could hurt if you shift and I miss. Don't move."

Hallr raises the hammer and strikes the chisel with force. The kid makes a noise but doesn't move. Hallr looks at the rivet and sees that the chisel has cut halfway through. He grabs both sides of the shackle and twists. The men around them see his arm muscles tense, and the metal bends.

Those close by talk as Hallr bends the steel shackle, twisting until the rivet breaks. "He can just bend the steel with his hands."

After the rivet snaps, Hallr expands the cuff to push it off the kid's ankle.

Hallr grabs the chisel and hammer. Standing, he says, "Come with me."

As they walk, the kid has a slight limp. Hallr looks down and sees blood on his ankle. "Are you okay?"

"I'm fine. I'll walk it off."

The smith is working on the axe. When Hallr tosses the chisel on the bench and makes a loud noise, the smith stops and puts the blade he was bending into the fire.

Hallr says, "I need a sword the right size for him and any armor we can find. Just point me in that direction, and I'll look for the armor.

The smith chuckles, looking up at the kid and then down at Hallr, "This is a joke, right?"

"No. This is going to make them run scared. They will run if we can make him look impressive. I need a long sword he can lift, but the armor is most important. We need to adjust something so he looks even bigger."

The smith looks at Hallr, saying, "I need help. I can't do the axe and him."

The kid looks down and says, "I'm not stupid. I can hear you, and I can help."

Hallr asks, "Can you sew?"

The kid shakes his head, "Ma sewed."

"Can you swing a hammer?"

"Course. The smith in our village wanted me to swing his big hammer."

Hallr turns toward the smith. "He's your hammer, man. I'll work on the armor. Kid, I'm looking for armor parts. Help him with the axe." To the smith, he says, "Feed him if you have anything."

The kid is clenching his fists hard.

The smith says, "Kid, what do they call you?"

In a slow voice, he says, "Never say I'm a kid. My name is Kaleb."

"Dwarf, not that you care, this is Kaleb."

Hallr says, "Kaleb. Why do you change the way you talk? You aren't good at faking stupid. Talk normally, or I will call you stupid, not a kid. You've got a story why you need to sound stupid?"

Kaleb replies, "Let old farts think they are smarter. Prevents a few arguments."

Hallr gives Kaleb a look as he shakes his head and turns, walking to another smith wagon, then leaving the area. He doesn't return for over an hour. When he does, the smith uses a small hammer for fine work. Kaleb is holding a large hammer and swinging hard when the smith tells him to hit.

Hallr tosses all the armor parts he has collected on the ground close to Kaleb and grabs one of the shoulder pauldrons. He says, "I can't reach. Bend down so we can try this."

The smith says, "He can swing a hammer. We could have this axe done before dawn."

Hallr says, "Tomorrow we put on a show. I want them to see and have time to stew on fighting a dwarf and a giant before the fighting starts. After the show, you can have more time to work."

Adjusting the pauldron, Hallr says, "I can make this work."

Two hours later, the smith stops. "That is enough for now. Let's take this to Hallr, then we'll take a break and eat."

Kaleb smiles when he says, "Eat."

The smith is carrying the double-bladed axe by the handle, with the blades hanging down. The smith is leaning as he holds the heavy axe.

Hallr is sitting on the ground sewing a metal plate onto a leather jerkin with leather thread and a needle from the smith. "This will be the last item before we do a simple test."

Putting the axe down close to Hallr, the smith says, "Let's get food, Kaleb."

Returning, they see Hallr standing, spinning the axe, twirling it, then tossing and catching it. The smith is watching with his jaw open. "That damn axe is over thirty kilos. That is crazy, you can do that."

Hallr is smiling. The axe is about half the size of his Mithril axe. Using iron, it is heavier than a half-sized Mithril axe would be. He is getting a feel for the weight and size.

Hallr smiles and immediately says, "Kaleb, come here, boy. Let's try this on you."

"Stop calling me, boy."

Hallr looks up at the tall teenager, "You're less than twenty, still growing. You're a kid, but I'll call you Kaleb. Okay?"

Kaleb nods.

Hallr picks up the armor he was working on. There are two shoulder pauldrons stacked on top of each other for each shoulder. For the chest, three breastplates overlap—a large one in the middle and smaller ones on each side.

Kaleb says, "Looks funny."

"It will look right when you put it on, and we will adjust the look. I need you to sit down."

Kaleb sits down on the ground. Hallr lifts the chest piece onto its end, and it is up to his chest. He lifts it and lowers it over Kaleb's head. "Okay, it is all open in the back. Because this is mostly a show. Now, stand up and pick up the axe."

Kaleb bends, stands, and has to grab the chest plates to keep them from falling. He stands. Hallr hands him the axe handle. "Put the top of the handle in one hand and the bottom in the other. Good. Now turn to the smith."

Kaleb turns, and the smith's eyes go wide. "Holy dragons!"

Hallr says, "Too bad we can't have two axes like that. Okay, Kaleb, here is a helmet. I've broken it in the back, so I think it will fit. Kneel."

Kaleb kneels, and Hallr puts the helmet on him. "Now stand."

The officer and Tobias are riding up when Kaleb is kneeling. When he stands and faces them, they jerk on their reins so hard that the horses both rear onto their hind legs. Even with the horses on their hind legs, the riders look just above eye level with Kaleb.

The smith and Hallr are smiling. Hallr looks at Tobias and sees fear. His leather breeches are getting darker in the saddle.

The officer says, "In the morning, we are going to put on a show. We will get every bugle, drum, and any other noise makers to go off. The troops will line up. Somebody will get dressed like a noble and ride their horse out in front alone. After he is there for a bit for them to see in all his finery, you two will walk out and stand next to him."

Tobias asks, "What is that supposed to do?"

Hallr says, "Show them they will fight a dwarf and a giant. Intimidate them. If they get scared, some will run off before the battle and more during the battle."

Teppo is upset, along with everyone in his group. Right now, Ranjeet is taking the brunt of Teppo's anger.

"We followed the dwarf. Where are the others, the wagons, and the box?"

"Teppo, you saw all the information; you were part of every decision. The people we asked said the dwarf traveled south. They must have split up, and I'm not surprised. A dwarf traveling with a witch wouldn't last."

"I want the dwarf, and I want the box."

"No problem, Teppo. The dwarf is here for war. When this battle is over, we get the dwarf. With the dwarf, we go back and find the

wagons and the box. Now, I'm going to bring this up again because the witches keep hearing about this dwarf fighting and killing magi. The horse we found was gruesome."

"They will get over it. My plan will work. Concentrated time with the dwarf, seeing us all as friends and not fighting him, not attacking. We got him to join our group. Then we can take on any kingdom, and we will eliminate every royal family that is against Magi."

"We need the teachings from the box to get the control witches strong enough to control the dwarf."

"Control will be the last resort. We need to influence and help him with other Magi. Let's put the word out for the outcast to attack him. We help him. Anyway, you don't think we can control one dwarf without the box. All of us together, projecting and reinforcing what he sees. The hard part will be us remaining calm. No aggression toward the dwarf; we are friends."

"No one has ever tried that. There aren't dwarves around so that we can try."

"Exactly right. All we hear is that covens attack dwarves. If we are friends, instead of attacking like everyone else, we can influence him with some gentle control nudges. We want the box information when we eventually have to fight other control covens. You want to suggest something different. What is your idea?"

"You take the witches and go find the box. I will stay with a few men for the dwarf. He will respond better to me with no witches in the area."

Teppo nods, "I can see that perspective. All right. You stay for the dwarf." Teppo looks at the sky. "I won't be able to get the wagons out of this area before dark."

"You will probably have to use control to leave. The soldiers won't let wagons leave, especially with fighting-age men. Wait until early tomorrow."

Teppo says, "I'll use the women as an excuse. We need to get them out of the way before the battle. The handmaidens are in the wagon."

The next morning, the entire army was up early. Everyone has heard about the dwarf and the giant show. The king and generals want everyone close to make noise.

Teppo is cursing under his breath. To the witches, "I know, I know. It's not your fault. Now they are saying no one can leave. We are going to war tomorrow morning."

The Giant's First Fight

The next morning, everything is ready. They will put on a for the enemy army. The soldiers cheer. The other army watches calmly.

This day is for preparation. Everyone is busy getting ready. Tomorrow morning, the battle will happen.

Hallr is finishing enough to get Kaleb's armor functional. It is not really battle-ready, but that takes more materials. He is also feeding Kaleb whenever he can. "I need you to be full of energy, and I need to put more meat on those bones. Eat."

At sunset, as the sun is halfway down on the horizon, there is a commotion. The officers yelled at everyone to assemble.

As an officer rides by, the group hears the enemy is now in formation. They could attack at any moment.

Hallr is confused, like everyone else. He is getting his axe and making sure Kaleb is ready. "Stay close to me. Your job is not to fight toe-to-toe. That is my job. You finish them. Use that long pig sticker on them."

The smith walks over and adjusts Kaleb's leather straps. That means he is pulling a strap with his foot on Kaleb's hip. He says, "Something is wrong. There is never a fight at nightfall."

Hallr says, "True. Humans like to fight in the morning, not at night. You people have a hard time seeing in low light."

Kaleb's head swings, looking intently at Hallr. "You are a dwarf, so you work in underground mines. You can see when it is dark."

Hallr chuckles, "Most humans never think of that when they try to sneak up on me when I camp."

The blacksmith asks, "Why would they fight at night?"

Kaleb replies, "Because they have an advantage. What could they have that we wouldn't expect?"

They are getting ready. The officers are yelling. Everyone is on edge already. Everyone hears an inhuman bellow.

Hallr says, "Don't know what makes that sound. Does anyone know what that is?"

Kaleb says, "That doesn't scare you."

Hallr smiles, "Naw. If it bleeds, it can die. I've never found something that wants to kill me that doesn't bleed."

They hear in the distance, "They have a troll. A huge troll."

Hallr says, "Never killed a troll before. They are probably tough."

Kaleb says, "You don't get scared?"

"I feel fear, but I use it. It doesn't control the way you think of fear. Why should you let fear control you? You going to cry, going to run away?"

Kaleb is looking at Hallr, thinking, not responding.

"Use it to help you be sharp."

The troll yells again.

Someone yells, "Trolls hate direct sunlight. They want to fight at night."

Kaleb nods to Hallr, "You chop 'em, I'll stick 'em," as he lifts his sword.

Hallr smiles and holds out his hand for a handshake. Kaleb bends down to shake hands, elbows bent, and the dwarf and the giant kid shake.

Hallr turns and yells, "I'm troll hunt'n tonight!"

Kaleb stands and yells with a surprisingly deep voice, "Troll hunt'n is my new favorite."

The soldiers around them pause and then yell. "Troll hunt, troll hunt, troll hunt."

It spreads through the ranks.

After a minute, Hallr walks to a soldier with a sword and shield. He grabs his arm. When the yell says 'hunt,' he smacks the shield with the flat part of the sword. Nodding, he does it again. The soldier nods and smacks his sword on the shield. "Troll hunt" shield smack.

In minutes, the entire army is moving to form its lines. "Troll hunt," smack.

Hallr grabs Kaleb's chest piece to bend him down. He says, "We've never fought a troll, so we don't know enough. I need you to be the bait."

Kaleb looks at Hallr, confused.

Hallr is frustrated because he didn't say this before the noise. Now the noise is too loud. "You look like the right target for a troll. Kite it. Dance around, jab, and move. Don't let it hit you. Let me have time to take their legs out."

Kaleb nods. He understands. Hallr doesn't let go. He yells, "Dance, move. DON'T let it hit you."

Hallr lets go and turns to see if he can find an officer. Tobias is riding close by, and Hallr yells and moves toward him. Kaleb follows. Tobias looks down at Hallr and says, "What do you want?"

"I want you to go tell the archers, especially the war bow archers, to fire at the troll as soon as they see it. If it dies before it gets to us, we don't have a problem, do we?"

Tobias looks at Hallr pathetically, "You don't think we've thought of that."

Tobias jerks the horse around and gallops off.

Kaleb says, "They didn't think of that. He is scared as shit."

Hallr says, "Let's go kill a troll."

Hallr gets his axe and gives the smith a fist bump, saying Thank you. He looks at Kaleb, who nods. They walk toward the front line.

Everyone parts to let them through. They walk to the front and step out, just the two of them. They stop for a moment just in front of the line. Hallr asks, "Are you ready for your first fight?"

Kaleb says, "How do you know it's my first?"

Hallr chuckles, "You look impressive, you're smart, but it shows. Stay focused. They will take advantage of any weakness. We got this."

Hallr walks forward. Kaleb takes a step and, with his longer legs, is at the same level as Hallr after Hallr's three steps. He pauses.

As they walk out, the army restarts the chant, "Troll hunt," smack.

After several meters, the other army shifted. They hear a bellow.

When the troll walks out, it sees the open area and comes to a stop. Looking and smelling, it bellows. Light grey skin, it seems four meters tall. It is wearing a leather cross-chest belt. At its waist is another belt. There are several leather strings at the waist, as it used to have a pouch. At the center, there is a flap hanging down. It is easy to see his dick and balls hanging down. The flap is a simple dress, not for genuine modesty. It is carrying a large tree stump. The root ball is the end, as a cudgel.

Hallr steps to the side and starts spinning and twirling his axe.

Kaleb sees him do this and starts swinging his axe, simply back and forth.

When Hallr walks, Kaleb follows. Soon after they walk, the troll fixates on them and moves.

Hallr yells, "Archers!"

When nothing happens, Kaleb bellows in his deep voice, "Archer's fire!"

In a second, arrows fly—most land short of the troll. A few hit the troll and bounced off. The troll's skin looks tough.

They watch as the troll shambles closer, and arrows hit and bounce off.

Hallr says, "I don't know if it's magic or troll skin. We are going to have to kill it the old-fashioned way."

Hallr walks forward. Kaleb is breathing shallow and fast, but he is following.

A few meters of walking, the troll bellows, goes into a knuckle-down stance and moves forward. It drops the stump and immediately stops. It stands, picks up the stump, and starts the shuffle forward toward them.

The enemy is shouting and moving around. Hallr sees this and yells, "Move forward."

Kaleb stops. Looks from one side to the other, between the armies as the troll heads toward him. He looks at his army behind him and yells, "Move! Destroy them!"

As if energized by his voice, the troops moved. Kaleb can see officers trying to stop them, but they keep moving. He yells. "Destroy them!"

Hallr, hearing this, smiles. Having lived through many battles, he knows that confidence, a firm voice, and stature can overcome fear.

The troll is ignoring Hallr while focusing on Kaleb. Kaleb has turned and focused. He raises his sword and runs forward past Hallr. The troll stops. It doesn't drop to move faster.

Hallr yells, "It learned. Be careful. It isn't a dump creature."

Kaleb slows and strides forward as the army runs to catch up. Hallr is a side story at this point. The troll watches Kaleb approaching, and at a few meters, it bellows. Mid-bellow, Kaleb charges fast and swings his sword. He swings wildly, missing the troll's head and grazing its cheeks with the blade.

The troll jerks back. Shaking its head, it puts its free hand to its mouth. Pulling it away, it sees blood. Its head jerks toward Kaleb, and it strides forward. Kaleb backs up.

The troll ignores Hallr as he now runs up and takes a step to the side of the troll's right leg. He brings up his axe, and with a heavy swing, he hits the troll in the leg, on the side, just below the knee. The blade sticks as Hallr holds the handle; the troll strides forward and pulls the handle out of his hands.

The troll yells in pain. Stopping, it looks down and sees the axe. It turns and growls at Hallr. Hallr is moving to the axe handle when Kaleb strides forward and shoves his sword at the troll. His shove barely penetrates. Kaleb, remembering what Hallr said, suddenly pulls back and pushes with all his strength into the troll.

The surrounding army cheered, watching him stab the troll. The troll has other ideas; it yells and swings its arm and knocks the sword out of Kaleb's hands and out of its belly.

Hallr grabs the axe handle and pushes down to cause a change. The troll yells, and for the first time, swings the stump as a club at Hallr. Seeing it coming, Hallr drops to the ground, prone, and rolls behind the troll.

Kaleb has a moment of disbelief when the troll knocks his sword out of his hands. When Hallr goes prone, he snaps back and goes for his sword.

The troll has missed Hallr and now turns so it can swing down toward him. With his back to Kaleb, he raises his club when Kaleb's sword tip comes out of his stomach. The troll feels the pain and pauses, looking down at this new thing. The blade pulls back and then goes through the troll again.

Hallr watches Kaleb stab the troll through the abdomen from behind. When Kaleb pulls out the blade, he jumps and reaches for the axe. He is to the side and slightly forward. He grabs the handle and pulls hard. This causes the troll's knee to twist, just as Kaleb's blade goes through it again.

The troll jerks from Kaleb's blade so Hallr can jerk his axe free. He steps behind the troll and swings his axe up into the troll's groin. The troll immediately makes a groaning sound, drops the tree, and drops to its knees. Kaleb steps back, looking at the troll. The troll looks at him, obviously in pain, but also with anguish on his face.

The troll is on its knees. It falls forward, dropping to his hands. Kaleb looks at Hallr and says, "This is not right. Something is wrong."

Hallr walks to Kaleb. "You're right. However, we have already passed the point of saving him. He was going to kill us."

Kaleb switches from watching the troll to looking at Hallr. "How is this right?"

"This war isn't right. There is never a right war. It usually boils down to some shithead wanting what another shithead's stuff. They get to tell people with less to fight and to die."

"I don't want to keep doing this."

"That is dangerous thinking. Those in charge don't take kindly to being directly opposed. You need to survive the day first."

With that, Hallr walks to the troll and pushes him. The troll falls over, groaning. Hallr turns around and yells to the sky. To Kaleb, he says, "We have to survive the day."

Hallr is facing the enemy, who is stunned that their unstoppable beast is down. There is yelling from the officers in the back. In moments, Hallr watches the faces change from shock to hatred. They are looking at him as the problem, as the thing to kill.

One soldier runs at Hallr, raising his sword. Hallr steps forward, raising his axe. As the man charges, Kaleb suddenly appears from Hallr's right, taking two steps and swinging his sword. The body hits the ground and slides to Hallr's feet, headless. Hallr looks at Kaleb, who is striding forward, saying, "We have to survive the day."

For the next few minutes, they fight as every enemy soldier that sees them charges forward.

Both armies are fighting now. With the troll down, the feel of the battle changed. The Fortholm troops fall back. Hallr looks at Kaleb and sees him breathing hard. He has been a target and is swinging the long sword fiercely.

Hallr says, "You don't have to chase them. Take a minute."

When Hallr separates them from the mass of troops and the fighting is far enough away, he gestures, and they pause. Tobias comes charging up on his horse, yelling, "Go kill them!"

Hallr yells back, "After you. Lead us."

Tobias has a flash of fear on his face, and he says, "I'm the one giving orders."

Kaleb puts his hand on Hallr's shoulder, and they turn and start following the mob.

As they catch up, several soldiers go down, and the enemy sees Hallr and Kaleb. They shift and charge forward. The fighting continues for a while, with Hallr getting concerned. Kaleb is a kid who excels by using his size and long sword, but he will eventually tire and fall.

After chopping the legs off a soldier, he looks around and sees

Kaleb six meters away with three soldiers around him. Kaleb stumbles, then stands back up, thrusting the sword and killing another. Two more charges at him, and he steps back and trips over a body. He falls backward and lands hard on the ground. Hallr strides forward, lifting his axe overhead.

One soldier yells and jumps forward, raising his sword above his head with both hands. As he steps toward Kaleb, the spinning axe blade impacts the soldier's chest, knocking him to the side and off his feet, tripping a second attacker.

Kaleb scrambled to his feet as the others surrounded him. Hallr grabs a sword from a fallen soldier. A pikeman appears from the right, stabbing a soldier about to attack Kaleb.

The soldier yells to his cohort, "Fight the giant." Quickly, a dozen soldiers are with Kaleb and Hallr as they push forward. The enemy only focuses on Kaleb or Hallr, and the others take advantage of the openings. As they move forward, the surrounding group grows.

After a short time, Hallr stops, grabs Kaleb's arm, and says, "We need water and rest. Stop moving." To the others, he yells, "Move forward. You've almost broken their line. Go take the win."

An hour later, victory was theirs, but pockets of fighting persisted. Kaleb and Hallr found water skins around them and drank. They haven't moved, but the fighting is now dozens of meters away. It has become so dark that the larger groups fighting now use torches to see.

Tobias is riding around the battle area with a torch. Kaleb says, "He's probably looking for us."

Hallr says, "He'll be a target riding around with that torch."

When Tobias sees them, he rides over, asking, "Why aren't you fighting?"

Hallr says, "We need to rest and have water. We don't just fight until we drop. If it bothers you so much, take our place until we get water."

Tobias glares at Hallr, then turns to Kaleb, saying, "Get back in the fight."

"Right, oh," as he walks away from the battle.

"*Where are you going?*"

"*The troll isn't dead. You want me to let it recover and attack. Oh, and I thought that was what you guys in the back were supposed to take care of while the actual soldiers were fighting.*"

Hallr smiles and starts walking towards the troll. He says, "*Yeah, why don't you come finish the troll?*"

Tobias says, "*Kill it, then get back into the fight.*"

As they walk away, Hallr, with his superior night vision, sees an enemy soldier moving among the bodies. He is following Tobias.

As they get to the troll, they hear it breathing, doubled over, holding its groin.

Kaleb walks up to the troll and kneels. He reaches over and shifts the metal helmet to see its face. The troll looks at him, then turns, closing its eyes.

Kaleb says, "*He's crying.*"

Hallr nods, "*Pain, loss.*"

The troll looks at Hallr as if seeing him for the first time. It says, "*Dwarf.*"

Hallr nods, "*Both of us caught in another human fight.*"

The troll's eyes are flicking back and forth between them. After a moment, it says something they don't understand. It holds its hand flat above the ground, about half a meter off the ground.

Hallr shakes his head, not knowing. The troll is thinking, mumbling words. It turns back to Hallr and says something, then another word, and another, and then they hear "*Bairn.*" Hallr looks, and the troll sees he understands. It puts its hand out again above the ground, "*Bairn.*"

Kaleb says, "*Bairn means baby.*"

Hallr points to the enemy camp and says, "*They have your baby?*"

The troll nods. It looks at Kaleb and says, "*Baby.*"

Kaleb nods and puts his hand on the troll. "*That is why he is fighting. They have his family, his baby, and are threatening to* kill them."

"They probably have his whole family. He could only make us understand the little one."

"What do we do, Hallr?"

"Right now, nothing. Nothing we can do. We need to rest, and in another hour, we'll go into the camp and find them. Wait here."

Hallr returns with several waterskins. He puts them down on the ground near the troll. Kaleb drinks and then offers the troll water. The troll nods and drinks as Kaleb pours water into its mouth. It coughs, which then worsens. Then, they see blood on the troll's mouth as it lies on its side.

Hallr says, "It knows it's dying."

They are sitting on the ground, not talking. Hallr knows Kaleb is in shock and battle-fatigued. His brain is overloaded, and he needs time not to think about what is happening.

While they are sitting there, a riderless horse gallops by. Hallr says, "That is Tobias' horse, minus the rider. I guess that guy caught up to him."

Kaleb says, "What guy?"

"Never mind. Let's walk."

As they stand, Kaleb touches the troll. Its eyes open, and it moves, then coughs, a hard, heaving cough. Blood is spewing out of its mouth with the coughing. After a minute, it stops and looks at Kaleb. Its eyes close, and it stops moving. "Let's go. We can't do anything else for him."

"His family?"

"Kaleb, if they are alive, we will have to fight most of these guys to keep them that way and get them out."

"We can get them home."

"Where is that? Trolls live in scattered caves. That army spent a whole lot of time and effort to capture that family to make him fight out in the open."

"We can try."

"Let's find them and see what we can do. Get ready to fight the enemy and our army to get them out."

Troll's Family

Hallr is walking through the corpses on the battlefield. It is now dark night, and they have stopped hearing fighting. There is a light to the right, but Hallr is not walking directly toward it. "We go to the side and approach from their side, from the flank."

On the way, they hear multiple humans moaning. Wounded, lying on the battlefield, waiting for help or death. Those who could move have left the battle area to seek medical help. The rest are close to death or can't walk. When they pass one, and it grabs at them, Hallr pulls his short sword and stabs the person. After the second one, Kaleb asks, "Why?"

"Kaleb, do you want to fight them later, be a nurse, find the troll family, or leave? Decide."

The next wounded person they see is an enemy soldier. He isn't moving; they can hear him breathing. Kaleb uses his long sword to finish him as they pass.

Having moved around the edge, Hallr is looking in the back area. He says, "We need to find cages."

They are passing through the wagon area, seeing scavengers rummaging through everything. After passing and checking several covered wagons, Kaleb hears someone talking. "That is a shame. Those would be worth their weight in gold alive. Some rich guy would have them for a collection or something."

Another voice says, "You believe what that guy said? They had orders to kill them when the big fighting troll went down."

"Well, someone killed them."

Hallr stops. He touches Kaleb's arm and points in a direction. They walk to a wagon. Inside is a female troll slumped down in a sitting position. Her limp arms are out toward a dead baby troll.

Kaleb clenches his fists, looks at Hallr, and sees his face—an intense, focused look. Hallr shifts the axe, looks at Kaleb, and whispers. "I'm going to do some hunting. Stay out of the way."

Without waiting for Kaleb to say or do anything, Hallr walks away. In a few steps, Kaleb can barely make him out in the dark.

Kaleb walks toward the fire. As he approaches, he can hear laughter and loud talking. As Kaleb approaches, he sees the king, dressed in his fine robes, sitting at a table. The king is enjoying the view as people bring him loot and captured individuals.

Kaleb moves behind a wagon and stops to watch for a minute. He hears people speaking to the king.

"This one claim is that she is from the extended royal family. She claims she will swear loyalty to you and provide a noble husband with many fine sons."

The king looks and asks, "Her age?"

The girl replies, "Sixteen, Your Majesty."

"Why are you not already wed and having children?"

"My father refused suitors, or they refused my father's meager dowry."

"Gag her."

The girl says, "Please," while someone puts a gag over her mouth.

Kaleb is confused and shifts to be less visible, watching.

The man finishes tying the gag and says, "Your Majesty?"

"There is an excellent reason one does not take fair maidens from your enemy and marry them into your own. Especially when they are past marrying age with no children, it is better to be cautious."

Everyone waits. The girl shakes her head, her eyes wide. Someone in the crowd says, "Witch."

The girl shakes her head more vigorously. She drops to her knees, moving her lips around the gag to say, "Please."

The king looks to an aide close by and asks something Kaleb can't hear. Looking back at the girl, he says, "For those who don't understand why I'm being diligent with captives, it is this. A witch can hide among us for years. They profess loyalty to the crown, but *in truth, their loyalty is only to their coven. They will kill any of us if directed by their coven. Behead her."*

A soldier standing to the side steps forward and grabs the girl. He drags the crying girl away from the king. Another soldier, not knowing how magic works, says, "Don't remove her gag. Don't let her speak."

Kaleb steps back to leave. He wants to be gone when he sees Tobias stumble into the area. He is bleeding from an arrow through his left shoulder. A guard is grabbing his arm to take him away.

Kaleb stops, turns back to watch, and listens.

Tobias shouts, "Your Majesty. I need to report."

An aide next to the king steps forward, saying, "Boy, the battle is done. We are deciding the fate of captives."

Men attacked me on the way here. Because the soldiers didn't kill the stragglers, they attacked me.

One of the experienced soldiers laughs out loud. "That would be your job, boy."

"The dwarf and that giant, the dwarf found. They left the troll alive, along with others."

After mumbling through the crowd, the king raises his hand for silence. "Is the troll alive? If it is, is it dangerous? We could use it in our army if we can control the beast."

An aide says, "We will have someone check, Your Majesty."

"As for you getting attacked and complaining. You are the son of my friend, so I will not have you dragged from this area by your hair. You are complaining to me instead of using the chain of command to deal with stragglers."

All eyes are on Tobias. His face is going from white to red. He realizes he is not getting dragged away, and he stands taller. "Someone should punish the dwarf and the giant for leaving fighters alive."

The king smiles, turns to his aide, and says, "Get him to the medical tent." Louder, he says, "Punish the two that did more to win today than anyone. They defeated a troll boy! They will not receive punishment; they will receive rewards. Have them found and fed, and I will speak with them tomorrow."

Away from the fire and the soldiers, where they can't hear the king and the guards can't listen to him. Hallr is looking at the man in charge of the trolls. He is now on his knees with his hands tied behind his back. "Ya already admitted your job was to take care of that mama and baby. You killed them instead of taking care of them."

"They told me to kill them if the big one died. If the fighter died, we didn't need the mom and baby."

"What did you tell Mom and the baby?"

"We told them they would be safe and return home after the battle."

"You lied. They were dead before the battle started."

During his search for the troll handler, Hallr found a rag on a wagon. It smelled, but Hallr didn't care. He now shoves the material into the troll handler's mouth so no one can hear his screams.

Once he finishes, Hallr moves to find Kaleb.

Kaleb is watching the people and items presented to the king. He hears a slight noise. Turning Hallr is there. He moves quietly when he wants to. Something is in his left hand, which is covered in blood. "Follow me."

He goes back to the troll wagon. He puts his bloody hand in and opens it. A thumb and an ear drop to the bottom of the wagon. He looks at Kaleb, "Not dead, but he will wish I had killed him for the rest of his existence. Everyone will know he lost that thumb, and it wasn't by accident."

Kaleb asks, "And the ear?"

"To make sure he gets noticed. He could hide a missing thumb. Much harder to hide a missing ear."

Kaleb nods and says, "They want us found, fed, and presented to the king tomorrow."

Hallr looks at Kaleb, "You want that?"

Kaleb shakes his head, "No. I want to go home. Do you want that?"

"Nah, when the troll keeper complains, they will listen to him over a dwarf. Where is your home?"

"North, but they burned it when they dragged me out to bring me here. Pa fought them, and he and Ma died. Home is gone."

Hallr turns and says, "Let's walk west for a while. We don't let them find us. In a day, we turn north, avoid all this."

Kaleb nods as they walk. As they pass wagons, Hallr looks into each one. By the time they get to the edge of camp, they have blankets and one pot.

Kaleb asks, "What about other stuff we need?"

Hallr replies, "We won't stop walking till we have the supplies we need. If we stop, they could catch us or find us. Keep walking."

Tobias Task

After getting bandaged, Tobias walks to the food area. While there, he overhears two guards talking.

The first guard says, "They found the troll mama and baby killed. The handler claims he was attacked by the dwarf. He also says that the dwarf killed the trolls."

The second guard replies, "That is bullshit. I went and looked. A small sword killed those trolls. The kind that the handler carries. The dwarf would have used the axe."

"What about the handler?"

"The handler is lying. He is missing his thumb and ear. If it were a fight, the dwarf would have killed him as well as the trolls. I say the dwarf punished the handler. He was sending a message."

Tobias walks over, "Where is the dwarf? He was supposed to be presented to the king this morning."

The first guard says, "Gone. Hasn't been seen since the battle."

The second guard says, "So he may not have even been in the camp. That handler could have been robbed and is covering it up."

Tobias asks, "Are they still looking for the dwarf?"

"I think so."

When Tobias looks toward the tent where he last saw the king, the king isn't there. When he asks, they chuckle and tell him the king has shifted his royal tent.

Tobias makes his way to the king's tent. When he gets close to a royal guard and states who he is, the reception surprises him.

"It is about time. You were requested hours ago. Come this way."

They take Tobias into the tent, and then he has to wait. After watching three others get time with the king, Tobias complains. "Present me to the king. I'm more important than those peasants."

The guard next to him glances at him and turns back. The sergeant gives a little laugh and doesn't turn.

A guard walks past Tobias and the guard with him. He goes to one of the King's aides and talks to him. The guard leaves, and the aide talks to the King, who nods.

The guard says to Tobias, "Move."

Tobias goes in front of the king and bows. The guard shoves him forward and says, "Kneel for the king."

Tobias looks back, angry, as he kneels. "Your Majesty."

The king looks at Tobias, "You do not know why you're here."

"To give news about what the dwarf has done."

"Yes. The dwarf YOU brought to our camp. The dwarf helped to win the war, but also killed the trolls. Where is the dwarf?"

At the mention of his bringing the dwarf, Tobias's face goes white, and beads of sweat appear on his temple. "I don't know where the dwarf went, Your Majesty."

"Your orders are to find the dwarf and bring him to me. I don't care where he has gone. Find him and bring him to me. I don't care how long it takes."

"Is Your Majesty going to punish him?"

Several people laugh.

"No. I want him kneeling and professing his loyalty to fight for the crown. I want him to be my warrior champion. Training and leading our troops."

Tobias nods, "Thank you, Your Majesty. Will the army provide men to help capture and return the dwarf?"

An advisor from the side steps forward and says softly, "Your Majesty, having troops with him will mean regular reports."

"Good point. Assign two soldiers to accompany him. They will help and also keep this one in line. They can rotate with others, so I get regular reports."

To Tobias, he says, "Find the dwarf."

After Tobias leaves, he inquiries about the soldiers assigned to him, but receives noncommittal answers. After being shuffled between different tents and officers, he is frustrated and goes to the food area. Sitting alone and eating the stew offered to him, after complaining about his station, he looks around, thinking,

"They don't know what I can do. I will bring back the shithead dwarf and secure my family's position in the royal court."

While finishing his stew, a skinny man walks up. Tobias raises the bowl to hand to him as if the man will take it away. The man ignores the bowl and sits down. "You need to find a dwarf. They are hard to find. The only one anyone has seen in years was the one you brought. I can help you find him. For a price."

Tobias is smirking, someone who can perform miracles for money. "What price?"

Ranjeet says, "Three gold to find him. Twenty gold to capture him."

"You can capture a dwarf?"

"My friends and I have some tricks."

"Find him, and you get three gold. That means you tell me, and I see him. This is not just a location, pay me and go find him bullshit."

"Do you want us to capture him?"

With a smirk, Tobias says, "Sure, if you can."

Ranjeet asks, "Where did you find the dwarf?"

When Tobias describes the location and the wagons, Ranjeet shifts. "He was with others. Describe them."

Tobias sits without speaking.

"If you want to find the dwarf, the people he was traveling with are a good start. He may try to get back with them. Describe them."

Tobias says, "That is a good place for me to start."

The Journey North

Hallr and Kaleb walk every day, avoiding people as much as possible. Kaleb learned quickly to walk slowly with smaller steps. The size difference meant Hallr would take three steps to his one. They started arguing about walking at that point.

Hallr was the first to say, "Ya need to learn to walk. If we don't walk at the same speed, you should leave."

"I'm walking normally. I don't usually walk with others. No one would walk with me. You need to walk faster."

Gesturing at his legs, Hallr says, "My legs are this size. That's it. You learn to walk or get on with ya."

The next several hours, Kaleb walks ahead, waits, and begins arguing when Hallr can hear, then walks ahead again.

When they encounter people, it often turns into a discussion or a request for them to solve everyone's problems. After days of walking and being stopped, they arrive at the intersection where Hallr and the group would turn and cross the river toward the mountains.

At the intersection of the road east, there is a makeshift town. There are vendors selling merchandise from the backs of wagons. Makeshift stalls with grills made from makeshift bricks. They hear a hammer from the blacksmith. About thirty meters away, off from the vendors, is a makeshift corral with horses and oxen. Behind that looks like a pen with pigs. Between the merchant area and the corral are a dozen tents.

They walk through the area toward the sound of the hammer. Everyone stops and watches them as they walk. A dwarf and a giant are walking together. They have accumulated gear, including backpacks and blankets. Everyone who looks at them sees that the gear is makeshift, patched together. Even the dwarf's axe is welded together from parts.

As they approach the sound of the hammer, it stops. A woman walks up and begins talking to Kaleb. "You need a place to bed down? We can provide food and a safe place for the night."

Hallr replies, "We are heading to the river. We need to get across and find our friends. They have two wagons heading toward the mountains."

The woman looks at Hallr, then at the woman next to her. She turns back and mumbles something as her eyes narrow, and Hallr immediately feels his head hurt. It is sudden, and he drops his iron axe and grabs his head. Kaleb holds his head as he collapses.

Both women are looking intently, one at Hallr and the other at Kaleb. One says, "We aren't your enemy. What is happening? We are friends. Let us help."

Hallr growls, standing, looking at the woman with pain and fury on his face. He knows he can't bend down to the axe. He reaches for his dagger when he hears Kaleb scream, "My head!"

The woman's face shows fear as Hallr looks at them and takes a step, dagger in hand. Suddenly, the woman to Hallr's right flies to the left and slams into a wagon. The woman next to her turns to her left and flies backward, hitting the wagon as well. The pain is gone. Hallr takes a breath and looks to see Agnarr walking toward him while focusing on the two women.

Turning, Hallr sees Kaleb on the ground, convulsing.

Hallr feels a hand on his arm and turns to see Sheyla. She looks at him intently, touching the side of his head. "I have to check. Sorry, we didn't know you would arrive today."

"Help my friend."

Sheyla nods and kneels next to Kaleb. She checks him, then, while her hand is on his head, she closes her eyes and concentrates. Sheyla focuses, and sweat rolls down her temple. In a moment, Kaleb's breathing changes. When she stops, she stands, wobbling. She grabs Hallr's outstretched arm. Sheyla says, "I need to practice more. She was trying to kill your friend. He may be out for a while."

Hallr turns to the two witches, bends to pick up his axe, and hears from Agnarr, "Not you. These two are mine."

Agnarr is standing next to the two unconscious women and makes motions with his hands. The unconscious bodies shift. He bends down and puts their hands behind their back.

Sheyla reaches down and grabs a piece of linen sticking out of Kaleb's pack. She winds up pulling out a torn and stained shirt Kaleb has been using as a cleaning rag. "I need this." She walks over to Agnarr and tears the rag into pieces.

Agnarr reaches, taking one part of the shirt. He ties the witch's hands behind her back. Sheyla ties the second witch.

Hallr pushes Kaleb with his toe. You need to wake up, Kaleb. Hallr kicks him softly.

Kaleb's eyes open, and he looks at Hallr, asking, "What?" Kaleb then doubles over on the ground, grabbing his head. "Bloody dragons, what happened?"

Hallr kneels next to Kaleb, "Witches attacked us."

Hallr reaches out a hand to help Kaleb stand.

Kaleb puts one hand on the ground, grabs Hallr's outstretched hand, and tries to stand. His legs shake, and he sits back down. "I need a minute."

Kneeling and tying one woman, Sheyla says, "He will be okay. They didn't have time to destroy his mind, but we need to get you away from the witches."

After a couple of minutes, Kaleb reaches for Hallr's hand and stands. When he is up, Sheyla says, "Head to the wagons. Distract the crowd for us."

They turn in the direction Sheyla is pointing, and the crowd has been watching. Hallr takes a step, and a path opens, allowing Hallr to see Milfred moving his great axe next to the wagon wheel. Sheyla says, "Agnarr and I have to do something with them. Go get your axe, put on a show."

Hallr looks at Kaleb and hands him the makeshift axe. He walks to his dwarven axe. Milfred comes forward, saying, "I worked on your axe. I could sharpen it a little. That metal is incredible."

Hallr picks up his axe, feeling the heft. Smiling, he steps away and spins it, twirls it, then tosses it and catches it as it comes down. The crowd is watching in awe. Many are mumbling. Kaleb says, "This is the famous axe with no name."

Milfred looks up at Kaleb, holding the makeshift axe that most people would struggle to use. He turns to Hallr, "Who is this? You didn't want children, now you have one?"

Kaleb says, "I'm sixteen, have been through a war, and helped him kill a troll. Don't call me a kid again."

Milfred gets a shocked look and says, "Sorry. What should I call you?"

"Kaleb."

Hallr is smiling. "Milfred, this is Kaleb. Kaleb, this is Milfred, the blacksmith. The two earlier are Agnarr and Sheyla, who healed you."

Turning to Milfred, Hallr says, "What the hell are you three doing here?"

"We're waiting for you, as we agreed, on the route you would take to get across the river. This is what we agreed. All these people started with people asking for blacksmithing help."

Hallr shakes his head. "I don't like this crowd. Witches were waiting. We need to get moving away from people."

Milfred looks intently at Hallr and says, "This all happened over several days—people who were leaving the fighting area. We dealt with shit waiting. You need to think about your group, your friends. We can talk tonight, pack everything, and leave in the morning."

Hallr is thinking about what Milfred says, then nods to Milfred, and he turns to Kaleb and gestures. Hallr and Kaleb put their packs down, and Hallr shows the axe to Kaleb, who nods. When Kaleb grabs it to pick it up, he pauses and grunts as he lifts it, "This has heft. I couldn't fight with this. It is too heavy."

It is almost dark when Agnarr and Sheyla return to the forge area. Kaleb asks, "What did you do, and what is happening to them?"

Sheyla asks, "Who is this?" looking at Hallr.

Kaleb says, "I'm Kaleb, troll killer, and friend of Hallr."

Agnarr smiles, "Well, alright."

Kaleb asks, "What did they do to me?"

Sheyla says, "They were trying to kill you with what is called a mind flay. It is a way to destroy your brain and mind."

Agnarr says, "From our questioning them, someone hired them to find and control Hallr, only Hallr. Get him to stay until others arrive. They don't know who hired the coven."

Sheyla says, "It is not a true coven, but a group of witches working together. These two are friends. The others are south, looking for Hallr. This is like the group after the village. Hallr wasn't exaggerating; witches are always trying something."

Kaleb asks, "Can you explain more about what happens with this mind flay?"

Sheyla nods, "At the lowest level, a healer gets your cells to heal. No one can explain exactly how, but you heal faster and better when magic applies to help. The other extreme is destructive. Witches tell your body to die. Parts of your body can decay; they die. It is extremely difficult and very dangerous."

Kaleb says, "Hallr talks about pain in his head from witches."

Sheyla replies, "Yes, they are trying to tell his body to die. Stronger witches can do more, so there is more pain. I believe the stronger witch focused on Hallr. That helped you because the weaker one couldn't do as much damage."

Agnarr says, "I think the approach to Hallr has changed. They want to control him, not just kill him."

Milfred says, "You said control him, not kill him. Why control?"

Agnarr says, "If they had a dwarf under their mental control, they could win wars."

Kaleb says, "The king's decisions make more sense now. He had a young woman beheaded, thinking she was a witch, thinking she could or would control the king. Why didn't it work on him?" looking at Hallr.

Sheyla says, "He is a dwarf and resistant to magi mind influence. I knew from the first time we met, but I didn't realize how strong he is until we arrived in the village. That little girl, Meriel, was trying to control you. To stay with us. Merial told me just before we left, no one can control you with normal methods. She must have been coached and told to try. You can't be controlled by those methods, which is dangerous for someone so young to say. She must have been coached by the witch that found them to try that with everyone."

Hallr says, "The two witches?"

Agnarr says, "They won't be a problem anymore."

Sheyla says, "Two witches concentrating couldn't stop you. It is your resistance is exceptional, or after so many years, you have developed the ability to prevent any control."

Hallr nods, "It was hard with two."

Kaleb asks, "Did you kill them?"

Agnarr asks, "Are you concerned about that?"

Kaleb shakes his head, saying, "If you have a problem, I'll do it. If they aren't dead, I want to know how you prevent them from being a problem."

Agnarr looks at Hallr, "This young man is hardened. Is this from your training? You're doing?"

Hallr looks back, "You can ask him. I helped him learn. The war we had to fight did the actual work."

Kaleb says, "We had to survive the day, and then I learned about cruelty and politics more than ever before."

Sheyla nods and says, "For the witches, I needed you two to distract the crowd while we took care of them."

Kaleb looks at Sheyla, "I don't know you. What does that mean?"

Agnarr says, "There is a pen beyond the corral with ten hogs. We took them there."

Hallr looks at Sheyla as Kaleb nods to Agnarr.

Kaleb says, "We need to leave before someone finds the bones."

Milfred says, "Just more bones in that pen. No one cares in this camp."

Hallr says, "Tomorrow, we head to the mountains and whatever misadventures are along the way. Kaleb, this is your chance to get *away and make your own way. These three are trouble, just like me."*

Kaleb looks down at each of them and says, "Are you joking? Look at me! All I do is attract trouble. I attracted you, didn't I? I'll stay with you, if you'll have me."

Hallr smiles, "You're in for an adventure."

Agnarr says, "I'm reluctant, but say yes. A dwarf and a giant."

Milfred says, "All in. Just all in. What could go wrong?"

Sheyla says, "We will have to be careful. The people who sent those two witches will try again. We don't know who sent them or why, but they are still trying to get you."

Kaleb says, "Now I'm learning about this after I agreed. I guess I'll need to be saving you more often than I thought."

Hallr laughs, "We're all outcasts. Saving each other is why we are a team, but you're way behind. After the battle, I figure you've got two, three hundred to catch up."

Kaleb blushes, smiles, and says, "You can't count."

Milfred asks, "Do you have any coins? We should get supplies if we can?"

Hallr smiles, "Have you been giving away your services?"

Milfred shakes his head, "No. I have money. I want to know if you were giving away your services. And I want to know what we can get while we are here."

Hallr unties his coin pouch and tosses it to Milfred.

Milfred turns to Agnarr, "We only get what is hard to buy on the trail. Hallr, you stay with the wagons. We will be back soon."

Kaleb turns to Sheyla, "I have money."

"Let's see if we can find some spices for cooking, maybe a couple of blankets."

Kaleb turns to Hallr, "You good to stay."

"Ay."

Walking through the stalls, Sheyla asks, "Where are you from?"

"Northwest, close to the coast. And you?"

"Originally, I was from way down south. I was taken from my

parents when I was really young for training."

"As a witch?"

"Yes. I'm a healer, in case you haven't figured that out."

"You and Hallr didn't talk. Is there something I need to be careful with?"

"Witches have attacked Hallr all his life. He doesn't trust me. I stay away so I don't antagonize him."

"Do you trust him?"

"Not much. He is a dwarf. He is single-minded about many things, but he can fight. Right after we first met, he fought a powerful witch. Except for two others causing problems, he would have probably defeated her alone."

"You think that is significant."

"Yes. How did you do against those two witches? He was pulling a dagger to kill them when we stepped in. He is not an enemy. I have been told he is more like me than we both want to admit, wandering, trying to survive in a world that doesn't want us."

After shopping for spices, they headed back with Kaleb carrying several bags. Sheyla stops to look at a jewelry vendor.

Kaleb asks, "What are you looking for?"

"A peace offering."

Rummaging through the odd box the vendor has on the side, she pulls out a worn, plain beard bead. Looking at the vendor, she says, "One copper?"

The vendor says, "Five."

Kaleb snorts, "Let's go."

Sheyla looks intently at the vendor. "You have more?"

The vendor turns, digs into a bag, and pulls out a small pouch. She dumped the contents onto the makeshift table with her other items. Kaleb leans over to look at two beard beads. These are larger, older, and have something carved on them. Sheyla turns one over to show a stylized D. The other also has a D.

Kaleb says, "D. Maybe a family name, or dwarven Drekhul, meaning hero. Maybe Dregnar, or a battle veteran."

Sheyla turns to Kaleb, "You know dwarven."

Kaleb blushes, "A little. I must have picked it up somewhere."

Sheyla looks at him for a second and says, "Sure."

Turning to the vendor, she says, "Five coppers for all three."

When the vendor shakes her head, Sheyla turns to walk away.

The vendor says, "Wait. Six for all three."

Sheyla says, "Done."

Back at camp, Sheyla made Kaleb put the spices on the wagon and showed him how she organized them. With his long arms, Kaleb can reach almost halfway into the wagon to put the spices with the others.

He then turns to Hallr. Sheyla has said nothing about the beads. He catches her eye and gives a questioning look. Sheyla compresses her lips, walks over, and hands the beads to Kaleb. "You do it."

Kaleb looks confused for a second, then turns to Hallr, "These are a peace offering from Sheyla. She found them and picked them out."

He puts the pouch in Hallr's hand and waits.

Hallr opens the pouch, dumps the beads, and looks at them. Then he turns to Sheyla, "Thanks."

Sheyla says, "The vendor gave us a good deal for them. I thought you might like something for your impressive beard."

Kaleb says, "Plain. Need some work. Yeah, he could use them."

Hallr punches Kaleb in the thigh. "She tried. First human in years."

"Are you two good with each other now?"

They both say, "No," and turn away from each other.

Tobias Learns About the World

Tobias is on the trail of Hallr. The stranger he sent off to find and bring back Hallr is gone. Tobias paid no gold upfront, refusing even to negotiate.

He is traveling with soldiers assigned to him by the king, and three more released conscripts who agreed to travel with him for ten silver coins.

Once he had a direction to start, he assembled his group and began following it. Following a dwarf and a giant is easy. Everyone will talk about them.

He is eager to find Hallr. He tells his group, "When we find them, kill the giant quickly. The king won't pay for him. After that, we capture the dwarf and take him back."

None of the group has ever dealt with a dwarf. They all heard about Hallr during and after the battle. They are simply following orders.

A crowd surrounded them when they reached the intersection camp area. Everyone is trying to offer them something. Tobias is trying to push through the area when he hears someone say, Giant. He stops and asks, "There was a giant. Was there a dwarf?"

An old woman with a blanket over her arm looks at Tobias with his nice clothes, well-fed horse, and says, "Buy a blanket, and I'll tell you."

Taking the queue, the others all start offering to provide the information if Tobias buys something.

Tobias is furious. His face is red. When a vendor gets close to his horse, he jerks the reins, making the horse move and knock the person backward. The crowd is getting agitated. Then they all stopped moving and talking. Tobias watches as they all turn toward the road he has just arrived from.

The stranger he spoke to, who was looking for the dwarf, is on horseback. There are two more on horses, and a wagon with several women and another man driving is behind it.

Tobias is turning his horse around to go to the man. He notices the riders with him all suddenly look like they're in rags, and the horses look starved, with saddles falling apart. "What the hell?"

The approaching riders and the wagon turn to their left and head off the road. Tobias and the group follow. When they stop, Tobias hears from one of the other men. Get off and park your horses. We need to talk.

Everyone looks normal again, and he hears, "It was a simple illusion to get them to leave you alone. We can do simple illusions to help you."

Two hours later, Tobias is looking at an older man, the actual leader of the group, named Teppo. He has been told a story that is hard to believe, but it makes sense. "The real reason they hunt magi is that controller groups can control a king's actions."

Tobias says, "This is why my king has outlawed witchcraft and executes magi."

Teppo says, "Yes. To them, the threat is too much. Even when we can help them against their enemies, they hunt us. We hide and help where we can. We help people like you by doing simple illusions."

Nodding Tobias says, "Finding the dwarf. Why is finding the dwarf important to you?"

"You're hunting the dwarf, not someone else. Are you searching for someone else?"

"Well, no."

"Tobias, we will help you with the dwarf. We can also help you with your dilemma in the royal court."

"What are you talking about?"

"People try to take advantage of you. You have been diligent and protected yourself. Being a good person, you are the primary target. By keeping you down, by making you look bad, they elevate themselves."

Ranjeet walks up to join the discussion.

Tobias nods as Teppo continues, "How many from the royal court were on the battlefield? How many found the dwarf? Your efforts are getting subverted."

Ranjeet says, "After we talked and I started searching for the dwarf, I found proof that the troll handler was lying. That made you look bad."

Tobias grits his teeth.

Ranjeet looks at Teppo and says, "The dwarf and giant were here. They left two days ago. They are heading to the mountains, searching for Molgan."

Tobias says, "We can catch them."

Teppo is looking intently at Ranjeet. When Tobias speaks, he turns and says, "We can, or we can follow. Why do you think they're going to Molgan?"

"I don't know, so that the dwarf can find relatives?"

Ranjeet says, "That is probably part of it. If they are still alive. Molgan is the lost Dwarven city. They are looking for it to find the treasure."

Teppo says, "Treasure, we can help you get Tobias."

Tobias looks between them, "Treasure. That is a children's story. Someone found and took treasure long ago if it existed."

"Then why are they looking for a deserted, dilapidated, dead city in the mountains? No one has found the treasure, but a dwarf was never looking before."

"I don't know why the dwarf would go there. I want to get the dwarf and take him back to the king."

Teppo says, "If there is a vast treasure in the city, you could take it all back to your king and become top in his court. The recognition you deserve."

Ranjeet says, "We are staying here tonight. You can think about it tonight. I recommend that we follow them until they find the city. Then we can go in and get the treasure. If there is no treasure, or when we get the treasure, we capture the dwarf."

Away from Tobias Teppo says, "That was good. It is better if he *decides on his own instead of us making a controlling suggestion."*

Ranjeet replies, "I picked up on your wanting to follow them to the city. Why do you think the dwarf wants to find the lost city?"

"I'm not sure. Treasure is one answer. Another answer is that he needs something in the city to open the box. Dwarves made the box. I know that if anyone finds the lost dwarven city, it will be a dwarf. We don't need to be anywhere urgently. We can follow. If there is nothing, we get the dwarf into the mountains away from help. If there is a city, we get that as well as the dwarf," as Teppo smiles.

"Assuming there is a city to find."

"The old stories must have some truth. It hurts nothing to follow instead of capturing the dwarf. If there is a key, we need to open the box. We need to let the dwarf find it before we take the box."

Ranjeet says, "If Tobias doesn't decide to follow on his own, we can still give him control commands. He will be useful for money, for supplies, as we follow the dwarf."

Teppo smiles, "We get the box, the treasure, then we can make Tobias powerful in the court and our benefactor. By the time the king dies, we could have everything set up."

The Trek

After crossing the river, they headed straight east towards the mountains. Along the way, they stop at towns where Milfred offers blacksmithing services. He has Agnarr, Kaleb, and Hallr as helpers. Together, they help with town construction, repairs, and any other work that will get them food and supplies to keep going.

The first winter is hard. They were high in the mountains when a blizzard hit, trapping them in a small village. They avoid using magic that the villagers can see. The town survives thanks to Agnarr's skill at hunting. His ability to hit targets with his shooting is unmatched. Kaleb and Hallr chop wood for fires. When spring comes, they don't leave right away. They helped the villagers build a new grand house to prepare for the next winter.

When they finally set out, they headed into the central valley below the mountain village. They find two abandoned farms close together, or so it seems. There are no farm animals; the pens are open, and everything is in disrepair.

Kaleb, curious, goes to investigate the barn at the second farm. He finds a shallow grave with bodies. The grave has a man, a woman, and three children. Someone killed the farmer's family, but they have no clue who committed the murders.

With no sign of Molgan, they turned north, heading toward the next group of mountains. This cycle of stopping, working, and staying in a village for the winter will continue.

The box is now under everything else they use or move. Almost forgotten, but ever-present in the back of their minds.

The second spring, when they travel again, they continue their travels north, looking for roads into the mountains to search.

According to the maps they have seen and the locals, they are approaching a river junction that marks the border between Icemoor and Harenhal. There are old stories about the city in this area. Like most areas, however, Hallr has commented, "The odd saying, the odd way of handling stone reminds me of dwarves, but nothing else. No dwarven roads, stonework."

On a village visit, Milfred has set up his forge and bellows to repair items for the locals. Like every village, the kids are curious about Hallr and Kaleb. The dwarf and the giant. While they work, Milfred is the smith, and Agnarr is the apprentice. Hallr is the hammer, and Kaleb mans the bellows, moving things around. Sheyla is the smiling face selling their services.

While working in this village, Agnarr comments to the others, "We are constantly being watched. I don't know what they are looking for, but this differs from other villages."

Hallr says, "The more we travel in this country, the more they whisper about me, but this village is different. I've heard two wagons being said. We need to be careful. Nothing but blacksmith work and trade," he says, looking at Sheyla. She nods in response.

The next afternoon, a kid fell off a structure they were climbing. They wanted to know if the strangers could help. Sheyla is the first one they talk to and immediately asks, "You don't have a healer in the village?"

The kid says, "No. Our village healer died, and a traveling healer won't be here for many days."

Agnarr walks over, wiping sweat from his head. "Sorry, kids, we rely on village healers just like you. If you have a scrape, we have salve and rags to wrap it."

The kid says, "It's bleeding a lot."

One of the village adults is walking over as the kid says, "Please, it hurts."

Sheyla has a concerned look on her face. "I'm sorry. I wish we could do some magic or something to help, but none of us can do magic."

The adult nods to Sheyla and Agnarr and tells the kids, "Go to the pub and ask Madalene to help."

He turns to Agnarr as Hallr walks up. "We heard rumors. A traveler said that the group with two wagons is magical. The guy said they controlled people around the village."

Hallr says, "Two wagons. That sounds like us, but we are very visible traveling smiths, not magic. You worried about magic?"

"Frankly, we are. The old stories talk about evil witchcraft. They come in, control people, and take our supplies. Hearing about magic and controlling other villages, we are concerned."

After the villagers leave, Agnarr gets everyone together. "The rumor about two wagons controlling villagers' concerns. If the villagers consider us that group, we will have issues."

Sheyla says, "If there are controller witches anywhere in the area, we will have serious problems. We need to move."

The next morning, they packed when several villagers approached with items needing repair. The man they talked to approached, saying, "We realized you can't be the wagons from the rumor. We can give you work. You don't have to leave."

Milfred says to the villagers, "The rumor about witches has us concerned, just like you. We need to move out of the area. We will stay one more day and repair whatever we can. In the morning, we need to move on, and good luck to you."

The man nods, "Yes, I would leave if I were you as well. We're sorry we stayed away and that you can't stay longer."

Sheyla says, "We're sorry we can't stay. If there are witches, we want to get out of the area."

Several days later, two wagons rolled into the village. As soon as the villagers see the wagons, they spread the word and all hide.

After a few questions, the witches huddled together. The older man walks out of one house and speaks with Teppo and Ranjeet.

Tobias is angry. "What else did he say?"

"Master Tobias, he said it was from a single traveler. He was repeating."

"Now the dwarf knows we are in the area. We can't lose them."

Teppo says, "Calm down. The plan hasn't changed. We follow them. We watch and wait. When they find the lost city, we move in."

"The direction they are traveling will take them to a desolate area. No villages, no one to spread rumors. We need to get provisions to continue to follow them."

Tobias says, "You are terrible at foraging. How much will this cost?"

Teppo says, "We will add it to the account to settle with the gold from the city. Let's go over and see the stables."

When Tobias leaves, Ranjeet turns to one witch, "Have them bring out everything we can carry."

The villagers are bringing out all their supplies. As they deposit their items near the wagons, several become agitated. Ranjeet is there and talks to them. His answers do not satisfy everyone.

Over the course of the day, they loaded their wagons. As they were leaving, Tobias asks Ranjeet, "Did you get an accounting of the cost?"

"Yes, my lord. I have all the details." Looking at his notes, Ranjeet says, "Sorry, sir. I missed a name for the accounting. Let me go get that detail before we leave."

"Very Good. I want details. We need to ensure we treat these locals with respect and pay them properly."

Ranjeet closes his blank notebook. Walking to the coven guard, he says, "Make sure the bodies are out of sight as the wagons leave."

In the camp, they are around the fire. Hallr stands, grabs his axe, saying, "I'm getting more wood."

After he leaves, Kaleb asks Sheyla, "The village was different and is making me think. I'm not sure what I should ask. How does control magic work?"

Sheyla turns, looking at Kaleb, and Agnarr shifts to face Kaleb. Agnarr says, "I think we can explain."

"Hallr said you've done it before. Why would you do that?"

Sheyla is glaring at Kaleb, "I was a kid and told that was what I was supposed to do. When I found out what it really was, I ran away. The only time I've done it around Hallr was protecting all of us."

Kaleb is looking at Sheyla. "Why do the others do it?"

Agnarr says, "Power, control, sometimes money. They don't do it for good reasons; they basically lie to people."

Sheyla interjects, "That is why it is bad and outlawed by magi and humans."

Kaleb says, "Why would a king have every magi killed, even people doing good? Is it that dangerous?"

Milfred nods, "They, the bad controllers, lie all the time. Someone saying they are a healer." Milfred gestures toward Sheyla, "But they really are a controller, or scouting for a control group."

Sheyla looks at Milfred and interjects, "Thanks for that attack."

Agnarr moves to stand next to Sheyla, "Not nice."

Milfred is shaking his head, "Wow. Let me finish my point." Turning back to Kaleb, he says, "When you actually have someone who won't do control, no one has a way to check or verify. It is the intention of that person."

Kaleb looks from Milfred to Sheyla, "The intent of a person, which one can't really know. Meaning you can never trust a witch?"

Milfred is shaking his head. "You've spent too much time with Hallr. People judge everyone by their actions."

Agnarr says, "You fought a troll. You were trying to kill it until you learned the real reason it was fighting. So, using your logic, you just said, no troll can trust you. You revealed your true intentions. You will fight trolls."

Kaleb furrows his eyebrows for a second as he listens, thinking about the discussion. "If I meet a witch, I can't trust them."

Milfred says, "If you meet a human, can you trust them? A dwarf or a troll. Witches are human, but you don't know if they are a witch when you first see them. By your logic, you can't trust anyone you meet."

"So, I'm supposed to trust everyone. That doesn't work for me."

Agnarr is clenching his fists. He takes a breath, looking at Kaleb, "I don't need to trust everyone immediately. They stay polite and nice, and we can get to learn more. If they behave badly, I won't trust them. Why is a magi different?"

Kaleb is silent for half a minute, thinking, then says, "The impact, the damage can be so bad that it's safer not to trust them."

Sheyla turns, saying, "I'm done with this."

Hallr returns with wood, looks at everyone, and says, "What did Kaleb do now?"

Kaleb says, "Me?"

Milfred says, "Hallr, you've poisoned his mind. He doesn't want to trust anyone."

Hallr replies, "Don't trust them until they prove themselves."

Sheyla looks at Hallr, "After everything we've been through, do you trust me?"

"We've been through some shit, fought with and for each other, so yes. When I met you, I didn't trust you. If you'd tried anything, I would have chopped you in half."

Milfred says, "Witches have attacked you most of your life, so that makes sense to me. Not for Kaleb."

Kaleb says, "I still don't know how it works. I can't determine how to treat witches if I don't know how it works."

Sheyla says, "You're not ready to listen and accept. I will not argue about it."

Agnarr states, "We are finished for now. You are frustrating, and we are done. Think about this. As much as you frustrated two mages today, we didn't use magic on you."

Kaleb says, "Everyone in the group has a past, secrets, something they don't want the others to know."

Milfred says, "Okay, Kaleb, what is your past, your secret?"

Hallr says, "He lied about being dumb to everyone in the war camp. I don't know why."

Kaleb glares and Hallr for a second, then says, "I was told never to tell anyone what I really know. They will use it against me."

Agnarr asks, "Who told you? They told you not to trust anyone with this information."

"Ma and Pa."

Sheyla asks, "Why?"

"I don't really know all the details. Ma and Pa came from Sunderal. Pa worked in the treasury, doing accounts, and then something happened. They never told me any details. They left everything behind. Started over with me. I wasn't supposed to tell anyone. They're both dead now, so it doesn't matter."

Hallr says, "There is more. Why do you talk stupidly sometimes?"

"Ma brought books or traded for books. She taught me to read, write, and do math. I read all the books. Ma and Pa said people would ask questions about a simple country boy who knows how to read and write."

Milfred says, "And if anyone found out, they might start asking awkward questions about where your ma and pa came from."

Kaleb looks back at Milfred, "What is your secret?"

Milfred shrugs and says, "I don't keep it a secret, but I don't shout it out. I want Mithril. I want to make stuff with Mithril. To do that, I need the forges of Molgan. It's that simple."

Agnarr gives a little smile as he grabs the kettle from the edge of the fire to put more water in his cup.

Kaleb turns to Hallr, "What about your past, your secret?"

"My past doesn't matter. No one can change my past."

"Tell me."

"No."

Milfred says, "Well, Kaleb, now you have Hallr grumpy, not just Sheyla and Agnarr. Great evening."

Learning About Magic

The group spent the next couple of years searching in the mountains. As they travel, they stop at every small town to offer blacksmithing services. Sometimes it's two days, sometimes it's several weeks. During the snowy winters, they stayed in whatever village they were in, usually in a valley. The villagers always try, in various ways, to make them stay.

During this time, Kaleb has grown. He is now over two meters tall and has added almost 50 kilos, most of it muscle. He can swing an axe and wield a hammer like Hallr. Villagers are always in awe when he helps erect a structure, lifting beams and logs no one else can move.

They continue traveling north, heading toward the river junction separating Ondel and Harenhal. During this time, Agnarr, and Sheyla avoid using magic. No one wants to argue about magic or everyone's past.

Without magic, they work closely on projects, especially moving things where Agnarr's magic could have made it easier.

Life tests their patience when the heavy wagon slides down into a rut, and the back wheel breaks several spokes.

After the initial discussion and trying to get the wagon out, they took a break and set up camp.

Milfred says, "We need to get the wagon out, the broken wheel off, and repaired. We might as well set up camp here."

Kaleb says, "I'll start digging."

Getting the hand tools, they don't have a shovel. Kaleb digs in front of the broken wheel and quickly hits a rock.

Hallr is smiling, watching him. When Kaleb pauses, he says, "There is a rut because of that big rock. You can't dig it out."

"Fine, I'll break the rock."

"You can't swing and hit the rock under the wagon."

"Okay, smart dwarf, what do we do?"

"We will have to cut several small trees to have levers and rollers."

Kaleb looks around. "There are no small trees close by."

Hallr chuckles, "Because the last people who had to do this cut them down. We aren't the first to have this problem. Look around, pay attention."

Milfred has been unloading the wagon to make it lighter so that they can lift it. He says, "What do you suggest, Hallr? I'm unloading to make it lighter so we can lift it."

Hallr nods, "What is your plan?"

"Lift the wagon and set it on a pole or tree with the wheel off the ground so we can pull it off and repair it. Then we put it back on and get the working wheel and wagon out."

"I like that plan better than breaking the rock. But if you want my idea, it is to take a wheel off the other wagon. Lift this one, change the wheel, get it out, and then fix the wheel for the lighter wagon."

Agnarr is smiling, "Unload both wagons, lift both wagons."

Hallr says, "Well, we have something most people don't have."

Kaleb is out from under the wagon, looking at Hallr, and says, "What?"

"We have a mage. Agnarr can help lift the wagons without unloading them. We use a small tree as a lever, and he uses magic. He can help push the wagon out and doesn't have to be touching it."

Two days later, they had everything repaired and were back on the road.

Sitting around the fire that night, Kaleb asked about magic again. Hallr rolls his eyes and leaves the fire. Kaleb says, "I want to know."

Agnarr asks, "What do you want to know?"

"How does it work?"

Sheyla says, "You have asked in the past, and from your

questions, you showed your opinions with no facts. If you're ready to listen with an open mind, I'll explain."

Kaleb nods, "Not just more talk about good and bad, but how it works. I'm ready."

"Get past the opinions like witches eat children. You never said where you heard that, and it is completely untrue."

Agnarr says, "That would only be a story to scare little kids."

Sheyla says, "Not true. Now, I'm going to tell you the secret of magic. I haven't talked about this before because most people don't believe what is possible. You won't believe me when I tell you. I have to show you so that you can understand. Are you ready?"

Kaleb nods, "How does it work?"

Sheyla turns to Agnarr, then back to Kaleb, "I use my mind to push ideas and thoughts into your mind. I don't know how I can do it, but it works."

Milfred says, "You want to know how it works, to see if you can do it."

Kaleb nods, "Yes. What is it? Can I do it?"

Agnarr says, "Probably not. Most people will exhibit signs when they are young. If found and trained, they can use their skills. If people do not train them, they can be wild and unpredictable."

"Okay, enough talking around it, what is it?"

"Most of magic is an illusion. It is what someone makes you think is real."

Agnarr says, "The other small part is important. It is moving physical objects. That you can hear about in a minute."

Kaleb is poking the fire, listening. He looks at Sheyla, "An illusion, not real, but we think it is real."

"Yes. The positive use of magic is to make you feel good. Make you have positive energy. It can help your body heal. Magic can also serve evil purposes."

Agnarr says, "It takes incredible power, skill, and training to make an illusion that could get you killed. It is possible to make a group of people see something that isn't true."

Kaleb looks from Agnarr to Sheyla. "The witches that attacked us, the ones trying to kill me. I didn't see anything. I felt hands crushing my head. That was the illusion."

"Yes. That, as well as some physical movement in your brain. They were literally using physical movement magic, trying to scramble your brain. Making the cells die."

Sheyla says, "You asked how it works. It is in our brains. It is all concentration and focus. I concentrate on you and the images I imagine get projected into your mind. That is all I can tell you about how it works."

Hallr walks back up to the fire and stands to the side. Kaleb is between Hallr and Sheyla. Sheyla says to Kaleb. "The illusions can be real to you." She closes her eyes, and suddenly Kaleb smells sulfur and hears a deep growl. He turns to see a giant dragon standing behind Hallr. The dragon is looking at him, smoke curling up from its nostrils.

Kaleb jumps and moves toward Sheyla. He points, turns to Sheyla.

When Kaleb jumps and points, Hallr turns to look behind him and says, "What?"

Kaleb turns back, and the dragon is gone. When he turns back to Sheyla, a banquet table is behind her, covered in food. Kaleb smells the freshly baked bread and roasted lamb. Sheyla stands, and her frock transforms into a striking emerald green ball gown.

Agnarr says, "It looks completely real, doesn't it?"

Hallr says, "What looks real?"

Kaleb looks at Hallr, gesturing, saying, "The food."

He turns back, and it is gone.

Sheyla sits down. "It takes a toll to create big illusions as a witch and maintain them. I don't normally do that. It would be easier if I practiced more."

Agnarr takes her a cup of water. He says, "Sit down. Think about your questions; don't just start asking nonsense."

Hallr says, "What happened?"

Kaleb looks at Hallr, turns back, and says, "Why didn't he see that?"

Agnarr says with a smile, "He's a dwarf."

Sheyla is putting down the water cup and says, "Dwarves are resistant to magic. That means they are resistant to being read and manipulated."

Agnarr says, "Hallr knows stories about Magi attacking dwarves. That was because the control covens couldn't manipulate them. Dwarves can protect people from manipulation. That is a problem for a control coven, so they have for decades been trying to wipe out dwarves."

Kaleb asks, "Is this control thing why kings outlaw magic and have them killed?"

Sheyla says, "Yes, exactly that."

Hallr asks, "What about healing? What about Agnarr's power?"

Agnarr nods, "The magic I focus on is movement magic. It is different for each person. I am best with push and pull, not healing."

Agnarr picks up a twig and holds it in his palm, with his palm facing up. The twig rises and hovers above his hand. "I'm pushing with my hand. It makes the stick rise, and I can effectively hold it there."

Sheyla says, "Everyone who does magic can do mental things and push and pull. But each has different strengths. Agnarr is good with power push-pull, not as much with fine control. He can also do mental reading, but not so much projection."

Hallr sits next to Kaleb and motions for him to take a seat. He says, "I get that. What about fire? Agnarr can start a fire, make an arrow burst into flames."

Agnarr smiles, "I move the smallest part of the wood I can focus on back and forth fast. It's the same as starting a fire with two sticks. I do it with my mind."

Sheyla says, "Making your body's cells grow achieves healing. They close a wound. Evil magic, the worst type, does the opposite. It breaks or rips your cells apart. The witches who tried to kill you were trying to make your brain mush. I think Hallr's head hurts *from witches because they are trying to do the same to him. He is just resistant."*

Kaleb asks, "Does practice strengthen you? What are the limits? Could you make me try to kill Hallr?"

Sheyla says, "Yes. It takes power and stamina. To control even a single person usually involves a control coven of at least a dozen members. They work together and overlap, so there are no gaps. If I tried to keep up an illusion for a long period, I would collapse with a tremendous headache."

Agnarr says, "If we encounter more witches, let Sheyla and me deal with them. If we have a problem, Hallr can kill them."

Hallr says, "Or I just kill them from the start."

Kaleb asks, "Is magic something I can learn?"

Sheyla replies, "Probably not. People who become witches and warlocks often exhibit signs during their childhood. It almost always starts with reading others. Reading unspoken thoughts. Thoughts and emotions, especially when someone feels excited, frightened, or angry."

Agnarr adds, "If gifted kids survive, people can train them to use their abilities. We won't know the abilities each child is best at using until they are older."

Sheyla says, "I'm good at illusion imagery and control magic. Because they outlaw it, and most importantly to me, I don't like it. I focused on healing."

Traveling And Searching

Arriving at the river fork at the boundary between Ondel and Harenhal, the group is arguing about which path to take.

After back-and-forth arguing, while they are preparing the camp and food, Hallr leaves the camp and walks up to the highest point in the area. Kaleb finds him there two hours later. He is sitting and scraping in the dirt with a stick.

Kaleb says, "We need to decide something. You are stubborn and not explaining. Now, I'm going to sit here while you explain it. Explain it until I understand."

Hallr looks up from his little dirt scratching. It looks like a map, at least to Hallr. He says to Kaleb, "When did you grow up?"

"With you, watching you. I didn't have a great childhood. Being the big, lanky kid caused problems. Ma and Pa were fine; everyone else wanted me to do something, thought I was older, and asked why I talked like a kid. The soldiers said I would fight. Pa said I was too young. They killed him and ma."

"Sorry about that, but you're shitting me when you say ma, pa, simple shit. I know you're smart. Why say that?"

"Ma and Pa were what I always called them. They hid my education, and we practiced speaking with different people."

Hallr is sitting for a minute, simply looking at Kaleb, not speaking.

Kaleb says, "I've got nothing but time. I don't understand a lot of things. I ask questions, and sometimes I need to listen and ask more questions. Explain which way you want to go."

Hallr says, "You always ask questions, pestering me to answer what to me seems obvious. This is different. I don't know exactly why. Okay. I see this in my head. It is telling me to take the left fork. It is longer to get to the mountains. There are no towns to get supplies; it is remote. One part of it is that I grew up east of here. I know the city isn't in that area. This fork in the river will take us much farther north."

"Yes, everyone says it's too remote."

"But isn't that part of what we need to consider? If the city were close to some well-traveled area, it would have been found by now."

Kaleb counters with, "If it were the great city, wouldn't there have been roads to get there? Things would travel to and from the city. How did the city get enough food in the mountains? It had to be brought from local farms. If there are excellent farms, people would still be there, farming."

"Kaleb, I hear you. I agree with your arguments. But maybe we don't know the complete story. Someone may have destroyed the roads, or someone might have taken the stones for another purpose. What about keeping the city hidden? Maybe they intentionally made things easy in one area, hard in another, to make people look the wrong way."

"Hallr, how much conviction do you have about this? You are acting weird."

Hallr is nodding. "I came up here to think and decide."

"Great."

"I'm going on my path. If you all decide against it, we'll part ways. That's it. The fork to the left is my path. I can't explain why I'm not sure myself. I know I need to go that way."

Kaleb looks at Hallr and smiles. "Friend, I apply my form of logic, but I don't care. I want to stay with my friends. With my battle buddy. You want to dig, I'll start digging. You want to go on the left fork, I'm ready."

Hallr looks at Kaleb intently, "Don't do this just for me."

"When you're ready, we'll go tell the others we're heading left in the morning. They can come or argue with the air if they want."

The next day, they all headed out toward the left and spent the next several weeks hunting and preserving food for the ascent into the mountains.

When they find a place where the water is a fast-flowing stream emerging from the mountains at a small waterfall, they stop. Hallr is looking at the area, at the mountains. He says, "It looks altered."

Kaleb, always eager to learn, asks, "Altered how? Show me what you see."

"Look at the stream. On the left side, there is a small distance from the water to the vertical of the solid rocks. On the right, you see boulders from a landslide. Someone may have altered the stream's path."

Milfred says, "When you describe it, that makes sense. How do you see that?"

"It is just the way I look at it."

Agnarr says, "He's a dwarf. They look at rocks differently."

Milfred nods, "Like when he can see a rock from a distance and know it has iron in it."

Sheyla asks, "Hallr, your family history? Were you miners?"

"We were miners in local mines where I grew up. My family has been miners for generations, and you're asking a good question, but not the right question."

Kaleb is suddenly curious, "Really? What is the right question?"

Hallr says, "To humans, dwarves are all the same. Dig and make stuff. To dwarves, those are two distinct skill sets. I'm a digger. I can't explain it except to say I'm not skilled at making fine crafts. A crafter or tinker makes things. They create intricate items, but also manufacture gears, levers, and gates. They look at stuff and make things that work, but they can't look at a rock and see if they should dig."

"And the right question?"

"If you're a digger, what do the rocks tell you? What do I see?"

Milfred, Sheyla, and Agnarr are looking frustrated. Kaleb is smiling. "I think you are trying to explain something you can't. What do you see?"

"I see a stream that is cutting into the rock, as all streams do. It is one path. It doesn't spread out. Over time, you expect the stream to erode the rock and change it. Water erodes the easy path. That *stream has been the same for hundreds of years. The depth of that one path through the hard rock. It is not the easiest path for water to create a natural flow. Someone made the water go that way."*

"Do you think we need to follow that stream?"

"Yes. There is no path to follow, but we need to go in that direction. Now, looking at it, if we dig, we might find a road under those boulders."

After a day of searching, Kaleb found a path. He tells them, "There are large rocks from a landslide. I think with some digging, we can get the wagons through. Otherwise, we are on horseback or on foot. We have to go south to the second opening sloping up to get to the landslide."

They turned the wagons and traveled to the section Kaleb described. Soon after the wagons start up the slope, Hallr stops, looking around. He walks to the left a couple of meters and kicks into the dirt. Kneeling, he scraped dirt to reveal cobblestones.

After opening the path for the wagons, Hallr follows the direction of the stream. Late in the day, he stops, kneeling. He pulls grass and shifts dirt. The group gathers around. Hallr uncovers another set of worn cobblestones for a road.

Tobias says, "We lost them."

"No, Master Tobias, this is the best sign we have. They left the obvious trail that everyone can see. The dwarf has found something and is taking the not-obvious path toward the city. Everyone on horseback needs to fan out and look for paths a wagon could take."

Hours later, Tobias is fuming when a rider returns. "I found a trail. It leads to a section that was just widened for the wagons to fit."

Teppo stands and says, "Show me."

It takes most of the day to get their wagons up the trail and through the opening, Teppo says, "See, Master Tobias. A little patience."

"I'm not patient when we are talking about this treasure. Have the riders go forward to scout. If they are close, we want to know so we don't stumble into them."

"Excellent thinking, Master Tobias. That is why you should be in charge."

Scouts ride ahead on the most likely path. The scouts return after dark when the group has made camp for the night. "They dwarf and group are taking an old road. They cleared spots, revealing cobblestones."

Teppo says to the rider, "Tomorrow you will go out again. If they are close to the city, we need to watch for new hidden paths they find. We don't want them to disappear again."

Tobias nods. "If you find them."

Teppo says, "No, WHEN you find them."

"When you find them, stay hidden. Watch until we are sure they have found the city."

The wagons travel slowly. Usually, the wagon with the witches has the canopy closed. Today, they pulled back the canopy for ventilation. Tobias can see the witches huddled around the old woman. He usually only sees them when they go from the wagon to the tent or back to the wagon. They are always around the old one. She needs help to walk, and they must lift her into the wagon.

Tobias notices the witches huddled together and muttering. "What are they doing?"

"Master Tobias, when we get to them, we have to deal with the witch, the warlock, the kid, and the blacksmith. They are practicing to be ready. They know what to do, but practicing gets them in top condition to deal with other magi."

A week later, Hallr is looking around as they trudge along the path. He has directed them to the old road when he can see it. They are

now high in the mountains. It is cold at night. They are past the area with trees, and even with Kaleb riding one of the two spare horses down and bringing back wood, they only have wood for cooking. Everyone is depressed.

Sheyla says, "I'll say it. No one else will, so I'll say it. We should go back down to the valley. Winter is approaching, and we can prepare and do this in the spring."

Hallr says, "I don't want to quit." Looking at Kaleb, he says, "You're trying to read everyone. I want to know what Kaleb thinks."

Kaleb says, "Hallr and Milfred want to continue; Sheyla and Agnarr want to go back and wait for spring. We have enough wood for two more fires. If we don't find it by the time we have the last fire, we turn around."

Hallr looks around and says, "It is a compromise. I agree with that approach."

Everyone nods, and they continue moving. As night falls and they decide on the camp layout, Hallr looks ahead. While they are working, he keeps glancing in that direction. Sheyla says, "Hallr. Hey man. What is it with you? I know how this works now. You see something, but you're not sure. Everyone needs to stop. Let's all go look."

Hallr says, "No. Wait. It needs to get darker. Don't light the fire."

Kaleb asks, "What do you see?"

I see they destroyed the path. They cut this drop-off to narrow the path.

Milfred says, "A good strategy if an army is approaching."

Hallr continues, "After the cut, to the right, the stones look different. The way we are supposed to travel is to the right, but it doesn't look old or used. The path is only wide enough for a wagon."

Everyone stops, and Kaleb grabs the crafted axe and starts walking up the path. They stopped here to camp because the path narrows, because of the cut and the trail beyond, making it difficult for a wagon to fit. Kaleb walks just past the cut part and stops. After a few seconds, he turns and waves for everyone to join him.

With them all together, Kaleb says, "The path goes to the right, but it looks different in this light. The stones aren't as smooth."

Milfred is looking, moving his head up and down, then side to side. "I think I see what you're saying. Milfred observes that someone made or patched it.

Hallr is looking at the wall, and they all see a solid wall of rock with small stones scattered on the ground. He walks up, kicking small stones. He placed his hand on the large rock. "I think it is this way."

"But Hallr, that is a huge, solid rock. How do we go forward there?"

"I don't know. My gut tells me that path is wrong. This is the way. Look at the top; there is a curve that doesn't look natural."

"We don't have a choice unless there is some secret way to move this massive rock."

That night, while everyone sleeps, Hallr has a dream. A dragon is talking to him.

"Hello Hallr."

"Who are you?"

"My name is Xylia. I need your help. I'm a dragon and I can only communicate with a dwarf."

"How are you talking to me? I'm resistant to magic."

"Dwarves and dragons can communicate. You are close. There is a path, a way in. Go to the right and look around the boulders. There is a way in."

Early in the morning, Hallr sits up and says, "Holy dragons, there is a way."

This causes Kaleb to sit up and look at Hallr.

"I had a dream about a dragon talking to me. I know what to do."

Only Kaleb hears Hallr say this. Hallr gets up and starts moving around, waking everyone.

When everyone is up, Hallr says, "We leave the wagons for now. We follow that false path for a distance and search."

As they walk, Sheyla says, "What are we searching for, and how do you suddenly know this?"

Kaleb says, "He had a dream about a dragon talking to him."

Agnarr and Sheyla suddenly stop and say, "Stop!"

Hallr turns, "What is it?"

Sheyla says, "Tell me about this dream. Did the dragon speak to you or show you things?"

"It spoke to me."

"What did it sound like? Hallr, this is important. What did it sound like?"

"It was deep, but not booming. It was more that I heard it in my head than heard it through my ears."

Sheyla and Agnarr lean together and whisper. Kaleb takes two steps to reach them. He is clearly concerned and now nervous. "Please explain. Is this magic?"

Sheyla looks up, startled, and takes a step back. She raises a hand, "Hang on."

Kaleb repeats, "Explain."

Agnarr shifts between Sheyla and Kaleb and says, "Dragons in dreams are a symbol of authority. They are used to influencing people to do things they wouldn't normally do. When you said a dragon talked to you, we need to know if someone is trying to influence you. Yes, Kaleb, using magic."

Sheyla says, "We have to consider you're a dwarf and are resistant to things like this."

Agnarr continues, "The voice one hears in the dream is critical. If they hear what sounds like a human voice, it is always, always a control dream."

Sheyla says, "When you say you hear it in your head, it doesn't sound like a control thing, but we don't know what it is then."

Hallr, hearing all this, begins walking again. They reach a section of small boulders, only twice the size of a person, compared to most of the others that are the size of a house. Hallr looks around the sides, then squeezes between two rocks. He can get through, and after a minute, they hear, "Come on through."

Kaleb looks at the opening and then at the others, "You all go first. I will probably get stuck."

As Kaleb goes through, he is squatting. His knee touches the ground multiple times. At one point, he wiggles and starts cursing. At the exit, he gets his head out and sees everyone looking at him, smiling. Hallr puts his hand out to help Kaleb get out.

Standing, Kaleb sees everyone looking to the right. He turns and looks to see the entrance to the city: the gate, parapets, and windows. The gate appears to be large enough for several wagons to enter side by side. It looks to be twenty meters tall. The proportions of all the parts around the gate are also massive to look correct.

Behind the gate, a set of parapets allows archers to fire into the courtyard. Behind that is the sloping rock of the mountain. The gate and walls around it are the only visible parts of the city. The gate and windows are the only means of entry.

Hallr says, "Look at that gate, ten meters wide, twenty meters high. There is a vertical seam in the middle. That is two massive stone blocks."

Kaleb turns to look thoroughly around. He says, "From this side, there is another gate. That boulder we saw outside is a gate. It is carved. I think it can open if we can figure out how it works."

Hallr is smiling; he looks at the others. They are all in awe of what they are looking at. "We found it."

Kaleb says, "We should get the wagons in this section. They will be safe while we look around."

Agnarr looks and sees the inside of the gate. He points at the gate and says, "It is much smaller than the city gate, maybe two wagons across. You know how to open that thing?"

Kaleb has a spring in his step as he walks forward, saying, "We'll figure it out. A gate that dwarfs built and was last used centuries ago."

Milfred says, "Hallr, what do we do? How do we open it?"

Hallr is looking at the gate. He shrugs and starts walking after Kaleb. "I do not know. That would be a tinker thing, not a digger thing."

Sheyla follows and walks up to where Kaleb is running his hand over the massive stones, where the edge meets a partially covered channel. "What do you think?"

"It is an enormous slab of rock, partially underground. I think it rolls, but I don't know how yet."

Hallr says, "You like this stuff? Figuring out how it works?"

"Love figuring out puzzles like this."

Milfred says, "I'm going back through the little path to take care of the horses."

Sheyla says, "I'll go with Milfred. You three get the gate open."

Over an hour later, Kaleb is talking to himself about what he sees. He has been searching everywhere in the courtyard. At the junction of the gate wall and the side wall, he points. "I'm sure that is a lock pin. Open that, then it will move, but how does it move?"

Agnarr is leaning against the gate, watching. "I see a slot for this big rock to go into, but this part in the ground here looks like it will leave a huge channel. We won't be able to drive the wagons across."

"I know. I'm working on it." Kaleb is standing next to the gate, looking at the other wall. Moss covers the wall in front of him. He steps over and wipes his hand across the moss to move it aside. "We need to pull moss off the walls."

"Hm, there is something under here." He grabs the moss and pulls. Large chunks are coming off the wall. Kaleb tosses it to the side and grabs more.

Kaleb's enthusiasm amuses Agnarr as he is pulling off the moss. Then he sees something and pushes off the gate. "What is that?"

Kaleb keeps pulling on moss and uncovering more of the wall. Agnarr pushes moss aside to show a curved stone. The hole, about eight centimeters in diameter, appeared then. A minute later, he uncovers another hole at the bottom of the wall. Kaleb shifts up on the wall and finds another hole higher. Even more significantly, he says, "It's curved."

Hallr has been at the big city gate. He yells, "Kaleb, I need your help."

"Just a minute, Hallr."

After waiting while pacing back and forth, Hallr walks over to Kaleb and Agnarr. "I need help. I think I've found how to get in a window, but it's too high. There are piles of rocks that look like someone climbed in before."

"Hallr, I know you want to get into the city. I do, too, but we need to get this gate open and bring the horses and wagons into this huge courtyard."

"Fine. What do you have here?"

Kaleb spends the next few minutes excitedly describing the parts and what he found.

Hallr says, "You think that if we stick a log in that hole, release the lock pin, and lift it, it will move the gate."

Kaleb has a huge smile, "Yah. It may not move fast, but it will move."

"So we need a wooden pole. You got a wooden pole?"

"Well, no. We have to find something."

"Hmm, maybe inside the city."

"Hallr, you have a one-track mind."

Agnarr is tuning them out while he walks along the moss-covered wall toward the city gate—ten meters from the small gate, the wall curves, making the courtyard larger. There are centuries of moss on every wall. Agnarr wants to know what else might have moss on it.

He kicks some of the mossy bumps at the base of the wall. They are spongy. His hand is running along the wall as he steps on the lumps. Then he steps, picking up his foot to get above the moss lump. He steps on something hard. Grabbing and pulling moss, he finds the end of the logs. "Hey, you two, come over here."

They are arguing and ignoring him.

"Hey!"

Hallr looks over at Agnarr, who holds both hands face up and shifts them as if serving something. His hands to his right, pointing at what he found.

Hallr walks over with Kaleb striding and overtaking him. "What have you got?"

Kaleb rips moss off the logs. As he pulls the moss off, the logs shift. Hallr goes next to Kaleb and grabs one log and pulls. About one meter of the log breaks off and pulls away. He looks at it and says, "Not much good for us."

Kaleb says, "Just one or two is all we need."

As Kaleb pulls moss away from the bottom logs, they can see that they have partially collapsed from rot. "We just need one or two."

After pulling the logs out, Kaleb has one that is just over two meters long. One end crumbled when he pulled it out, and then when Hallr tested it, more broke off.

Kaleb has a log just over a meter long. He goes to the section and inserts one end of the solid pole into the hole. It fits easily with little space. Kaleb puts both arms under and lifts, but there is no effect. He squats and puts the log on his shoulder to lift it. They hear the rock move, as if he has broken it free, but nothing else.

Agnarr says, "You said something about a lock pin."

Kaleb lets go of the pole and looks flushed, says, "Forgot."

Hallr says, "Show me."

They gather around to look at the lock pin. They can all clearly see a square stone. It has a hole or slot in the top and extends into the larger rock. Above the pin, in the larger rock, is a protrusion. Hallr says, "It's manual. Insert a stick or bar into the hole and slide it out."

Kaleb looks around for something. Pausing after a second, he goes over to where they laid down their gear and grabs his sword. Hallr says, "You will bend the sword."

Kaleb nods, "If I do it wrong."

Kaleb inserts the tip of the sword into the slot on top of the pin. The edge of the blade is in the direction he wants to move it. He says, "This is the strong side. It would bend if I turned it to the flat side. Here goes."

Kaleb pushes the sword with the blade against the protrusion to give him leverage. The pin doesn't move.

Agnarr says, "Just like the wheel. It has been in that spot for centuries. It will take some effort."

Hallr is looking at the pin, thinking, then the wheel with the log in it. He looks back at the pin, saying, "If it is there to lock or prevent the gate from opening, then turning the wheel frees the pressure. I'm going to lift on the little wheel, then you try."

They spent a minute getting set up and coordinating. After several tries where Hallr pushed and Kaleb didn't push, Agnarr says, "You both go on my signal."

Hallr and Kaleb nod.

Agnarr continues, "Ready, NOW!"

Hallr lifts hard on the pole, and Kaleb pushes on the sword at the same time. They all hear the sound as the pin moves.

Kaleb keeps pushing, grunting out a "Yes."

The pin stops, and Kaleb stands full upright and says, "Take a breath, and we'll do it again."

Hallr nods, looks at Agnarr, saying, "What about your magic? Can you help pull that out?"

Agnarr looks back, considering his words, "I'm not a miracle worker. My strength is primarily pushing. Pulling is weaker. I'll try."

The next attempt, the pin slides out of the hole twenty centimeters.

Hallr is nodding, "That helped a lot, Agnarr."

Kaleb looks at the big gate, walks to the pole, and pushes it up. The movement of the poles causes the small wheel to turn and then stop. Kaleb says, "We had to break loose each of the parts. Now it is the big gate. This time, Agnarr can use his push."

Agnarr smiles, "I can help with this," as he walks to the other side of the gate.

Hallr says, "Move the pole down to this other hole in the wheel."

Kaleb says, "That is too low for me to squat."

Hallr replies, "We will both pull it up this time."

Nodding, Kaleb moves the pole to the lower hole in the wheel. They get ready, and Hallr says loudly, "Agnarr, give us the go."

Agnarr concentrates, shifts, and focuses on the gate. He is reaching deep, calming himself, as if practicing. He is going to push the gate with his magic. "Ready, go!"

Hallr and Kaleb lift hard, and the little wheel moves. They all hear a very loud crack, and the big gate shifts. The pole gets to the top of the wheel, where it enters the larger wall, and they must stop.

Pulling the pole out, Kaleb steps back, looking at the wheel. "Hey, Agnarr, can you try something?"

Agnarr walks to them and says, "Sure."

"Do your push thing, but only at the top of this wheel. If you can spin the wheel, the gate should open."

"Okay, give me a minute."

When Agnarr is ready, he focuses, and the wheel moves. Hallr is using his hands to push and help turn the wheel. Kaleb walks to the big gate and watches it move. He observes the gate as it shifts up. Kaleb takes a step back, looking across the gate as it lifts.

"Guys, it doesn't roll; it is on a pivot. It is moving up. That makes perfect sense. Pivot so there is a counterweight we can't see to make this small wheel work with gears."

Kaleb looks up as the edge of the gate moves up. Squatting down, he could see Milfred and Sheyla smiling.

Milfred says, "You did it."

Agnarr keeps rotating the wheel, and the gate is moving, showing a twenty-centimeter-wide channel that the wagons would have to cross, which is clearly visible.

Sheyla gestures to the gap and asks, "What about this gap?"

Kaleb says, "I don't know. They had to have something."

Hallr says, "Agnarr, keep going, you're doing great. Kaleb, you could help."

After several minutes, the gate had reached almost halfway up when Agnarr stopped pushing. "I need to rest for a minute and drink water."

Sheyla looks up at the massive gate rising into the air, which a little wheel moved. "The dwarven craftsmen were amazing."

When Agnarr stops pushing with his magic, Kaleb grabs the pole and inserts it into one hole in the small wheel to prevent it from turning. They all stopped to rest.

While Agnarr is drinking, Sheyla walks over saying, "Don't overdo it and exhaust yourself on this. We don't know what is inside the big gate."

"We don't know how to get in or open that big gate."

"Kaleb is showing he can figure it out. What if something is in there that we need to use magic to deal with?"

Agnarr nods, "This is easier once it moves. I'll be okay."

After a few minutes, while Agnarr is still resting, Hallr and Kaleb turn the wheel to keep the gate moving. After several minutes, they are sweating and complaining. Hallr says, "They didn't open or close this gate often."

Kaleb asks, "Why a second gate?"

Milfred comes over to help and says, "The courtyard would protect us better from the elements, like the storm we see up in the mountains."

Hallr says, "Makes sense. They would close it for storms or attacks.

When the gate reaches about 90 percent open, it stops. Kaleb looks at the situation, saying, "It's like we've reached another stop; we have to break loose. Agnarr, you can help. Push guys."

They hear a muffled groan from under the big gate, and the wheel moves again, but it is harder to move now. After a moment, Sheyla says, "Hey, look. A section of stone rises within the gap. It's filling the gap."

Hallr says, "Don't stop pushing. We're getting pushback now and have to keep pressure so it doesn't turn back on us."

Milfred says, "It feels like we're lifting that stone. If we let go, will it push down, and the momentum will start closing the gate?"

Kaleb says, "We'll try that when the wagons are in the courtyard.

After minutes of grunting and sweating, Agnarr says, "I've got to rest."

Sheyla says, "Don't stop, guys, it is almost flat across."

When it is flat, Sheyla says, "There."

Milfred says, "Probably should have asked this before, but how do we keep it from going back?"

Hallr says, "The pole, put it into the hole, and it will stop the rotation."

Agnarr is squinting while rubbing his temple. "Will the pin work?"

Kaleb says, "Yes, the lock pin."

Hallr inserts the pole and holds it with the leverage provided while Milfred and Kaleb step back.

Kaleb goes to the pin and tries to push it in. "It won't go in."

Milfred says, "It has to be aligned with a slot. Hallr lifts the pole as high as you can while Kaleb pushes.

Hallr lifts and pushes on the pole. Milfred gets on the end to help with his longer reach while Kaleb pushes. Hallr gets on his toes and pushes up, and suddenly the pin slides in partway and stops as the pole in the wheel moves down.

Milfred says, "Switch with me, Kaleb."

They switch, and Kaleb pushes the pole up, and immediately Milfred slides the pin into position.

Sheyla says, "That was easy."

The guys all give her a perplexed look.

Hallr looks at the city gate, "Now we can get into the city."

Milfred says, "No. Now we can bring the wagons into the courtyard."

Kaleb asks, "Do we close the courtyard gate once the wagons are inside?"

Agnarr replies, "That was a lot of work. Don't close the gate."

Milfred says, "There is a storm approaching. We should probably close the gate to get full protection of this courtyard. Right Hallr?"

Hallr is walking toward the city gate and does not respond.

Molgan City Gate

The Window

They have the courtyard gate open. They brought both wagons and horses into the protected area. As they get the wagons into the area, Milfred comments, "The winds are picking up. We wouldn't be able to have a fire outside the gate. This courtyard is great."

Kaleb asks, "If the winds are picking up outside the gate, are you sure we don't close the gate?"

Milfred looks at Agnarr and gestures to Hallr, who is staring at the city gate. "With no input from Hallr, I say leave it open. That is a lot of work to open the gate. We may need to head back down for food and wood."

Kaleb looks at Hallr and says, "He won't leave."

Sheyla says, "I don't want to enter the city today. We put in the time and effort to get that gate open. We don't know what we will have to deal with when we get inside. Let's find a way in tomorrow."

Agnarr nods, "A good rest is what I need now."

Kaleb walks over to Hallr and gently punches him on the shoulder. "We found it."

"Yes, I need your help to get in. Under that window to the left is a pile of stones. It looks like someone went through that window before."

"The rest of us talked while you were staring. We can go inside tomorrow. Tonight, we rest and get ready."

Hallr looks up at Kaleb, "Seriously."

"It's not going anywhere. You can see it, so it isn't an illusion."

That night, after Hallr is deep asleep, his dream starts, at least that is how he describes it.

"Hello Hallr."

"Your Xylia, the dragon? How do I know you're a dragon?"

Hallr sees an enormous red dragon. The scales are bright ruby-red. She extends her leather wings and flaps them. He says, "You're beautiful."

"This is what I look like now."

The image changes. It is a dragon lying on the floor. Her face is the same. She has a broken left wing and her scales are falling off. The scales are cloudy red. Her body is frail. Her skin is hanging off her bones.

"I'm weak, dying. You are close enough now, and the only one I can communicate with. If you don't help me soon, I will die."

"What do I do?"

"I need food. I have been trapped without food for decades. Please help."

"What food? Where are you in the city?"

"Get into the city; I will guide you to me. Bring meat. Please help and please hurry."

"Xylia......Xylia."

It is before dawn. Kaleb needs to pee. They agreed to go outside the gate to relieve themselves until they found something better. The winds are stronger, gusting, and Kaleb reaches out to steady himself. As he returns, he feels something on his face. Looking up at the sky, he can make out snow falling.

When he is almost back to the wagons, Kaleb sees Hallr leading one horse toward the city window. Hallr is carrying his enormous axe. "He can't wait. He's going into the city. But why the horse?"

As Kaleb walks toward Hallr, thirty meters away, he watches him stop with the horse. Then swing around with his axe and chop the horse's head off in one swing. He yells, "What the hell?"

His yelling awakens Milfred, Agnarr, and Sheyla as he runs to

Hallr. "What are you doing?"

"Xylia needs help. She is going to die if I don't get her food."

They are all running up and surrounding Hallr, and Sheyla asks, "Who is Xylia?"

"The dragon in the city. She talked to me. She told me she is trapped and hungry."

Milfred looks at the body of the horse and says, "It's a little late to argue about killing the horse."

Hallr says, "We have two extras. And if you haven't thought about it. We are going to need to eat, too."

Hallr puts down his axe, grabs the horse's head, and takes several steps. He spins and throws the head toward the window. Blood is flying out everywhere. Hallr picks up the axe and chops on the front of the horse, taking off a front leg and shoulder. He grabs that and tosses it into the window as well.

"I need to get in there."

He goes to a large rock off to the side, picks it up, and, straining, slowly shuffles over to place it on the pile under the window.

Milfred says, "The window is too high. It will take an immense pile of rocks to get up there."

Hallr stops, looking up at the window. After a few seconds, he looks around. "The wagon. I will back the wagon to be directly under the window, then pile the rocks in the wagon."

Kaleb says, "Won't be high enough."

Hallr looks at Kaleb, "Boost me up, or throw me."

Sheyla is watching and grabs Agnarr's arm. "He is obsessed, as if he is being controlled. But I don't think he is being controlled."

Agnarr focuses on Hallr. When Sheyla grabs his arm, he turns to look at her, nods at what she says, then says, "Okay, Kaleb, we play along. Throw him, and I'll push."

Kaleb looks at Agnarr as if he is crazy. "You are actually going along with this?"

Hallr grabs Kaleb's arm. "Do it."

Kaleb grabs Hallr's collar behind his neck when Hallr shouts, "Wait."

Wiggling free, he picked up his axe, swung it over his head, and threw it into the window. "Now throw me."

Kaleb grabs Hallr by the collar and the belt. He swings him back and forth twice, then heaves, launching Hallr into the air.

Agnarr is ready. When Hallr is flying up, he pushes with his mind. The problem is, he pushes on Hallr's butt, which causes Hallr to tumble. Hallr enters the window, head down. They hear grunts, then curses. After a pause, they heard, "I'm good," followed immediately by a scraping and a thump.

Kaleb says, "What happened?"

"I slipped on the blood. I'm going to find the dragon."

Kaleb looks at the others, "If you think he is being controlled, someone else should follow him."

Sheyla says, "He sounds controlled, but he's not acting controlled."

Kaleb says, "How do you know?"

"I know what controlled looks like."

Milfred says, "What should we look for?"

Sheyla says, "A sudden shift in focus, in what is important. Like Hallr is suddenly obsessed with getting into the city."

<<<>>>

Tanisha says, "There are more this time. I think they have two controllers."

Zevran says, "We need to get everyone positioned."

Neriah says, "We've been through this. Get everyone ready. Kids, we don't want to have you fighting these outcasts."

Feliu says, "I'm ready. I will help."

Merial says, "The last attack was almost a year ago. I've been studying, practicing."

Neriah asks, "What have you been practicing?"

"Illusions, not control. It is different."

Elin shakes her head, "Most people can't tell the difference."

Tanisha smiles, "I've been practicing too. When they get

close, we are going to project that we have twice as many guardians."

Merial says, "We will scare them without using control."

Zevran says, "Let's go. We need to get ready."

When they leave, and Elin and Neriah remain, Elin says, "Those three are scaring me. What is worse is that the outcasts have grown. This will scare them, but it won't stop them."

Neriah says, "I've been putting this off. We have kids who are 16, 14, and 9. They are excelling, chewing through every training we give them."

Elin is shifting her dagger. "I need to get ready. I will say they are gifted and are integrating well with the village. But."

"But they are also making many people nervous. The villagers understand those kids were taken to be controllers. They were going to be trained to be evil. If they project all the extra guardians, it will make people concerned."

"Neriah, we need to discuss finding the dwarf. The attacks will continue until they think the box is gone."

"I know Elin. I know. The village doesn't even know about the mythical, magical box. They think the outcasts are trying to steal the kids."

Zevran enters the room, "Elin, let's go."

Neriah says, "Zevran, when this is done, start planning to find the dwarf. We. No, I have put this off too long."

Zevran nods, "It will be winter soon. We will get to the mountains, but we will have to wait for spring to go in. First, we need to know where the dwarf is. I will send scouts out to find where the group went. That will take months."

Neriah replies, "Understood. Get a wagon ready. You will take a few men, Elin, and the children as soon as we know a direction. Elin must adjust the children's training. You don't know what you will encounter while traveling.

Find the Dragon

Hallr has the horse's front leg and a chunk of the front shoulder over his left shoulder. He is carrying his axe as he walks down a hallway in the city of Molgan. His dwarf's ability to see in low light is all he has. Like a human, when there are torches and shadows, he can't see some areas well. He doesn't know where to go; he is walking down the path that seems most logical.

After walking down ramps and stairs, he gets to a large tunnel. There is enough room to have a wagon in this tunnel. Hallr doesn't know which way to turn. He yells, "Dragon, which way?"

He waits a full minute, then yells again.

A vision appears in his head, like a movie. It was only seconds, but it shows this tunnel, large doorways, stairs, and symbols.

Hallr turns left and starts moving quickly. He is following the path. He sees the symbols on the walls and the turns, and he knows which way to go. The wagon path is what he needs to follow. After the visual, he understood the symbols and the directions on the walls.

He sees an archway with double, open doors. This is where the vision ended, but there is no dragon. Hallr has been carrying several hundred pounds of horse and his axe, moving fast. He is breathing hard. He keeps going and steps through the archway.

Before him lies a vast cavern. He has been in a few caverns before, but he has never seen a cavern this large before. He can't see the other side because it's so dark. What he can see in front of him is a ramp down to an area. Gold plates, goblets, and jewelry cover the floor he can see. Hallr thinks, "The treasure. It's real."

The stench is awful. Rotting something. He breathes through his mouth, so he isn't smelling it as much.

174

He hears and sees a slight movement. Squinting, he can see the dragon. Huge, lying close to the other side of the room. Hallr looks happy and satisfied. He found the dragon, and it's still breathing.

Hallr moves down the ramp quickly and heads to the dragon's head. Its skin is hanging down like rags on bones. Hallr's euphoria changes to despair. It is obviously dying.

He drops his axe, puts the leg in both arms, and runs to the dragon's head. He is standing in front of the dragon's head, looking. The dragon's eyes are closed, and it is breathing slowly. Hallr says, "Dragon, open your mouth."

The dragon takes a deep breath. Its head shifts, and then it lifts its head to open its mouth. Hallr smiles as he lifts the leg over his head and throws it into the dragon's mouth. "Swallow it."

The dragon tilts its head back, swallowing the horse's leg, then its head falls, slamming into the gold items below. Hallr waits a few minutes, then turns and starts running back out. His brain has etched the path, so he remembers it and can follow the symbols. Getting close to the window, he had to check the direction.

Hallr walks to the edge of the window. The walls are two meters thick, and the window sill slopes down so rain will run out of the city. Hallr has his hand on the wall as he walks. Some of the blood is draining to the opening, making it slippery. At the edge, where he can see everyone, he yells, "I need Sheyla to help. Get a rope and a torch. Kaleb, I need you to chop up the horse. I need more meat."

Milfred says, "You're sure he isn't being controlled?"

Sheyla replies, "If he is, it is the best control I've seen. I can't tell."

Kaleb looks at Sheyla, "You'd better get up there, or he's going to get pissed."

"How do I get up there?"

Agnarr says, "Listen to what he said. Get the long rope and a torch."

With the rope, Kaleb throws a large loop up to Hallr to grab. Hallr nods, "I'll tie it up here," as he disappears, dragging the rope.

He is back in a few minutes. "Now, Sheyla."

Agnarr says, "I'll boost you with my push. Climb the rope."

Kaleb brings a torch, saying, "We only have the one. I don't know how long it will last."

Milfred says, "The wind is getting bad. Don't light it until you are inside."

A few minutes later, Hallr is carrying the horse's head, leading Sheyla, with the torch, through the path to the dragon.

When they enter the chamber, the light from the torch reflects off the gold, casting light all around the room and making the dragon look bigger.

Sheyla starts, gagging from the smell. She is bent over. Hallr says, "Try to breathe through your mouth."

Taking in the sight of an actual dragon, she looks at Hallr. "A real dragon. Oh my gosh, a real dragon."

"She needs your help. She's dying. You need to do something."

"What do you want me to do? Why are you mad at me?"

"You're a witch. You can help."

"What can I do for a dragon?"

"I don't know. You're a healer. Heal the dragon."

"What do I heal? What, what am I saying? Hallr, that is a full-size dragon." Sheyla holds up her hand with her thumb and index finger together. Looking at Hallr, she says, "I'm this big compared to the dragon. What can I do?"

Hallr looks intently back and says, "You can try!"

"What's wrong with her? How do you know it is she?"

"When she was in my dream. I don't know. I didn't lift her tail."

"What's wrong with her?"

"I don't know the details. She's starving. She hasn't eaten in years, maybe centuries."

Sheyla is looking at the dragon with its molted scales all around the ground, her loose skin just hanging onto bones. She is thinking, "What can I do?" as she steps toward the dragon.

"Hallr, is it okay? Can I go up and touch her?"

"Yes. I don't know. She has passed out."

Hallr walks up to the dragon next to Sheyla. Up close, Sheyla looks at the skin, at the dragon's shallow breathing. "I don't know if I'm strong enough to help."

"Try!"

"What do I do to help?"

Sheyla is looking at the starving dragon, and Hallr's words now sink in. She has helped people whom rescuers had freed from dungeons before. Locked up and left to starve. She helped them digest the food. "Hallr, I know what I'll try. I don't know if I'm strong enough, if this will even work."

Sheyla has the torch in her hand. She looks around and sets it on top of some of the crushed gold ornamentation. Walking up to the dragon, she puts both hands on one hand on a massive dragon scale and the other hand directly on the dragon's skin. She touches the dragon, and the dragon's presence overshadows her mind. Her legs are wobbly.

Hallr grabs her shoulders to steady her.

Sheyla hears Hallr say, "I've got you." It is distant, through a tunnel. The dragon's presence is in front of her and around her. It is everywhere, a massive presence in her mind. It is quiet, not trying to dominate her. Sheyla takes several slow breaths before she begins.

From helping people who have starved in a dungeon, she needs to kick the digestive system. Give it a shove to make it work naturally. For that to help, there needs to be something easy to digest. It has to be small pieces, bits. She knows Hallr got the dragon to swallow the horse's leg, so there is something.

Focusing her mind on the horse's leg. She can't see the details; she can only project. Reaching out to the horse's leg with images of it being ripped, torn, and shredded. She is shifting mentally to the dark magic, the worst part of magic. Rip tissues apart; destroy them. She is using every term she can think of to describe the leg breaking into smaller pieces.

This should also cause the dragon's stomach to get stimulated, if she is strong enough.

She is touching the dragon and feels no change. When she has *done this before to humans, she can feel their bodies respond. Sometimes the muscles and stomach move, and a burp occurs. There is a sign. With the dragon, she gets nothing. She has to work harder to make something happen.*

Taking a deep breath, she leans into the dragon. She felt Hallr shift his hands, holding her steady.

Push harder; she needs to focus. Tear, rip, shred, rend, tear, rip, shred, and rend. She repeats as she concentrates as hard as she can.

Her body is tensing as she concentrates. She is concentrating intensely and holding her breath. Hallr wraps his arms around her stomach and squeezes. Sheyla feels the air leave her lungs, but her focus intensifies as she tears, rips, and shreds.

Hallr squeezes again, and Sheyla feels her chest burning from not breathing. She takes a deep breath to push as hard as she can. TEAR, RIP, SHRED. Her head is splitting. She hears someone yelling and realizes it is her own voice. She can't keep this up. TEAR, RIP, SHRED...

Hallr grabs Sheyla as she collapses, "Wow, I got you."

He lays her gently on the ground when he hears a shift in the dragon. Its stomach is moving, and he hears a large, loud burp from the dragon. The dragon shifts, and Hallr grabs Sheyla's arms to drag her away so the dragon doesn't roll onto both of them, when the smell assaults him.

He drops Sheyla's arms, bends over, and starts coughing. "That... is... bad."

Recovering from the smell assault, Hallr picks up Sheyla and carries her up the stairs to the entrance archway and sets her down.

When the dragon shifted, it rolled onto the torch, so they are now in darkness. Hallr doesn't know what he should do now. Does he wait, try to wake up Sheyla, or get more help? He sits next to Sheyla, watching the dragon. It hasn't changed; it is breathing softly.

After a few minutes, he hears distant yelling. Milfred and

Agnarr must have come in through the window. They are yelling his and Sheyla's names.

Hallr decides and leaves Sheyla. Taking several steps into the large hallway, he stops, turns back, and looks at Sheyla, "Thank you."

Going quickly through the city, following the path he has taken several times now. He yells, "Stay still. I'm heading to ya."

The Courtyard Gate

Kaleb is still outside. Agnarr helped Milfred get up into the window, then they helped Agnarr. Kaleb tossed chunks of meat up to them, and they left to find Hallr while he finished butchering.

They have been gone for some time. The weather is getting worse. Snow now covers the courtyard and the wagons. He knows he needs to prepare things. The horses need to be moved out of the wind. The wagons shifted.

Looking at the wind moves the snow around, he realizes the open gate is allowing the wind to blow into the courtyard.

He resolves in his head to close the gate. Agnarr wanted to keep it open because it had been so hard to open, but they needed the courtyard's shelter.

Now he has to figure out how to close it himself. Pull the lock pin out, but to do that, he must release the pressure. Using the original pole, he grabs a shorter pole as well. Putting the long pole into the lowest hole in the rotating wheel, he lifts and puts the short one under to hold it.

He grabs his sword and, using the same process as before, levers the lock pin out, pulling it with his hands the last several centimeters. Then he grabs the longer pole in the wheel, lifts slightly, and jerks it out of the wheel.

The wheel rotates and stops. Kaleb growls, "You're supposed to close." He lifts his foot and stomps on the wheel, which gets it moving slowly.

The big gate moves. Reversing what it did before, the gate swings down. The stone filling the channel lowers, making a gap. Wagons can't enter or leave now. The small lifting wheel is spinning faster.

At the end, Kaleb hears scraping, then a crash as stone hits stone. The wind blocks most of the noise. Looking at his handiwork, Kaleb nods. Turning around, he smiles. With the gate closed, the winds are swirling high, and the snow is getting blown around. Very little snow is now landing in the courtyard.

It is close to noon, and the storm is now at full intensity. The scouts for the Tobias group have been out since daybreak. They need to ensure they know the path the dwarf and group wagons take through the mountains. Not able to see more than a couple of meters now because of the storm and blowing snow.

The gate closes when they are about one hundred meters away. They hear the gate crash shut. One of the two is from the control coven, and the other is a soldier assigned to Tobias by the King's guard.

The guard says, "That sounded like a big rock falling. We can't see anything and won't know if a large rock is about to fall on us. We need to head back and wait out the storm."

"I agree. The snow is covering every trail. The snow is already up to the horse's knee. They will have to push through this fresh snow. We go slow so we don't get lost."

After another hour of work, Kaleb had the horses tethered, fed, and out of the wind. Kaleb shifted the wagons and butchered the dead horse. Kaleb collected the organs except the stomach and intestines, which he takes to the edge to dump. Looking for an out-of-the-way spot to dispose of the remains, he examines the walls. When the gate was open, the wind shifted the hanging moss, exposing parts of the wall. This is when he finds a doorway partially covered in moss. The wind pushed moss into the doorway.

Ripping down the moss, he enters to check and finds a latrine. There are seats, and the hole underneath is deep. He can't see the bottom. He says, "I knew there had to be a latrine close by."

181

In go the horse entrails, and he heads back to wait. He won't be able to get the horse meat and himself up without help.

Tobias is in his tent after his midday meal. People outside yell. The wind has been strong, causing his tent to lean. He has the only private tent, as his station deserves. The others are in two standard tents, one for the women and one for the men. He is unsure why they are yelling.

Putting on his cloak, he opens the tent to see the wind blowing snow everywhere.

One of his assigned soldiers runs up, "Sir, Teppo is requesting you in the men's tent. He needs help to manage this mess. Lead the way, Master Tobias."

Entering the tent, Teppo is talking to two of the men. He immediately stops when he notices Tobias. Turning, "Master Tobias, this storm is getting worse. We need to break camp, load the wagons, and head down."

"Why don't we just hunker down and wait out the storm?"

"That would be the right thing with a typical winter storm. This one is much worse than usual. Scouts looking for the dwarf have just returned. They reported that the snow was already up to the horses' knees. They also reported falling rocks, which would be fatal to anyone. We will get stuck in the mountains. If we get stuck here with no shelter, we will probably freeze and possibly starve."

Tobias has his arms folded, listening intently. He looks around at people packing and scurrying. The sides of the tent are moving in the wind. The side facing the storm is bending toward them. Looking back at Teppo, he says, "You made a good decision without consulting me. I agree we need to travel down."

"Very good, master Tobias. If you can dress warmly for the journey, that would be helpful. We will start moving as soon as the wagons finish loading.

"Yes, of course. I will get dressed appropriately. When we get down the mountain far enough, one man needs to ride to inform the king. We need to report that we are close and will be in the city in the spring."

"Master Tobias, that is a little soon. We aren't rushing. The dwarf will find the city and stop. We can take our time."

Teppo, you insist we would find the city soon. When we discover the city, we will need additional troops to take and hold it. I'm not stupid. As soon as we find the city, thieves, and scavengers will swarm, looking to take the treasure.

"I can agree with that part, but that isn't all, Master Tobias. We will need workers. We will need people to bring supplies and to work in the city. Cooks, cleaners, merchants. All the things we need to have a living city. Getting those people to the city will take time. But we will need to have soldiers to guard the treasure."

Tobias says, "I'm glad we agree. After your input, I will ask that we have a large enough group to help and hold the city. The request will be for 50 soldiers."

After Tobias steps out, Ranjeet steps over. "Why did you talk about having workers in the city?"

"We need to find the city, get control, and then how will we take the treasure? We will need many workers and wagons. The timing is a concern of mine. The time to find the city, take control, and investigate the rumored treasure. We don't know how long it will take. We want to take any treasure as soon as we find it, but we don't want a bunch of people to manage mentally waiting around with nothing to do."

"If the city is that great, have you considered that we stay and take over the city? The workers can be part of rebuilding it as a city."

"Yes, I have. That will depend on the city. If the city is usable, we can stay. Falling apart, a piece of crap, we won't stay. If we stay, our people can use the dungeon to hold the people we need to keep alive, but who need to disappear. We will make the city the coven stronghold, grow our power."

Nodding, Ranjeet says, "That would be a great help. It takes a lot of work to keep those people hidden. With the learning from the box, the city will become the premier training location for controllers."

"It was my grandmother's dream to have a controller city where we could be safe."

"She won't see you accomplish her dream."

"She will know. We will have a place to live and train, and they will not hunt witches there."

A powerful gust of wind pushes the tent's side, almost hitting them both on the head. "Go finish getting the camp packed. We need to get down the mountain. I'm going to send two ahead to break the path and hunt for meat."

Back to the Dragon

Hallr left Sheyla and headed to find Agnarr and Milfred.

They are close to the window, only partway to the stairs going down. With the light from the window, they can see. They have the dilemma of horse meat. What do they take?

When Hallr finds them, he says, "The torch is gone. You will need to hold on as I lead you down into the city."

Agnarr gets a look of realization, "Of course. Dwarf night vision. You can see."

Hallr replies, "Well enough. I'll take the largest hunk of meat. Let's go."

Hallr has to lead them while carrying several hundred kilos of horse meat. He quickly realized he had to talk to them and describe what they were doing, or they would run into everything.

Hallr didn't pay attention until Milfred says, "My head is just below the ceiling in these tunnels."

Agnarr says, "The city probably has some tunnels that are only for dwarves."

"We are on the stairs now. We will go down about forty steps."

As they slowly descend, Milfred says, "I can't see anything. It makes it harder to judge distance. I feel like I've already gone down hundreds of meters."

Hallr replies, "I'm going slow, so it takes longer. It's not much further."

When they arrive at the chamber, he has them sit next to the unconscious Sheyla as he goes over to the dragon. Her breathing is slightly stronger, but she is asleep. He rummages around the area and can grab the end of the torch and yank it out. What he gets is a destroyed stick that won't do anything. He says, "We need to light a fire."

Going to Agnarr, he hands him the torch stick. "The dragon

rolled on it. I'm going to find more to start a fire so you can see."

Hallr disappears from view, and Agnarr says, "This is wild. We are in a room with an actual dragon. We can hear its breathing, but we can't see it. The stench is awful. It seems the dragon has been trapped here for decades, maybe centuries. All the meat is to feed it. What happens when it wakes up and finishes the horse? Are we next?"

Milfred says, "Can't do much about it. I don't think Hallr will let the dragon...."

"You're shitting me. Hallr can't stop a dragon from eating us."

Their talking makes Sheyla move. She wakes and groans, "My head."

Agnarr helps her sit up. "No water. Can you tell us what happened?"

"There is a dragon. I tried to get its stomach working again. I passed out from the effort. Now my head is pounding. I'm going to stay lying down. The dark is good for my head."

Minutes later, Hallr returns with a few small pieces of wood. "Not much to scrounge down here."

He creates a spot in the middle of all the gold items. A large golden bowl receives the broken wood. He goes to Agnarr, "I'm going to lead you to the sticks so you can use your magic and start a fire to give us light."

Agnarr says, "Let's do it."

Agnarr can't see anything. Hallr leads him a few feet and says, "It is at your feet."

Agnarr kneels, touches the bowl, and sticks. Picking up a single stick, he concentrates. Holding the stick vertically, just above his fingers, he visualizes the wood particles moving rapidly back and forth.

After a few seconds, a tiny fire appears. The small light is perfect for Agnarr's eyes. He looks down at the bowl, then out in front of him. He drops the stick into the bowl because he sees the floor covered in gold and jewels. Most of it consists of gold plates, bowls, jewelry, and coins which the dragon has crushed flat. "Holy crap."

He looks to his right and can see the enormous dragon's head lying on crushed gold.

Milfred is behind him, saying in a whisper, "A dragon, holy crap." Then, after a pause, loudly, "Holy crap, this room is full of gold."

Sheyla says, "Quiet. Don't wake her."

Sheyla hears and quickly realizes it is the dragon, "Too late, I'm awake."

In the dim light, Milfred sees Sheyla's face as it goes white, and he says, "Are you okay?"

Sheyla says, "She's awake. Didn't you hear that?"

In her head, Sheyla hears, "You touched me so that I can link to your mind. Don't be afraid. You're with Hallr. You helped me. I will not eat you."

Hallr has experienced all this and is smiling. He hurries to the horse's head, close to the dragon, and says, "Open up."

Agnarr shakes his head. "I heard nothing except you."

The dragon lifts its head and opens its jaw. Hallr spins and throws the horse's head into its mouth. The dragon puts its head back and swallows when Hallr says, "We have more."

Sheyla says, "She's talking to me mentally. I touched her, and we can communicate now."

The dragon lays its head down, not slamming down this time, and watches Hallr in the low light bring all the horse meat. When he says open, she lifts her head and opens her mouth. He throws in all the chunks of meat. She moves the meat and chews on something for the first time in centuries, then tosses her head back and swallows.

Lying her head down, she looks at them with her left eye.

Milfred says, "What just happened?"

Hallr is smiling as he looks up at the dragon. He turns, almost bouncing, and says, "We just saved a dragon."

In his head, he hears, "I'm not saved. I'm still very weak. I need water. There is a water source over there, but it hasn't worked in a while."

Hallr turns, saying, "Show me."

The pipe appears in Hallr's mind, and he runs under it and searches. "I'll be back," as he runs off through a doorway. As he is running away, Milfred yells, "Don't leave us..."

Agnarr says, "I don't think I've ever seen Hallr this excited. He just ran off and left us with a hungry dragon."

Sheyla hears in her mind, "Reassure them. I will not eat Hallr friends."

Sheyla is thinking, "Then why do I feel uneasy?"

Immediately in her head, she hears, "I will not eat you, but I don't trust you, human."

"Why don't you trust us?"

"Humans are the reason this great city fell. You're that kind of witch. Those who control others are why I've been trapped here for centuries."

Sheyla gets a huge chill and shivers. Agnarr asks, "What did she say?"

"She doesn't trust humans, Magi. A control witch is the reason the city died."

Sheyla shifts in the doorway, sitting outside. In her head, she hears the question, "Are you scared?"

"Yes."

"Of what?"

"I'm a natural control witch."

"I can read your concerns and the memories they trigger. You have controlled many and caused them to kill for you. You don't control the other humans with you now."

"How much of my memory can you see?"

"I know what you focus on and what you dream about. What bothers you, and you dwell on. Back to my question. You don't control the humans with you now."

"I controlled people when I had to. When I didn't have any other options."

"You're concerned you won't have a choice in the city?

"I don't know. We just got here and the first thing I did was

meet a dragon. I don't want to control others. I want to be left alone. If I'm pushed, I could get angry and lash out."

"Against me? Girl, your magic won't affect Hallr or me. The city fell when our human allies were under control. Not me or the dwarves. You are safer in this dead city than anywhere else right now. Why is Hallr so watchful around you?"

"He thinks I'm going to do just what I said, lash out and use control magic and make everyone attack him."

"Are you going to attack him?"

"NO! Just no. Why would I do that?"

"Why do you think the other witches attack dwarves?"

"I've never been involved in anything like that. Hallr is the first dwarf I've ever seen in my life. I never did a chitchat with a control witch about dwarves."

"You need to resolve this with Hallr somehow. And just to be clear with you, I will be on Hallr's side if there is a fight."

Sheyla is still sitting next to the door. She looks at the dragon, shaking her head. "How did we get to this? I don't want to fight you, or Hallr."

"You need to resolve something with Hallr."

"You mean tell him about my past?"

"That is one part. Learn his past. Why are you afraid of your past?"

"You know what it is. You don't think I should be worried?"

"I think Hallr would consider you less of an enemy if he knew how hard you fought to get out of that situation."

"Dragon, do you have a name?"

"Xylia."

"Can I call you Xylia?"

"Yes, you can all call me Xylia."

"Xylia, I will try to talk to Hallr. He will need to talk to me. Will you help convince him to talk?"

"I will help. You will have to stop being afraid to talk about your past."

Sheyla is shaking her head. "Later. This room is a problem. We *can't see without light. Is there a way to get light into this room without a fire?"*

"Yes. There is a tube at the top that goes out. It is for air and light. The tube is now overgrown. I haven't seen sunlight in many years."

Sheyla looks around for Agnarr. She can barely see him in the small firelight. He is close to the door where Hallr disappeared. "Agnarr, I need your help."

As she stands, her headache intensifies. She puts one hand on her head and drops to one knee. Agnarr quickly kneels next to her. "What is it?"

"Give me a minute. Healing the dragon took a toll."

Agnarr says, "We all need water. I should go look for Hallr."

Sheyla says, "Not yet. Help me up."

Sheyla stands, holding Agnarr's arm. When she is steady, she walks toward the dragon, saying, "Xylia, the dragon, said there used to be a tube going up, letting in light and air. She said it has been covered. You think you can open it?"

"I don't know where it is."

Sheyla hears, "Walk closer to me and look for light. At the brightest part of the day, there is sometimes a sliver of light."

Sheyla asks, "What time is it outside?"

Hallr walks back into the room, saying, "I can't find how to turn the water back on. I'm going to get Kaleb to help figure it out. It is an hour after noon outside."

"How do you know?"

"Dwarves know. Don't know how, we always know."

Xylia says in their mind, "Dwarves live mostly underground. They have developed the ability to track time way better than humans or dragons. Don't look up. Look for a spot of light on the floor, or me."

Sheyla repeats, "Look for a spot of light on the ground or the dragon. We may find the opening."

Milfred comes over, and they spread out to look. Their little stick fire burns down to embers, so there is much less light. After a few minutes, Xylia says, "There. Girl, walk to your left."

They gather around and watch the floor. After a minute, a faint light plays across the gold on the floor, then vanishes. Agnarr looks up, shifting around. After moving several times, he says, "I'm not sure of the exact spot."

Hallr says, "You can use your push. You won't do anything to the ceiling of solid stone."

"Good point. Here goes."

Agnarr focuses as he brings his hands together, then shoves them up. On the third try, they see light. It is not bright, but there is light. Xylia says, "Gray, it must be cloudy or a storm outside."

Milfred says, "Kaleb is out in the storm."

Xylia replies, "I'm getting stronger. I can sense the human outside. The courtyard is now protected because he closed the gate. You think of him as a giant. Go get the interesting young one."

Hallr says, "I'll get him," as he walks toward the door and out of the room.

Now, with a target, Agnarr pushes hard. He shoves over whatever is covering the opening, and a large circle of soft gray light hits the floor. They hear a soft whistle from another room. Xylia says, "Hot air is going out the hole, causing other air to come in."

Sheyla repeats the information for the others.

Sheyla then says, "Agnarr, Xylia tells me I need to resolve something with Hallr."

"You'll listen to the dragon."

"What does that mean?"

"When we first became a group, I told you we needed to trust him. What I didn't say is that we need to trust each other. That includes yourself."

"How does that affect Hallr and me?"

"Whatever you're afraid of us knowing about your past is going to keep being a block."

Xylia says, "You can tell them."

Sheyla turns to Xylia, "Tell them? You know the memory. Do you *know how it makes me feel?"*

"We share a connection. When you dwell on it, when you think hard about it, I can tell. In a full city, I can't get clear visuals, but with you, a few, I can sense your terrible memories. Yes. I can tell how bad it makes you feel. Holding it in doesn't make it better."

"I'm not ready to talk about what happened."

Water

Kaleb is sitting in the wagon, waiting. He has done every chore he always puts off while he is waiting for the others. He hears a noise and looks up at the window. Hallr appears and yells, "Enough goofing off for you. Come on and meet the dragon."

Kaleb walks over to the window where the rope hangs and looks up.

Hallr says, "Why haven't you come up?"

"I'm too heavy, and I can't haul myself up that far on a rope. I also can't get the remaining horse meat up without help."

"Let's get the meat up here. Then you tie the end of the rope around your waist. Grab the rope and walk up the wall while I pull you."

Hallr has the remaining meat, and the liver piled behind him. He braces his legs and pulls on the rope to bring Kaleb up. Minutes later, Hallr is grabbing Kaleb's wrist and pulling him into the window. "Leave the rope and follow me."

They are carrying the last horse meat. Right after they get situated and moving, Kaleb says, "I can't see anything. Are you sure..." Kaleb smacks his head on the top of a doorway and knocks himself out.

Hallr turns and kneels next to Kaleb, gently slapping him. "Sorry about that. I don't have to look up and watch where your head will hit something."

Kaleb groans and sits up. "This place is for short people."

Hallr chuckles, "That it is. Get up."

Hallr is now watching the height and multiple times tells Kaleb to duck or reach up to feel the opening.

They step into the dragon's room. There is faint light from the ceiling. Kaleb stops as soon as he gets through the doorway. He is looking at the dragon.

Hallr walks toward the dragon's head. When he is close, he says, "Open up."

Xylia opens her mouth, and Hallr throws in the meat. He says, "That is also the liver. It is good for you. Kaleb, bring the meat."

Kaleb is simply staring at the dragon. The dragon's head turns to get a better view of Kaleb. With its head up, it swings over the heads of Agnarr, Sheyla, and Milfred. The dragon puts its snout close to Kaleb and draws in air, smelling him.

The air intake is so strong that Kaleb stumbles forward, dropping the meat he is carrying, and puts his hand on the dragon's nose. Instantly, the dragon's presence overwhelms his mind. His knees go weak, and he falters, then stands back up.

The dragon pulls its head away, back to its original, comfortable position. Kaleb hears in his head, "Not a real giant. Just a really tall human."

Sheyla says verbally, "Not a giant. You needed to check?"

"Yes. People said that humans killed off giants centuries ago. I need to smell him to see if you could be like Hallr. The last of your kind."

Kaleb says, "Thanks for confirming. I'm Kaleb. And you are?"

"Xylia. I like your manners, boy. Being a fake giant, I wasn't sure I would like you."

Kaleb shakes his head, "I'm not trying to fake it, just tall."

Hallr yells, "Kaleb, let's go. Bring the meat, and then we need water."

With all the meat piled close to Xylia's head, Hallr says, "Open up."

Xylia says in their mind, "You need to be warned if you have the tall one with you. There are traps in parts of the city. The dwarves set up defenses so that attackers wouldn't control certain parts of the city. Things like water are essential."

Kaleb says, "Am I going to have a problem?"

"Yes. If you find a place with many human skeletons, you are in a trap."

With Xylia swallowing the last of the meat, they head

through a doorway into the dark, talking to each other about how water could get to the room.

At an intersection of hallways, Kaleb says, "We need to be looking for pipes. Right now, I can't see anything in this dark, so you need to notice the pipes."

Hallr replies, "I think I'm seeing the obvious ones. There are probably more I don't see."

"So, tell me, Hallr, where does the water come from? What is the source?"

"I figure we are inside a mountain covered in snow. The water is from snowmelt. The heat from the city melts the snow that is collected."

"We need to find the input point and trace from there."

More than an hour later, they are breathing hard from climbing stairs. "Hallr, are you sure?"

"No. I'm just going up because the water has to flow down."

"I'm climbing stairs, hunched over in the dark. The next place I can stand, we are going to take a break."

Two more sections of steps, and Hallr says, "There is a door. The door fits dwarves. I can see a bit of light at the bottom."

"Can we open it?"

"You sit on the steps and let me look."

The sliver of light helps Hallr to see details. There is a stone crossbar at the top third. He pulls that off and sets it aside carefully. Looking at the door, there is a handle carved into the left side, but a vertical stone bar partially obscures it.

Looking at the vertical stone, he can't move it up. After trying several directions, he caused the top to shift to the right. "Figured it out. It swings to the right as you lift it."

Setting the vertical stone down, he grabs the handle and pulls. The door shifts a few millimeters and stops.

Kaleb is in position and is watching. He says, "It's stuck. Can you put a foot on the side to help pull?"

"Right."

Hallr gets his foot on the side, takes a breath, then jerks hard on *the handle. The door swings in, and light pours into the stairwell, along with snow. The light is grey, but still blinding them.*

Kaleb has his hand in front of his eyes, palm facing out, while squinting to see.

Hallr is facing the wall. "Bloody hell, that is bright. I need a minute."

Kaleb crawls to get through the small door. Outside, he stands, still blinking. It is cold and snowing. The snow is not falling straight down; it is swirling and blowing sideways because of the wind. He says, "The storm isn't over."

Hallr steps out to see his breath in the cold air. Looking out across the landscape, with snow swirling, he considers a flat area through it. "Let's go check that out."

The flat area has swirling snow covering it. With the movement, they can see ice. Hallr tests the ice, then walks out, followed by Kaleb. Kaleb says, "Never walked on ice before.

Looking around, Hallr says, "There is a stone structure."

Turning, Kaleb takes a step, then slips. Hallr chuckles, looking down at Kaleb lying on his back, rubbing the back of his head.

They walk over and look at the structure. It has a rectangular top and slopes down into the water through the ice.

"Okay, Kaleb, here is the input."

Looking around the outside of the rectangle, Kaleb says, "We need to see if water is going in. If not, we need to clear the input."

"Going down in that frozen water. Your daft, man."

"Hallr, I can't think with all the smart things we've seen; they wouldn't have something for this. Let's search this box."

Hallr finds a stone blocking a small hole. "The entrance. Looks like I'm going inside."

Kaleb helps, and they shift the stone so Hallr can go into the hole. When they let go, it moves back to cover the opening. Kaleb says, "It looks like I'm holding the door for you. Don't take too long; it's cold."

After a minute, Kaleb hears Hallr chuckling. He asks, "What's so funny?"

"No swimming needed. Three Mithril poles are going into the water. It looks like they clear any debris from the input."

A minute later, Kaleb hears water splashing. A few minutes later, Hallr crawls out of the hole. Putting the stone back, they walk back to the doorway. Hallr says, "There is a ladder inside. That stone water entry goes down some distance."

It takes ten minutes to walk back to the door. At the door, they feel the air moving out. Hallr says, "Warm air from inside the city is rising in the stairwell. Maybe the air in the city won't be so stale."

Kaleb takes a breath, "Back into the cramped stairs."

Hallr says, "Let's close the door and see what else is happening with the water."

Their travel direction comes from looking for pipes, and by sound when they can't see any.

Kaleb says, "I can't see with it so dark, but I think it helps me focus on hearing."

At a large intersection, Hallr stops and says, "You can stand over in this corner. This corridor intersection is full of pipes."

"Which pipes are working?"

They quickly begin arguing. Hallr says, "There are two directions to check. I want to try the one with no water noise. There should be water moving in those pipes. Then we can check yours."

"I want to get out of these short hallways more than I want to argue, so we'll do it your way."

Walking down the hallway, Kaleb is grumbling about being stooped over. Hallr makes out the first skeleton in the hallway. There are no weapons, no armor, just a skeleton lying on the floor.

Hallr says, "Human skeleton. Xylia's warning. This must be something important ahead."

As they progress, more skeletons appear. Kaleb says, "They are all just skeletons. Someone stripped them at some point."

After twenty more meters, Hallr says, "I think you should wait here. Ahead, there are more skeletons; some of them don't have a head next to them."

Hallr moves forward. The doorway to the room has four skeletons. All are leaving, as if trying to get away from something. Hallr kicks the bones out of the way as he slowly enters. There are a dozen more skeletons. He says loudly, "Most of the skeletons in the room had their heads chopped off."

Hallr takes two more steps, hits a trigger in the floor, and Mithril spikes shoot down out of the ceiling, stopping just a few centimeters above his head. The spikes retract into the ceiling as Hallr hears water and gears. The sound stops when the spikes have completely retract.

Hallr steps to his left and triggers another trap. This time, Mithril blades swing out from slots in the wall. They are ten centimeters above his head. A different water-and-gear sound occurs as it retracts.

Additional steps trigger these same traps again. Getting across the room, he looks around. He has to touch the wall as he looks around. There is a small lever he can see. From his height and from this spot in the room, he can see it. A taller human wouldn't realize what they are seeing.

The lever is hard to move, but after he turns it, nothing happens. He walks into the room to trigger the traps, and nothing happens.

"Kaleb, it should be safe to come in now."

Kaleb can't see and is following Hallr's voice. His feet are kicking bones from multiple skeletons as he walks stooped over. He says, "Traps for humans."

Hallr is looking at the equipment, pipes, and valves.

"Kaleb, something here isn't working for the water."

"This room, this trap, is incredible. After the triggers, the system resets. That sound of water and gears must be the resetting action. I would bet these guys were trying to turn off the water to stop the trap reset system. They turned off the water to Xylia at the same time."

"Look at the bloody equipment."

Kaleb says, "Sure, with my dark vision. What equipment do you see?"

Hallr replies, "Yeah. I can barely see. Lots of pipes. There are some valves with handles."

"Are any handles turned differently?"

Looking around, Hallr moves across the room. "Here. This valve is different. The others all have the handle in line with the pipe, except this one."

He grabs the handle and tries to turn it. "The handle won't move."

Kaleb reaches down and rummages. He stands and holds out a femur bone. "Hit the handle with this."

Hallr hits the handle twice, hard. With the second hit, the bone breaks. He grabs the handle and jerks it. They hear water moving through the stone pipe when they align it with the pipe.

Hallr says, "They must have thought, turn off the water for Xylia. No water, she dies."

Kaleb says, "I don't think they understood dragons. She has obviously been without water for many years."

They hear Xylia say, "Human thieves are like grapes, full of liquid."

In the chamber, they hear a groan from inside the walls, followed by silence. A few minutes later, they all hear a soft noise in the walls. Xylia says, "Water is moving."

The sounds continue with some gurgles, slurps, belches, and pops. With the light almost gone, they hear rushing air, then sputtering. A stream of water, approximately six centimeters across, emerges from a hole in the wall, located just below the ceiling and two meters from the side wall.

Water shoots out in an arc, dropping into a collection pool. There are objects in the stream of water, as well as mud. After several minutes, the water flows clear, and the pool is now full. As *the water flows, some of it spills over the edge and into a hole in the wall, disappearing.*

While the pool is filling, Xylia shifts on the floor. Sheyla hears, "Muscles I haven't used in many years."

Xylia shifts her body and groans. The humans watching can tell this is a struggle and probably hurts. She doesn't move far, then stretches out her neck. She is just able to get her snout into the stream of water and open her jaws. Water flows into her mouth, out the sides onto gold items. They see her swallow several times, then she pulls her head back and lies down.

Sheyla hears, "That was hard, but good. I already feel better. Girl, what do you want me to call you?"

"My name is Sheyla."

"Is that what you want me to call you? I can say anything. Some humans don't like me to use their names."

"Sheyla says, Sheyla is fine with me."

"All right, thank you for helping me, Sheyla. One little thing can make a big difference."

"I'm glad I could help. I wasn't sure I could do enough. You're an enormous dragon."

"Tell me about the others. What do you know about their past? Start with Hallr."

"Why are you asking about Hallr?"

"I haven't seen a dwarf in centuries. Where did this one grow up? What was his experience?"

"I don't know a lot. He grew up south of here. He said his family had lived there for years. They worked in the local mines."

"He seems like a digger, not a tinker."

"He is a digger. I don't think he knows much about his distant ancestors or what happened."

"What about the others?"

"Milfred is a blacksmith. He wants to make tools, weapons, and armor. Only this place can produce Mithril things.

"Not anymore. And the other one?"

"Agnarr is a warlock but doesn't use magic unless he must.

He is strong in magic. Now he's Milfred's apprentice. He won't tell me about his past and why he doesn't use magic."

Xylia replies, "Interesting."

Sheyla says, "You seem to like Kaleb. Why is that?"

"He could have become evil and dangerous. Hallr and the rest of you gave him a chance. He dreams about building things, not destroying them."

My Treasure

Milfred and Agnarr have been wandering around the room while there is light. They are picking up various gold items, examining them, and then returning them. Milfred says, "The gold is pure, but the craftsmanship varies."

"Agree, some look amazing, and others look like a child did them."

Finding a very intricate coin as large as his palm, Agnarr says, "Like this one. This workmanship is amazing. Let's ask about this."

They walk toward Sheyla, who is sometimes speaking to the dragon, sometimes silent, and nods. Agnarr walks up and says, "Can I ask about this?" holding up the large, intricate coin.

The dragon turns its head and says to Sheyla, "They want the gold. It didn't take long for their true intentions to show."

Sheyla says, "You want to take the gold? Xylia says, your intentions are obvious."

Agnarr says, "That is presumptuous. Really presumptuous. I wanted to ask about who made this, about who made the stuff in this room. The coin shows incredible workmanship, but other items in the room look like kids' projects."

Xylia listens to Agnarr and shoots her head forward toward him, her mouth opening. She snaps her jaws shut less than a meter from his face. Agnarr says, "What, you don't like getting called out for your bullshit?"

Xylia breathes in and then quickly exhales through her nostrils right at Agnarr, who falls and tumbles backward from the force.

Sheyla says, "He's right. You're mad for getting called out."

"I've had no contact for centuries, and the first time I do is a human telling me I'm presumptuous about a human not trying to steal the gold. Do you know how rare it is for a human not to take the gold?"

Sheyla asks, "Agnarr asked a reasonable question about who made the coin."

Only hearing what Sheyla is saying, Agnarr says, "I'll be clear with you. This treasure could help get supplies and gear. There is enough to help people."

"You want to take it."

Sheyla repeats, "You want to take it."

Agnarr looks at Xylia, then shakes his head. "I would use it, but... but taking any of it would bring out the worst in humans who know about it. People would swarm the city in search of treasure. You keep it. Just answer my question."

Raising her head and moving it back and forth, "The hands of a child made everything. They make them part of their art and craft classes and give them to me to keep for them. The little ones make simple items. The older and more skilled ones make very intricate ones, like the one you are holding."

Sheyla repeats what Xylia says and fumbles with the wording about the kids. Xylia makes a low growl, causing Sheyla to back up. Xylia says, "They need to touch me so we can communicate. Tell them."

Hearing this from Sheyla, Milfred walks toward the dragon. The closest part of the dragon to her mouth is the front leg. Milfred is looking up at Xylia and realizes her wing is wrong. He says, "Agnarr, her wing is wrong. It looks broken."

Agnarr is now looking up as he approaches the dragon. When they are next to each other, Xylia's front leg swings up and out, then down on them, pinning both to the gold floor while covering them.

When they contact the dragon, they both stiffen and collapse onto the gold items. Large, overwhelming, dominating. Xylia's presence is everywhere in their minds.

Agnarr groans, then says, "My private thoughts. Those aren't yours to take."

The foot raises and moves away from them. Agnarr groans and

yells, *"That was cruel and unfair."*

He hears Xylia talking in his head. *"Unfair was my human friends being controlled by witches and killing dwarf children. Unfair was humans blew up the tunnel I used to get out, trapping me in this room, blowing up the rooms above me where the little ones have school. Cruel is watching all this happen, and the ceiling collapses, breaking my wing and pinning me down. I couldn't do anything."*

Sheyla says, *"Wow, you're dealing with serious issues. I'm sorry."*

Milfred slowly stands back up and says, *"Your wing bends the wrong way. That doesn't look natural."*

Agnarr is glaring at Xylia. He says, *"Don't talk about taking gold when you take from us."*

Xylia lays her head down. *"I will not apologize to a human. I'm tired."*

Milfred says, *"Talking doesn't use much energy. What happened?"*

"My wing got broken. When a dwarf was digging me out of the rocks, I had to shift my body. The only way to get me out was to shove me onto my side. Rocks moved, then more fell. I had to twist, and it made the wing fold over. It was the worst pain I have ever had."

After several minutes, Agnarr is calmer and realizes what she said. Agnarr says, *"The kids who made the treasures were all killed?"*

Xylia says, *"Yes. My little ones. They learned their craft by making things in gold. Sometimes they would collect gold items and melt them to make something better. This is my treasure. My kids made these for me."*

Agnarr says, *"I have another question. They are significant to you, but you can make them from any substance. Why gold?"*

Xylia replies, *"Finally, an intelligent question. The dwarves mine many things in these mountains. Iron, Mithril, copper, silver, coal, and gold. They mined more gold than they needed.*

Gold is also easy for the kids to use. They take what the elders don't need, and the kids do things to practice their craft skills."

Kaleb and Hallr re-enter the room, both hearing Xylia speak. Kaleb says, "I heard the discussion on your broken wing. Sheyla can fix it. She's a healer."

Sheyla turns with a surprised expression that turns angry, "Don't commit me to what you don't understand. I can't fix a broken and already healed dragon wing." She dramatically points back and up at Xylia, "A dragon."

Kaleb says, "Sorry. I thought you would help her."

Sheyla turns toward Agnarr, shaking her head, "I swear that kid."

"Don't call me a kid."

"Then stop acting like one!"

Milfred asks, "How did you get the water working?"

Kaleb says, "We climbed lots of stairs, went outside to a lake of snowmelt water. Hallr cleared the intake, and water started flowing."

Hallr continues, "Then, following pipes, we found a room with traps that had valves controlling water flow. Kaleb figured out the key valve to open."

Xylia says, "I need to rest. You humans are making me move more than I have in years. I need to rest and eat again soon."

Hallr nods, "We will get you food."

Milfred says, "Wait. Hold on. We can't just keep feeding her our horses. We need to get down the mountain before we are trapped by winter snow."

Kaleb looks at Milfred and then at Hallr. "You don't know, or don't realize. That is a huge storm outside. We are stuck here. This is not bad inside the city."

Milfred replies, "Except for food."

Xylia lays her head down, and they hear, "There are always mushrooms," as her breathing quickly changes.

Sheyla motions for everyone to head to the entrance. At the entrance, Agnarr stops and says, "We can't see. The light is almost gone from outside, but the hallway is completely black."

Hallr says, "We need to get back to the window, then to the wagons. I'll lead the way."

Kaleb says, "Why can't we open the gate and bring the wagons inside? What is on the inside of the big gate?"

Milfred asks, "Can we open the gate? How do we do that?"

Agnarr looks at Hallr. "You do not know, do you?"

"None."

Kaleb says, "It's probably like the courtyard gate. We find the solution, and it opens easily."

Sheyla is looking at them, talking to each other. She turns and starts walking across the gold. "I'm going to drink some water while I can."

Agnarr and Milfred turn and start following her. After a pause, Kaleb shrugs his shoulders and follows. Hallr says, "Fine," and follows.

After drinking, as they are walking back toward the entrance tunnel, Kaleb says, "What we need are torches to light the path. Even candles. We have a couple of candles in the wagon, but we need a dozen or more."

Milfred is walking with them and thinking. He stops halfway to the entrance archway and starts looking around. "Agnarr, I want you to try something."

"Okay, what?"

"Think about this. If I put an iron bar in the fire, it gets hot and glows. We could use that as a light. But that is too much. We need iron and a forge. What about a smaller version using your magic?"

"I'm not tracking with you."

"You use your magic to make it hot, like starting a fire, but something that will glow for a while. The problem is, I don't know what. I'm looking for anything different."

Kaleb walks down Xylia's side, looking at all the jewels. He finds a gray stone that seems out of place and picks it up. He picks up several more that look different from all the others.

The others have brought items to Agnarr to try. When Agnarr had tried all those, he called out, "Kaleb, you got anything?"

Kaleb takes what he found back to them. He says, "Here are some to try." He puts them down in front of Agnarr, who looks, pushes them with the tip of his shoe, and nods. "I'll try."

With each gemstone, he focuses and pushes back and forth in the middle to get it hot. After a few seconds, the first one glows. Kaleb says, "It's working."

As soon as Agnarr stops, the glow fades quickly. "That was a dud. Let's try another." After several tries, Agnarr looks at Kaleb, "I don't think this is going to work."

Kaleb picks up the last one. Yellow color with gray flakes inside. "Maybe the flakes inside will do something."

Agnarr concentrates, and one flake glows softly, becoming brighter. Agnarr stops, and the crystal continues to glow, slowly fading. Kaleb says, "I can use that."

Hallr is not at the entrance, and they don't see him. Kaleb holds up the crystal, casting its light around the room. It is faint, but the room is visible. Hallr is not there.

Milfred says, "I think we are more accustomed to the dark and see with less light, but we still need something."

Kaleb says, "Hallr must already be on his way to the window."

Sheyla says, "We have one light now. We need more, and we need a plan. Are we going to open the city gate? How do we do that?"

Agnarr says, "Let's go. We can explore some of this city on the way to the window. See if we can find anything useful."

The group of four is walking in the city. They quickly got lost. Every few minutes, Agnarr focuses on the crystal, making it bright again. Everywhere they search, they find empty rooms and empty shelves. When they find something, it is worthless trash. Kaleb often walks hunched over because he is so tall. At some intersections, the ceiling is higher, allowing him to stand upright.

After walking and turning at different intersections, they found nothing familiar. They have also been looking in the rooms they *pass. Sheyla says, "Nothing. The city is empty."*

Xylia's voice echoed in her head, saying, "They plundered and stripped the city, taking everything useful. Anyone who could fit through the windows took anything of value, or they broke down anything of value to fit through the windows. The only things of value are behind locked doors that no one has a key to open anymore."

Milfred asks, "What about forges, tools, armor?"

"The equipment to make things is too heavy to haul away, so it stayed. There are no ore, coal, or tools. That was all taken," says Xylia.

They continue walking. Agnarr asks, "Xylia, can you help us know which direction?"

"I've never been in those corridors. I can show you images of common spaces that the dwarves shared with me for reference. You need to head toward the gate."

An image of the gate's interior appears in their mind. "That is all I can provide."

Milfred says, "I'll say it, we got ourselves lost."

Kaleb says, "We will find our way. We can't just stop. Let's go to the right at the next corridor."

As Agnarr focuses on the stone to make it light up again, he says, "We're completely lost. We need Hallr."

Agnarr and Milfred alternate yelling, "Hallr!"

Walking down a corridor, not knowing where they are, they stop to brighten the crystal. They hear footsteps, and in a short time, Hallr comes around a corner. "You four are much deeper in the city. Did you get lost?"

Kaleb replies sarcastically, "Yes. We didn't have a guide. You ran off."

"Hey, I don't have a map, but I can read."

Agnarr says, "Read what?"

Hallr points to the top of the wall at the intersection, "The hallway designation. Look at the top of each intersection of corridors. The symbols show your location. The top is a number;

how many floors down you are. Below that, you have an arrow and a direction. The second one on that row is how far from the main forge or factory."

Milfred says, "The forge is the center?"

"Forge or factory. It depends on where you started and where you're going."

They all hear Xylia say, "Facing the gate, from outside, the furnaces, and forges are inside on the left, and the factory or construction is on the right."

Milfred looks and says, "Six marks, so we are six levels down. Heading down this corridor will take us toward the forges, the other way toward the gate."

Hallr says, "Very good. You don't even need light to know where you are. You can feel the writing on the corners. Which way should you be going?"

Kaleb says, "To the gate," as he swings around, taking a step, and hits his head, knocking himself out.

Kaleb wakes to see faint faces looking at him. "My head hurts."

Sheyla puts her hand on his head and closes her eyes. Kaleb feels his headache subsiding. "Thanks."

Hallr says, "We need to figure something out before you break the city."

Kaleb sits up, saying, "Not funny."

Open The Gate

After a day of searching and Xylia telling them what little she knows, they have a plan for the gate. Hallr and Kaleb are searching for the floors close to the gate.

Kaleb says, "The entrance area has three sides, all with three levels. We are on the third level, looking into the gate. The bottom level is twice the normal height. Obviously, wagons come in and out loaded with material. There is nothing visible to move the gate. No ropes or chains. How would you even lift something that big?"

Hallr walks toward the side. "I do not know. We need to start at the gate, walk around the side rooms, and look for something. If it's like the courtyard gate, it will tilt to the side."

"Hallr, the gate looks big. I don't know what a typical size is. I've never seen a large castle gate in person. Is that gate normal? I don't see how that could be a tilt open."

"Like I would know. I've seen one other city gate up close. I usually go around the back and enter a city through the least-traveled gate. That gate is big, huge—ten meters wide, twenty meters high, and probably two meters thick. Nothing will get through that. The problem is, I don't know how it could move. No hinges we can see. If it needs to go up, how do you lift it?"

"Yeah, I know. Lifting that is not simple."

They reach the side of the gate on the third floor and look at it up close. Hallr says, "Nothing to lift, no hinges to open. I don't see any tilt."

Kaleb says, "I need to go into the rooms and hallways. There has to be something. There is that seam in the middle. Maybe the two sides slide into the mountain to open."

Hallr nods as they look into rooms and to the side. Going through the rooms, they found nothing. They are all empty or have piles of decayed wood. Kaleb examines each pile, looking for sticks to make torches. The rest of the time, he dumps some wood chips outside the door so they can find it again quickly. He tells Hallr, "Wood chips we can use for cooking."

Hallr says, "This isn't working. Nothing to open the gate. We need to go down a corridor and go deeper into the side, check above and below. We see nothing on these three levels: what is above, what is below the gate."

Kaleb is looking at Hallr, frowning. "We know why the gate isn't open. If it were easy, someone would have opened it. What could be below the gate except solid rock to hold up the gate?"

Late in the night, Hallr says, "No, nothing. We looked on both sides and above. The hallway above, with the archer windows, means there is no way to lift it. Could the whole thing be fake? Someone made it look like a gate, but it can't open. I'm heading back to the window, or the dragon hall. We can start looking below the main level tomorrow."

Kaleb says, "Not fake, but also not obvious. I think the two parts slide into the mountain on the side. We have to go further to the side."

In the corridor close to the window they have been using, Milfred says, "We need to get the wagons, well, at least our stuff inside. Are you going to get the gate open?"

Kaleb says, "We're working on it."

Milfred asks, "Did you find the gatehouse?"

Kaleb asks, "What is a gatehouse?"

"It is a small house close to the gate where guards and inspectors will check people and wagons entering and leaving."

Hallr looks at Kaleb, who shrugs. Hallr says, "We weren't looking for the gatehouse. I don't care about anything not related to opening the gate.

Kaleb asks, "There is a gatehouse. Is there one specific to gate control, or gate working? Where are the people who open and close the gate?"

Agnarr has been shaking his head. Guys, the gatehouse is the *gate. There are rooms on the side for people. It is all one big thing called the gatehouse. Some people use different names, but it is all the same.*

Hallr says, "Not helpful. Where do we look?"

The next morning, they started going down below the entry level. Sheyla hears Kaleb and Hallr yelling about direction and where to look. Over the next hour, the yelling doesn't stop; it just gets fainter.

Hallr says, "Look, I'm telling you, this is a dwarf city. A gate room opens the gate, and it will only fit a dwarf, not tall humans. Remember Xylia's warning about traps to stop humans."

"Moving that big, heavy gate will take a lot of muscle. They would get everyone they could to help or use horses. The point is, it will take up a lot of room. Not just dwarf-size."

"Have we checked this hallway?"

"No. After all that talk, that is where you want me to go. In that tiny hallway."

"Sucks to be you."

"If I get stuck, I'm going..."

"You're going to cry. Then I have to find grease to ..."

"Shut up, short man."

A few minutes later, Hallr says, "It's got more space over here. You want to see this."

"What?"

"Get your ass over here."

To fit, Kaleb begins by stooping, then squatting, and shuffling. He has to lie down and crawl through the last section. On his left side, pulling himself along with his left arm. He is holding a torch up with his right hand. On the ground, crawling, he gets out and then stands slowly, afraid he will hit his head.

Hallr says, "You can stand."

Standing, Kaleb looks around the chamber. He can't tell the actual size. They are standing on a ledge walkway about one meter wide. In front of them is a stone wall. Looking, Kaleb realizes it isn't a wall. To the left, it slopes down.

Hallr has walked to the left and is looking over the edge. He gestures for Kaleb to approach. When he is next to Hallr, Kaleb can see that the sloping rock looks to be four meters across. There is a gap from where he is standing to the stone, then another gap and another wall.

Looking to the left and down, the end is at least twenty meters away. It is going into another rock.

Hallr asks, "What is it?"

Kaleb says, "It looks like a huge lever, like a pry bar, used to lift a wagon when we change the wheel. The gate has a counterweight just as big as the other end of this enormous arm. We remove the locks or pins, then move the system. It is easy."

They both step on the huge rock and turn. They are standing close to the pivot point of the lever, looking up toward the gate. Hallr says, "Okay, I see it. Pretty simple. No one would expect the gate to go down into the floor."

Kaleb says, "Meaning the counterweight has to go up. Let's walk down this arm."

When they reach the counterweight, the lever connection point is approximately 10 meters wide and 1.5 meters tall. Looking at the top of the counterweight, Hallr says, "I see a lock pin."

"Where? Even with this torch, you can see better."

"We need to jump down."

"Ha, shorty. It's just a hop for me."

As he hops down, the entire counterweight groans, but doesn't move. They walk to the lock pin on top of the counterweight and look. Kaleb says, "It has pressure on it, so we can't move it. We have to shift something for this to unlock."

Hallr says, "This is a meter square block sticking out of the wall by a meter. It is amazing workmanship. There won't be just one. I'm going to walk across and check."

At the midpoint, Hallr stops. "Put your torch over here. Look."

Kaleb sees smooth stones with lines sticking out slightly. "What?"

"These lines are distinct, deeper."

Hallr runs his hand over the stone and the seams. A portion of the square is sticking out slightly. Stepping back, he looks up for anything else. Kaleb says, "Nothing can stick out when the counterweight moves. Anything protruding will stop the movement. This has to be it."

"What?"

Hallr says, "Come here. See these lines. About a meter on each side. This is a button."

"You're daft now. A button that is a meter across."

"Look at the size of this gate. That is a small button in comparison."

"How do you know it's a button?"

"You said it can't stick out. It is sticking out a couple of centimeters. It has to go in. Now push."

"They both put their hands on the stone and pushed with no effect."

Kaleb says, "Move aside."

Kaleb steps back and rushes forward, hitting the stone with his shoulder. They hear a soft click. Hallr says, "That was the rock laughing at you."

"Well, I can't get back far enough to run. This big trough, tank, or something is taking up room."

"Why would they need a tank on top?"

"Don't know. We'll figure that out later."

"Okay, we hit the button together."

When they both hit the button, there is a crack, the stone shifts by less than a centimeter, and it stops.

"Keep pushing."

They push with no effect until Hallr says, "Stop. We're missing something."

Kaleb says, "Let's check this other lock pin," as he walks toward the pin sticking out that they haven't examined.

Hallr is looking at the pin and comments, "It looks just like the other one."

Kaleb is looking at the pin, then across to the other pin, then up the lever arm. "Hallr, everything like this we have encountered has been sitting for centuries and is stuck. We need to get everything unstuck."

"Sure, I get that. What do we do?"

"Let me think about this for a second. When we did the gate at each step, we had to free the next part. We want to free the lock pins, but they are holding down the counterweight. I think I've got it. JUMP."

Kaleb jumps up and slams his feet on the counterweight. "JUMP."

Hallr jumps and lands. They can't see any effect. Kaleb says, "Jump together. One, two, three, jump."

When they land together, they don't feel any movement, but they hear a bunch of pops and cracks. In a second, dust rained down on them. Kaleb says, "Now we push on the button again."

Pushing hard, the button moves in about 25 centimeters before coming to a stop. They feel the counterweight shift beneath their feet. Looking at the sides of the new opening. Hallr says, "Look. There is a lever on each side. We pull them down."

Kaleb says, "I think our weight is pushing the counterweight down just enough so the pins can move now."

They jerk on the levers to loosen them, starting with the left one. It swings down and lies in the opening about halfway across the button slot. At the last part, they hear a noise, and the counterweight shifts. Pulling the others, they feel the counterweight move and stop.

Kaleb says, "Now we need to get off and push it up."

They go to one side where they expect to see stairs carved into the rock. Instead, they see slots carved into the rock. Kaleb looks and says, "No stairs. This is a ladder. Everything about this gate shows balance. This can't be just one side. I'm going to the other side."

Kaleb runs off into the dark, holding the little torch up high. In a couple of minutes, he yells, "Now get off the wait and on the ladder."

When both step off, the counterweight shifts up several centimeters and then stops. "Now look on the side of the counterweight. A slot, handle, or something to push up."

Hallr yells, "Got it. I'm pushing."

Kaleb can see the counterweight move up as they climb the ladder. The counterweight is moving with simple pressure. Every ten meters, there is a small landing. They shift fifteen centimeters and continue climbing. The ladder slots are standard size for a dwarf, and Kaleb takes them two at a time. This causes the weight to tilt and jam.

Hallr yells, "You're going up too fast."

"You're too slow."

They both adjust their movement speed and continue to move up, with Hallr calling a step cadence. With consistent movement, they reach the top together. At the top, there is a flat area. Hallr can climb off the ladder and stand on the platform with the counterweight behind him. The platform is four meters deep into the rock and spans the length of the counterweight.

Kaleb is holding the counterweight from the ladder on the side. Above him is the platform. He checks and sees that the gap between the landing and the counterweight is approximately one centimeter. Kaleb is looking around and says, "Really great work. I'm holding up a rock that weighs as much as most human castles."

Meanwhile, Hallr is looking around for something to hold up the counterweight. Moving along the landing, he sees a stone pole leaning toward the counterweight. In the center is a set of stairs leading toward a small door. Past the stairs is another leaning pole.

Hallr walks back to the first pole. It is square, about twenty-five centimeters on each side. The base does not attach to the landing, but it goes through a hole. He gets under the stone pole on the side closest to the counterweight and pushes, with no effect.

Kaleb is watching. When he sees Hallr pushing on the pole,

he nods. When it doesn't move, Kaleb yells, "It's probably stuck."

Hallr nods, looking at Kaleb. He takes a step back as he looks at the pole, then moves forward, slamming his shoulder into the pole. On the floor, he hears a scraping sound as the pole moves. Hallr keeps pushing until the top of the pole is leaning toward the back wall of the landing.

Kaleb watches as Hallr moves the pole, spotting a moving stone shelf beneath the landing area. It looks four meters wide and a meter thick. He is smiling as he watches. When Hallr has fully moved the pole, the shelf is sticking out of the wall by about 50 centimeters. He yells, "Look over the side, under the counterweight."

Hallr walks over and looks at the gap between the counterweight and the shelf. He smiles at Kaleb as he walks to the other pole to move it the same way.

With both shelves out, Kaleb lowers the counterweight. The counterweight settles down on the shelf. Hallr is standing on the landing with the top of the counterweight at his head height.

Kaleb walks on the landing toward Hallr. He says, "To close the gate, we shift these two levers and jump on top. Simple and easy to close quickly. I like it."

Hallr points up. Kaleb looks up to see a water pipe. It has a valve with a stone connection going to the wall, where someone can shift the stone and open the valve. Below the valve is a group of four spouts for water to drop. They are a few meters above the tank on top of the counterweight.

Kaleb says, "A way to make the gate close quickly. That valve causes water to fall into the tank. The water drains from the tank when you need to open the gate."

Hallr says, "That is smart," as he walks up the small stairs to the door and pushes hard. The door swings into a tunnel, "This way."

Kaleb gets to the door, looking in, says, "I've got to crawl."

Hallr laughs and starts walking down the tunnel. Kaleb says, "It isn't funny, Shorty." Kaleb puts the torch out, puts it in his belt, and crawls.

The tunnel is twenty meters long. Hallr is working on the door when Kaleb crawls up. Hallr says, "It's locked."

Kaleb says, "I can't see anything without the torch. There should be a lock release if there is no keyhole."

Hallr looks and feels around the lock. On the hinge side, a metal bar protrudes. On top is a small metal bar that fits into a slot on the larger bar. He moves the little bar to the left, shoving hard. The large bar shifts, "Maybe this will do something."

He pushes the bar down, and they hear several things shifting. Ultimately, the door shifts.

Kaleb says, "That sounds promising. Let's get through."

Hallr pushes the door open. The other side of the door is a chamber. Hallr says, "This is dark."

Kaleb crawls out and stands. Hallr says, "Don't stand. Sit. If there are traps here that get triggered, you could get hurt."

Kaleb asks, "Where are we?"

Hallr says, "I'm not sure. We need to light the torch."

Kaleb pulls the torch out and then his flint. He makes sparks with the back of his knife to relight the torch.

It is so dark that Hallr can't see. He is not speaking as he stands waiting. When the torch lights up, he looks around at the walls covered in real dwarven Mithril armor and weapons.

Hallr says, "This chamber is full of Dwarven weapons and armor."

Xylia says in their heads, "The gate is open for the first time in centuries. From your reaction, you found one of the locked rooms."

Kaleb puts his flint and knife away, shifts to a knee, and looks around. "That is hard on my back. Xylia, you mentioned earlier that the city had been looted, apart from the locked rooms. This means someone locked the gate and prevented anyone from entering the gate room."

Hallr says, "Which is in the middle of the mountain, not next to the gate. Brilliant."

Kaleb says, "Can we get out?"

Hallr moves around the chamber on the left. He says, "I see a suit of armor on the floor." As he approaches closer, he says, "It's a dwarf skeleton covered in armor. Next to one hand is a large key, next to the other is a dagger. Xylia, there is a skeleton. A dwarf locked himself in and died here."

"One of the few dwarves who saved a few lives before the control witches destroyed the city."

Hallr steps over to get the key and steps on a trigger block. Spikes shoot down from the ceiling. As they descend, Kaleb goes prone, saying, "Shit."

Hallr says, "Sorry. I have the key to unlock the door."

Kaleb says, "That was close. Watch where you step."

"I'll take care where I step."

They hear water moving, and the spikes retract into the ceiling.

Looking around the walls with the torchlight, Kaleb says, "Wow. Milfred is going to scream like a girl with all this."

Hallr, with the key in hand, is looking around. Kaleb has shifted to kneeling, and from his angle, Hallr views Kaleb and the dwarven armor behind him on the wall. There are armor body parts that are way too small for him, but that helmet.

Hallr walks over, looking at Kaleb. "I want you to try something."

Kaleb furrows his brow, "We are in a locked chamber and need to get out before I get cut up, and you want to try something?"

"I found the key, but I also see something interesting."

Hallr reaches up and pulls down a large dwarven helmet. It has a nose guard in the front; otherwise; the front is open for the eyes and mouth. It is obviously Dwarven and made of Mithril. Flaps are creating an opening at the back. It will fit on a larger head. He hands it to Kaleb and says, "Put this on."

Kaleb looks perplexed. Hallr says, "Just try. If you're wearing that, you won't knock yourself out when you try to break the city walls with your head."

"Ha, hilarious."

"I'm serious. Try it on."

With a shrug, Kaleb puts on the helmet. The flaps at the back don't close. There is a four-centimeter gap.

Xylia asks, "Does it fit?"

Kaleb replies, "Yes, I need to adjust something or replace some leather. The flaps in the back don't close, but it works."

Xylia says, "Good, very good."

Hallr asks, "Xylia, why is that good? What is with him wearing the helmet?"

"It will protect his head from the walls. The others are now asking why you two haven't returned."

Hallr chuckles, and Kaleb says, "Really. That caused a very good comment."

Xylia continues, "It will also protect your mind. Mithril armor protects from control witches. That would have helped when the city fell."

Hallr holds up the key, "Time to get out of here."

Kaleb nods and shifts to follow Hallr to the door. When Hallr steps on a trigger, he yells. Kaleb reacts, trying to get down, but it is too late. The Mithril blade swings out of the wall and across Kaleb's back at the shoulders.

Hallr is holding the key, looking at Kaleb. He steps toward Kaleb, stops, turns to the door, and says, "Stay there while I open the door and get ready."

With the door open, Hallr is standing outside. "Okay, I'm not in the room, stepping on anything. You need to crawl out."

Kaleb's breathing is labored, and blood is streaming to the floor.

Hallr says, "Don't stand, just crawl."

Kaleb looks up at Hallr and, forearm over forearm, crawls toward the door. On his third arm movement, he triggers the spikes.

Hallr says, "Good, nothing will hit you when you stay low. Now move!"

Kaleb triggers traps twice before he gets to the door. Hallr grabs his arm and drags him out. "Stay there. I'm going to lock *the door."*

With the door locked, he kneels next to Kaleb. "I've got to get you to Sheyla. Can you walk, or do you want me to carry or drag you?"

"Help me up. I can walk."

Hallr says, "Xylia, tell Sheyla that Kaleb is hurt. One trap cut him on the back."

"I will tell her to be ready. Take him to the open gate."

Ask Xylia

Hallr is helping injured Kaleb to the group. He is bleeding a lot from a Mithril blade that cut across his back.

When they arrive at the gate area, he sees the wagons inside. Sheyla is standing by the wagons, not knowing where they will arrive from. She says, "Take him to one wagon and get his shirt off."

He shifts Kaleb to move him to a wagon. Milfred comes over to help, saying, "What happened, and what are you wearing?"

Kaleb says, "Mithril helmet. There is a room full of armor and weapons."

Sheyla says, "Celebrate later. Xylia, something's wrong. I can't read him; my healing isn't working."

Xylia says, "The helmet."

Sheyla blushes with embarrassment, "Of course, Mithril is blocking me. Get the helmet off him."

Agnarr has walked up after putting wagon items in a room. "Hand it to me. I'll take it to a room so that it won't impact Sheyla."

Sheyla has Kaleb sit on the floor with his back to her. She says, "Taking this leather shirt off will hurt and cause more damage. I need you to cut this off or open this area more."

Hallr nods, grunts, pulls his dagger, and grabs the cut edge of the leather to cut it off.

Kaleb asks, "I don't get a say?"

Hallr says, "No. I need you. We need you healed, healthy."

Sheyla says, "You can mend the shirt."

Hallr says, "Not by him. He can't sew."

Sheyla replies, "Perfect time for him to learn."

Now Milfred says, "The gate is open, and that's great. Tell me about finding the weapons and armor."

Kaleb says, "The gate control room. It is full of armor and weapons. A dwarf locked the room, and the only way to get to it was to open the gate and follow a tunnel."

Sheyla says, "Kaleb needs to stop talking now."

Hallr says, "There is a dwarf skeleton in the room, and that dwarf locked the room from the inside. The problem for Kaleb is the traps designed to kill anyone taller than a dwarf. Kaleb dodged a couple."

Milfred asks, "How many weapons? How much armor?"

"Enough for a dozen dwarves."

"Is there anything else, books, scrolls?"

Hallr shakes his head, "Don't remember seeing any, but I wasn't looking. Why?"

"I want to know if there are any instructions. Something for the gate function, records. Maybe there will be something about how other parts of the city work."

Hallr looks at Kaleb's back. The cut is only deep in one area. The bleeding has stopped. He says, "It's not that bad. You'll be back to normal in a day."

Kaleb says, "I'll be back to work tomorrow."

Sheyla says, "No. If I do all this work and you rip open the wound, I will not fix you again. You rest."

Hallr says, "You will be sewing. You need to learn about patching."

"What do you mean? I sew the leather along the cut."

"Then the stitching will rub your wound."

"Oh."

Agnarr says, "If you need to do something before you sew, you can help search this area of the city."

Hallr says, "I need to get the horse to Xylia."

Agnarr says, "We are in the gate, but now what? Where do we set up camp? There is no kitchen here; there are no apartments."

Milfred says, "There has to be something for guards to stay close to the gate. Some rooms or a barracks."

Agnarr says, "Sure. Something like that will work."

Kaleb says, "I'm going to look for rooms," as he stands and winces as he tries to adjust his cut-up shirt.

Sheyla says, "Sit down. I'll look. We need latrines, bathing, and cooking."

Kaleb replies, "I'll walk. Sitting on the ground isn't comfortable."

Agnarr says, "Hang on."

Hallr chuckles as Agnarr pulls out the helmet and hands it to Kaleb. "Protect your head."

Hallr gets one horse to feed Xylia. He says, "Xylia, I have a horse. I haven't traveled to your chamber from the gate area."

"I only know one path from the gate. Take the second wagon path from the left. Two hallways to the left will get you to the chamber. Someone had used this path before. The horse will become frantic when it smells me. That is why there are gates. As you travel down the hallway, you will see two enormous gates. Close them after you go through."

When Hallr closes the second gate, he turns the horse toward the dragon hall, takes off the halter, and uses the lead to smack it on the rump.

Xylia has moved. When the horse comes out of the tunnel, she picks it up, chomping down. The horse dies immediately. Xylia tilts her head up and shifts the horse. Hallr watches her bite, chewing the horse to be small enough to swallow.

Agnarr and Sheyla have found the guard barracks area. It is a two-level open area. Around the outside walls are rooms for the guards. In the middle is a long stone table with stone benches. At one end are a latrine and showers. Simple water valves to turn on the frigid water. On the lower level, on the other side, is a food preparation area. There are pits for fires and places for stoves, but there is no equipment.

After finding the area, they moved their food items from the wagons into it and began preparing dinner.

During the preparation, Kaleb says, "I'm doing nothing right now."

Hallr says, "Yes, you are, you're complaining."

When the food is ready, they are all sitting at the long table.

Agnarr says, "It has been two days since we found the city. We have saved a dragon, figured out how to open the gate, and found a place to camp. Now we need to talk about our next steps."

Sheyla says, "We need to ask Xylia more about the city. What other secrets can you tell us, Xylia?"

"My memory right now isn't the best. It has been centuries since the city was alive. Talking or asking about specific things helps me to remember things."

Kaleb asks, "Is this from starving for so long?"

"I don't know. Probably. Many things have faded."

Milfred says, "You asked what we do next. I want to know about Mithril armor. It is the most valuable armor anywhere. It is so rare now because it is all lost or destroyed. Now we can make more."

Hallr says, "Hang on. How do you destroy Mithril armor?"

Milfred says, "Not really destroy, just put it where no one can get to it. Drop it in the deep ocean, throw it into a volcano. Witches pay gold for anything Mithril."

Agnarr says, "Witches?"

When I was an apprentice, the blacksmith trainer shared a story about his childhood. Someone brought a hunk of metal the size of my fist to the blacksmith, his trainer, and asked to be made into a sword. The blacksmith couldn't melt it. That is when he knew it was Mithril. Witches showed up to buy it. They gave him ten gold coins for a small hunk of otherwise worthless metal. It was an actual exchange.

Sheyla says, "He received gold, not an illusion, because he was resistant when holding the Mithril."

Milfred nods, then says, "He then gambled it away. A man who had never gambled was then sure he would win."

Agnarr says sarcastically, "Witches."

Sheyla looks at him. Agnarr says, "Not you. You know what I mean."

"I do, but making it generic to include me does not feel good."

Xylia asks, "Now you have your treasure, it is more valuable than gold. Will you load your wagon and leave?"

Hallr says, "No. I don't give a dragon's turd about that. I'm staying."

Milfred says, "You're naturally resistant."

Sheyla says, "Completely immune when wearing a Mithril helmet."

Milfred says, "The only way to stop a powerful control coven is with Mithril as protection or a dwarf. Hallr, why do you think there are no other dwarves? Why is Mithril armor so rare?"

Kaleb looks from Milfred to Hallr, then Sheyla, "The witches. I mean, the control witches are eliminating the only thing that can stop them. Witches hunt dwarves to kill them. You said there are stories about this."

Hallr says, "Not leaving."

Agnarr laughs, "Sure. Stay. This is all about you."

Xylia says, "Old stories about control covens starting wars so humans have armies to attack dwarves."

"Without dwarves, which is most of the time, Mithril is our only defense against witches," Milfred stated, his forehead veins bulging.

Kaleb grabs Hallr's shoulder. "You have talked about doing the right thing since we met. The right thing is to stop controlling covens. We can give regular people armor to fight."

Hallr says, "I don't do that wandering around, beating my chest, saying come fight me."

Milfred says, "Hallr is right. The best thing we can do is to make as much Mithril armor as we can. Get it into the hands of fighters who will stop the covens."

Agnarr says, "I want to make armor."

Kaleb is shifting, adjusting his shirt. "I'm going to need help to get this shirt off. Where will I get the material to fix it?"

Hallr says, "From the bottom of the shirt."

Agnarr is looking around the group, "We came together from different backgrounds and started searching for this city, and now we are discussing restarting the Molgan forges. Not bad for a bunch of misfits."

Sheyla says, "Our little group of misfits."

Kaleb says, "Everyone knows my background, but I know little about any of you. Why are you here? What brought us together?"

Agnarr says, "No, we don't really know your background. You say your parents taught you. What do you know?"

"I grew up out in the country. There was farm work or studying when I was small. I studied so I wouldn't have to dig fence post holes, chop wood."

"That sounds like good stuff," says Hallr.

"I learned math, accounts, reading, and writing. I read books in multiple languages. Then Pa hurt his back. I had to work on the farm."

Sheyla says, "When we first met, you talked and understood dwarven words. How many languages do you know? Can you speak all of them?"

"I know six languages, but only reading, not speaking. I tried once, and the way the native speaker says the words is different. They couldn't understand me, and I couldn't understand them. I haven't tried since that one time."

"Working on the farm was a big change for you," says Milfred.

Kaleb says, "Yes, I had a hard time at first, until I got stronger. The local village blacksmith wanted me to help because I was big. I could make a few coppers to buy supplies by working for the blacksmith. Now I want to know about Hallr. You're so old, there are stories from back when Xylia was born."

Xylia says, "When dirt was first forming."

There are smiles from everyone except Hallr. Hallr looks at

Kaleb and says, "I created the first dirt so I would have something to dig."

Sheyla says, "Kaleb, there is more detail about your background that you need to tell us, but right now I want to hear about Hallr."

Sheyla's Past

Hallr says, "You want to know about my past. I'm simple. I grew up south of here, in Southern Stonebridge, close to Harenhal. When I lost my ma, I started wondering. It quickly became clear, when I arrived in Ondel City, that I was going to have a problem. Three different witches attacked me."

Agnarr asks, "How long ago was that?"

"Don't know for sure, something like fifty years."

Kaleb says, "Wow."

Agnarr is looking at Hallr. Shaking his head, he says, "Everyone in this group has a past. Kaleb is not as much because he is wet behind the ears. I want to know about yours."

Hallr is looking at Agnarr. He turns to each of the others, looking them each in the eyes. He takes a breath and says, "Not going to talk about it."

Xylia says, "You will need to tell them at some point."

"What could you have in your past that you're afraid to talk about?" asks Kaleb, looking confused.

Hallr turns to Milfred, "How did you become the traveling blacksmith?"

"I'll share, but you only get the short version. I've only been traveling for about ten years. The army forced me to work. After the battle we lost, the town was sacked and destroyed. My usefulness as a blacksmith saved me from death. I had to leave. Eventually, I got my wagon outfitted.

"I'm not usually one to be noticed, in the background, so I've seen many situations where control covens do bad things. Wanting to help and fight back against the covens, I needed to find Mithril. I need to make Mithril weapons and armor. If I found a dwarf along the way, even better."

After Milfred stops, there is a long minute of silence. Hallr says to Sheyla, "Will you tell us why you're considered an outcast?"

Sheyla grits her teeth and making a fist. "I don't like to talk about this."

Hallr asks, "Why?"

"Everyone who hears my story has the same reaction. They don't want to be around me or deal with me. Humans because of what I can do, and witches for the way I did it. I made the humans involved hate witches more."

Kaleb says, "It must be terrible. I can't think of anything to make us not want to be around you."

Agnarr says, "I don't want to tell my past either. You start."

Sheyla hangs her head, takes a breath. Looking up at everyone, she starts.

"My parents had a problem with me. I was like Meriel. I would ask, and people would do what I wanted. It started causing problems. As a little kid, I didn't have boundaries with what I asked people to do. My parents didn't know what to do with me. My parents locked me in a room most days so that I couldn't do anything bad. Then the witch came. She told my parents she would take care of me and train me."

"Saying the witch took me is wrong. My parents told her to take me. They never wanted to see me again. The witch took me, and I was told I could be a controller. In the first few weeks of training, she changed her statements about the controllers. She said I could be a top controller witch, but she needed to take me to a coven for that kind of training. The problem for me was that I found out the cost and what control covens actually do. The witch took me to an ancient witch and gave me to her. She was very old and very crazy. I was told I could be a powerful controller. She was my leader."

"The top controller, witch is the primary illusion creator. They always go crazy, or their minds turn to mush. Not what I wanted. They go crazy because they spend all their time trapped in an illusion they've created. The more they stay in the illusion, the harder it becomes to go back to reality."

Kaleb says, "Seriously. They get stuck in their own illusions. I wouldn't do the control thing if that were the result."

Sheyla nods, "After learning what they did to others' lives, I decided I needed to leave, but that is a problem. Covens don't let people leave. I was learning to control, getting powerful. After a couple of years, I was stronger than everyone else except the top witch. I was strong enough to get away. I was nine years old."

Hallr says, "You were like Merial."

She nods and continues, "They wanted me to take the lead on a few projects. We were getting merchants to give the coven money, lots of money. With a little push, a merchant hired a gang to hunt us down. There were attempts to talk, negotiate, and control, and it kept getting worse. In the chaos of everyone trying to escape, I tried to run. The controller had the men bring me back."

"I was fighting back when the gang returned. Adding to the chaos of the fighting, I ran. The next three days I spent afraid and hiding."

Agnarr is looking at Sheyla, his eyes narrowed. "You need to give us the entire story."

Lips compressed, staring back at Agnarr, she shook her head and continued. "Not every detail. I found a farmer leaving the city after selling his crops at the market. I used control to make him hide me. To get me out of the city."

Milfred shrugs, "That doesn't sound terrible."

Sheyla takes a breath, "He got me out. That night, I slipped away from his wagon. I didn't want to control him anymore. I was walking on the road at night when I heard the riders. They followed the farmer. Someone must have seen me getting into his wagon. They killed him when he wouldn't tell them where I was. He didn't know, but they didn't believe him."

Agnarr shakes his head, "But you didn't stop them and expose yourself. That was good, smart."

"More days of hiding, hunger, and walking. I found a ride, a real ask, not controlling someone for a ride into the next town. As soon as I got out of the wagon, I sensed her."

Hallr shifts, "Maybe something interesting now."

"What does that mean?" asks Sheyla.

"Your story so far is you doing things to survive. I have no issues with what you said. Even the farmer. If you hadn't done those things, you would probably have been dead."

Sheyla looks at Hallr, who is dismissive of what she went through. Frustrated, she continues, "I sensed a powerful witch. At that point, she didn't know I could sense her. I tried to disappear into the market crowd, but she knew the town and followed. When she caught up to me, she was more than simply aggressive. She was territorial and wanted to know why I was in her town. I was told I couldn't stay in her town."

Kaleb gives a confused look and asks, "Is that a normal thing?"

Agnarr replies, "Yes, just like any vendor. You live by selling services. Competition can hurt your ability to make a living."

Sheyla continues, "She was the town healer and thought I was coming in to compete or take over her town. I didn't tell her I was trying to escape the coven at that point. I explained my coven was dead, and I was just hiding, searching for a teacher."

Milfred says, "She became your mentor, your teacher."

"Yes. Because I was so young, she took a chance. It took time to work out our relationship. I was learning to heal. I liked it. Then, a year later, it changed. A gang came into the town with several injured members. This is when I learned a new term. A new enemy. They were witch bounty hunters. They tracked witches, captured them, and collected a bounty for delivering them to a king or magistrate for execution.

Agnarr says, "They would search for control witches, but they didn't care."

Sheyla nods, "After healing the members, they drugged me. I never saw the other witch again. To keep their captives controlled, they forced us to swallow drugs. I have vague memories of being raped, of traveling in a cage."

Hallr shifts, looking at Sheyla, "Did you kill them?"

Agnarr shifts his gaze from Sheyla to Hallr and says, "Let her tell the story."

"My next clear memory was waking in a cage wagon with four other witches. We were taken out of the cage and into an underground cell. They didn't drug us as much. They were collecting witches to take to another kingdom."

Kaleb is now working on the leather flaps of the helmet. Hallr is showing him how to work the leather thread into the metal flaps. Hallr says, "Just like sewing."

Kaleb says, "You obviously got away. You look like this is making you upset."

They all hear Xylia comment, "Sheyla, you did what was necessary. You seem just as concerned about them learning how powerful you are, not just what you did or how you did it. Don't worry."

Milfred looks surprised at that comment. He looks at Agnarr, who is showing no expression.

Sheyla continues, "There were eight of us when we went back into the cage wagon. Drugged and traveling for I don't know how long. One day, they didn't apply the drugs, and I focused. I learned they didn't give us the drugs because they were fighting another bounty hunter group. The next day, I could apply enough control to the guy giving us the drugs to convince him that he had given us the drugs. But he didn't give us any drugs."

Kaleb is nodding and says, "Yes."

"I waited. The drugs needed to wear off more. I needed to be less fuzzy. In the middle of the night, I started. I had the leader convinced that the other group would give up their captives. Combine the captives to get a better deal. He needed to meet with the other leader. Two men, with no weapons, just to talk. Then the real work started. He needed to send a messenger to have a meeting."

Xylia says, "Your discipline, at that age, at this point was perfect. I have encountered many individuals who have maintained that level of discipline under those conditions. That is a reason for me to trust you."

Sheyla takes a shaky breath. She wipes away a tear. "I didn't know the other leader. I needed the leader of the gang holding me to be close to read him, to control the other leader."

Milfred's face changes as he realizes what he is hearing. He sits back, "Holy crap. Someone you've never met, someone you've never seen. That specific person was the target. Is that normal to use one person to get to another?"

"Control witches don't have to see the person. They have to sense them and be close. Usually, they focus on the highest person, the king, the leader, and they work to get close to them. This is different. To control one specific person from a long distance, someone you've never met and don't know, is virtually impossible. I use the connection person and sense when he is talking to the actual target."

Agnarr is looking intently, interested. "I've never heard of this. Did the coven teach you this?"

Sheyla shakes her head. "I learned it from the healer. She showed me how to connect with an injured person through someone they knew. A kid could find the witch, then run to the wounded person. The witch could begin healing before she was close to the person."

"I used it, corrupted it. When I connected with the other leader, I frightened him. I got him to believe that the original leader was a controller trying to trap him. It was intense. At the same time, I had the original leader being passive, and the rest of both groups thinking the others were really witches."

Hallr says, "Bloody dragons. You make it sound so easy."

Sheyla grits her teeth and says, "NO. I had blood dripping from my nose while bent over, holding my head. My head felt as if it was being ripped apart. I was also projecting to the rest of the group. The other witches in the wagon no longer felt drugged. They reacted. They saw the men fighting. First, they backed away from me, screaming. Then they got aggressive."

Sheyla stops. Xylia says, "Tell them."

Sheyla says, "I had to be aggressive back to them. I had to hurt several of them. They yelled at me, screaming that I was evil. In those moments of intense conflict, the two leaders clashed. One smashed the other's head in with a rock. After that, chaos ensued, and I got one hunter to unlock the cage. The other witches ran out, leaving me alone to deal with the remaining hunters."

"When I woke up, there was only one hunter left alive. He was wounded and needed help. We made a bargain. He would get me to a safe city if I healed him and helped us both get away from the area."

Kaleb says, "Wait. Hang on. What happened to the rest of them?"

Sheyla is hanging her head, breathing slowly. Tears were dripping from her nose. "I projected to all of them that the others were witches. I made them all think the others were controlling them, so they saw witches. The only way to stop it was to kill them all until they found the real controller."

Hallr chuckles. "You were the real controller, but they didn't know. That is so clever, and a little evil."

Sheyla nods.

Xylia says, "The technique you described was not what I sensed in your memory. I'm impressed. I've never heard of someone projecting a control illusion that multiple people experience, and each is different."

Hallr gets up, looks at Sheyla while she is hanging her head crying, and walks around the table. He sits on the bench next to Sheyla. Just sits down, saying nothing.

Milfred says, "The hunter you helped? He didn't think it was you?"

"He thought I was a healer. That is all I ever said. I was ten, not an old controller witch."

Agnarr leans forward, "What happened to the hunter you helped?"

"I healed him, and we got out of the area. When we got to the next city, I left. I stole different clothes and was heading away when I heard yelling. Several of the witches who escaped were working *together and found the hunter. They used daggers when they killed him."*

Agnarr asks, "What did you do then?"

"I looked for a coven of healers. None would accept me. They are hard to find and very protective. The story about the witch hunters fighting the evil controller made them paranoid. I lived on the fringe."

Milfred shifts, "Ten. You had to survive on your own."

Sheyla smirks, "I'm the evil one. When I could do a healing for money, I did, which was rare. I spent several years trading services for training in magic. Healing mostly, but whatever I could find. Including controlling when I didn't have other options."

Agnarr says, "Then you heard about the kids."

"No. I would cause issues in a town and have to move. I became a wanderer like Hallr. Then I learned about options for healing wealthy people. I traveled from war to war. I would heal and get money to travel, which turned into looking for the next war."

Agnarr says, "War areas are dangerous."

"Not as much when I ride in a supply wagon and stay around the medical area. If they pissed me off and I had no other choice, I would leave a body to be found later. If anyone suspected I was involved, I used control magic to change their mind."

Agnarr says, "You were at the battle on the Graystone side, and you heard about the kids."

"Yes. I had to get to them. Prevent them from getting trapped like I almost was."

Hallr says, "What about you, Agnarr? What is your terrible past?"

Sheyla looks at Hallr, "What. You don't care what I did? I thought you would be horrified. You're the one who hates witches."

Hallr smiles.

Kaleb says, "I don't know. Was that bad?"

Hallr says, "I have spent half my life fighting witches. They wanted to control me, to kill me. Every witch that I interacted with would attack me. Then I met you. You wanted to talk and would get frustrated but wouldn't argue very hard. You would walk away when I pushed. Together, we have faced attacks, fought other controllers, discovered a lost city, and you saved a dragon from death. You've proven to me you're a capable member of our little outcast group. You did what needed to be done."

Agnarr says, "You kept a dragon from dying. Right after we met, you said you could have done more with the witch that attacked Hallr. How strong are you?"

Xylia says, "I have met many strong humans; only a couple could have done what she did to keep me alive. There are many more disgusting human minds I've read. Sheyla said she is the evil one. She could have been much more evil, easily. Her integrity is also a strength; her power."

Hallr shifts, leans toward Sheyla. "Sheyla. I don't say your name often. Sheyla, I don't have a problem with what you did. Now that you've finally told me, I'm thinking I have an ally in a fight."

Sheyla smiles, tears streaming down, then laughs. "A dwarf and a controller witch, allies fighting covens. That would be a story people would say is from ancient times."

Taking a breath, Sheyla wipes the back of her arm across her eyes, then uses her hand to wipe her nose and mouth. She turns and wipes her hand on Hallr's sleeve. "Enough of that. I'm changing the subject."

Hallr looks down at his sleeve where she wiped her hand, then says, "What subject? Something depressing this time?"

Kaleb smiles, "Let's talk about food."

Sheyla says, "No. Xylia told me I need to share my past with Hallr, and he needed to share his past. The new subject is Hallr's past."

Hallr shifts away from Sheyla, shaking his head.

Xylia says, "Now is the time."

Hallr puts both arms on top of the table, making fists with both hands. "My story is way worse than yours."

Kaleb says, "So you say, but you have said nothing yet."

"I was traveling, getting attacked frequently. I had been injured in the last big fight and spent time in a forest just recovering. Out of food, I went to town. I think they had been waiting for days."

Kaleb asks, "Who was waiting?"

"A group of witches, the remains of the coven I fought before when I was wounded. The attack started with a couple of large men. I think they were surprised when I actually walked into town, and those two were the first they could send at me."

Milfred says, "It started with two men. That doesn't sound bad for you."

"After the two, there were three more. I was getting frustrated and hungry. I could fight. Then it all changed." Hallr makes a fist, pounds the table, and shakes his head. "I love children, but that day changed me."

Sheyla stretches her arm, putting her hand on Hallr, "I didn't realize."

Kaleb asks, "What?"

Hallr says, "They got all the children from the village, gave them knives and sent them to attack me. I tried to leave. I didn't realize they channeled me to the traps. Bear traps. My leg was in a trap; I couldn't escape, and they were stabbing me."

Agnarr says, "That was cruel. Wrong."

"I started killing them." Hallr pauses, shaking his head. "When the kids were dead, I pried the trap open and hunted them down. That was the day I changed. I vowed to kill the controller witches. To hunt any witch that would hurt children."

Sheyla shakes her head. "I'm sorry."

Agnarr says, "That explains so many things. The way you acted around the children, with Merial. The way you first acted with Sheyla."

Hallr says, "You were close to getting an axe until you talked about helping the children."

Milfred smiles. "The only ones who can stand each other are all outcasts concerned the others won't accept our secrets."

Xylia says, "You all have a past. You are all afraid of others knowing because they will judge you. Because they will reject you. Yet you travel together, fight together, and support each other without knowing the information. Now that you know what has really changed. The people you see around the table are no different from before they told their story."

Hallr smiles, "Yes, we are different. Now they all know my secret. That is a commitment."

Xylia says, "You committed to each other when you started looking for the city. We need to talk about food."

Kaleb says, "Yes, as bad as your stories are, can we talk about food now?"

Sheyla smiles, "Always start with your stomach. We are in the city, trapped by a storm, but we don't have food to stay."

Milfred growls, "We have to find a way. We can't abandon the city now."

Agnarr says, "To bring supplies to the city, we will need two horses and a wagon. We need to feed the other horses to Xylia and plan on leaving."

Hallr says, "No."

"Hang on. Xylia said something about mushrooms yesterday. What is that about?" asks Kaleb.

Xylia says, "Mushrooms are grown in deep levels of the city."

Sheyla feels Hallr shift. Looking at him, she can see his mind churning. "What is it?"

"The city can't run on just mushrooms. There has to be something else. You grow mushrooms with human and dwarf shit, but that can't be all."

Xylia says, "And dragon shit. And the mushrooms feed the humans and dwarves, but mostly they feed the chickens."

Kaleb, looking confused, asks, "Chickens?"

Agnarr asks, "Xylia, please explain."

"Certainly. Mushrooms are grown to feed multiple levels of

chickens in multiple large coop areas. They lay eggs, and the chickens can be eaten. My diet was mostly chicken for centuries. For the people, add vegetables from the valley, and everything works."

"The valley. What valley?" asks Agnarr.

There is silence for half a minute. "Xylia?"

"Sorry. Memories of the fight when the city died. There is a hidden valley. It has no passes or any other way to get to it except through the city."

Hallr asks, "How did the dwarves get to it?"

"Let me finish. This location for the city, where it was built, was chosen because of the mountain and the valley together. They dug and built here for two reasons. The ore in the mountain and to have access to the valley. Unless you can fly, the only way to get to the valley is through the city."

Kaleb asks, "Where is the path?"

"It is sealed. During the fight for the city, a dwarf was instructed to seal the gates on the path to the valley. Without access to the valley, the city can't survive."

Milfred says, "This is one of the locked areas no one can access."

"Yes, but I don't know if the valley access can be opened with a key. I've never seen the gates. I know there was more than one gate, so simply breaking one is futile."

Milfred says, "They must have tried and given up. That is why the attackers stripped and abandoned the city."

Agnarr says, "The information that the valley existed was lost."

Hallr adds, "The treasure was the focus."

Xylia says, "Exactly. I was trapped. They knew about my treasure and kept coming for that. It was how I survived all this time. My food came to me."

Kaleb shudders, "Wow."

Sheyla says, "That is all nice to know. How do we get food now? Mushrooms? Chickens? How do we get to this hidden *valley?*

Hallr says, "We need to search the city and find the gates."

The Fertile Valley Gate

The next day, while they are eating at midday, Agnarr says, "We will need to feed Xylia again soon. She is getting much stronger, but she was so emaciated that we can't stop feeding her. Hallr, unless you find the gate to that valley today, we will have to feed her another horse."

Hallr says, "We're looking. Kaleb found the rubble of a broken door. After checking the wall that seemed like a dead end, I realized it was a hidden door. It is locked somehow. There is also a path that leads to a collapsed rock area. The path to the valley has to be one of those two."

Kaleb says, "That solid rock door they destroyed was over a meter thick, with three centimeter-thick steel on the back. It took a while for the attackers to get through.

Agnarr says, "I'll try to help with the door. My lock-picking skills are pretty bad, but I'll try."

Sheyla says, "I'll finish setting up a living area. We need to organize the supplies we have and set up the cooking area. We will start rationing until we find another food source."

Kaleb says, "I found the water valve for the cooking area. Just leave it running for now."

"That is a great help. Instead of hauling water from the shower area to clean and cook. Thanks."

Kaleb says, "Check my shoulder, then Agnarr, and I will pick a lock."

Sheyla says, "Not bleeding. The scar is forming. No heavy lifting for several days."

At the broken door area, Agnarr is looking at the remains of a solid rock door, twelve meters across and over a meter thick. He says, "Wide enough for wagons and people to move in both directions. How did it move?"

Kaleb asks, "Right here in the middle. That hole was the pivot. The gate was balanced on both sides, so it just took some work to swing it. What are you looking for?"

"We opened the gate to the courtyard when we figured out the puzzle to move the rock. I'm looking to see if there are any parts of the lock for the broken gate I can see. It will help with the next door."

"That is over here," says Kaleb.

Kaleb takes Agnarr to a large rock with a steel plate attached to it. He bends to push the rock, and Agnarr says, "No. Don't move it and hurt your back."

Agnarr shifts around and puts his hand out, using his push magic to shift the rock to show the steel.

Kaleb says, "This is the only part of the steel left, probably because it is attached so well. I think they poured the molten metal into the section to attach it."

Agnarr moves around the rock to get another angle. He looks at the wall. "How does it lock into the wall?"

Kaleb says, "It looks like a steel plate that slides is attached to the back of the door. It goes into this slot. But the rock here has grooves on the sides. I think this moves up."

"The door is pulled closed, then the steel bar slides into the lock." Looking at the opening, then putting his hand in, Agnarr says, "The rock has a notch inside. This rock would need to go up for the steel to slide in."

Kaleb nods, "I think the bar on the door had a spring. There is scraping on the wall."

"To close this, someone moves the rock up, and another person closes the door and slides the steel in, lowers the rock, and it is locked."

Xylia says, "That doesn't sound right."

Kaleb asks, "What do you mean?"

Xylia says, "One of the last with a helmet was commanded to lock the gates to the valley. They were alone when they locked the gate. I don't know what happened to them after the explosion *dropped the ceiling on me."*

"Xylia, do you know how this works?"

"No. Never seen it, can't describe it, but one dwarf operated it."

Agnarr says, "So the steel plate would slide in when the rock is lifted. It would need to be pushing, ready to lock; that would be the spring."

Kaleb says, "One dwarf can operate it. All you need to do is use your push magic, make that go up."

Agnarr shakes his head, then looks at Kaleb. "I'm not all-powerful. Also, if the lock is the same as this door, after the rock is lifted, the steel plate has to slide out. How am I supposed to move both at the same time through a meter-thick door?"

"They made everything so it would be easy if you know how it works. One dwarf to lock and unlock it."

"Kaleb, looking at the next door, it was only accessed from the inside. It was designed to lock people out," says Agnarr.

Kaleb says, "Stay with your original idea; figure out how this one works. Let's be systematic. Use your push on the wall and see if something moves."

"Sure, that is a good suggestion."

Kaleb has his head bent down as usual, watching the wall while Agnarr is a couple of meters back and pushing. Kaleb comments, "The seams for the blocks in the wall have a pattern. It must be hiding a part that moves."

About three meters from the lock, Agnarr pushes, and Kaleb says, "I heard something."

Kaleb pushes against parts of the wall, but nothing moves. He kneels to examine a seam lower down. "There has to be something."

Standing, he puts his hand up to prevent himself from hitting the ceiling with his head, and a stone moves. "Wow, look at this."

Agnarr looks at Kaleb, pushing against a stone in the ceiling. It is a lever arm with another section lowering in the middle of the wide hallway. At the wall, there is a small gap at the top of the stone.

Agnarr pushes on the top of the stone, and it pivots, causing the bottom to move out and revealing a slot to grab.

Kaleb chuckles, "Simple, easy, once you know."

Kaleb lets go of the ceiling stone, grabs the bottom handle, and lifts. He grunts and lets go.

Agnarr says, "Stop. You're going to rip open that wound."

Grabbing the bottom, Agnarr lifts the lever and pivots the arm. After a few centimeters of movement, he says, "Okay, it is now touching something inside."

Continuing to lift the handle, the stone inside the wall scrapes as the lever within it moves, and the lock stone shifts upward.

Agnarr is shaking his head, "That is incredible workmanship to make that big stone move so easily."

"Yep, a kid could do this."

Hallr is walking up to them and says, "Did you figure it out?"

Looking at the situation, Agnarr says, "Yes. Now we know how it works, and I know I can't do that for the other door."

Hallr asks, "What? Why not?"

"I can't push a lever down three meters that way. I need to be above it."

"Kaleb, show me where to push and pull. Let me see while Agnarr explains what he CAN do again."

Agnarr lets go of his lever, and it swings down into place, stopping just before being flush because of the ceiling part. He pushes the bottom with the toe of his boot, and it locks into place with a thud.

Agnarr says, "I push or pull to me. I can't make a rock go sideways across the room. It has to be me pushing it with my magic, just like if I were pushing it with my hands."

Kaleb points and says to Hallr, "Push here. Then push at the top here. Now the bottom is out enough to reach down and pull up. That causes the connection inside the wall to make the lock column over there move up."

Kaleb says, "Can you push the lever on the other side, or just what you see?"

"I've never tried to push something I'm not looking at. I don't know."

Hallr says, "I can see what Kaleb is getting at. You need to practice. I have to go look at what is above this hallway."

Hallr turns and walks off, and Agnarr says, "Above this hallway, what does that do?"

Kaleb is shifting stones on the floor. One as a tiny wall. Behind it, away from Agnarr, he places a smaller stone. He describes what he wants to try: "If you can push the lever inside the wall, the one you can't see, we may be able to do this. I will describe more after you try this. Squat down so you can't see this smaller stone, then push it through the larger stone. Don't move the larger one."

After a couple of attempts, Agnarr can get the smaller stone to move, but he also moves the larger stone. Kaleb says, "We need to practice this."

"We? You got a magic mouse in a pouch?"

"If you can do this and Hallr can find the area above, we can open that door. If you are above the lever, you can push it down, just like this stone here. I lift, and the top pushes down on a lever in the wall to move the lock."

"What about the metal bar that goes into the wall lock?"

"For that part, I'm counting on one dwarf to lock and unlock it. Let me show you what I think."

Kaleb goes to the ceiling to release the wall lever. He says, "Pull that up so I can grab it."

He grabs the lower handle and pulls the lever up. It pushes down on the lever in the wall, which lifts the lock stone. When Kaleb has the handle lifted all the way, they can see that the slot for the lock stone has a ramp at the bottom. Kaleb says, "See that ramp. I think the stone will push out the steel lock bar."

Nodding Agnarr walks to the wall, looking past the lever stone Kaleb is holding, and looking into the wall. "That is a bigger lever with a huge part on the end."

Kaleb says, "The counterweight makes it easy to lift the lock stone."

Agnarr says, "Seeing it inside the wall makes an enormous difference. I know what to do; I don't know if my push will work."

A couple of hours later, Agnarr can move the small rock without shifting the larger one. Hallr walks down the hall, carrying something. "Time to take some measurements."

Agnarr looks at Hallr, questioning. Kaleb says, "Measure what?"

"There are rooms above here. I don't know the exact spot, so I have a string, and we will measure a few things to get Agnarr close in the room above and see what happens. First, we measure the distance from the lock stone to that lever."

Hallr takes the long string and ties a knot to mark the distance. "Now, the distance between doors. Then the distance from this first door to the hallway intersection back there."

In the rooms above, Kaleb says, "I didn't follow your measurements to get here. Are you sure this is above the door lever below?"

"It's not perfect, but it should be good enough for Agnarr. From my point of view, Agnarr, we can't get to the lever directly because of this wall. You push down through the floor in this area. Push hard several times."

Agnarr nods, "I'm going to be systematic again. I will start here, move that way, then shift and repeat the pattern. I will need to push on the end of the counterweight lever to get the door unlocked."

Hallr says, "Kaleb, go down to the door. Yell when it opens."

"You won't be able to hear me."

"Xylia can, and she can tell us."

Xylia says, "Smart dwarf. With a city full of humans and dwarves, I would only hear noise from all the minds. With only you five, I can hear what you say."

After six pushes, Xylia says, "Kaleb said there was a noise, something moved. More in that area."

Agnarr shifts to the center of the area next to the wall and *pushes again in a pattern.*

Xylia says, "Kaleb says it's open."

Agnarr turns to Hallr, who has his fist out toward Agnarr. Agnarr returns the fist bump, and Hallr says, "That's using magic."

When they reach the hallway, Kaleb opens the door, and thirty meters away, they see light. The hallway is now bright from the light coming in. They walk to the opening together to look at the hidden valley.

Just before the opening, the hallway expands to twice its original width. Hallr says, "I would say forty meters across with the ceiling high enough for a wagon with a driver. They probably had wagons going in and out all the time."

On the left side, there are the remains of a collapsed wagon. It was there and decayed over the centuries.

To the right, against the wall, is a pile of armor. Agnarr walks toward it, looking around. He says, "What happened here?"

They walk to a skeleton with a suit of mithril armor. It is on its side with a sword through its ribs. Hallr says, "Xylia, there is a dead dwarf with a sword through it. I thought a dwarf locked the doors and was alone."

"That is what I understood."

Agnarr puts his hand on Hallr's shoulder, "They killed themselves. If witches could get into their minds, influence or threaten them, they could have them open the gates. This one dwarf stopped them."

Kaleb says, "Hallr, the dwarf at the gate control, had a dagger in his hand. Their sacrifice prevented the attackers from occupying the city. But dwarves are resistant to magic, especially with Mithril helmets. I don't understand."

Xylia says, "A lot was going on during the fighting. I couldn't hear much. One thing repeated by the leaders was, 'Don't let them guilt you into opening doors'; they will threaten to kill your family."

Agnarr shakes his head. "Covens can be cruel."

Hallr's jaw is set. He squats next to the skeleton and says, "Thank you. I'll put you to rest where you deserve to be."

Kaleb asks, "Xylia, what is the dwarf custom for burial?"

"Back to the land. They would clear a section of land to bury the dead. Let the bodies renew the land. After that section was full of burials, they would plant trees and move to another section. Eventually, they would get back to that section after the trees had been harvested. Any bones they found would be crushed and mixed with the soil. The cycle was trees to farmland to graves to trees in a cycle, taking decades."

Hallr says, "We'll start that again. We will have to start with the clearing."

Walking out of the wide opening, they look across the valley. Agnarr says, "This valley is huge. Trees for lumber, an enormous lake in the center."

They all see their breath in the cold air, gazing out at the valley floor covered in snow.

Kaleb is nodding, looking out. "The road is serpentine to make it easier for heavy wagons. That looks like a collapsed structure."

Agnarr says, "I see another one on the right. That one in the trees could be a mill."

Xylia says, "Farms for food and wool, timber production. There was even a vineyard on the other side of the valley from that entrance. They told me the wine was good, but it was only used on special occasions. Beer. Dwarves drank lots of beer."

Hallr nods, "I can get into that."

Kaleb asks, "Xylia, what does it take to make beer?"

"Barley, as the grain, water, yeast, and hops. No fire, just put it into a barrel and drink when fermentation is done. I know this because dwarves love to talk about the finer points of brewing beer. They don't shut up about it. Or they didn't. I miss that."

Kaleb asks, "You said there are chickens?"

"There should be, I can't say for sure."

As Xylia is talking, they hear a faint chicken squawk, then another. They see a deer bound out of the trees, followed by several *chickens running, being chased by a wolf.*

Kaleb says, "Let's see if we can have chicken for dinner," as he heads down the road.

Agnarr says, "I'm heading back. We need to bring the wagons and the horses over here."

Hallr nods, "Good thinking. Hey Kaleb, we're going back. You should get some armor before you venture into wolf territory." To Agnarr, "Let's go."

The next day, everyone is at the valley entrance. They have moved the wagons and they have their horses that can be taken down to graze. The air is frosty, but they can see the snow beginning to melt.

Sheyla asks, "Xylia, are there structures, something we should check?"

Agnarr says, "First, we need to know about the horses; we can't take them down to be attacked by wolves."

"Yes, there were several structures. It is hard to tell you exactly where they are located. I flew over them centuries ago. There was a logging facility closer to the city entrance on the south side of the valley. East and west were farming, while the north side was devoted to sheep. They kept the sheep away from me, so I wasn't tempted. Up the slopes are vineyards, hops growing, and a bean they called coffee."

Kaleb asks, "Sheep for wool?"

"And leather, and meat. They also milked them for butter and cheese."

Hallr has a pep in his step, smiling. Kaleb says, "You like that. Your ancestors had it all figured out."

"Dam straight. If they've been left alone for centuries, there will probably be lots of sheep. We can get meat and hide going."

Milfred says, "You already said there are wolves."

Xylia says, "And bears in the hills."

Sheyla says, "Great. Wolves can be dangerous. Kaleb, you should wear full armor before you venture far."

Kaleb replies, "Doesn't fit. I'll make do with forearms."

Agnarr says, "We can take a horse and check everything in a couple of days."

Hallr says, "No horses. They will be targets for the wolves. Kaleb and I will go out on day trips."

Agnarr says, "That will take weeks to cover the valley. The snow will slow you down."

Hallr asks, "Are you in a hurry for something?"

Kaleb says, "You don't ride a horse, so you don't want to use them."

"You're so big you shouldn't be riding a horse either."

Explore the Valley

After the first day walking in the valley, Kaleb says, "This is ridiculous. Agnarr is right. We need to use the horses."

Hallr says, "Then I guess Agnarr and Milfred are exploring. I'm not riding a horse, and you can focus on getting the chicken farming going."

"And what are you going to do?"

"I need to find tools, coal, iron, and some Mithril to mine."

Each night at the evening meal, they gather to share what they have accomplished and what they plan to do. On the second day of exploring, they each gave a summary.

Agnarr tells them, "I only got partway around the north side of the valley. What Xylia described is there, but everything is collapsed, broken, and unusable. We may be able to dig out usable tools. The fields have a mixture of whatever was there. Everything is overgrown. The area with grazing deer is slightly better. Inside one of the old buildings, I got the chicken for dinner and found a chicken nest with a dozen eggs. I plan to go south tomorrow and check toward the mill."

Kaleb says, "I have the eggs in a warm box. With what we have collected, we could hatch over thirty chicks. That will be a great start to the farm."

Milfred says, "I checked the furnaces, forges, and know what we need. Two of the biggest issues I see right now are that everything needs maintenance and that I need to turn on the drive power for some equipment. I need to figure out the power source for the bellows. They are big, turned by a stone shaft. I don't know what makes the shaft turn. Without those bellows, we can't turn the ore into iron and forge any new tools we need. I'll be searching for the power source tomorrow."

Kaleb says, "The power is probably water. You will need to find *out how they turn falling water into power."*

<<<>>>

During breakfast, Milfred asks Hallr and Kaleb about the gate guardhouse's location and what else they saw.

"Yes, we heard water," says Kaleb.

Hallr says, "It sounded like a waterfall."

An hour later, Milfred is cursing, "Damm dwarf tunnels. I need a helmet. Just follow the water sound, they said."

After multiple wrong turns, Milfred steps onto a balcony overlooking a chamber. In front of him is a large, broken water wheel. To the right is a large waterfall, with water flowing from the wall five meters above the wheel.

The wheel is large, made of steel with wooden paddles that have fallen apart over the centuries. An internal structure allows for the wooden paddles to be spaced every 2 meters along its 10 meters of width. The wheel sits in a large base and connects to the stone shaft that goes into the wall.

"This is what drives the bellows and the factory machines. I have to fix the largest water wheel I've ever seen. Each paddle on the wheel is about one meter across and ten meters wide. I can't make those. Maybe I can make two-meter sections to get it moving."

Back at the barracks area, Milfred asks Agnarr, "Did you see a sawmill? Something that can make lumber?"

"Yes, but it is broken. It will have to be repaired to make anything. Why?"

"I found a water wheel that drives the shaft I need for the bellows. The wheel needs wooden boards to be repaired and turned."

"We can talk to Kaleb about working on it in the spring."

Milfred says, "At dinner, we need to talk about what is in the valley."

At dinner, they are giving the update, and Milfred asks about *what is in the valley.*

Agnarr says, "What I have explored matches what Xylia told us. Nothing is working. Everything is falling apart. I'm going to work on a corral or pen for the sheep. Keep them in a confined area and help keep the wolves out. I will need help with chopping saplings for the fence."

Kaleb asks, "Can we keep wolves out?"

Hallr is shaking his head. "You can't keep them out. You need to create traps."

Broken Wing

A month later, they are on the second day of a powerful storm. The snow in the valley is getting too deep, so they can't work or explore. Kaleb is working on his chicken farm inside. "Xylia, I've got chicks, some slightly older ones. When will we start getting eggs?"

"I don't know, Kaleb, I'm not a chicken farmer. I'm a chicken eater. The dwarves talked about the egg-laying hens being in the top pens. They receive more light through skylights. The breeders are also all at the top. Chickens will eat a lot of mushrooms. There are many things you are going to have to figure out."

"By spring, I may have enough adults to have the cycle going continuously."

"Hate to burst your big bubble, fake giant, but it will be months before that farm can feed me. You will spend more time harvesting mushrooms. You need to keep those farms going."

"The mushrooms are so overgrown that it will take months to get to the growing beds. I will not harvest more than I need and have it go bad," says Kaleb. "That is too much effort when the mushrooms could go bad."

"I will be on a sheep diet for months."

Kaleb says, "I know. We get a sheep, take meat for stew or kabobs, and you get the rest. We see fewer wolves, but we will have a few carcasses. While I'm working on the chicken stuff, tell me about the forges. I want to talk about Mithril."

"I don't want to talk about that."

"Why?"

"I can't help with that anymore."

"Tell me the details. What did you help with? Why can't you?"

"Come to the chamber, and I will tell you."

Kaleb furrows his brow as he throws a chicken into the pen and closes the door. "Okay, that doesn't sound like something I want to hear. Milfred will also want to hear this story."

"It's not a cheerful story."

Sitting in the gold chamber, next to the fountain, Kaleb is watching Xylia. "It has been about a month, and you are looking better. Are those new scales forming?"

"Yes, I'm doing much better. There are some new scales. Those will take about a year to fully grow back."

Milfred walks into the chamber, sees Kaleb, and walks over. "Are we going to learn some Mithril secrets?"

Xylia says, "Yes. The punchline first. We can't smelt Mithril anymore."

Milfred looks confused. "Why not? We have the forges, the molds, and there is even an ore that is ready."

"There is no smelting without dragon fire."

Kaleb sits up, looking at Xylia. "Say that again."

"It takes dragon fire to smelt Mithril. The furnaces you have, using coal, will get hot enough to smelt iron, but won't get hot enough for Mithril."

"Okay, but we have you to make dragon fire."

Xylia points her snout up, toward the ceiling, and makes a noise, and a fire ring, like a smoke ring, rises to the ceiling. "I can make fire, but a puff that will burn you to a crisp isn't the same as Mithril."

Milfred is standing and looking at Xylia. "I thought that as you get stronger, you can make stronger dragon fire."

"Yes, but not enough. Let me be clear. To smelt Mithril, you need the hottest fire. That level of fire takes everything I have. I strain to get that hot and to keep it going long enough. The dwarves planned for a month for a few minutes of my fire. It takes a strong, healthy dragon. I can't do that anymore."

"Why not? What do you need?"

"I need a healed wing that doesn't hurt to strain. When I strain or tense, my wing hurts. The pain is extreme."

"Can we help? Can Sheyla do something?"

"The little healer could barely keep me from dying. She would need to break the wing, position it, and start the healing process. You think that little human can do that?"

Kaleb is intent, "We will all help. Sorry, Xylia, I'm not even talking about making Mithril. Just getting you healed. We will help."

Xylia puts her head down. "Having a dream will be good for you."

That evening, while they are eating, they are around the table. Hallr had brought potatoes, carrots, and turnips from the valley. They were eating lamb stew.

Kaleb says, "We need to fix Xylia's wing."

Sheyla says, "Stop fixating on Mithril."

"Not Mithril. We need to heal Xylia. She is stronger; she could fly again. I'll dig her out."

Sheyla replies, "Back to you thinking I can heal a dragon. You are delusional."

"We will all help. The more important part is that you don't have to heal her. WE need to get her wing in the right spot. You start the healing, and then it will just take time. You don't have to be all-powerful."

Hallr is finishing his bowl, sets it down, and says, "The wing is healed wrong. To fix it, you have to break a dragon's wing, then move the whole thing. The entire time, a dragon is in extreme pain. Let's break your arm and see how that will go."

"I don't have all the answers. Maybe we knock her out."

Milfred and Agnarr laugh. Milfred says, "Knock out a dragon."

"Agnarr, help. Don't just sit there."

Agnarr is sitting, holding the sides of his bowl. He looks up. "I don't know if it is possible to break a healthy dragon bone. But I think I could break Xylia's bones in her condition."

Kaleb is looking at Agnarr intently. "You're that strong?"

"Breaking a bone is not the same as pushing a rock. The push on a rock is constant and hard. The push to break something is *focused, sharp, hard, and powerful."*

"You've done this, or something like this?"

"Yes. It is not something I'm proud of."

Milfred looks intently at Agnarr. "Are you going to talk about it?"

Sheyla says, "Yes, will we hear what drove you out. What are you afraid of?"

Hallr sits up to listen. Agnarr looks at Hallr, "Do you really care?"

"Not about what bothers you. I don't pry or try to make it worse for you. You said fixing the dragon is possible."

"I was part of a group, a coven. We were hunted, chased from our village by witch hunters. I grew up and lived on the ocean coast in southern Broadleaf. We were traveling northwest."

"I wasn't happy with the group, the leadership, or the direction. My plan was to travel to Harendal. I wanted to be a teacher in the town where we took the kids. It all changed one day in Kyrgall City."

"I wasn't with the group. I was actually looking for the city healers. That is when they found me."

Kaleb asks, "Who?"

"A controller coven, or several members."

Sheyla shifts, saying, "I've never asked how the controllers we have encountered haven't been able to control you fully."

"I'll get to that. I found out the group was showing off their power during an audition for a servant of the Greystone king. Show control, something dramatic."

Milfred says, "I was in the city when all this happened, but I wasn't there at the start."

"They controlled me, took me to a building. It was old and looked abandoned. Two stories, brick with no glass in the windows. It looked as if part of the roof had fallen in. There were families inside—refugees from Whitbeck trying to survive."

"They told me there were warriors and spies inside. They had gotten the families out, and I need to help collapse a wall on the warriors."

"Three men and three women focused on me, but I resisted. It was hard and I couldn't stop. I pushed the walls, two walls."

Agnarr pauses, takes a breath.

Kaleb says, "The families were still inside."

Agnarr nods, lips firm, jaw clenched. "I pushed hard enough to make two walls collapse, then the other two fell. The building became a burial mound for dozens of families."

Hallr asks, "How did you get free?"

"The power I showed, the building collapsing, shocked them. They lost concentration, which let me get back to myself."

Taking a deep breath, Agnarr says, "I heard the screaming. Kids screaming. I went into a rage, using a neck breaking technique I learned, I killed them."

Kaleb says, "That's why you know you can fix Xylia's wing."

Sheyla says, "You killed them?"

Agnarr nods, "I broke their necks. It was fast. They were all dead in seconds. The problem was that it was all seen by others on the street."

Milfred says, "The city leaders declared martial law and started hunting magi. They were arresting anyone remotely magical."

Agnarr says, "I ran for a while. Stole clothes and a cape. I was walking with a crowd toward the city exit, just trying to get out. In the shoving close to the gate, a kid was pushed down. I helped him get up. The mother looked at me."

Milfred says, "This is where I become part of the story. The soldiers were questioning everyone, what do you do? Many were pulled aside. I had my wagon trying to get through the checkpoint to set up and start working. Ahead, the soldiers stopped a man. I heard you're not a baker. The next thing I saw was a soldier flying, and hell broke loose. The soldiers just started killing people."

Agnarr says, "When the fighting started, I looked and started looking for a path to leave, then stopped. The woman looked at me, and I think she was about to yell Wizard!"

Milfred says, "They were next to me, and I saw Agnarr shift and the woman's face. I yelled Apprentice, stop helping these fools. Get back in the wagon."

Agnarr nods, "I was confused for a second, then said sorry and climbed into the wagon. Milfred kept yelling at me at that point."

Milfred says, "I looked at the woman, and she was going to yell, so I started yelling first. I called him an idiot, a lazy bum, and a bunch of other things. I said to stop helping the stupid ones who don't appreciate help, those who want to complain about everything."

Agnarr smiles, "That shut her up. We made it through the soldiers' checkpoint, and I've been an apprentice from that point."

Sheyla looks at Milfred, "Why would you help a wizard?"

"I hadn't seen him do any magic. The checkpoint was in chaos, and he couldn't see anyone trying to get through. He was alone. Not acting like part of a coven. In my travels, I've learned that if they aren't acting like an ass, they may not be an ass. Another wanderer like me could be company. And if it turned out he was really an ass, I could leave. That was before I saw him use his magic."

Sheyla asks, "So why can't they fully control you?"

Milfred smiles, begins to speak, and Agnarr says, "My charm."

Kaleb says, "You're that charming."

"No, my necklace charm," as he reaches into his shirt and pulls out a small object on a leather string.

They see a dull piece of metal inside a small net of leather to hold it.

Milfred says, "Mithril. It had been mine for many years. A couple of days after we met, we were at a camp with several other groups. Riders appeared and started searching."

"They sensed magi. They were searching for me. When they found me, they started controlling me."

Milfred says, "I was showing him items in the wagon, trying to make him an apprentice people would believe, when he changed. Suddenly, he put down the tongs, turned, and started walking *away with these guys."*

"I was being led away from the camp area."

"They were leading him away. I was wearing the necklace and pulled it out, holding it so they couldn't control me. I watched them walk toward another camp group. Then Agnarr started raising his arms toward the group. I ran up behind him and dropped the necklace over his head."

"I was totally going to push, topple, and destroy wagons. Then I felt the necklace and had a pain in my head. Massive pain and clarity. I turned to the four behind me as they started drawing swords."

Milfred says, "I collected the horses, and we went back to the wagon. I said nothing for hours. I was shaking after watching that. Back at the wagon, I started packing and said, we are leaving."

"I knew he was upset, frightened. I just followed and did what he wanted. When we were traveling, after it got dark, we didn't stop. I said, Thank you and asked, do you want to talk?"

Milfred says, "I wasn't mad. I thought I probably should be. I was now implicated in killing four people with magic. When Agnarr asked if I wanted to talk, it brought me back."

Agnarr says, "We talked and agreed to travel together to help where we could. To find more Mithril to fight control covens."

Milfred says, "That was about a year before we met Hallr and Sheyla at the battle."

Sheyla says, "I understand you better now. I'm sorry for what they made you do."

Hallr says, "Is this necklace why you resisted when we met control witches before?"

"Yes. It is hard, but I can resist."

Kaleb is smiling, "We need to make Mithril."

Hallr nods, "Now, back to the question before we heard your life story. You can help the dragon."

Kaleb looks at Hallr, then punches him in the shoulder. "Give him a minute."

"Naw. He says he doesn't want to talk about it. He doesn't want to dwell on it. So, I move on."

Agnarr smiles, "You're an ass sometimes. Good intentions, but an ass all the same."

Sheyla looks sternly at Agnarr. "You can break the dragon's wing. You're that strong?"

Agnarr nods, "I was the best in the group."

Hallr says, "You didn't want to stay in the village because of what you had done."

Agnarr nodded. "I wouldn't be fully accepted or trusted after that."

Kaleb asks, "Now that we are back to talking about Xylia's wing, what do we do?"

"It will need to be coordinated. I need to get on her back to examine the situation. I can break the bone, but it will be extremely painful. From what I saw of the wing position, breaking the bone will be the easy part. Then I need to lift and flip the wing."

Milfred says, "That is going to hurt like mad."

"Yes, and it will be hard. I have to be on her back. Flipping the wing will be harder than collapsing the wall. I will need to practice for many days before we even try. Now, the complicated part."

Hallr chuckles, "It can't be easy."

"There are muscles involved. They haven't been used in a long time. The muscles won't move the way we need them to. They will need help. That is where Sheyla is going to have to spend time with Xylia getting ready."

Sheyla shakes her head, "You think I can somehow heal the dragon wing muscle? Every muscle is bigger than Kaleb."

"I've been thinking about this. You can help get her muscles ready before we break the bone. You get the muscles to move, to twitch for a couple of days. We do this, then you push them to heal. It isn't the best, but it will work."

Xylia says in all their heads, "If I don't want to?"

Hallr says, "Then you get to hear Kaleb whine and complain until you eat him."

Kaleb says, "Hey, now. Xylia, don't you want to have the pain gone?"

"I know how much it will hurt to go through this. Even if you do all this, it doesn't mean I will fly, or create the dragon fire you want."

Agnarr says, "If we agree and start tomorrow, it will be several weeks before we are ready. Then Xylia will need to heal. You won't be able to create dragon fire or fly for months."

Kaleb says, "We will talk more about it if you say no after we prepare."

Hallr gets off the bench and says, "My update is that I have found a rail line that probably goes to coal. I'll head to that mine tomorrow. First, I need to find a dwarf hammer. I'll be doing some digging."

Kaleb says, "Digging what?"

"Digging Mithril ore, digging coal, digging Xylia out of that room."

Kaleb says, "I'll help."

Hallr shakes his head, saying, "No. If Xylia is going to fly, we need to feed her. That means you're now the primary chicken farmer. Chickens, mushrooms, and shit, that is your focus."

Kaleb glares at Hallr, "While you get the glamours' work."

Milfred laughs, "You want glamorous? You can help get the forges and molds ready. That will take muscle: dwarf muscle or giant muscle. Based on Xylia's description, we get everything set up, the Mithril melts into the molds, and we wait for it to cool. There is a huge amount of preparation and then waiting."

Agnarr asks, "Xylia, the first step is for us to look at your wing. Are you okay if we look at it?"

"Sure."

<<<>>>

The next several days, Kaleb is working on the chicken farm. Some days, they hear one CLANG; some days, two. Followed by a faint voice, "I'm okay."

Sheyla and Agnarr debated how to get to the top of Xylia's back. After discussing options for almost an hour, Xylia says, "Okay, I can't take it anymore. The only way to get on my back is to climb in my mouth, and I turn my neck so you can get out on my back."

Sheyla freezes for a second, and they hear a rumble from Xylia. Agnarr says, "She's laughing."

Xylia says, "Yes. Girl, Sheyla. I won't eat you." After a brief pause, "Maybe crunch a little."

Agnarr turns to look at Xylia. Sheyla says, "Not funny. Seriously, not funny. We all grow up with the idea that dragons eat people. The first dragon I meet jokes about chewing."

Xylia replies, "I didn't have that perspective before. I was joking. You're the first person I could consider having in my mouth and not chewing. And Kaleb would say, because she tastes bad."

Agnarr chuckles, "Yes, he would."

On Xylia's back, going to the wing, Sheyla immediately says, "Part of this wing skin is dead. Xylia, do you feel anything here?"

"Are you touching it? I feel you standing on my back."

Agnarr asks, "It looks bad. Does this mean she won't be able to fly after healing?"

"This is worse. The circulation isn't good. The wing won't heal at all. It might simply die and fall off. We need to get her circulation moving and help this skin heal. Help me up on the bone."

Agnarr helps Sheyla get onto the main wing bone. She walks toward the joint, examining the skin and muscles. Near a joint, she kneels and pushes on the skin.

Xylia says, "What are you doing?"

"I'm pushing on skin and veins to see how flexible they are. So far, we need to get you moving."

"Moving the wing hurts."

Agnarr says, "I know it hurts, but it is important for me to know the right place. Let's do this right so we only do it once."

"I agree with that plan, and I will try."

"Extend your wingtip, moving nothing else. That worked well.

Now, the next part of your wing."

Xylia groans.

Agnarr says, "Now that wasn't from the bone position. That was from lack of use. You don't move this wing, and it shows. Your muscles and bones are weak. I probably couldn't do this if you were at full health."

"My assessment of your bones is that they are extremely weak. Breaking your wing will be easier than I thought. That means healing will be harder. If it were a human arm, I would say we should put it in a sling to limit excessive movement. In your case, we can't strap your wing down."

Sheyla comes from the other side, where she has been examining the good wing. "I see how the muscles are positioned and look. From that, this wing healed wrong along here, but it is not good. The healing added bone material that we don't need."

Agnarr says, "That isn't good. That will prevent good movement if it stays in her shoulder."

"Agreed, but there is another point to discuss. Her transition from the leathery skin of the wing to scales on her side. On the other side, there are small scales that gradually get bigger. It allows for easy movement. On this side, there are several larger scales on what will be the underside when we put the wing back in position."

"Show me which ones."

Sheyla points out several larger scales. The scale is milky red, not the bright red of the new scales or some of the older scales. Agnarr moves around and pushes on a scale with his shoe, and the scale pops off. Xylia shifts and grunts. "Hey."

"Sorry. It looks like our preparation is going to include some scale grooming on your left side."

"Hm. I expected as much. Those scales haven't been rubbed or pruned in many years. Just let me know next time."

Sheyla looks at the scales around the one Agnarr has removed. "Several will need to be removed. Smaller scales are needed around the high-movement area of the shoulder. We could use Kaleb's long arms to help."

Agnarr nods, "Or we drop Hallr down her side to grab them on the way down."

Xylia says, "Kaleb has been collecting the old scales. He wants to make dragon armor that no weapon can penetrate. Not even Mithril-tipped arrows."

Agnarr says, "Good luck to him."

Later, after they are off Xylia's back and walking to the living area, Agnarr says, "We may have to break her wing to fix the circulation. We will definitely need to break it in two places."

"It has been centuries; she has been like this. Enduring the pain. Her systems are working normally. The recovery with food is going well. Her lack of movement is the problem. We need to dig her out of that room and get her moving."

"I can hear you. You need to know that the ceiling collapsed after the fight. I wouldn't let the dwarves dig me out. The children's bodies are in the rubble. I couldn't deal with that."

Sheyla says, "We understand. They will be skeletons, know."

Xylia says, "Agnarr, two breaks?"

"Yes, when the broken bone healed, your wing was flipped onto your back. The bone grew to fill the gap. There is too much bone. I will need to break it in two spots, then shift the excess part out of the way."

Sheyla says, "We need to take it out."

"We can't operate on Xylia without something to numb the pain."

Sheyla replies, "We need to figure something out."

Agnarr says, "Back to the idea of getting you moving. Hallr said he was going to dig you out. If we get you more space, you can move and help your muscles."

Sheyla asks, "Where is he, by the way?"

Xylia says, "He is searching the coal mine. The primary mine is located many kilometers away and is accessed via a deep rail line. He said he needed a good hammer. The tools are probably in the mine."

"Can't you communicate with him now, like us, like this?"

"No, as my strength increases, my mental distance increases, but I have limits. He is much farther."

Late that evening, after everyone else has eaten and Hallr hasn't returned, Kaleb says, "I may have to go look for him."

Milfred says, "He is a dwarf in a dwarf mine. You think you can find him?"

"What if he's in trouble and needs help?"

Sheyla says, "Tomorrow."

Milfred says, "You don't know what you're saying. If he went to the railway line to get to the mine, would there be a car here? Is the car something you can move? If there is no car, you will have to walk. It could take you all day to get there."

Kaleb says, "I'm going to look in the morning."

Shit and Mushrooms

Milfred wakes up to a noise. He gets up and looks out the door of his sleeping room. He looks over to see Hallr carrying a big dwarven hammer. One side has a spike, and the other is flat. Black covers him from head to foot.

Milfred asks, "Is that coal dust?"

Two white eyeballs turn to look at him. "Aye. I brought two railcars full of coal. Now I need to wash."

Kaleb awakens to the voices. He looks at Hallr and starts laughing. "Two eyes floating in the black."

Hallr grunts, "Hey, I didn't bang my head once."

"Shut up, short man."

Milfred sees the beard shift and some teeth as Hallr smiles. Turning, he walks into the dark. "I need a bath."

Kaleb says, "The cold waterfall shower is working."

Milfred says, "I'm going back to bed. I have to finish cleaning the inside of the left forge tomorrow. Then, following Xylia's instructions, I need to fix broken bricks and get the whole thing lined with ceramic powder."

Kaleb says, "Yeah, back to bed."

In the morning, Kaleb wakes up and goes to the common area. Passing Hallr's room, he hears him snoring. He looks around for the hammer and doesn't see it. Bending down and looking into Hallr's room, he sees a line of objects against the wall. There is the hammer, his new axe from the gate guardhouse, his old axe, and lastly a small pack, Hallr size, leaning against the wall.

Kaleb grabs the hammer, strains to lift it, and pulls it out. "Heavy, like an axe. It must be a standard thing. They weigh the same, so dwarves are used to swinging them. Good balance for swinging. This will probably break anything."

In his head, Xylia says, "Except Mithril. The old stories talk about two dwarves with those hammers carving a tunnel through granite. They break a path, and a dozen follow to clear the rubble and smooth the walls. Only the top diggers could do that two wide. Hallr swigs like that."

"How about my swing?"

"You are young, learning, but Hallr is teaching you the right way. Leave his hammer and come talk to me."

In the chamber with Xylia, Kaleb walks close to her front leg and plops down on the ground. Xylia says, "I need to look at something. Get up and go under my neck."

Kaleb goes to the back of the room, which they haven't been to. Xylia has always been lying next to rubble on this side. As he walks under her neck, he asks, "What are you hiding back here?"

"Don't get mad. I had to eat."

Kaleb felt perplexed while walking around her right front leg before halting. "Wow, that is a lot of armor, and shit."

Kaleb is looking at the remnants of soldiers, or their armor. He turns to look back under Xylia's neck at all the gold, back at the armor, "That is a lot of thieves trying to take your gold."

Xylia says, "That results from the rumor of gold. It attracts thieves. I kept myself fed for a couple of centuries. The problem is that the big vertical chute that takes my shit down to the lower levels for the mushrooms is blocked. I don't know if it's blocked by their armor, part of the ceiling collapses, or if it's just full. I need help."

Kaleb walks to the pile and grabs one piece sticking out. It is a forearm guard. There are holes in it. Holding it up and turning it, Kaleb asks, "This is partially gone. Did your stomach do this?"

"Yes, leather, cloth, and thin metal are digested. Thicker parts are consumed but not entirely gone. It makes it easy. It used to be easy. Thieves come in, I make a fire ring, and I've cooked dinner. I eat them, armor and all."

"It used to be easy?"

"Over time, fewer came. As I got weaker, I couldn't cook them; I had to catch them and eat them."

Contemplating the mountain of shit, Kaleb says, "This will take a while to deal with. I'll have to go down and check."

"If it is just full, you can get the bottom shifting it to tunnels for the mushrooms. I can shove up here to get it in the chute."

Walking back toward the archway exit, Kaleb says, "Pretty smart for you and the dwarves. There is gold in the mountain. It is bait for thieves and food for you. At the same time, the kids use gold to learn their craft, so the treasure looks like it is constantly changing."

"The dwarves and I had a good thing going."

Down in the caves, Kaleb hasn't reached the chute from Xylia. Mushrooms choke the tunnels. So, think in places where his sword barely penetrates. He hacks, digs, and pulls out mushrooms. The small but growing chicken population is receiving piles. They are happy to eat all the mushrooms he puts into the coop.

After several days, he knows he is close because he digs out an armor boot.

When he digs his way to an intersection, he asks Xylia what she knows.

"I don't know a lot of details. There are many sections and caves. We never ran out of mushrooms.

"Are all the mushrooms the same? Just one kind?"

After a pause, "No. Haven't thought about that for centuries. There were several types, I think. The bulk was for chickens, with some designated for human and dwarf food, and the medical ones. The medical ones were in a different area."

"What medical ones?"

"They had mushrooms to help with some infections. They called them fungi. There were also the Mycojoy mushrooms."

"Never heard of Mycojoy."

"They said it meant pure happiness and joy from mushrooms."

"What are the Mycojoy ones used for? What do they do?"

"I never had any of those mushrooms. The dwarves and humans said that, in small doses, it was like getting drunk. Larger doses would make them unconscious. They used them with them badly injured."

Kaleb stops chopping mushrooms. He asks, "If you took enough of those, would you pass out? Could we use that when we fix your wing?"

"Interesting idea. It would take a very large number of mushrooms. However, having me drunk while confined in this room could be a bad idea."

"Okay. Do you know the area where they grew this Mycojoy?"

"It was in the upper levels, toward the mountain peak, inside where they grew herbs and other medicinal items. Be careful about going there. If the lower areas are overgrown, the medicinal mushroom area may be as well. The spores from the Mycojoy could overwhelm you."

"Is there anything we can do so that we aren't overwhelmed?"

"Sure, hold your breath."

At the evening meal, Milfred asks, "Has anyone seen Kaleb? He is never late for a meal."

Sheyla says, "He was going to look for a medicinal mushroom area. There was something about some Mycojoy mushrooms. I don't know, I tune him out about mushrooms this, mushrooms that."

Agnarr smiles, "I get that. He mentioned that people eat some mushrooms. I'm going to skip that meal. Kaleb can eat, and we'll see how he does."

They hear a distant clang.

Hallr says, "There he is."

Clang. Clang.

Milfred says, "What is going on?"

They hear multiple clangs growing louder.

Xylia says, "He got into the Mycojoy spores. He is drunk."

Kaleb stumbles to the table, sits, and says, "I'm hungry."

Agnarr says, "I'll get you a bowl, but tell us what happened."

Kaleb takes the helmet off and nods. "Xylia talked about medicinal mushrooms, so I went to find them. The room door was stuck, as usual. When I shoved it open, it barely moved. The room is overgrown with several types of mushrooms. I was holding my breath, so I didn't breathe in the spores. I shoved the door to get it open enough to get into the room. When I stepped into the room, I slipped on mushroom juice."

Hallr chuckles.

"I landed hard, and it knocked the wind out of me. I naturally took a deep breath. Being laid out on the floor, I also avoided the spikes shooting down."

Hallr is laughing now. Everyone else is smiling, and Sheyla is smacking Hallr on the arm. "It's not that funny," she says, laughing.

"I crawled out of the room. Then I woke up, and everything was moving; two torches separated, then came together. I only had one torch with me."

Milfred says, "You're drunk from these mushrooms."

Kaleb nods, "Xylia said they were fun."

He focuses on the bowl in front of him, slowly reaching for it as if his arm doesn't work. He takes several spoonfuls without talking. Pausing eating, he says, "We can use these to knock out Xylia when we fix her wing."

Hallr smiles, "Great idea."

Agnarr says, "I like that. We can do all the things we need to while she is asleep."

Sheyla is looking at Kaleb while he eats. "Kaleb, I need you to face me, then look up, just moving your eyes so that I can see the sides of your eyes."

Kaleb does as she asks. He holds the position and suddenly closes his eyes, shaking his head. "That is starting to hurt."

Agnarr says, "What was that?"

"Making him look up is the simple way to check his pain threshold. It started to hurt. In his case, it took twice as long as I would have expected. The mushrooms help with pain. The problem with this idea is that it will take over one hundred kilograms to knock out Xylia."

Kaleb says, "I knew it as he shifts and spills his bowl and drink glass."

Milfred says, "You're done. Time to go to bed."

The next morning, Hallr is up early as usual. He walks to Kaleb's door and yells, "Get up!"

Kaleb jerks in bed, rolls over to get up, "What is it?"

"Those mushrooms messed you up. We are going to hit some rocks this morning to get your blood flowing."

In the dragon chamber, Hallr says, "We need to dig out Xylia's tunnel so she can get out. I've looked at the rubble. Someone pulled out most of the smaller rubble. Now the bigger rocks are different."

Kaleb is looking at the wall, a pile of large rocks that is blocking the tunnel. "Will I start on one side and you on the other?"

Hallr says loudly, "NO."

Kaleb shrugs, "What?"

"If we do this wrong, the rubble above what we see will come down. We have to start on this side. We dig our way to the tunnel, then we dig and remove rock from the tunnel's side."

"How long will this take?"

"Weeks, months. That mostly depends on how much time we spend on this instead of some other work."

Xylia asks, "Why so long?"

Hallr says, "I could dig through this in a week. What do we do with the rubble I create? I will need to gather rubble, put it in a wagon to take it to the valley, and dump it somewhere. That all takes time."

Xylia says, "The kids' skeletons will slow you down."

Kaleb says, "Haven't thought about that part. Yes. We need to collect them and bury them properly. That is depressing."

Hallr is looking at Kaleb, jaw clenched. He says, "We will take care of the kids properly. I will not be a happy dwarf on those *days."*

"*Do you have happy days?" Gesturing up and down at Hallr's figure, Kaleb says, "Is this happy or grumpy today? It is hard to tell with you.*"

"*You keep hitting your head and can't see properly.*"

They hear Xylia saying to the others, "They never stop."

Is it Spring

After exploring initially, they designated Agnarr the fertile valley leader. He would spend all day working in various areas. Hallr and Kaleb always helped when Agnarr needed help.

At the evening update, Agnarr tells everyone, "The corral for the sheep is complete. And I moved the pregnant ewes inside just in time. We have our first lamb today. It is spring in the valley."

Kaleb says, "Great news. Do you think we can get down to a village? We could use tools, rope, cloth, lots of stuff to help."

Sheyla says, "We need to talk about this. First, are we staying?"

Hallr says, "Staying. You can stop talking about it now."

Sheyla continues, "If we go to a village, we will need to pay for things."

Xylia says, "I have plenty of gold."

Sheyla shakes her head. "Most important. Are we going to talk about the city? We found it. Do others need to know? What happens if they know?"

Milfred says, "I'm staying, but I will take a wagon down for supplies. We could use help to bring the city back to life. There are too many things to get done."

Agnarr is looking at Sheyla intently. He shifts to Milfred. Sheyla says, "What is it, Agnarr?"

"We can't defend the city. The only thing protected is the gold, but Xylia is still weak. If we tell people, they will come. They will come for gold, for opportunity, for whatever dream they have."

Hallr asks, "What is your point? I won't let just anyone in."

"Can you stop a thousand? What happens when soldiers arrive to take the city? I have those concerns and more. My biggest concern is Xylia."

Xylia and Kaleb both say, "What?"

"If we are going to fix her wing, we need to do it before anyone goes out of the city. She needs a couple of weeks to heal before anyone shows up. We won't be able to knock her out, fix her wing, and let her heal when people are pounding to get it."

As Hallr and Sheyla nod, Kaleb says, "He's right. We need to focus on Xylia and get ready."

Agnarr is on Xylia's back, rubbing the bone of her wing. "I know it hurts, but I need to know the right place. I want to do this once, not have to break your wing multiple times."

"I agree with that plan, and I will try."

"Extend your wingtip, moving nothing else. That worked well. Now, the next part of your wing."

Xylia groans.

"Now, that wasn't from the bone position. That was from lack of use. You don't move this wing, and it shows. Your muscles and bones are weak. I probably couldn't do this if you were at full health."

"My assessment of your bones is that they are extremely weak. Breaking your wing will be easier than I thought. That means healing will be harder. If it were a human arm, I would say we should put it in a sling to limit excessive movement. In your case, we can't strap your wing down."

Sheyla comes from the other side, where she has been examining the good wing. "I see how the muscles are positioned and look. From that, this wing healed wrongly along here. The healing added bone material that we don't need in this area."

Agnarr says, "That isn't good. To get that out of her shoulder, we will need to make a bigger cut than I thought. That will be more healing.

"Agreed, now we need to talk about the scales."

Agnarr is nodding, "We talked about this, and Kaleb said he was *doing some grooming."*

Xylia says, *"He only did what he could reach from the ground."*

Sheyla says, *"The simple option right now is for Agnarr to use push to dislodge the easy ones."*

"I can do that. It will be a simple exercise to get ready."

Two weeks later, Hallr is at the archway entrance to the dragon chamber. He asks Agnarr, *"Is she sleeping? That was a lot for our little healer."*

Agnarr nods, *"She did great. She will be asleep for hours. How is our patient?"*

"She is still sleeping. I was concerned when you cut into her shoulder and pulled out that bone sliver. You called that huge piece of bone a sliver. I thought she might wake up. Her breathing changed a lot."

"I felt her breathing change. The Mithril blade is sharp, but it still took effort to get through her skin. I had to remove the bone, or she would never use that wing again. That cut concerns me for another reason, Hallr."

"Dragon's blood is thought to be magical?"

"What? No! The lack of blood. Her condition is way better than when we arrived, but she is not healthy. There should have been more blood."

"What are you saying? Is she dying?"

"I don't know. What I know is that we need to give her those infection-fighting mushrooms, far more than we planned. We need to feed her more. And you need to dig her out. She needs to get out in the sun."

"That is the plan. I checked everything with Kaleb before. The only thing that stops us is one boulder. Let me show you."

They walk across the chamber and around Xylia's head. Up close, they hear her raspy breathing. Hallr says, *"She can't die.*

Not now, after we saved her."

"She's centuries old. How long do dragons live?"

"I don't know."

Hallr points to a large, jagged boulder close to Xylia's right wing. "That boulder is the key. If it is broken, that entire wall of rubble will come down on her. Kaleb and I have to start over here, at the top. Remove rocks from the sides."

Agnarr asks, "What's on the other side? Is it open?"

"Don't know. If there is another way to get to her access tunnel, we don't know. It would be better if we worked from that side. Kaleb is helping, but it takes time to take the rock out with the wagon. Once we get through the tunnel, it will be faster."

The next day, Sheyla brings a bowl to Hallr. "Still not leaving her? Here is a bowl of stew, but I can stay with her."

Handing the bowl to Hallr, Sheyla walks up to Xylia and places her hand on the dragon. Closing her eyes, she mentally reaches out to the bone and, in her mind, touches the bone cells, causing them to divide. While she is going through this, she feels Xylia's mental presence. She goes from distant and quiet to approaching and asking, "What?"

Sheyla says, "It's over. You did great. Rest."

Xylia says, "Hungry."

Sheyla takes her hand off Xylia, turns to Hallr, and says, "She's waking up and hungry."

Hallr jumps up, spilling his bowl as Xylia's eyes open. They mentally hear, "Intruders," as Xylia swings her head toward the entrance.

Sheyla stands near Xylia's front leg to avoid being hit, yet she suddenly becomes startled and scared. Her swinging head hits Hallr, sending him flying across the room toward the entrance.

Sheyla reacts when she hears Hallr grunt. She turns, extends her arm, and focuses on Hallr. Mentally, she is directing everything she knows, "Focus, focus, pull, PULL."

Hallr's flight slows, not what anyone would consider significant, just before he hits the wall and falls to the floor.

Xylia is confused, groggy, and now feeling the pain.

Sheyla places both hands on her and says, "It's okay. You're safe. No intruders."

Xylia stops moving, frozen by the touch, the voice. Mentally, she says, "Who is in my chamber?"

Sheyla is shaking in fear. If she talks, Xylia will know. Mentally, she says in a calm voice, "Remember Hallr. Remember his friends. We are not stealing your gold."

Xylia replies, "Not gold, treasure. My kids made my treasure."

Sheyla says, "We fixed your wing. It will hurt for some time. Please don't move your wing."

Xylia says, "Girl? Is that you?"

"Yes, I'm here."

"I feel weird. It is like diving out of the sky, then swooping. Is this drunk?"

"Yes, I think so. How about the pain?"

"There is a lot. Not sharp pain like before, but the whole shoulder area hurts."

"That is a good sign. Now we need to feed you and give you medicine. If you are calm, I need to check Hallr. You knocked him across the room."

"Sure."

Running to Hallr, Sheyla kneels. He is on his side, in a crumpled lump. He is breathing. She checks for broken bones and slowly rolls him onto his back.

Xylia, with a clearer voice, asks, "Is Hallr okay?"

"He is unconscious. You accidentally hit him and knocked him out."

Sheyla feels the reaction from Xylia, "NO. NO. NO. Hallr."

Sheyla stands and turns to see Xylia focused on her. Both dragon eyes locked on her. Xylia says, "Help him."

Sheyla replies, "I am. I will. YOU need to calm down. It was an accident. You didn't mean to."

"I did it. Can't change it. How do I help?"

Sheyla kneels to continue her examination. The side of Hallr's head is swelling and turning a purplish color. "He hit his head. I need to focus on him."

Sheyla spends several minutes focused on Hallr. When she pauses, she turns to see Agnarr, Kaleb, and Milfred looking at her.

"He hit his head and his side hard. He will have bruises on his side and leg. His hard head is the worst. I'm focusing on him. I need water and some time with him. Don't move him."

Over an hour later, she stands and says, "He needs to sleep."

Xylia shifts her head and sets it down close to Hallr. "I'll watch him. Get rest, girl. Sheyla. Sheyla...Thank you."

Hallr is unconscious. The side of his head is black and blue and swollen. The day after the accident, Kaleb is grumpy. "You're the healer. Heal him."

"I've done what I can."

"Fix it."

"Look. I can't reverse what was done. All I can do is help his body heal itself. I don't make the injury go away. Coxing his cells to divide, which speeds healing. That is all I can do. You have a scar from the guardroom. I can't make the injury disappear, but help heal after."

"There has to be more you can do."

Sheyla stands and walks toward the exit.

"Where are you going?"

"Away from you people and dragon."

Agnarr walks into the room, steps to the side, and sees Sheyla's face as she walks out. He looks at Kaleb and says, "What's going on?"

"She needs to do more."

Agnarr rolls his eyes, "More, like what?"

"I don't know, something."

"That's right, you don't know. You don't know, do you? Stop demanding. You piss her off, and she can't or won't help as much."

"She ...."

"Shut up! The last two days, she has kept a dragon and a dwarf from dying. What have you done? When you can do anything like that, you can complain."

Walking in the hallway in the dark, Sheyla hears Xylia in her head, "I'm sorry."

"For what?"

"Being short and rude to you. You're helping so much."

"I'm tired and hungry. I'm going to sleep."

"Yes, I won't bother you."

After sleeping for several hours and eating, Sheyla returns to the dragon chamber. Xylia senses her approach and says, "Feeling rested and better?"

"Yes, I feel better. How is Hallr? Can you sense him with your mental abilities?"

"No, he is still fully asleep."

Sheyla walks over to the Hallr, sits down, and puts her hand on his head. Ten minutes later, she gets up and walks to Xylia, saying, "Your turn."

"Whatever you have done, the pain is so much less."

"I'm getting your bones to heal, which will be the biggest part before you move. Most of the pain is from the muscles that haven't been used and are adjusting. Have you tried to move your wing?"

"I haven't tried, but it's moved twice."

"With the bones set, you can begin small, tiny movements which will help the muscles."

The next day, a couple of hours after Hallr wakes up, Xylia says, "You love to argue, but only with each other."

Kaleb replies, "That's all on him."

Hallr says, "I can't swing the hammer, and you're barely able. Bloody Dragons, Kaleb, focus on your swing."

"You're the one who can't take a little dragon smack."

Xylia says, "Not funny.

Kaleb says, "Sorry."

Hallr says, "It's a reaction because you proved he has the hardest head in the city."

Several hours later, Xylia is annoyed. They continue to argue. She is mentally talking with Sheyla, "I could puff a fire ring. No, I could smack the floor to scare them. How about I get a mouthful of water and shoot it on them?"

Sheyla replies, "They love arguing. Just tune them out. Why are they still there?"

"Kaleb said he is going to get through to the tunnel tonight. Hallr has moved more. He is carrying rocks to the wagon to haul out. Kaleb now wants to dig faster to make Hallr work harder."

Sheyla smiles, shaking her head. "It is good for Hallr to be moving, but he could easily overdo it. You can mess with them by making them take breaks at different times."

Xylia makes a noise, a kind of grunt. "That could be interesting. I'll mess with them until they learn to coordinate better.

The Army Gathers

"Master Tobias, a rider is approaching."

"A soldier? Have the troops I requested arrived?"

Teppo steps over so they are together for the rider. Teppo says, "The snow is melting slowly, but we have gathered supplies. We should be ready when the troops arrive."

Tobias nods as the rider stops by one man who is working on a wagon. The man points toward Tobias and Teppo, and then the soldier rides over.

"Greetings. I was commanded to ride ahead and inform you that the troop of soldiers, two hundred strong, will arrive tomorrow. Captain Ulgary will meet with you and plan our assault on the dwarf city."

Teppo looks at the man, squints, and says, "You said two hundred soldiers?"

"Yes."

"That is four times what we expected and planned supplies to accommodate. We will need to discuss with Captain Ulgary."

Tobias asks, "I asked for fifty soldiers. Why are there two hundred?"

"Sir, if you were aware of military decorum and practice, you would understand. A city's guard contingent is commanded by a captain or higher, and a captain will command a minimum of two hundred troops. Captain Ulgary will take the city and hold it in the king's name."

Teppo turns to Tobias, "The minimum number of troops for a Captain. We aren't ready for this many troops."

Tobias replies, "This is what the king sent. We will support them."

Teppo arranges for the soldier to have food and a bunk. He also directs people to mark an area for the troop to set up camp.

Ranjeet meets him an hour later. "Two hundred. That is an impossible number to control. What is your plan?"

"I plan to let them do all the work. We only need to control the captain and his lieutenants after they take the city."

"We were planning for Tobias and one or two. This will be six, maybe seven to control at the same time, all doing different things."

"An old city is a dangerous place."

Teppo stops because Tobias is approaching. "Master Tobias. I had the area over here designated for the troops to set up their camp. We will meet with the captain in his tent, I'm presuming, and talk about next steps."

Tobias is looking over the area. "What about a food prep area for them? Latrines?"

Teppo holds up both hands, "Hang on. I will not get presumptuous about some details. The captain's men will decide where they want those things, and they have the manpower to make it happen."

At midday the next day, the two hundred soldiers arrive. Half the soldiers are riding horses and are in formation. The other soldiers are marching behind the horses. Following them is a large group of wagons. Captain Ulgary is leading with three lieutenants flanking him.

Tobias is smiling as they watch them approach.

Teppo is standing next to Tobias, and Ranjeet is behind him. As they approach, Ranjeet says, "Two hundred troops, and it looks like another two hundred support people with them. That's four hundred more mouths to feed, not fifty."

After the initial greetings and introductions, Teppo instructs Ranjeet to take the lieutenants around and help get their camp set up.

Teppo says to Captain Ulgary, "Captain, I have to say I'm shocked at the numbers you have with you. Master Tobias asked for a small group of fifty to take and hold the city. This is two hundred soldiers and at least that number of others."

Raising his hand for silence, Captain Ulgary says, "We heard the request. What happens after the fifty soldiers are here and take the city? What is next?"

With a flash of insight in his eyes, Tobias says, "After the city is taken, we will need more troops and other people to work and transport supplies and the treasure back. The captain was thinking ahead."

Teppo says, "We haven't gathered enough supplies to feed this large group up in the mountains. With your men helping, we could hunt and process everything. It may be several weeks before we can be ready."

Captain Ulgary says, "In two weeks, we will start heading to the city. We will continue to gather along the way."

Teppo nods, "I'm glad to hear that, Captain. We want to get to the city as quickly as possible. There is one more thing. We know snow has melted part of the way from our scouts. Higher in the mountains, the path may still be covered in snow. Two more weeks of melting will help."

"I'm going to monitor my troops and the camp setup. When my tent is ready, we will meet to discuss more details."

After meeting with the captain and his team, dealing with some details, and planning, they break for the evening.

Tobias requested, and the captain agreed to support him. They moved his tent to the troop area.

At the troops' evening meal, they called it chow time. Tobias walks to the officer's tent to eat, and a guard spots him at the door. "Only officers eat here."

"Excuse me. I'm a member of the royal court. This entire mission is on the king's orders to me. You will let me pass."

"I will not let you pass without authorization from an officer."

Storming off, Tobias finds a lieutenant late to the evening meal gathering. He stops him and says, "The common soldier is refusing me. Escort me into the meal area."

"I'm not sure about the protocol. I will have to check, but I'm late. Captain Ulgary does not take lightly to tardiness for the company mealtime."

The officer enters the tent while Tobias waits. He hears arguing for a minute, then silence. A different officer moves the tent flap, steps out, and addresses the soldier on guard. "Master Tobias is a guest of the captain and will be treated as such. He will have access to the officer's tent, especially at meals. Pass the word."

He turns to Tobias, saying, "My apologies; we didn't communicate with our troops well enough. Please join us for dinner."

Tobias nods and follows the officer into the tent. Inside, there is a table. They have moved things around to shove the lieutenants closer together and provide a space diagonally across from the captain for Tobias to sit and converse.

Captain Ulgary says, "Sorry about the confusion. It should all be cleared up now."

In front of them is fresh venison. Tobias knows hunters brought several deer into camp today after a two-day hunt. They are taking the best supplies and consuming them immediately.

Before he can ask, one lieutenant says, "We are enjoying the fresh kills for dinner. In the mountains, we will only have jerky."

Tobias looks around at the group. The lieutenants are young, except for one who looks maybe ten years older. They are all following the rules of etiquette. "Captain, thank you for letting me join your table. It is refreshing to see a group following proper etiquette."

Captain Ulgary nods, "The reports from the men that returned said you were insistent on many things, but also practical. We need to talk about this group you have been with."

Tobias nods, "That is the practical side: more men, a common goal. I've been consistent in sending reports to keep the king informed. They haven't liked all, but I insisted."

"What is their goal, the goal they told you, and their actual goal?"

"They want the city's treasure. I'm sure part of their plan is to take a large cut of the treasure for themselves. That obviously won't happen with your troop here. The request for fifty men *would be enough to stop their plan. The request of only fifty soldiers was small enough that they wouldn't stop me from sending the soldiers to report."*

Captain Ulgary looks at Tobias, his eyes narrowing slightly. "That was shrewd of you. Not what the reports would show."

"Captain, people think I'm simple and single-minded. I've made mistakes, but not because of being simple-minded. The mistake was that I didn't show my authority and capability. I let them see me as easy to manipulate."

"How big is this group you have been traveling with?"

"There are ten men and nine women. The women do domestic work around the camp and stay out of the way."

"We will be four hundred and fifty traveling into the mountains. This movement will need careful coordination. My lieutenant will be in charge."

One lieutenant introduces himself as Lieutenant Stonesplitter.

"He will begin sending troops hunting and gathering. Another group will set up our next camp. Your group will need to follow behind."

Lieutenant Stonesplitter says, "They will follow our supply and equipment wagons. Also, just to be clear. Everyone will be up getting food an hour before sunrise. The camp takedown and packing needs to be complete so we can move an hour after sunrise."

Tobias smiles and nods, saying, "I will feel less frustrated in the morning if I focus on getting work done."

<<<>>>

Two weeks later, Lieutenant Stonesplitter is telling the Captain and Tobias, "The snow hasn't melted enough. It hampers hunting, but the biggest impact is that we are not traveling far enough each day. The wagons are moving slowly."

"Your solution, Lieutenant?"

"I will send most of the men out ahead each day. Some will find our next camp location and begin working without the wagons. They will have fires and clear an area."

Tobias says, "Captain, I recommend slowing down. Spend an extra day at some camp locations. Give the men time to get through the snow and prepare."

"Mr. Tobias, we need to move. We need to find this city."

"Why the rush, Captain? The city isn't moving. No treasure is leaving the city. You sound like this is a compulsion you have to get there quickly."

Captain Ulgary replies after considering for a few seconds. "I see what you're saying. I do want to get to the city quickly, and I didn't realize I was pushing so hard."

A soldier riding up to the camp interrupts them. The soldier shouts, "Wagon approaching."

The Kids Return

Teppo is at the women's tent. The tent is not entirely set up for the night, but there is a big problem. The lead controller, Willow, is his grandmother, a seventy-eight-year-old woman who is very ill. Even at seventy-eight, she is mentally the strongest one for illusions and control. She has been feeling unwell for several days, but today it got worse.

"Master Teppo, she is very sick, and it is sudden. She has thrown up several times; she can't keep food down."

Another witch says, "She keeps saying the girl. We don't know what that means."

Teppo replies, "With her not controlling, are we influencing Tobias or the Captain?"

"No, Teppo. Esme has been preparing and practicing, but she has never been a primary while others have been supporting. She has only done solo, focused control in the past. We have to be careful."

Hearing the shout about the wagon, Teppo decides to investigate. As he leaves, he says, "Esme will lead until Willow recovers."

Teppo walks up to Tobias and Captain Ulgary as a rider dismounts.

The rider turns and says, "A wagon. A day behind, following our trail. If they were pushing through raw snow instead of using our trail, they would be two days behind."

Tobias asks, "What is the group, and do you know their intentions?"

"Eight men, a woman, and three children."

Captain Ulgary is looking at the rider, turns to Tobias, "This makes little sense. A wagon with children following us."

Tobias is looking at the rider with furrowed brows. He looks

290

at Captain Ulgary and says, "The only thing that makes sense is that they are going for the city and the treasure."

Teppo says, "That is unusual. Pushing through the snow or following us to get to the city with kids. I have another thought about the situation."

Captain Ulgary says, "This is now a military operation. We will use military protocols. Your analysis needs to provide those aspects."

"Yes, Captain. I think they could be a rescue party. The dwarf and the group were in the mountains as winter began. We don't know if they found the city. We don't know if they had food to survive the winter. This group would be the spring follow-up and support group."

Tobias is looking at Teppo. He turns to the captain and says, "This is an aspect no one considered. Teppo, thank you for the insight."

Captain Ulgary says, "Explain."

Tobias nods, "The dwarf group has been the focus; however, before our interaction, we knew they took children to a village. This could always have been the plan. The dwarf finds the city and the treasure. The second group follows later and meets them to provide provisions and support."

Teppo is nodding, his brain racing. His statement was a long shot to disrupt the discussion. Now Tobias is using it. He needs to stall everything while Esme gets into her role. He will have to follow this line of thinking.

Teppo says, "That is what I think as well. We need to be careful now. We can act as an explorer group, not aware of this group. Let them travel through, and we'll follow. The alternative is to stop them and find out what they know."

Captain Ulgary is smiling. "We are going to keep moving; follow the orders I've given. Let them catch us, and we will question them."

Teppo is gritting his teeth. Ulgary is amused by Teppo's statement. Willow obviously does not influence him. Esma needs to get in control, or this could get dangerous for them.

Returning to his group, Teppo receives more bad news. Willow's condition is worse, and Esma is sick. She is throwing up. "What happened? What is going on?"

Ranjeet replies, "It must be from the food. The others are all taking medicinal herbs to prevent anyone else from getting sick.

Teppo is watching when Ranjeet touches his temple. Teppo feels a headache and touches his temple. "This is control from someone."

Ranjeet is looking at him funny. "There is no one here who could impact us like this."

Teppo nods, "It is happening."

One witch leaves Willow and walks over. "Teppo, your grandmother is ashen. I'm afraid she is dying."

Teppo clenches his jaw. Ranjeet says, "I'll go out and deal with the army. Sit with your grandmother."

"Grandmother is a distraction. I need to focus on the captain. This could all turn against us in minutes."

"Go to Willow."

Ranjeet goes to Esma to check on her. "Are you feeling better?"

"My stomach is better. Now it's my head. It feels like after I spend too many hours controlling. I should be ready after some rest."

<<<>>>

Tanisha tells the lead escort rider, Zevran, "Merial has made their controller feel sick. She said the controller is older and weaker. She made her stomach upset."

Zevran nods, "You understand we can't fight that army. If Merial can't influence the captain and the other key people, we will be in danger."

The lead witch, Elin, walks up, "I have put Merial to bed. She needs to rest before we get to the army."

Tanisha feels agitated and says, "We must reach Hallr and

the others as soon as possible."

Elin says, "We understand what is at stake. We are going to do everything possible to prevent these people from getting the box."

Zevran says, "I agreed to make this journey with kids because of two things. The danger of that box and watching Merial overwhelm the controller, who attacked the village."

Elin says, "We are breaking our laws with Merial. We shouldn't be controlling and letting a ten-year-old be the primary controller. I'm still in awe of her ability."

Tanisha is nodding, "When we met, the witch wanted each of us to try controlling. Merial did it, as she had always done, effortlessly. She is amazing."

Elin replies, "And vulnerable, and naive. Zevran, if we run into trouble, we need to get Merial away, protect her, or hide her."

Tanisha says, "We can't let the others know what she can do."

Zevran looks at Elin and says, "If it comes to that, I will get her out. My job is to make sure it doesn't get to that point."

Elin replies, "You can't just kill everyone. I know you're a powerful Guardian and a trained assassin who protects magi. We have to get through that army and to Hallr."

Tanisha looks at Zevran and asks, "If the army gets to the city, what do you think will happen?"

"The controller group with them will get the humans to open the gates, letting them enter and take over. If they get in and fortify the city, it will be almost impossible to get them out."

Elin says, "We are assuming Hallr and his group found the city. They could be stuck in a high valley, waiting for spring."

One of the guardian riders returns. Stopping at the three, he says, "Their scout saw us and went back. We are within a day of catching them as planned."

Zevran nods and says, "Now we follow. Let them do the work, getting through the high snow."

The rider asks, "Now we're within a day of the army. Will we get to find out why we have done all this?"

Elin says, "Yes, we will let the entire group know what's

happening."

Later, around the fire as they are finishing eating, Elin says, "Gather around so we can give everyone an update."

Merial puts her bowl with the others, then sits next to Elin.

Elin begins, "We are doing this because of the most dangerous object any magi could possess and use. There is a box that contains instructions on how to teach anyone how to control a dwarf. A witch with that power can control any group of humans."

"That is just a story. It isn't real, so why do we care? We don't do control."

"We care because it is so dangerous. Because it would put someone in a position to control any of us easily. Break our laws. The last person known to have the box was the dwarf who dropped off these children."

"What do we do when we get the box?"

"We don't want the box. We want to make sure it is hidden where no one can get it or destroy it. That also means we need to make sure no one else gets the box."

"Are you going to tell us why we have three kids with this group? Going into dangerous areas where we could fight?"

Elin stands now to make sure they hear what she says, "The children traveled with and were protected by the dwarf. Controller magi have been hunting dwarves for centuries. He has no reason to trust or protect magi children, yet this dwarf did just that. They have a connection with him that no other magi can have. They are here to show our commitment to destroy the box, not to use it."

"Will we have to fight the army?"

Zevran stands and says, "Probably. There are 200 soldiers plus an equal number of support personnel. We also have to deal with a controller group that has been following the dwarf group."

Merial says, "They tell people they want the treasure in the city. That is true, but they want the box."

Elin repeats what Merial says, so everyone hears.

One guardian comments to others: "Merial and Tanisha are really gifted, empathetic readers. They would know."

Zevran looks from Merial to the group and says, "We don't need Merial to tell us. The facts tell us everything. That controller group was at the battle where the kids were freed. Where the box was being traded, they wanted the kids and the box. After the battle, Hallr got the box. The controller group that wants the kids, instead, has been following the dwarf and the box, not stopping for the kids."

Snow

At the evening meeting, after the meal, they are planning. Milfred says, "I'm going to take a wagon and head to a village. I will take all the wool we sheared, two dozen sheepskins, and a box of crude gold coins I made from melting a large bowl."

Sheyla says, "I need you to get seeds. Medicinal herb sprouts or seeds."

Hallr says, "Spices. Kaleb needs to experience making chicken with some spices."

Kaleb shoves Hallr's shoulder and says, "Yeast would be good. See if Hallr really knows how to make beer, or if he's all talk."

Agnarr asks, "What about the snow? We haven't opened the courtyard gate to know if a wagon can make it down to the valley. This is the worst time. There will be more ice than snow, with the ice hidden by the snow."

Milfred says, "We won't know until we try."

Kaleb says, "We can open the gate and check tomorrow. Ride a horse down for a day to check."

<<<>>>

Teppo is asking the captain, "Can we stop and camp for more than a day? Let the snow melt. I would like to have a day to dig a grave in the frozen ground to bury my grandmother."

Captain Ulgary looks at the camp and says, "We made half the distance today because of the snow depth. We will camp for two days."

Turning to a lieutenant, he says, "Make camp and send out multiple hunting parties. They can range out for a day."

Merial asks, "Elin, it is cold here. When will we get to the city?"

"I'm not sure. We have been traveling up into the mountains for a couple of days, so I hope it is close."

Tanisha waves to Zevran as she walks to Elin. Zevran arrives and asks, "What?"

"The army has stopped, and I sense them sending out riders."

"The snow is impacting them. They probably stopped to let more snow melt, clear the path, and hunt. I will let the men know to expect riders."

Tanisha puts her arm around Merial and says, "We can try to reach out and see how close Hallr is. You ready to try?"

Merial smiles.

Milfred, Hallr, and Kaleb are at the courtyard gate. They are using new logs from the valley to make it easier to open the gate. Milfred will ride a horse for a day to see if a wagon can travel to a town.

Xylia is lying in the chamber. Her wing and shoulder are doing better. As soon as Kaleb finishes opening the tunnel, she will go to the valley and open her wings in the sun. This little group of humans is making her feel better about humans.

She feels a presence. With the continued healing, her ability to sense magic has increased to almost normal levels. This is a new presence reaching out from far away.

Humans are normally strong enough to reach this far. Humans will only reach out this far trying to find someone specific. That can only be Hallr, not another human.

Shifting, this is not good. They know Hallr is in the mountains; they know him from his past.

The group has the gate almost halfway up when Xylia says, "Don't open the gate."

Hallr asks, "What is it?"

This presence agitates her, and the people sense it in her voice, "Close the gate, and I will tell you."

Kaleb pulls one polis from the small wheel and puts it aside. Hallr and Milfred are looking at each other with confusion. Kaleb grabs the other pole, removes it, and stomps down on the wheel.

The wheel spins slowly. As the gate closes, Kaleb says, "It's closing. What is happening?"

"People are approaching the city. I sensed a magi reaching out. I don't know how many."

Hallr asks, "Why are you upset?"

Xylia replies, "I know nothing about them. I can't tell from a distance. They could be dangerous. Every human needs to wear Mithril helmets."

Agnarr says, "That sounds ominous."

Hallr asks, "Xylia, talk to me. Why?"

"The magi reaching out at this distance is strong. Maybe as strong as Sheyla. The last witch I encountered that was that strong was the controller who tried to take the city."

Sheyla says, "As strong as I?"

Xylia says so that everyone can hear, "Yes, Sheyla, as strong as you. Your strength and power are exceptional. Your focus on healing is clear. Thank you again. That strength is not common. The magi reaching out is looking for Hallr. Looking for the city."

Hallr asks, "Xylia, is there a way out so I can go investigate? If I can intercept them, there is less danger."

"There is no other exit you can use other than the small path in the rocks. That was by design, by intent. No secret ways in or out of the city."

Agnarr says, with a sarcastic, inquisitive voice, "What are you thinking? Oh, I'll walk out into the attacker's arms. It will be okay."

"If I'm wearing a Mithril helmet, that can't control me."

Milfred says, "I say no. Sorry, Hallr. If a group of magi is approaching, we don't take chances. I won't be nice until they prove their intentions are not bad."

Agnarr says, "They could try to help. They may have good intentions, but they could be forced or controlled. It is not bad to have skepticism; treat them as not friends until we know more."

Kaleb is standing after placing the last log they used for the gate in a pile. He turns to see Sheyla walking toward them out of the city gate. He says, "I can see both sides of what you are saying. My experience with a control witch was bad, and I'm more inclined to show them my sword than share a dinner table."

Sheyla nods at Kaleb, "That is a good attitude. If they want to apply control magic, they want to control someone. They want power."

Agnarr asks, "Sheyla, can you sense them?"

Sheyla replies, "I will not try. Why? If they want the city, they need to find it and then get in. If they are friendly, they can approach and ask politely."

Milfred laughs, then says, "Hi, friend who found the lost city high in the mountains where no one travels. I'm not here for treasure or to take over the city, just saying hi."

Xylia says, "I like Milfred more now. That is exactly the way to consider them."

Agnarr says, "Well, Milfred, you're not going for supplies. Let's get the horses back to the valley."

Kaleb asks, "Why would they be pushing through snow this early in spring to get to the city? Is the gold that enticing?"

Sheyla's face goes white. "I haven't thought about it in months. They are looking for the box."

Kaleb asks, "What box?"

Xylia screams, "NO! You brought it to the city."

Rage, fear, despair. The box that she helped to create. It is evil.

Reaching down, she feels the rage; the city is dead because of the box. Her doing, her failure. Her fire is there; it has been so long.

Swinging her head up, she sends flames at the ceiling.

They all turn to look at the city and see dragon flames shooting out of the vents at the top of the mountain.

Hallr says, "She is pissed. We know she can make dragon fire again."

Kaleb says, "Brought what to the city?"

Milfred says, "An evil object that is supposed to contain instructions on how to control dwarves and other witches."

Agnarr says, "Interesting that we have been so focused on getting in, then saving Xylia, then opening the gate and the valley. We have been focused on everything but the box."

Sheyla says, "Xylia, we have to talk about this. It pissed you off enough to use dragon fire for the first time in centuries."

Merial sucks in her breath.

Tanisha asks, "What is it? Did you find Hallr?"

"Yes, and something else. Something powerful and big. It doesn't want us to approach the city."

"What is it?"

"I don't know."

"Do you know how to find Hallr?"

"No. The other presence blocked me. I know he is in the mountains, the way we are moving."

"Okay, little sister. That is enough. We need to get ready. I worried that the army we are following would attack Hallr or us. We need to be ready to turn them to our side. It will be hard."

"You asked me to make one of their witches sick to slow them down. The easy one to sense and make dizzy, I can't sense her anymore. She was strong; she wanted to talk."

"What, when. You didn't tell me this."

"The night after I touched her. She said she would train me. She sounded like the witch at the wagon. The one before we found Sheyla and Hallr. I told her No."

"That was good. You need to tell me these things."

"I simply said no. It wasn't a big deal."

"I want to know who could try to influence you. Who would try to control or separate me from my little sister? We are family."

Merial continues, "We became a family in the cage. Now we focus on us first."

"That is right. We focus on us. There will be others who claim to be friends, like that witch, but only want us to control others for their own benefit. We need to resist them by focusing on us, our family."

Merial says, "Feliu said the village trainers are friends."

"They are friends for now. When they need us to become their control puppets, it will change. Why are we here except to be controllers for them?"

"Zevran talked about the army, and we may need to fight."

"Exactly. We will be forced to protect ourselves. Merial, I'm concerned we won't be able to get to Hallr if you don't control the army people."

"With the old witch sick, I can control them."

Army Control

Teppo is talking to the witches, "We lost Willow, Esma is sick. We are going to lose control if we don't figure this out. I want Ranjeet to help with the control of the lieutenants."

Ranjeet says, "I'm not the best at control. You know this. I've spent years only doing short-term spot control when needed. With simple guards, with merchants. These army people are smarter, stronger."

Teppo asks, "What do the women think? They have a say in our combined future."

"Without Willow, we are weak. She was so strong, so powerful; we were all better because of her. We need to leave. If we stay, we need to be in the background. Let the army fight the dwarf. After they are weak, we can retake control. That will give Esma time to recover, to practice at being the primary controller."

Teppo clenches his jaw. He is losing control of his coven, the army, and the prize of obtaining the box.

"I'm worried that with no influence, the army will simply tell us to leave."

Ranjeet says, "Let them. We will be better able to feed ourselves, to get ready. We follow them. Once they've found the city, we can plan our next move. Maybe, just maybe, we can help the dwarf for a short time."

Several of the women nod and glance at each other. "Let the army deal with the dwarf."

Teppo raises his voice, "What if the army gets the box? What do we do then? With that box, we could control it all."

"We don't have the box. They don't have the box. We need to be patient and strike when we have the chance."

Ranjeet nods, "That is simple, easy. Teppo, you're worried

about the wrong thing. After the army is out of the way, getting the box will be easy."

Teppo says, "If the box was taken to the city for an opening tool, we'll need the humans to reveal that after we retrieve it."

It is late, after most people are in bed. Captain Ulgary is meeting with his lieutenants and Tobias. "I know I told the leech two days ago so he could bury his grandmother. The reality is that they are additional mouths to feed and protect in the mountains. We don't need them for any reason I can think of."

Tobias says, "You're correct. They have been helpful up to this point, and we have accounts to settle."

Lieutenant Stonesplitter asks, "Accounts? They have been paying for things along the journey?"

Tobias says, "Yes."

"Have they been paying for supplies all this time, for several years? Where was this money? They have been hauling money around?"

Tobias looks confused. "No, they have been creating accounts with the villages and farmers. Those need to be paid."

Captain Ulgary says, "Those will never be paid. This has been an elaborate sham. They had you to be legitimate; you were following the king's orders. It was about finding the city. Now..."

Tobias continues, "Now they need an army to take the city and then get the treasure. They have been using me."

Captain Ulgary nods, "It isn't all bad. Several years of travel while they protected you and focused on the common interest. However, now we have an army to finish the job. We don't need them."

Lieutenant Stonesplitter says, "We leave in the morning. We will break camp before sunrise to help make up time. I don't care if they complain, want us to wait, or try to follow. I will give the orders to break camp before first light."

<<<>>>

At sunrise, the control camp wakes. The early risers, upon seeing the army marching away, start waking everyone up. The army wagons are still loading, but the troops are moving.

Teppo walks out of the tent, and seeing the army leaving, starts yelling. "Ranjeet! Where is Tobias?"

A minute later, Ranjeet says, "Tobias isn't in our camp. He moved his things yesterday."

"They are leaving without us."

Ranjeet is nodding and replies, "We talked about this. Let them go. Let them find the city and fight the dwarf. Then we go in and pick up the pieces."

Teppo is clenching his fists, looking at Ranjeet. One witch says, "We need to head down to a valley. We aren't ready."

Teppo turns, "Why?"

"Esma is sick with morning sickness. She is pregnant. That is why she is having problems. Our top controller can't spend hours focusing on controlling a group when she is pregnant."

Ranjeet says, "Congratulations to Esma."

The witch replies, "And to you, Daddy. You couldn't keep it in your trousers with our best witch after Willow."

Teppo looks at Ranjeet, shakes his head, and says, "Pack up the camp. We are heading back to the valley. I want the riders to go ahead. Scout for campsites and hunt. We need to find a safe place and prepare."

Tanisha is returning to the tent where they all sleep. She yells, "Elin, Elin opens the tent and looks at Tanisha, "What? Come inside. What are you saying?"

"They are leaving. I'm confused. The army is moving into the mountains. The others are not with them. They are, I don't know, upset."

"The controller group isn't staying with the army? That isn't good. We need to talk to Zevran."

After listening, Zevran says, "We need to wait here to assess. I will send riders to check. Tanisha, you're our best empath. What do you sense about the controllers?"

"They are mixed, not focused, not together. I can't sense the top witch anymore. She is gone. The others are mad, upset, and confused."

Elin says, "Tanisha, this will sound weird, but tell me what you think if the top controller witch is sick, or maybe even dead. Would that feel right?"

"Yes. That would feel right."

"Zevran, if they lost the top controller, they are neutered."

Zevran nods, "That confirmation helps us how?"

"They can't control the army. The army is leaving them. We could take the controller group and eliminate them."

Tanisha's eyes go wide. "Why?"

Zevran says, "They are still a threat. They want the box. They will fight for the box. Are we trying to destroy the box?"

Elin replies, "The only reason we are here is to destroy the box. No other reason."

Tanisha nods, "Destroy the box."

A few minutes later, Tanisha sits next to Merial at the fire. They are alone while the adults are working around the camp. Merial asks, "Where were you?"

Tanisha replies, "The army left and is heading into the mountains. The controller group is not with them. They are heading back down to the valley."

"That sounds good. They won't be a problem."

"They followed Hallr to find the city, the treasure, and then get the box. If they don't follow the army, they don't get any of the treasure."

"I think that is good news; they are not heading to the city."

"I wanted to have them use the army to get into the city."

Merial says, "The presence stopping me from Hallr. I think it is a dragon."

"What? There aren't dragons."

"Just like there are no dwarves. Tanisha, this is awesome. Hallr and a dragon. We can talk to an actual dragon."

Tanisha is looking at the ground, thinking, "Can you talk to the dragon now?"

"No."

"Do you think you could control a dragon?"

"I don't know. Why do I need to control a dragon?"

"If we need to control people to get into the city, that could include the dragon, just for a minute or two."

"I don't know. Why is this so important to you?"

"The witch. The one who was talking to us at the cage wagon. She told me the strongest would be top-control witches with their own covens. The rest would become servant witches under the witch's direct control. The way she said it, we don't get a choice. It is just another case of me, I mean us, under someone's thumb."

"You're scared by that."

"Yes, you should be, too. We are just servants. I grew up with my parents as servants. They worked for wealthy landowners. As soon as I could clean, I started working. A small part of each day is not spent working. My only time for myself. That is what we will be: servants controlled by social and money situations."

"We do nothing unless we are told to. They use us to enrich themselves. Use us to hurt other people. I don't even know all the ways they will treat us as servants to help THEM have control."

"What do you want to do, Tanisha?"

"I'm not sure you're ready."

"I'm family. You need to tell me."

"I want to get the box and use it, learn from it. I want us to be so powerful that no coven can control us. Then, if they try to attack, we will be strong enough to stop them. We can stop them from hurting other people."

"Why would they attack?"

"To get the box. Have the power it can teach. To control us."

"If we are living in the city with Hallr, a dragon, and we have the box, no one can beat us."

"I know that is what we want, but they will try. They won't know how powerful we are if we are just in the city. They will come, try to take the box, and we will need to stop them."

"I want to be like Sheyla. I want to be a healer, not a controller."

"When we are in the city, we can have Sheyla teach us how to be healers. We have to get to the city and then make the army go away."

That afternoon, Elin asks Zevran for an update, and Zevran replies, "All the scouts have returned except one. The army is pushing hard into the mountains. They have riders trailing, watching for us."

As he is talking, a riderless horse comes trotting toward camp. Kaelor says, "The scout Thalen's horse," as he moves to catch the horse.

Elin says, "Where was he scouting?"

"He was sent to watch the coven group."

Elin nods, "He could have been injured falling in the snow."

"We don't know the story. Get Tanisha to sense him."

When Tanisha joins them and understands, she closes her eyes, thinking about what the scout looks like. She is reaching out to him. "He is alive, in pain. His chest and shoulder hurt."

Zevran asks, "Can you tell if it is from a fall, or from an attack?"

"He is in one spot. I think he is hiding. I can't tell what is causing the pain."

Zevran nods, "Thanks, Tanisha. I'm going to send three to get him back."

Feliu has walked up and asks, "Can I travel with the group? I can help Eldric with healing."

Zevran says, "Not going to happen, young man. How old are you?"

Feliu says, "Fifteen. The age at which you recruit people for your guardian group."

Elin smiles, "You knew this was going to happen. He has been training for the trials to be a guardian. He is also training to heal and is doing well. The witch, Sheyla, was an enormous influence on all three."

Feliu says, "I can also shoot and hit a target over one hundred paces away."

One of the other men nods.

Zevran turns to Eldric and says, "Okay, you're his guardian on the ride then."

The man, Eldric, nods, "Feliu, let's get ready."

Zevran says, "We leave as soon as we are ready."

Elin says, "Hang on. You're going?"

Zevran looks at her, saying, "My man is injured, and now I'm taking a teenager with no actual experience. Yes, I'm going."

On the trail left by Thalen's horse, they stop several hundred meters from where they sense he is hiding. Zevran says, "We go on foot. All dark clothing stays with the horse. We blend in with the snow."

Feliu is following his new mentor, Eldric, listening, watching, and trying to sense Thalen. When he feels a presence that is not from their group, he touches Eldric. With a soft voice, he says, "There are others. I think they are looking or waiting."

"They are waiting for us to come and rescue Thalen. This is a trap."

"What do we do?"

"We get Thalen and leave. That doesn't change for us. The others will deal with the trap. Listen Feliu. This is our job: get Thalen and get out. We focus on our job, or this is all a waste."

Feliu nods and says, "Wait just a minute."

He closes his eyes and reaches for Thalen. Sensing him, he opens his eyes and shifts his head until he is sure of the direction.

"That way."

Feliu's confidence in the direction slightly surprised Eldric. He can barely sense Thalen and is not sure of the direction.

It is dark, but they all know Magi can shoot arrows even in the dark. They have been moving in a crouch, following the trail left by the horse, which the others also know. When they get closer, Eldric goes from crouching while moving to crawling. He and Feliu are now just below the snow line.

Thalen senses them and says softly, "There are four waiting."

Feliu replies, "I know, two directly ahead and one to each side."

Eldric looks back at Feliu and puts his finger to his lips.

Thalen says, "That sounded like Feliu. Young for a rescue."

When they are a few meters from Thalen, Feliu stops, closes his eyes, and concentrates. Thalen shifts after a few seconds and says, "I can feel that. I have an arrow in my upper chest that has to come out."

Feliu says, "I need to stop what is bleeding now."

Eldric moves forward, saying, "Feliu, stay and keep working. Thalen, I will be with you in a second to help get you out."

"You're going to cause them....."

"I'm triggering the trap. Relax."

Feliu concentrates and scarcely hears the scuffle to his left and right. When the yelling starts, he opens his eyes and listens with his ears and his mind. Thinking quickly, he shifts his bow, nocks an arrow, and points it up.

He has been told no flames. The others can see your location if you light an arrow on fire before you fire it. Feliu knows a flaming arrow will let everyone see, and his group will have an advantage.

Pulling back the string, he let the arrow fly. The arrow flies up at a steep angle while Feliu concentrates. Halfway up its arc, it bursts into flames, lighting the entire area. The coven men aren't wearing white, which makes them stand out in the snow.

Eldric says, "Time to go. That was good thinking, Feliu. Where did you learn that?"

As they both begin helping Thalen walk toward the horses, Feliu says, "His name is Agnarr. He is strong with push magic and starting fires. He is a great teacher and showed me how."

Back at camp, with Thalen getting healing help, Eldric tells Zevran that Feliu did well, giving him details. Another man received a minor cut during a fight.

Zevran says, "An arrow burst into flames while flying, not before it was shot. That is something."

Eldric says, "He needs to be put into security training. He could be a real asset on missions with his healing."

Zevran nods, "We don't have all the training facilities. Let's get him started with what we can now."

<<<>>>

Teppo's world is upside down. Four men have not returned, and he is being told that Esma, the new controller, just had a miscarriage. She is physically and mentally unable to control anyone right now.

Ranjeet is stressed, trying to handle things and wanting to stay away from Teppo. He has arranged things for Esma. She should be okay with time and support.

Taking a deep breath, knowing what needs to happen for the good of the group. If they don't follow through, the group won't survive. Walking to Teppo, he says, "Teppo, tomorrow we turn around and start following the army. We get to the city and help them take over the city."

"What?" Shaking his head, Teppo looks at Ranjeet, "Sorry. I guess losing Willow and Esma losing the baby had more of an impact on me than I realized."

"Tomorrow, we follow the army. We will never get the box if we don't go to the city."

"What about the missing riders?"

"We don't know what happened, and we don't wait. We need to re-focus on the objective, or the coven won't survive."

Teppo nods, "You're right. Let's get everyone together. We all have to commit to seeing this through as a group. Esma lost the baby. She needs to grieve, but she can be a leader when we need her. Tell the men we will be aggressive and dangerous in any attack."

The next morning, they break camp early and begin moving. Teppo says, "Ranjeet, ride ahead and talk to them. We need them to understand they need us to have the humans open the city gate."

"Will we have a controller?"

"They don't need to know that right now. We give Esma as much time as possible."

"I'm supposed to influence them, not control them. This is crazy enough to work."

They Came for the Box

The city is quiet, and smoke is rising from the top of the mountain, where all the vegetation is on fire from Xylia's fire breath. They are waiting outside the main gate.

Hallr asks, "Xylia, are you okay? Can we come into the city? Will you talk to us?"

After a pause, they hear, "Yes."

Sheyla walks to the gate and says, "Will you tell us why that evil box upset you?"

Kaleb asks, "Can I see this thing?"

Xylia says, "You know it is evil, but you brought it here."

Hallr asks, "Where else could we take it to be safe, to keep it out of the control of a witch's hands?"

They hear a mental growl, "You're right. The group coming is looking for it. That means they know about it and what it means."

Milfred asks, "You showed your fire breath. Can you destroy it?"

Xylia says, "I'm not strong enough yet."

Agnarr says, "It won't matter. They won't believe us if we tell them it was destroyed."

Xylia says, "The biggest mistake."

Kaleb is walking into the gate area and feels the heat from one tunnel. The walls are radiating heat. He says, "What mistake?"

Sheyla says, "Xylia, tell us about this box. Where did it come from? Why was it made?"

Xylia says, "Come to the chamber with that thing."

As they enter the chamber, Sheyla, and Milfred are holding torches. Agnarr is carrying the pack with the box. They stop on the steps leading down to the gold. The floor is no longer plates, cups, coins, and other items. It is now a smooth gold floor with jewels sitting on the surface.

Hallr says, "Your breath melted all the gold, making a smooth floor."

"Yes, it will be easier to walk now."

Agnarr says, "The treasures are gone."

Xylia is simply lying on the golden floor. "I ruined that as well now."

Sheyla stops in the middle of the golden floor, saying, "What did you say?"

"You need to learn about my dark past. My thing, I don't like to talk about."

Kaleb walks back to the doorway. "There is cool air from the corridor. The room is still hot."

Agnarr looks up, "The vent hole is letting the hot air escape, drawing in cooler air."

Milfred wipes sweat from his forehead and moves to the doorway as well. "Xylia, are you okay? I mean, are you mad at us for bringing the box?"

"Yes, I'm mad, but I can't be angry at you for bringing that thing.

Kaleb asks, "I do not know what is happening. Can I see this thing? Where did it come from?"

Milfred says, "We found it after the war, where we met Hallr. A witch attacked him to get it."

Agnarr is turning over the pack to dump the box. "He almost died. Sheyla saved him."

Kaleb walks over and picks up the box, turning it over and looking at all sides.

Xylia takes a breath, "You should know the real story. It was my idea."

Sheyla looks at Xylia, squinting, "What?"

"It was centuries ago now. The control covens were new but gaining power. They were trying to take over. Originally, control witches were wicked and never had a coven. They were always single witches, outcasts."

Agnarr says, "That limited their power and threat."

"When they organized, they were a problem. The dwarves wanted a way to prevent covens from getting too powerful. I suggested something to make them fight each other."

Sheyla says, "Something they would all want more than anything, so they would destroy other covens to get it."

"Yes. It took many years of planning to get this right. There were other attempts, but they were destroyed, so there would be only one."

Kaleb is looking at the cover and says, "Bring the torch over here so I can see better."

Hallr says, "The box was built and sent out."

"It was great in the beginning. We spread the word about the powerful box. After several years, the covens began fighting for it. Then it quickly went wrong."

Milfred is holding the torch up for Kaleb and asks, "How?"

The covens began using their control over kings and generals to command human armies.

Milfred says, "That was centuries ago. The century of wars, when kingdoms were constantly fighting."

"That was the covens. Then it got worse."

Sheyla asks, "Worse than making humans kill each other for control of this evil thing?"

"Yes. The dwarves tried to help stop the wars. When a coven was directly involved on one side, they would fight against the coven-controlled army. Then the coven's tactics changed. They used the human army to kill the dwarves. The fight would start, then the soldiers would only attack dwarves."

Agnarr says, "That is when the covens started eliminating dwarves."

Xylia says, "What I think is worse is the whole idea backfired. Instead of eliminating control covens, it strengthened them. They fought, and the stronger coven would win. Over a century, the coven of witches grew stronger and stronger."

Kaleb says, "This writing is in six different languages."

Sheyla turns around to look at Kaleb. "Can you read what it says?"

"Yes. There are lots of warnings, but the way it is worded seems like a riddle."

Hallr is looking at Kaleb, "Your Ma taught you. What does it say?"

Kaleb is rereading part of the text several times. "Ah, okay."

Hallr says, "What?"

Xylia lifts her head to look at Kaleb, "Puzzle solver."

"It is a kind of riddle. After being in the city, this makes sense. If you don't know how the dwarves built the key part of the city, or how to enter, you won't understand. Counterweights."

"Its key message translates to: they crafted them to make the big ones easy. The last part means accessed in dwarven order. The sides of the box have the gates and doors as reliefs."

Kaleb shifts his hands around the sides. He moves one of his large hands to the opposite side of the box. Fingers moving, then everyone hears three clicks.

Kaleb straightens up and holds two parts of the box. Agnarr moves to see what is inside.

Xylia says, "There is nothing inside. There is no secret training."

They all look inside the box and see the details of a lock mechanism, nothing else. Kaleb says, "To open it, you need to know where to push and in the right sequence that causes the counterweights to align. The wrong sequence, and it won't open."

Hallr laughs, "The whole thing is a hoax."

Sheyla yells, "That... that's it. I'm mad. It is a hoax. No one will believe that. We can't say we destroyed it."

Agnarr says, "Yes, we can. We destroyed it in the city. That is why we brought it back."

Xylia says, "They are coming for the box. They have to be shown its destruction, then they need to leave and spread the word."

Milfred says, "They will want the box, and then the city and the treasure." He gestures around and continues, "Even though they can't carry it away easily."

At The Gate

Tobias says, "Captain, he isn't lying. If the city gate is closed, they will get the humans to open the gate."

Captain Ulgary asks, "What if the gate is open? We don't need them."

Ranjeet caught up with them two days ago. None of the soldiers would take a message or get him to the officers until he applied a little control to influence them.

The entire troop has been pushing through thick snow for days. Soldiers are tired. The horses can move through the snow, but the men have to find a place to camp, clear a spot for tents and cooking fires, and then set up camp. The next morning, it all gets taken down, and they move again.

When Teppo and the wagons catch up, Ranjeet gives him a report on what happened. "Now we are relegated to the back of the wagons. They won't include me in discussions."

Teppo says, "We wait and be patient. Esma is feeling better. We let them do the work now."

Midday the next day, the lead troops reach a narrow area. Captain Ulgary is talking with the scouts.

"Sir, about three hundred meters up the slope, the path narrows so only one wagon can go through. I would say it looks like part of the path or road was altered or destroyed to make a chokepoint."

"Good scouting, Sergeant. We are getting close to the city."

Tobias is looking down the slope at the line of soldiers, followed by the wagons and support personnel. There is no place that is flat and large enough for a camp. They will need to split up or make camp several hundred meters down the slope.

He steps over to Captain Ulgary. "Sir, when I look at the path of the wagons and at the line of troops, we may have a problem."

One lieutenant says, "We can deal with it."

Tobias continues, "There is no place ahead to make camp. It is too narrow and sloped."

Captain Ulgary is smiling, "Master Tobias. This is called a choke point area. No place to camp, no stops. It gets narrow and possible for a small force to prevent anyone from advancing."

"How will this work?"

"Lieutenant. Stop the advance. We need the siege wagon at the front. Tomorrow, we search for the city gates."

Milfred asks, "Xylia, any update on the troops?"

"The scouts went back. They were just outside the courtyard gate when they stopped and turned. The entire army has stopped now."

Kaleb asks, "Can you read their minds? Do you know what they plan to do?"

Hallr is heading to the main gate. Seeing this, Sheyla asks, "You have a plan?"

Hallr stops, walks back, and says, "Aye. They can't get in through the courtyard gate. If it won't open, they will begin searching and eventually find the little rock path we used. I want to take the stones out front, under the window, and block the path."

Agnarr says, "Xylia can't sense any magi with the army, which is good. That would make your little plan harder. You can't start making lots of noise now."

Kaleb asks, "What are we doing? Hiding, but making noise and not really hiding. If they know, or think the city is in this area, they will stay for some time trying to find it."

Milfred and Hallr say, "We need to get ready."

Sheyla says, "What does that mean?"

Agnarr says, "We need to close the main gate. Even if they get into the courtyard, they can't get through. We can defend the window we used."

Milfred is looking at Hallr, then at the gate. "I have a problem. There are only two of us who know how to close the gate. One of those was seriously injured opening the gate. Hallr, you need to show us how to close that gate."

Xylia says, "Yes, and the door to the valley."

Sheyla is looking at the group. "I need to know how to close the gates. If they get into the courtyard, you will all be fighting. I'll be the only one to do it. That also means, Hallr, you will not move rocks right now."

Kaleb is shaking his head. "We don't need to talk about just stopping them. How do we make them go away?"

Agnarr smiles, "We do nothing. We wait. They can't get in. We have food and water, while they don't. They will have to go back to the valley."

Hallr says, "From the description, there is enough to go to the valley and bring supplies up. They could be there all summer. We need to send them away or defeat them."

"Hallr and I can do it," says Kaleb.

Agnarr smiles. "How do you get out to them? Through the little path with full armor and weapons? You won't fit. Or do you open the gate that they want opened to get in?"

Kaleb says, "We're trapped."

Milfred says, "Snow trapped us, and we did just fine. Now it is an army. I would have gone to get supplies, but we can survive in the city with no problem."

Sheyla says, "To fight them, we will have to open the courtyard gate while an army is outside waiting to attack and take over the city. Does that sound like a smart thing to do?"

Hallr has been looking at everyone talking and says, "We have multiple issues. If we close the main gate, how do we get in and out to the courtyard gate, much less open the gate?"

Kaleb turns and walks toward the barracks. He returns with two axes, plus a dwarven shield. He places them inside the gate to the right. "I need to take care of the chickens. You guys figure something out."

The Last Dwarf

Two hours later, Sheyla and Hallr return to the barracks area. Sheyla says, "I know how to close the main gate and the gate to the valley."

Hallr nods, pointing to the Mithril helmet Sheyla is now carrying, "We found a helmet that will fit well enough."

Xylia says, "Everyone should get a helmet and wear it."

Milfred adjusts his helmet, saying, "I got helmets for Agnarr and myself. Hallr is the only one who doesn't have a helmet."

"I have one in the room. I've tried every helmet that might fit. The one in the room is the best."

Kaleb replies, "Big enough for even your head to fit."

"I'm not the one with a problem fitting through the door."

"Captain, past this narrow area, there is a small path to the right. It is just wide enough for one wagon."

"Tobias, where is this city?" demands Captain Ulgary, glaring at Tobias.

"I think it is time to try the witches. Have Teppo brought to us."

When Teppo arrives, Tobias says, "When we first met, you showed me illusions and said your group could do them. You have told me throughout the search for the city that you can get the dwarves and the humans to come out of the city. Now is the time."

"Master Tobias, not that simple."

Tobias replies, "It is now. In the fall, the scouts got here when the storm made us turn back. The city is somewhere here. You will get the dwarf companions to reveal the city and let us in, or you will be put in irons for deceiving the king."

"Master Tobias, you need to understand what has changed in my group. You know, my grandmother has passed away. She could easily do what you are asking. Our best witch, Esma, has been ill. I will go work with her, but don't expect a band to appear showing you into the city suddenly."

"I'm not an idiot. This will be coordinated and planned. You will start at night. At first light, we need to know about the city and how to get into it. Captain Ulgary will have his troops ready to enter and take the city."

"Merial, for the last couple of days, you have been a pain. Why are you grumpy?"

"Elin, the dragon is upset."

"What dragon? Why am I just now hearing about a dragon?"

"I wasn't sure. We are close enough to the city for me to know how the dragon is feeling."

"Tanisha, did you know about this?"

"Merial thought she sensed a dragon, but we weren't sure."

Elin puts her head out of the wagon and yells, "Someone call Zevran. We have to talk."

"A dragon? Is this dragon good? Bad? Do we know?" asks Zevran.

Merial says, "I think it is friendly to Hallr."

"Well, the army has stopped. We are catching them. We need to decide to stop or start the confrontation."

Tanisha says, "I think it is time."

Elin interrupts, "We can't let the army get entrenched in the city."

Zevran says, "I will send men in during the night. We will take out the leadership."

Elin nods, "The girls and I will deal with the magi group."

"No. My men will deal with them as well. You have already determined that their top controller is gone. The grave we passed confirms that. We will end this."

Elin asks, "When the leadership is removed, then what?"

"Without a leader, the army won't fight. We will deal with the controller group. That is the point; the girls need to reach out to Hallr and the witch. We make a contract, get into the city, and defend it. Then we destroy the box."

Elin says, "We won't know when your men are done until they return. We will need to wait until morning to reach out to Sheyla."

Tanisha says, "What will the army do without leaders? Do we need to focus on anything during the night?"

Zevran says, "No. Get some rest. You will have a long day tomorrow. The army will churn trying to find who to report the problem to. They won't do anything drastic during the night."

Let Me In

It is after midnight. Esma and the witches are starting. Teppo is with them as a coach.

"Esma, we start with the humans: the young giant and the blacksmith. Reach out. Get them to show themselves."

Esma and the attending witches are sitting together to begin the coven control process. Esma will be with the illusion and bring the other witches into the world. Together, they will reach out to control the humans.

Kaleb is asleep without a helmet. He hears a voice. Deep and strong, like Xylia. *"Come join us. We need to celebrate finding the lost city."*

The voice asks, *"Do you have the box?"*

Kaleb replies, "Yes."

He immediately feels elation and joy, *"It is time to celebrate. Come join us."*

Kaleb gets up, bends over to exit the room, and sees Milfred coming out of his room as well.

They are both smiling as they walk out of the city gate to the courtyard gate. As they approach the courtyard gate, they hear music, singing, and laughter outside. Together, they grab the poles and begin to open the gate.

They keep hearing, *"Join us. It is time to celebrate."*

Teppo is tapped on the shoulder. He immediately felt irritated. Softly, he says, "What?"

Ranjeet grabs his shoulder and turns him.

Teppo, realizing something is wrong, turns and leaves the group.

Ranjeet, red-faced, says, "Assassins. Magi assassins. The captain and his lieutenants are dead. We lost everyone except Rafferty and me before we killed them."

"The magi group that was following. We can't disrupt the witches. We need the army to attack them."

"I need your help. Tobias is the only one left; they might listen to him."

Teppo rolls his eyes. "Dragons save us."

At Tobias' tent, Ranjeet doesn't even wait to untie the tent flap. He uses his dagger to slice down the seam and jerks open the tent. Teppo walks in and says loudly, "Master Tobias, we are under attack."

Tobias wakes up. "What?"

Teppo shakes him. "Wake up. Tell the army. Attack the witches following us."

Tobias is focusing and says, "Where is the captain?"

Talking fast, upset Teppo says, "Dead. Assassins have killed him and the lieutenants. They also attacked us. We killed them, but we are all that is left."

Tobias shoves Teppo back, "Get out of my way." He yells at Sergeant Atonal, "Get up."

Ranjeet asks, "Who is Sergeant Atonal

"If the officers are dead, he is in command."

Tobias is pulling on his boots, grabbing his cloak, when a soldier opens the flap, "Sir. Oh, you're already awake."

"Take me to Sergeant Atonal. Teppo has already dealt with the assassins."

Sergeant Atonal knows the Army process well. He needs an officer to give the objectives, and he will make it happen. A soldier jerked him out of sleep talking about assassins, and the officers are all dead.

"Sergeant, what do we do?"

"Neutralize the threat."

"They are dead. They also attacked the group with us, killing most of the men before they were killed."

"Where is Tobias?"

"We have someone getting him."

Less than a minute later, Tobias enters the command tent,

"There you are, Sergeant. We need to deal with the group that has been following us. Send troops to capture or kill them all."

The Sergeant points to Teppo, "These guys."

"No. They are with us, not following. The wagon that had been behind a day, following. They sent assassins and killed the officers," says Tobias in an irritated tone.

Sergeant Atonal calls for men. He is having men prepare and asking scouts to report their locations.

During this time, a soldier appears at the command tent. He salutes the sergeant and asks, "Where is the lieutenant? I need to report something urgent."

"The officers are dead. What do you have to report?"

"Just past the narrow part of the path, a hidden gate is opening."

Tobias asks, "Are you sure?"

"Yes, sir."

Teppo is smiling, "That is the lost city being revealed. We need troops ready to enter. They will need to fight the dwarf and his human friends."

Tobias asks, "Why are they opening the gate now?"

Teppo replies, "In the dark of night versus in the day when everyone is watching. This is the plan you wanted."

Tobias looks at Teppo for a second, then turns to the Sergeant. "Split the troops: a dozen to the wagon behind, the rest to the city gate."

"Wake up!"

Hallr is sound asleep, snoring. Now, a dragon's voice is yelling in his head to get up. "What?"

"They have Kaleb and Milfred. Get the others."

As Hallr stumbles out of bed, he asks, "Who's got them?"

"Controller witches, several. A coven. They are having them open the courtyard gate."

Hallr walks into the common area and yells, "Everyone up!"

Hallr turns back to the room and grabs his axe. Turning around, Agnarr is ducking to exit his room, wiping sleep from his eyes. "Sheyla!"

"I'm up. What is going on?"

Xylia says, "Controllers have Kaleb and Milfred. They are opening the courtyard gate. I'm also sensing that the army people are upset. I don't know why."

Agnarr adjusts the Mithril necklace. "What do we do?"

Hallr shifts the axe, "We get ready to fight."

Sheyla looks at him, thinking. She shakes her head, "Fight Kaleb and Milfred? What are you saying?"

"Fight the army."

Xylia says, "Get your helmets on."

Agnarr nods, "Right, the helmet."

Sheyla says, "It is still very early, and I just woke up. I'm not running out the gate. I'm getting water and going to pee first."

Hallr's face shifts from confusion to amusement. "Practical. I'll be at the gate. You get done so that I can go."

Agnarr is looking undecided, and Hallr says, "Go."

On his way to the latrine, Agnarr stops, turns, and says, "Hallr, you talked about putting on a show for the army when you met Kaleb. Get the armor on. You need to look unbeatable."

Hallr nods, "After I pee."

Several minutes later, Sheyla walks out to the barracks common area wearing the helmet and carrying a short sword. Agnarr follows right after, wearing his helmet. He is holding a bow and quiver, with a sword at his waist.

Hallr walks from the latrine to his room. They hear him shift armor, clinking. When he walks out, he is wearing full dwarven Mithril armor, carrying his great axe.

Agnarr says, "That looks impressive, wow."

Sheyla stands next to Hallr and says, "We need to follow our plan. I have to close the gate."

Hallr looks up at her, "What about Kaleb and Milfred?"

"*Xylia will be a better help to them in the short term. If I don't close the gate, you have to close it.*"

Xylia says, "Yes, closing the gate is the priority."

Agnarr says, "We will be isolated with the army. Just the two of us."

Sheyla says, "Once the gates are closed, I can focus on counteracting the coven."

Xylia says, "It will take time to get to the gate controls and get them moving. Go now. Hallr, you need to walk out and stand as the block, the guard."

Sheyla says, "I'm going. Please don't kill Kaleb or Milfred."

Tobias is with Teppo and the Sergeant, watching the gate slowly rise. Looking across the courtyard, they can see the city gate.

Tobias says, "The city. We need troops to get into that city gate. Don't let them close it."

Teppo says, "The two opening the gate won't fight us. They are letting us in. We need troops to ignore them and go for the main gate."

The sergeant yells orders, and the troops run toward the main gate. They jump over the channel in the ground, and the courtyard gate fills.

As a dozen get across the channel, they see two figures walk out of the city gate. A human with a bow, wearing a helmet, and a fully armored dwarf with a great axe.

The troops stop, some sliding to a halt as they see the pair. The sergeant yells, "Take that gate."

"Sergeant, that is a fully armored dwarf. We can't; our weapons are not effective."

"Tackle him, overwhelm him."

Tobias is at the gate watching it continue to pivot. The giant is bigger than he remembers. He and the blacksmith are working away to open the gate, not caring that troops are entering the courtyard.

Teppo says, "They will stay focused until the gate is completely open."

"Will they fight the dwarf?"

"It won't be easy, but yes."

Tanisha is tossing in her sleep. Something is happening. She wakes to hear Merial mumbling in her sleep. Something has her upset. Reaching out to sense what is happening, she gets multiple different inputs. Zevran is upset. The coven is focused on people, probably controlling them. And the powerful presence, it must be the dragon is upset, mad.

The dragon must be making Merial upset. She gets up and touches Elin to wake her. "Something is happening."

A minute later, they walk out of the tent. They see Zevran at the fire talking to two men. When they walk over, they hear, "Get everyone up."

Elin asks, "What's going on?"

"I sent assassins to take out the leadership of the army and the coven. They haven't come back. The indications are that they were killed. Four men dead."

"Did they succeed?"

"It looks like the army leadership is gone. They have no officers left. However, the coven fought and killed my men. Their leadership is still active."

Tanisha is wrapping a blanket around herself, over her coat. Everyone's breath is visible. She closes her eyes to focus.

Elin notices and raises a hand for Zevran to wait. "What do you sense, Tanisha?"

"The coven is controlling someone, maybe two. The army is splitting, dividing. They want us and the city. Oh. The controllers have people opening a gate so they can get into the city."

Tanisha's brow furrows; she shakes her head, bends her head down, focused.

Merial comes out of the tent and starts talking. "They are controlling Milfred to open the gate. Xylia is very upset."

Tanisha says, "The dragon is upset, and her presence is overpowering, making it hard to read details. The army is coming."

Merial says, "I need to help Milfred."

Elin says, "No. Merial, if he isn't being hurt right now, we focus on the Army. The army is coming for us. We need to control the army so that they don't attack us."

Merial asks, "What do they do instead?"

Tanisha says, "Take us to the city."

Agnar is standing next to Hallr as they look at dozens of soldiers entering the courtyard by ducking under the rising gate. "The odds don't look good."

"For them."

"Are you crazy? Are you going to fight that entire army?"

"Yes. It will take a lot more than this bunch to bring down a fully armored dwarf."

"What do I do?"

"Kill the stragglers. Whatever I don't kill right away, you take care of."

Hallr takes a step forward and twirls, spins, and flips the axe.

"I'm telling you that's him."

"How can you be sure it is the same dwarf?"

"First, that is a stupid question. It is a fully armored dwarf. That means tough to kill. Second, yes, I'm sure. I was there when he killed a troll. Now they want us to fight him."

"Our orders are to take the city. Maybe he will let us in."

As they watch Hallr flip the axe, the reply is, "Or we get chopped in half by that axe."

"Are you going to refuse the order?"

"I'm going to wait for someone to lead us into the fight."

Sheyla is following the path Hallr showed her before. She is gripping the key in one hand and a burning torch in the other. The only one in the city now, she has to close the gate before the army gets in.

"Xylia, when I close the gate, Hallr, and Agnarr will be trapped, isolated. How can I help?"

"You need to close the main gate, then the gate to the valley. Keep your helmet on so they can't attack you."

"I heard the story about the attackers when the city fell, threatening to kill the guards' families. That is a different way to control the dwarves."

"They will try everything possible. You shouldn't hear mental threats with the helmet on."

"That is the problem. They got Kaleb and Milfred when they were asleep, without the helmet. I can't sleep with the helmet on."

"Close the gate first."

Sheyla unlocks the door, pushes it open, and slips in. She stays low in a squat as she closes and locks the door.

Waddling across the room, she opens the door to the tunnel. "Bloody dragons, they didn't want this to be easy for humans."

Xylia says, "You're doing great."

Crawling out of the tunnel, Sheyla stands, and stretches. She quickly goes to the levers that lock the counterweight. The first one moves easily. The second moves partway and stops. "No, no. Move you stupid lever."

She takes a step back and uses her body to hit the lever. It moves quickly, making her stumble and fall to her hands and knees. The helmet slides off her head and rolls to the edge, coming to a stop *between the platform and the counterweight.*

Putting the helmet back on, Sheyla says, "Hallr talked about using water to help the gate close faster. If I turn the water on with the valve on that wall, I can't ride the counterweight down to lock it in place."

Xylia repeats, "Close the gate. There is a ladder on the side that you can descend. Hallr and Kaleb climbed on each side to open the gate."

"I'll lock the gate, then I can follow the path he described to get to the valley gate."

"Correct. It is important to lock the gate so they can't just open it. You need to make sure that happens. Use the water to close the gate faster."

Nodding, Sheyla picks up the torch and goes to the pipes. Hallr showed her the valve that will pour water into the trough on top of the counterweight. She grabs the valve handle with her free hand, and it won't move.

Taking a step back and thinking. She puts the torch down and tries both hands with no effect. "I need to hit it."

She looks down at the torch, thinking she will use it to hit the valve, when the helmet shifts. She takes the helmet off and hits the handle several times until it moves.

With the helmet back on, she grabs the handle and turns the valve full open.

The pipes make noise. Air hisses out of the nozzles above the trough; first sludge, then reddish-brown water, and finally, clear water drops into the trough from all four nozzles. The counterweight immediately begins to sink. "I can't leave the water running, or I will never get the gate open again later."

Sheyla jerks the valve handle closed and runs for the counterweight before it gets too far down.

Jumping down and landing hard in the dark, she realizes she had forgotten the torch.

"Xylia, good news, and bad news. The good news is that the

gate is closing. The bad news is that I left the torch. I can't see anything. I never saw the lock pins at the bottom, only what Hallr told me."

"Can you check if water is flowing out of the trough?"

"I'll try."

As the counterweight is descending, Sheyla, with hands outstretched in front of her, slowly walks toward where she thinks the trough is located. If she misses, she could walk off the side of the counterweight.

After several tentative steps, she gets on her hands and knees and crawls. She stops when she moves her hand forward and puts it down in the air. She is on the edge. Turning left, she crawls, finding the trough as she hears and feels the counterweight settle. "Xylia, the gate is closed."

Agnarr turns back when he hears the gate moving. Watching it rise out of the ground, blocking access to the city, he gets nervous. "I don't know why I'm nervous now versus a few minutes ago."

"We can't run; they know it and will act differently," says Hallr.

"What are they waiting for?"

"Orders, a leader, I don't know. They are scared. The first ones up here will die, and they know it."

"You look very intimidating, tossing that axe around."

"That is the point. Avoid the fight by scaring them."

Dismounted, six soldiers are at the wagon. There are dozens more still mounted. The sergeant in charge says, "Take them into custody."

Merial says, "I want to go to the city."

One soldier backhands Merial, "Shut up."

Tanisha suddenly has a dagger in her hand. She is over a meter *away from the soldier. Her arm shoots forward, the dagger flies straight and fast, hitting the soldier in the chest so hard that he flies backward.*

Before he hits the ground, the dagger is flying back into her hand, "To not touch my sister!"

The soldiers turn toward Tanisha and take two steps toward her. The dagger flies again, then again.

One soldier says, "Witches," as they all stop and look at the Sergeant.

Merial stands, wipes blood off her lip as she steps over to Tanisha. Putting her hand on Tanisha's arm, she says, "Stop. You stop."

Merial sees Zevran looking at the remaining soldiers with their swords out. He puts his sword back in its scabbard and turns to Merial, "Maybe we should do this your way."

Merial looks at the sergeant next to Zevran and says, "Why are you being mean? Stop being mean to us."

The sergeant is watching Tanisha. He shifts to Merial, "We were told you are dangerous witches. Witchcraft is outlawed."

"Stop being mean. Tell your men you will take us to the city."

Zevran says, "Outlawed in your country, not here."

The sergeant turns to his men and says, "We are going to take them to the city to talk to Master Tobias."

Tanisha whispers to Merial, then nods to Feliu, turns to Elin, and says, "We need to get to the city quickly. Most of the army will stay and follow with the wagons."

Elin replies, "How will you go if not with the wagons?"

"We will ride behind mounted soldiers."

Feliu says, "Zevran and I will ride our own horses. Tanisha can ride behind me."

Zevran is looking at Elin and says, "I don't think you're in charge anymore."

"Obviously not. However, I feel like my head is clear now. I don't know if I was ever in charge," as she looks at Tanisha.

"Merial will ride with me," says Zevran.

The riders mounted and turned, moving, returning on the path broken through the snow.

When they pass the coven tent, Merial is gazing. Tanisha says to Merial, "Don't disturb them yet. We need to be at the gate."

The sergeant asks, "What are they doing?"

"They are controlling our friend, making him open the gate."

"Like witches?"

"Yes. They are witches."

"Witchcraft is outlawed."

Feliu shouts, "That is why we need to get to the city to stop this."

Tanisha says to Feliu, "We are almost there. We won't have to worry about covens anymore."

Feliu replies, "We will have the box."

When they get to the narrow area, the sergeant yells for them to clear a path.

With the slight rise in the path up to the courtyard, they can see Agnarr and Hallr standing in front of the gate. Merial says, "There is Hallr, and Agnarr. Where are Milfred and Sheyla?"

Feliu says, "He is opening that gate with a giant."

Sheyla's Illusion

"The gate is closed. I searched around the trough, and there is one small hole for the water to drain. I put dirt into it to slow it down."

Xylia replies, "Good. Now you need to close the valley gate."

"How do I do that? I can't see; I can't climb out. I'm stuck. Can you at least tell me what is happening?"

"Hallr and Agnarr are in the courtyard. None of the soldiers approached. Milfred and Kaleb have the gate almost completely open. Now, the bad news."

"That was the good news? What?"

"There are more witches. The witch I sensed before is getting closer. This is not the coven controlling the boys. It is another strong witch controller. Sheyla, history is repeating. They have come for that blasted box."

"Hang on. Another controller. What do you know about them?"

"There are three young magi who are strong. The strongest one is much younger."

"How young do you think?"

"I can tell she is prepubescent. There is another boy and an even older girl, maybe a teenager."

Sheyla says, "This is not good. Coven, controllers, an army converging. Many people are going to die today unless I can figure something out."

"Can we get the witches to fight each other?"

"They will simply get the army to fight itself. We need something they both have to focus on. Another army would be great."

"There is no other army. That would be different fighting."

Sheyla growls, "I can't even pace to think. I could step off this counterweight. This is frustrating, being literally in the dark. I can't see where I am. Can't see the battle. Can sense anything with this damn helmet on."

Sheyla sits down cross-legged, reaches to take the helmet off, when Xylia says, "Don't take the helmet off. I need you to stay out of their control."

"Xylia, I've never been controlled. I don't think they can."

Xylia replies, "Because it hasn't happened doesn't mean it isn't possible."

Sheyla thinks aloud. "Stronger, bigger. Something they can't fight and win. Like a dragon."

"They don't know about me. I can't crawl out and frighten them."

Mind racing, Sheyla is going through options in her head: what she will need to do to make this work. "Xylia, I have a plan. I need you to back me up."

"How? What are you talking about?"

"They are going to see a witch riding a massive dragon."

"That is crazy. I can't fly. A human can't ride on my back when I'm flying. The wind would rip you off my back."

Sheyla shouts, "Xylia, stop! I'm going to make an illusion that they all see. I need you to project so that they mentally believe it. Are Hallr and Agnarr still there, waiting?"

"Yes."

"Perfect. I need you to tell them I'm going to the project. When we land on the parapets, they need to turn and wave. Hallr needs to wave to the illusion he can't see."

"You sound a little crazy right now, but I understand what you want to do."

"We are going to destroy the box with dragon fire. They will all see it happen. I'm taking the helmet off."

With the helmet off, Sheyla reaches out. She will have to project this illusion to everyone. The first thing she can sense is the two witches. She immediately says, "Merial. What is she doing? Xylia, the two witches are the girls we took to the village. The boy is Feliu."

"What are you going to do?"

"Same plan. Get ready to roar."

"Tell me when."

Settled and relaxed, she takes a breath. Sheyla begins to concentrate and tense, "Now."

<<<>>>

In the courtyard, Agnarr, and Hallr hear Xylia, "Sheyla is going to create an illusion to stop them and destroy the box. Hallr, follow Agnarr's lead to wave at Sheyla."

"Sure, but she is supposed to be locked in the city."

Xylia says, "She is going to fly out."

Everyone hears a dragon roar coming from inside the city. It is clear, loud, and real. Everyone in the courtyard stops. Esma hears the roar, disrupting her concentration. She quickly regains her composure.

Everyone hears a noise, another roar, but this one is distant, from the mountain. As everyone looks toward the sound, they see it. A large, bright red dragon is climbing in the sky, wings flapping.

They watch it turn toward the courtyard. The army men are talking, mumbling. They have never seen an actual dragon, but from the stories they have heard, they know this isn't good.

Wings flapping, the dragon flies around the mountain peak, heading for the gate. Then, with the wings flapping hard to slow it, it lands on the parapets above the gate.

The wind buffets everyone when the dragon's wings flap. Then they realize there is a rider in the saddle on the back of the dragon.

She is wearing Mithril armor, holding the reins of the dragon in one hand and a box in the other.

They watch as the dragon looks across the courtyard.

Agnarr turns back to look, telling Hallr what is happening. "Now wave up to Sheyla riding Xylia. She is the boss."

Hallr turns, laughs, and waves.

Xylia rears back, inhales, and then lunges forward, unleashing dragon fire across the courtyard with a side-to-side head swing.

The flames go over everyone and past the courtyard gate. Everyone flinches from the heat. Smoke comes off things. Everyone backs out of the gate.

Sheyla says, "Xylia. Let Hallr and Agnarr know about Merial, Feliu, and Tanisha. Tell them to get to the courtyard gate fast."

After the crowd reaches the gate, Agnarr, and Hallr run to it. Everyone watches as the image of Sheyla throws the box out into the empty courtyard.

Teppo yells, "It's an illusion. There are no dragons. Get the box."

Everyone hears the powerful, booming voice of Xylia in their head, "I'm no illusion. If you think I'm an illusion, come over here, and I'll eat you as a snack."

Teppo goes white, his face going from fright to anguish as he watches.

Milfred and Kaleb stop opening the gate. Blinking, Kaleb turns to see Sheyla riding Xylia, who is sitting on the gate.

Kaleb exclaims, "You can fly."

Kaleb and Milfred hear Xylia, "You're not being controlled. Can you get helmets on?"

The image of Xylia takes a large breath, and the dragon fire starts. All directed at the box in the courtyard.

The watchers can't see the box. The flames are blocking the view. Even from the full distance across the courtyard, they are all cringing away from the intense heat of the dragon's fire.

Agnarr uses his magic and lights cloth items on fire around him as they watch, including his own cloak.

People are trying to put out the small fires created by the dragon.

When Xylia stops, they all look at the box, eager to see its condition. They see a melted blob on the ground. Small flames and smoke are coming out of the box. Whatever was inside is burning.

Teppo hyperventilates, clenching his fists. "No, No, No? All this time, all the work."

Tanisha already knew about the dragon and knows it is real. But this can't be happening. She almost falls off as she gets off the horse, stumbling toward the courtyard, crying. The box was going to save her, save them all. Now it is gone.

Everyone stops when they hear the rider yell, "There is no box. Nothing to fight over. This city is mine. The treasure is mine. Your survival now depends on not pissing me off. Leave my city."

Agnarr smiles at the statement and assumes Hallr will be mad about her claiming the city as hers. He turns to see Hallr smiling, completely unaware. He didn't see or hear anything; it was all an illusion. Agnarr says, "She destroyed the box and told them all to leave her city."

Hallr laughs out loud. "That turned out better than I expected. She is a smart cookie. Now, get helmets on those two, and we need to find Merial?"

Hallr yells, "Merial!"

Chaos is breaking out as the soldiers mill about. Agnarr sees a rider pushing through the crowd, with a young girl behind him. As they shift, he sees it is Merial; behind is another rider, Feliu, on horseback, and Tanisha is walking quickly behind.

"There she is."

Hallr walks toward them. Everyone shifts to get out of his way.

At the edge of the group, Teppo is now standing, just staring at the ruined box. He walks toward it.

Milfred watched the whole thing. As he walks toward the main gate, he realizes it's closed. He can't get his helmet. He says, "Xylia, we can't get our helmets with the gate closed."

Turning back, he sees one man looking at the box's remains. He says, "Xylia, a man is trying to approach the box.

Teppo watches the man call to another and step between him and the box. He gives a slight smile as he concentrates. The man starts to step aside when Teppo hears in his head, "My snack is approaching."

Teppo looks up at the dragon that is looking down into the courtyard by the gate. He turns and walks back to the group of soldiers while clenching his fists.

Merial sees Hallr and says to Zevran, "Stop," as she slides off the horse.

Tanisha hurries to catch up and puts her arm around Merial. She recognizes Sheyla, and now she knows it is an illusion. It is almost perfect, but she knows Sheyla does illusions. This whole situation has gone entirely out of her control.

Tanisha has been controlling from the background since Sheyla and Hallr left the village. The attacks, the fights, getting Neriah to agree to follow Hallr. She needed to get the box. She needed to get strong enough so no one else could challenge her, to enslave her.

Merial is stronger than she is, but she has influenced Merial to help. Now that she has seen Sheyla create an illusion, she could never have accomplished it. This will be different. She can learn from Sheyla. This is an illusion, so the box is still there.

They walk together, meet Hallr, and stop, not sure what to do. Hallr holds out his arms, one hand holding the axe out, and says, "Welcome to the city. I said you could join me in the city. I didn't think it would be this quick."

Merial hugs Hallr. She is slightly taller than Hallr now. She whispers, "She is still projecting the illusion. That means we need to help keep it going."

Tanisha is standing taller next to them. She hears someone behind them say, "Watch the dwarf; he can't see illusions."

Merial and Hallr both turn to look toward the dragon as everyone hears movement.

As they look up, Xylia spreads her wings and leaps into the air, flapping once, then swoops over everyone's head. Turning and flapping, they all watch the dragon and rider begin to climb.

Hallr and Merial, together, turn and watch Xylia fly.

Xylia turns and circles the courtyard twice, flapping and climbing. She turns and flies over the mountain toward the valley and is gone.

Tanisha hears, "Teppo, it's real. We need to go to Esma. The box is gone."

Family

Sheyla is dripping sweat. She is leaning forward with her hands on the rock. She says, "That was hard. I'm already getting a headache."

Xylia says, "That was great. You did a great job."

"I'm not done. The illusion of the dragon, you is gone, but the remains of the box are still there. Kaleb needs to get that blob and throw it into the window."

Xylia says, "I'll get him to get it."

"Next thing. I'm still stuck in the dark. No one can get to me to help."

"I have an idea, but we need to wait a little while before we can try it."

"Why do we have to wait?"

"The water needs to drain from the trough on the counterweight."

Tanisha is smiling, watching Merial direct and move Hallr to watch the illusion dragon fly. Merial says loudly, "A real dragon, flying."

She is also looking up and watching the imaginary dragon.

Merial hugs Hallr again and turns to Tanisha, "We can meet the dragon now."

Hallr says, "Her name is Xylia."

Tanisha asks, "How do we get into the city? The gate is closed."

<<<>>>

Tobias is talking to Sergeant Atonal, "I want you to take that *city."*

"You are not in charge. Our officers are dead. A dragon is protecting the city. You do not know what you are doing."

"I'm a representative of the king. That is enough for you to follow my orders."

"We report to the officers who report to the king, not someone representing."

"What are you going to do?"

"We will return to the king and report. He will decide if we bring an army back to fight a dragon and take the city."

"And what about me?"

"You will return with us to make your report."

Tobias is looking for Teppo. He says to the sergeant, "You need to wait until I talk to Teppo."

Ranjeet and Teppo are approaching Esma. She left the tent to meet with Teppo when the dragon broke her control. Ranjeet says, "That was a real dragon. You think it was an illusion, but it was real. Esma felt the dragon. She can't be fooled."

Esma says, "There is a dragon. A real dragon."

Ranjeet says, "You watched the dragon destroy the box. I was confused watching. Why destroy it with hundreds of people watching? Then I realized that was the only way for anyone to believe the box was destroyed. They couldn't just say it was destroyed."

Teppo looks distraught. "All this time and effort. We lost Willow. Now we don't have the city, or the box."

They hear Tobias yell, "Teppo, what are you doing?"

"We will be leaving."

"You are giving up. You just heard that there is a treasure in that city. Get your witches to control the sergeant and take the city."

Ranjeet steps between Teppo and Tobias, "How will the army

open that gate?"

"*Use your magic. Someone is inside. Make them open it. We are here after several years of searching. I'm not giving up now.*"

Teppo asks, "*Esma, is there someone in the city?*"

Agnarr is with Kaleb and Milfred. Milfred says, "*We can't get our helmets with the gate closed.*

Agnarr nods, "*Bad planning. I should have grabbed them before Sheyla closed it. Xylia, can Sheyla open the main gate?*"

Xylia replies, "*Eventually, it is a problem right now.*"

"*Why?*"

She is on top of the counterweight with no torch. She can't see and has to wait for the water to drain from the weight trough. Then she can work on opening the gate.

Kaleb says, "*I can help guide her.*"

Xylia says, "*First, Kaleb, you need to get the melted blob and throw it into the window. Everyone needs to see it disappear.*"

Agnarr says, "*The illusion is powerful. I'm supposed to see through illusions like this. It is fuzzy, but I see it clearly. Why, how am I still seeing this?*"

Xylia replies, "*She is very focused on making the box disappear. You need to do it or risk pissing her off really badly.*"

Kaleb says, "*Yes, ma'am. I mean, yes,*" as he turns and runs for the melted blob. A thin trail of smoke is still rising. When he puts his hand out to pick it up, he jerks back, "*It's still hot.*"

He turns back to the group, "*I need something to grab it.*"

Agnarr pulls off his singed cloak and tosses it to Kaleb, who has run back to the group.

With the cloak, Kaleb wraps the blob and runs toward the window, yelling, "*It's hot.*"

He drops the blob, shaking his hands trying to cool them.

He looks at Agnarr, shakes his head, then grabs the blob, stands, spins, and throws it up to the window. Everyone hears a clang as it hits the wall, then another clang.

Kaleb is shaking his hands as he walks toward Agnarr.

Tanisha turns, looks up at Zevran, still on his horse, "Zevran, this is Hallr. You hadn't met before."

Feliu pulls his horse up next to Zevran and says, "It's good to see you again, Hallr."

Hallr is smiling, "You've grown. All of you have. It is good to meet you, Zevran, and see you again, Feliu. Let's head to the, what the bloody...."

They watch Kaleb throw the blob, and Merial asks, "Is he a giant? Who is he?"

Hallr says, "He is tall. He is Kaleb. I met him after we left you at the village."

Zevran and Feliu have dismounted, and they all walk toward Milfred and Agnarr inside the courtyard.

Tanisha is looking, fixated on Kaleb, tall, strong, rubbing his hands as he reaches Agnarr and Milfred.

The soldiers are getting orders and moving away. Milfred is looking around, "I think we were controlled to open the gate. Now that the army has seen Xylia and Sheyla pissed off, they are going to leave. Can we close the gate?"

Feliu says, "Not yet. The rest of our group is in a wagon. They need to get here before we close this gate."

Hallr says, "Then we don't open the main gate."

Turning Hallr spots Tobias walking with Teppo and Ranjeet. He says, "Kaleb, is that the guy from the war?"

Kaleb looks and says, "The guy who told the king we left stragglers."

Sheyla is now fully relaxed. She crawled to the trough and, using her cupped hand, drank several handfuls of water.

"Xylia, I unplugged the drain hole. It will still take a while to empty. Then what do I do?"

"You will go to the side where there is a ladder and push the counterweight up."

"I can't lift this thing."

"You will use your push magic. With no water, the system is balanced. It will stay in place where you stop so you can lock it in."

Sheyla feels a witch reaching out. Not knowing who or what is happening, she projects back to see who it is, "Xylia, someone is trying to read or control me."

"I think it is from the coven."

Sheyla closes her eyes to listen, read, and reach out. It isn't Merial or Tanisha; someone else. She says, "I'm not in the mood for games today."

Sheyla aggressively applies a control illusion to make the person sick: "Tell me who you are."

Esma screams and grabs her head. "No. Who are you?"

Teppo grabs her hands while Ranjeet puts his arms around her as she collapses. Esma says, "I'm Esma. I'm going to open the gate."

Esma breathes hard, "I'm strong. You can't...."

Esma throws up on Teppo's shoes as she collapses.

Ranjeet is holding her. "What is happening?"

Teppo replies, "I don't know. Maybe the dragon is fighting her."

Ranjeet picks her up and says, "I'm taking her to the tent."

Tobias has been watching and says, "You can't get the gate open. The dragon is stopping you?"

Teppo says, "Possibly, or a powerful control witch."

"Get your witches in line. Get control of the army."

"You are going to have to wait. Convince them without magic to take the city."

Elin says, "Rielan, we are leaving the wagon. It doesn't matter anymore. Tanisha and Merial were right. There is a dragon. The dragon and the witch are protecting the city. If the dwarf is still friendly, we don't need the wagon."

Rielan nods, "Let's unhitch the horses and take them."

They are passing through the army support people milling around, and then the soldiers are waiting for orders. They are approaching three men and a woman when the woman grabs her head and screams.

Elin stops and closes her eyes. Sucking in her breath, she says, "That one is a witch from the coven. The witch on the dragon just did something. It was painful."

Rielan says, "Keep moving."

When they get close to the courtyard gate, Rielan yells to Zevran.

<<<>>>

Feliu turns and says, "The rest of our group. All that is left."

Agnarr says, "I remember the rider. He met us on the road."

Kaleb says, "Hallr, that annoying guy is walking this way now."

They watch Tobias walking toward the group. When he is close, he yells, "Dwarf, you deserted your post."

Hallr smiles, "Let him come."

Tobias says, "You were never relieved. You are still under the king's command. That means under my command. You open that gate and surrender the city to the king."

Hallr holds out his hand to stop Kaleb from walking forward. He says, "I never swore allegiance to the king. The agreement was that I would fight the war. When the war was over, the agreement was made."

"Not until you are relieved by me. You will kneel and swear

allegiance to the king and become his army fighter."

Tanisha asks, "Like a slave?"

Milfred says, "Something like that."

Tanisha pulls her dagger and tosses it in the air. Shifting her hands, getting ready to push the dagger, she says, "Hallr will be no one's slave!"

Kaleb reaches over, puts his hand on Tanisha's arm, saying, "No, he won't, and you don't need to do this. I will."

Tanisha lets the dagger clatter to the ground. Looking up at Kaleb, she slowly pulls her arm back. "I don't like people being slaves."

Kaleb says, "They tried to make me one, until Hallr rescued me. This little shit will do nothing."

Kaleb steps up to Agnarr and grabs his sword, pulling it out. It looks like a large dagger when Kaleb is holding it. He turns to Tobias, who has gone white. Tobias turns and runs toward the army.

Kaleb watches him for a few seconds, then turns back. Handing Agnarr his sword, he says, "Thanks."

He steps over to Tanisha, kneels, and picks up her dagger, then hands it to her. They are looking eye to eye as he is kneeling. Tanisha takes the dagger and says, "Thank you."

Milfred gives Agnarr a gentle elbow. "Those two young ones will need to be chaperoned."

Agnarr smiles, "It is too late. The courtship is already done."

Zevran says, "Let's clear the courtyard and close this gate. Let them figure out they need to leave."

Feliu and Rielan nod. They walk toward the last part of the army at the edge of the gate and tell them to leave. Kaleb walks over to the gate control, pulls the pole holding the small wheel, and kicks it to get it moving.

The gate closes slowly; the stone lowering to create a twenty-centimeter gap. The remaining people are scrambling to get out of the way.

Agnarr says, "Xylia, you can tell Sheyla we are closing the

courtyard gate."

"She is passed out right now. She had to deal with a control witch after the big illusion. It all took its toll."

Agnarr replies, "Let her sleep."

Merial asks, "How do we get into the city? I want to meet the dragon."

Kaleb says, "I need to get into the window so I can go help Sheyla open the gate."

Agnarr says, "I'll help."

Feliu says, "How will you get in the window, which is very high?"

Agnarr says, "You're going to help with your push."

Welcome to the City

Sheyla feels sticky from dried sweat. She moves, realizing she is still on the counterweight in the dark. She hears a noise in the dark. "Xylia, what's happening?"

"Kaleb and Agnarr are coming to help you."

Sheyla looks around and sees light, diffused and bouncing off stones.

"I can see light from the torch. They will be here soon. Why are they coming that way?"

"You have the only key to the gate guardhouse."

"Oh, right."

She sees the torch and can now make out Kaleb and Agnarr. They hop down on the counterweight, and Sheyla can feel it shift. She sees Agnarr has a rope over his shoulder.

Agnarr says, "You get some rest? That was an amazing illusion. It was fuzzy, but clear. It was fantastic."

"I gave it everything. I had to make it work for everyone watching."

Kaleb says, "Agnarr and the kid Feliu boosted me to the window. I put the rope down for Agnarr, and we came to help."

Agnarr says, "Xylia said you were exhausted, so we are going to open the gate."

Xylia says, "I think Agnarr can use his push and do it. Did you get the rope?"

Agnarr says, "Yes, let's do this."

Sheyla asks, "What do I do?"

"Sit and relax."

They tie the rope to the water trough, and Kaleb lowers Agnarr over the side of the counterweight. "I hope the rope is long enough."

After lower Agnarr for most of the rope, it goes slack. "I'm down, put the rest of the rope over."

Kaleb sits down next to Sheyla in the middle of the counterweight and says, "We're ready when you are."

They feel the counterweight move up slowly, then move faster. Sheyla asks, "What is Agnarr doing?"

"He got to the bottom and used his push on the counterweight. Because it is balanced, we are hoping it will travel all the way up, and we don't have to climb the ladder."

"But Agnarr is at the bottom."

"Tied to the trough. He should ride up the rope. When we get to the top, I will pull him back up."

Merial is asking everyone questions about the city. After Kaleb and Agnarr went through the window, the group walked over to the big gate and sat, except for Zevran. He started pacing.

Milfred has answered most of Merial's questions, with Hallr answering a few. Milfred says, "That is the short version of what happened to the Xylia and the city."

"Sheyla and Agnarr healed a dragon. Oh my gosh. I knew she was a great healer."

Hallr says, "We haven't even talked about the chickens or the valley."

Feliu asks, "Is the treasure a story or is it real? You didn't say anything about that."

"There is gold, but the treasure is gone."

Rieland asks, "Stolen?"

Hallr says, "Not really. Talk to Xylia about those details."

Rieland says, "I have to ask the dragon?"

"Yep."

"When I started on this journey, I never considered someone would say, talk to the dragon."

Merial says, "I can't wait."

Elin asks Tanisha, "What's wrong? You are upset about

something."

"The box was a fake."

Hallr says, "That is a whole other thing we will discuss. You need to know the story. In fact, Kaleb can show you the fake box. He opened it."

Tanisha looks at Hallr intently. "He opened it. But I thought only a dwarf could open it."

"No, a really smart guy with big hands was all it took."

Zevran walks up after pacing at the closed courtyard gate. "What happens next? We found the city, the dwarf. There are no more attacks on the village. Elin, do we head back?"

Milfred says, "Hang on. We all need to be together to talk about this."

Elin asks, "Why?"

Milfred replies, "I have many questions about you leaving. Do you leave and not come back? Do you bring the entire village here? If you do, what will the arrangement be? Hallr and I get kicked out. If everyone is here, who will be in charge?"

Merial says, "Hallr and Sheyla will be in charge. One dwarf, one human, and she is a witch."

Tanisha smiles, "They will never let Sheyla be in charge. She is an outcast."

Milfred shifts, and Hallr stands up. Hallr says, "She is not an outcast from us. She is part of our group."

Tanisha gives a slight smile and a slight shrug, looking at Elin. "You have never liked controllers, but you tolerated Merial and me."

"I did what I was ordered to do. I found on this trip that control isn't black-and-white. You used control at times to nudge people."

Milfred says, "Interesting. The character of the person and their intent are more important. Tanisha, what was your intention in coming here?"

Merial shifts to look at Tanisha. Tanisha knows she can't lie. "I wanted the box."

Merial interjects, "She is focused on a different type of control.

When people control others as slaves or servants, not when they control people with magic. She will fight not to be a slave to someone else."

Elin asks, "When would that happen to you?"

"That was how I grew up. The child of servants, which meant I was a servant, nothing more. The controller who evaluated us said I would be a top controller or a servant to a controller, nothing else, not another option."

Elin is frowning, forehead crinkled, "That wouldn't happen when you were with us."

"Unless someone had the power from the box."

Elin looks at Tanisha, then sees Feliu nodding, "You both felt that way. That you would become servants to a controller?"

Feliu says, "We are not as strong as Merial or Sheyla, so I focused on becoming a guardian assassin, not a controller. They won't make me a servant."

Hallr walks over to be between Feliu and Tanisha. "That is not an issue anymore. You three are staying. No matter what the others decide."

Elin turns to Merial, "And what about you?"

"I want to be a healer, like Sheyla, and not a controller."

The next morning, they are all gathering in the barracks' common area.

Merial says, "I met Xylia last night."

Sheyla is smiling and shaking her head, "You couldn't wait. You just wandered the hallways until you found her."

Xylia says, "I helped. I had to send her to bed after a couple of hours. Does she ever stop asking questions?"

Hallr laughs.

Kaleb and Tanisha come to the area from different rooms at different times and keep glancing at each other.

Sheyla says, "You two, stop it. Both of you come here."

When they are together, Sheyla asks, "You both like each other. Yes or no?"

They both nod. "Now sit down next to each other. After we eat, Kaleb will take Tanisha to meet Xylia."

Hallr says, "Before anyone goes anywhere, we need to talk about the future and the city. Milfred proposed that Elin and Zevran go back to the village and bring everyone to the city."

Sheyla nods, "Okay, and? You wouldn't bring it up if there weren't something else."

Tanisha says, "Who will be in charge when they return? If you are an outcast, what happens?"

Sheyla turns and sits. "Interesting question. What does everyone else think?"

Xylia says, "Not everyone can hear what I say."

Hallr raises a hand, "Xylia is telling us something."

Xylia continues, "Sheyla has already declared, while riding a dragon, that this is her city. Anyone coming to live here will have to accept that an outcast is part of the leadership. If they don't like it, don't come."

Sheyla says, "Thanks, Xylia," then repeats what Xylia says.

Milfred says, "We need people in the city. I think having the village move here is a good start. It will become a place for humans and mages to build, learn, and work together."

Agnarr says, "When did you become a philosopher?"

Milfred replies, "I can't make Mithril armor to fight the control covens. Building a city that the covens can't take over is just as good."

Sheyla says, "Bring the village."

Two Years Later

Neriah says, "Sheyla, she is out of control, not a pun. You are the only one with any sway."

"Merial is now a teenager, and the more you try to force her into a box, the more she will rebel. I've talked to her, and I think part of the problem is that she doesn't see the magic she can do as bad. It is all magic; it is how it is used."

They are walking to the barracks' common area, where everyone still meets to talk. Sheyla is very pregnant and walking slowly.

"Were you like this? Young and wild witch who could control."

"Neriah, when I was her age, I was living on the street, by my wits and my magic. It isn't the same. The difference is that I was in a coven when I was very young. A control coven and watched them do bad things to people. I saw how magic could be used for evil. Merial hasn't seen that."

"Please talk to her. She can't be using control on merchants that come to the city."

"That merchant was trying to steal Mithril. She simply made him confess. Of all the things she could have done, that was extremely mild."

"I KNOW. That is the problem. Control is so easy for her. People are not happy. They are complaining. Talk to her. If she would settle down like Tanisha."

"Tanisha is a completely different story. If she hadn't found Kaleb, we would talk about expelling her from the city. I eventually got her to tell me she was controlling you in the village so you would send her away to find the city."

"I've had to accept that a teenager manipulated me. Look at Tanisha now, they are great together, and they will be great parents."

Sheyla nods, "The baby will be a year old in the spring. Tanisha is asking about being a magic teacher. Did you hear she wants to teach Guardians how to heal?"

Neriah moves her staff and hits the ground harder. "Talk to Merial. People are saying if she is wild, we need to expel her."

"That is not a good idea."

"What alternative do we have?"

As they approach the barracks' common area, Sheyla asks, "Xylia, do you know why Hallr wants to talk?"

"He told me and asked me not to say anything until he talks to the council."

Sheyla asks Neriah, "Do you have any idea?"

Neriah replies, "No idea."

They arrive, and Hallr is sitting, waiting.

When they get to the table, Hallr says, "I'm leaving to look for more dwarves. The city is alive again. There are children here. You don't need me here."

Pregnant Sheyla is slowly sitting at the end of the bench, holding her belly. She replies, "But no dwarves."

Neriah says, "Hallr, when you asked for this meeting, I never expected this. We should talk about this as something we agree on. Talk about how we can help you."

Hallr says, "I'm taking Merial with me."

Xylia says, "Hallr talked to me, and I have mixed feelings. I know one thing. Feliu will follow you even if he is told not to go. He is ready for his next adventure."

Sheyla says, "We should wait until the others get here, but are you crazy? You want to go on a search with a teenage girl, a control witch."

Neriah says, "If you are going to do this, we need to talk about what you will have to deal with, having a witch going through puberty. This sounds completely crazy."

Xylia says, "He is crazy, but he knows what he is doing. You are trying to figure out how to change Merial or expel her. Hallr is solving the problem."

Agnarr walks in and sits next to Sheyla. Sheyla says, "We are waiting for the others," as Milfred walks in.

Milfred says, "Kaleb told me he would be very late and to start without him."

Hallr says, "We shouldn't wait anymore. I talked to Kaleb about this already."

Neriah says, "Hallr told us he is leaving. He wants to search for other dwarves. He said he is taking Merial. Xylia says that Feliu will follow him."

Xylia says, "I told Merial to come to the meeting."

Agnarr says, "I was wondering when this would happen. I won't be going; my adventuring days are past. We need to get the farms going, finish rebuilding the mill."

Milfred says, "If he weren't about to be a father, he would consider it."

Sheyla asks, "What did Kaleb say?"

"Tanisha was there, holding the baby. They were with Xylia at the tunnel opening, taking in the sun."

Xylia interjects, "Kaleb says he's going to annoy me until I try to fly."

Hallr continues, "He looked at me, got mad, and said I was a tiny, hard-headed old goat that needed lookin after."

Neriah asks, "And?"

"He said that because he wasn't going, I couldn't leave. Then he said, if I do, I need to bring back books."

Merial walks into the room wearing leather pants, a shirt, and a cloak. She braided her long hair, unlike her usual mane that looks unbrushed. "Sorry I'm late and I didn't change. Xylia said it was urgent, that Hallr wanted me at the meeting."

Sheyla asks, "What were you doing?"

"I promised Zevran I would help gather the new foals to the corrals to protect them from the wolves. Feliu and I are good at herding the stock. What is happening?"

"Hallr is leaving. He is going to look for more dwarves," says Sheyla.

Merial looks at Hallr and says, "Okay. Feliu and I will go with you. You need someone to take care of you."

Milfred and Agnarr laugh.

Neriah says, "Two teenage magi traveling with an old dwarf. This sounds like we will turn chaos loose on the world."

Sheyla is smiling and looking intently at Merial. "You and Feliu are both teenagers and are wild together. Traveling with an old dwarf could be dangerous. You could do with more training."

Merial says, "It's settled then. I will talk to Feliu and get ready."

Sheyla says, "Did you hear anything we said?"

Agnarr says, "She heard you. She is going with Hallr, unless you can lock her up. Also, you didn't say no because you agree he needs someone to take care of him."

Xylia says to Sheyla, "This is just for you. Turn her loose, don't confine her, or Feliu."

Hallr says, "Merial, I don't need you to travel with me cause I need lookin after. I need a healer witch because the covens are still hunting dwarves, and we'll probably be fighting covens."

"Uh - huh, so looking after you and fighting witches. Sounds like fun."

END

Requesting Your Review

Thank you for reading the book. I hope you enjoyed the story, and I would love to have a review. This will let everyone else know what you like and maybe don't like about the book. I'm always looking for ways to improve my storytelling, and I will read every review. I appreciate your feedback. The direct links are;

Amazon:
    https://authorbdmurphy.com/TLDapR

Barnes and Noble:
    https://authorbdmurphy.com/TLDbpR

Goodreads:
    https://authorbdmurphy.com/TLDgpR

Acknowledgments

Thank you to my family and friends for their support and patience throughout my learning process. They provided editing assistance and offered positive encouragement.

About the Author

B.D. Murphy started writing when the world hit pause—and he hasn't stopped since. He's the kind of author who sees a mystery in every machine, a plot twist in every algorithm, and a story hiding in your Wi-Fi signal. With a brain wired for engineering and a heart full of curiosity, Murphy crafts sci-fi that's clever, sneaky, and just a little bit subversive. If you like techy thrillers, real-talk characters, and endings that make you say "wait, WHAT?"—he's your guy.

Awards:

- *Feathered Quill first place–Science Fiction 2025–Sidney and Watson*
- *Readers' favorite Silver 5-star winner–Science Fiction 2023–Pandemic Hacker*
- *Readers' Choice Book Awards Finalist - Science Fiction 2025–Nanite Evolution*
- *Literary Titan 5 Star Gold Award - Nanite Evolution*

Website: authorbdmurphy.com
Facebook: facebook.com/bdmurph73
BlueSky: bsky.app/profile/bdmurphy.bsky.social
All the links are available at:
https://authorbdmurphy.com/about-b-d-murphy/

https://authorbdmurphy.com

Other Titles

Pandemic Hacker
Deal Hunter
Sidney and Watson
Nanite Evolution
Pandemic Hacker 2